Dear Melanie,

THE LONG DESERT ROAD

Wishing you all the best!

Alex Sirotkin

ALEX SIROTKIN

ARCHWAY
PUBLISHING

Archway Publishing books may be ordered through booksellers or by contacting:

Archway Publishing
1663 Liberty Drive
Bloomington, IN 47403
www.archwaypublishing.com
844-669-3957

ISBN: 978-1-4808-9370-2 (sc)
ISBN: 978-1-4808-9369-6 (hc)
ISBN: 978-1-4808-9371-9 (e)

Library of Congress Control Number: 2020914147

Printed in the United States of America.

Archway Publishing rev. date: 11/11/2020

To Stephanie,
and all the children.

CONTENTS

CHAPTER 1

Henry

I'm starting to think a lot about death; my own, that is. Surprisingly, I'm okay with it, I figure, so long as there are no scheduling conflicts.

Seriously? Death is as natural as it is final. It comes to everyone, and everything. It's just a matter of time. Nevertheless, I don't want to be alone on that day nor all the other days leading up to it.

At forty-four, my moment here on Earth is about half over if I'm lucky. Mom wasn't so fortunate, so who knows?

Death, like most things in life, is relative. If giant tortoises were self-aware, they could expect to live well past a hundred. It's a scientific fact that one survived for over 250 years. As far as I know, tortoises aren't enlightened in the manner of Descartes; they don't perceive their own interminable existence. Yet, they take their sweet time to do whatever it is they do to get by.

On the other hand, take your common house fly. It has a lifespan of three weeks. This would explain a lot. For one, its frantic leap away from the targeted flick of my dishtowel against the kitchen window. Every moment has meaning to these little interlopers.

As for me, I'm still out here, searching. For a woman? Sure. But sometimes, in between raindrops of doubt, I wonder if I'm missing something else in life. It's a matter of purpose and consequence. Do I have a role to play, or do I just take up space on this beautiful yet chaotic planet of ours? Of course, these are existential questions that border on cliché for those middle-aged folks like me that don't have the answers. It's a lot like: "How much for that gorgeous Maserati Gran Turismo?" If you have to ask, you probably can't afford it.

My uncertainty derives in part from my scientific nature. While I don't consider myself to be particularly gloomy, how can one measure the worth of a man against the unimaginable vastness of space and the inevitability of death? If anything, these realities impede my spirited participation in life. Why can't I be more like the desperate fly, personified? Gazing into its bulging and creepy eyes, one might see panic in its recognition of an imminent demise, and hence, the need to make haste! Not me; but along with finding a good woman, I'm working on it.

CHAPTER 2

Isabel

"Oh hey, Mare. One sec. I'm putting you on speaker."

Isabel, a forty-two-year-old attorney, places her cell phone onto her granite kitchen counter and resumes beating four eggs in a large glass bowl. She's an attractive woman, five-four, with Mediterranean coloring and subtly tinted brown hair, cut short and cute. Today, Isabel is dressed for work in a navy key-hole blouse, gray slacks, and black pumps, and she's protected herself with a blue butcher-apron.

"How are things going, Iz?"

"Too early to say," Isabel responds, adding a pinch of salt to the egg mixture. "She's still in bed. Frankly, Mare, I don't know if I can do this."

"You can! You're smart and patient. You'll figure it out."

"Yeah, I may be smart with my clients, but the jury's still out on the rest."

Isabel puts down the bowl and leans over the sink to wash her hands.

"Don't be down on yourself. You care so much about her. You're the one constant in her life. Without you, who knows where she'd be." Isabel hears this pep talk over the sound of running water.

"I do love her, when she's not making me crazy."

"You're a good mother, Iz. I can't imagine how hard this must be, but you'll get through it. She will too."

"Thanks, Mare," Isabel says. She shuts off the water and picks up a dish towel. "But as my mother used to say, 'from your lips, to God's ears.' I would think that, at twenty-one, Lauren would...."

Isabel is interrupted by the sound of her daughter's bloodcurdling scream, like that of a doe being attacked by a mountain lion.

"Oh crap! I've got to go," Isabel blurts out as she lays the phone onto the counter and rushes down the hall, the towel still in her hand. She bursts into Lauren's room and turns on the lights to find her daughter sitting up in bed, eyes closed, arms flailing, still screeching like a doomed animal.

"Lauren! Wake up!" Isabel demands. "You're having a nightmare!"

It's a second or two before Lauren responds. Silent now, she brings her hands down to rub her eyes open. Her dark hair is tousled; sweat covers her face. She brings up the bottom of her night shirt – a Dolphins football jersey – to dry herself off.

"Oh my God. You're drenched. Are you all right?" Isabel asks.

Lauren hesitates.

Isabel sits down onto the edge of the bed.

"Answer me. Are you okay?"

Isabel starts to bring the dish towel up to her daughter's clammy face, but Lauren grabs her mother's hand and pushes it away.

"I'm fine, Mom! It was a dream. I'm fine. Leave me alone!" Lauren insists, as she wipes her brow with her sleeve.

"Would you like to talk about it?" Isabel asks.

"No! It was just a bad dream. I'm fine," she repeats, with a certain edge.

"Okay. I'm glad. You know I'm here for you. Do you want to get up now? I'm making breakfast."

"Not yet. Soon."

Lauren turns over as if to go back to sleep. Isabel sighs, stands up, flicks out the lights, and shuts the door behind her. Shaking her head, she thinks out loud.

"Her second day back and already there's drama."

CHAPTER 3

Steinmetz

It's almost 8:00 p.m., and I'm late. Grasping a hand-rail, I find my way up a dimly lit flight of stairs and come upon an open-air circular metal platform, some twenty-five feet in diameter. The lights have been turned off. I fear that I'll crash into some valuable equipment and be scolded by one Dr. Daniel Steinmetz, whose reputation is that of a stickler. I don't want to piss off a source, especially a local one. So, I zip up my fleece against a cold and forceful autumn wind and wait a half minute for my eyes to adjust.

Steinmetz emailed me to meet him here atop this mini-observatory, one flight up and adjacent to the visitor center. He's going to explain his recent discovery that, at least according to Steinmetz, may blow a hole through the widely accepted theories on redshift and the speed at which the universe is coming apart. This may have bearing on the book that I'm researching, and journalistic diligence requires that I flesh it out. But I'm behind in my own self-imposed schedule, so I hope whatever Steinmetz has to say doesn't also blow a hole through *my* plans.

I head toward a silhouette of a man sitting in a chair. I have never met Steinmetz, but from an internet photo, I know that he looks like the dated stereotype of an astrophysicist: mid-sixties, five-five, five-six, wide around the middle, thick black-rimmed glasses, with a gray comb-over of what's left of his thinning hair. All that would be needed are a polypropylene protector and a slide rule in his shirt pocket to place his online image among black and white photos of scientists in the Mercury Program back in the fifties.

Steinmetz looks away from the eyepiece and turns toward me. "You're Spinoza, yes? Welcome to Kitt Peak."

He must have been sitting there in his gray ski parka for some time looking through the 200-millimeter amateur telescope as he apparently sees me a lot better than I see him in the dim starlight. Of course, I've been to this mountaintop facility before; it's only fifty-five miles west from my condo in Tucson.

"Please, sir, call me Henry," I offer, extending my hand.

"Well then, good to meet you, Henry. Thanks for coming up on a Friday night."

"No, it's I who should be thanking you, sir. Sorry to be late," I say with purposeful correctness, as if meeting a future father-in-law for the first time.

"Not at all and forgive me for bringing you out into the cold. It's not often that I get to hobby this way like a teenager."

The good old days of Hubble and the long, hopeful nights he spent in solitude peering through the eyepiece of the 100-inch Hooker are long gone. This research today gets done in front of a computer and in the comfort of a climate-adjusted control room.

"No problem, Doctor." I'm being more than polite. While my weakness in complex math kept me from an advanced degree in science, I adore the mysterious beauty of the night sky.

"Here, Henry, take a look." So far, he seems quite fatherly. I regret not having sought him out earlier.

"What are we looking at, Doctor?"

"You'll recognize it." He stands up so that I can sit at the telescope. With my right eye, I stare into the aperture, adjusting the lens slightly to bring Saturn into focus. This small telescope is used mostly by paying astro-tourists at Kitt Peak. The bright-white image of Saturn with its famous rings is small and in perfect proportion. The planet appears cartoonlike, so much so that one might be convinced that what one's looking at is an illustration of Saturn sitting somewhere within the instrument itself. As the night is clear, and Earth's moon is absent, I'm also able to count three of Saturn's own satellites that appear as tiny dots in the viewfinder.

Most who see Saturn this way for the first time gasp in astonishment, amazed there truly is a giant gas planet out there surrounded by an even larger perfect circle of ice crystals, like some sort of planetary life preserver. This is how as a child I was first awed by the amazing universe.

"Beautiful, as always."

"Yes, I know you've seen it before, Henry. I just need to be out here in the open sky from time to time. It's where I do my best thinking."

He pauses, then asks. "So, Spinoza, huh? Any relation?"

"You mean to the philosopher?" Steinmetz nods, so I continue. "I did a genealogy, and, yes, it's possible, but he lived 400 years ago. It's hard to say."

"Fascinating," he responds. "If there *is* a connection, you'd have a lot to live up to. Now, let's get in before we freeze our asses off."

I follow him back down the stairs, which by now are visible to me. I clutch a list of questions in my fleece's left pocket. I'm happy to head inside and away from the unrelenting mountaintop wind.

CHAPTER 4

The Negotiation

I sabel cringes as she listens to the fast-paced lament of her troubled and immature twenty-one year-old daughter.

"Mom, like, I haven't been out with any friends for so long. I need to get out. We're going to a meeting. Then these girls invited me to dinner. You know I need to make girl friends here. I want to be happy for once in my life. I'm really trying to make it work, don't you see? You haven't given me anything, like, for a long time."

Isabel thinks. *This is Friday evening, and I'm pretty sure I just paid sixty dollars on Wednesday for a haircut that she said was "so pivotal to her self-esteem."* But she's right, Isabel concludes; she needs female friends.

Isabel has given her daughter a wide berth since she moved back from Florida ten days ago. Lauren has been forever fixated on boys, bouncing from one "serious" relationship to another. Little boys have turned into big men, and she's gotten herself into major trouble on account of it.

Yet, Isabel second-guesses her own intuition. *Am I being strong enough on this, or am I just going with what's easy?*

"Dinner so late?" Isabel asks.

Lauren's expression is enough.

"Mom, it's the weekend. I'm not twelve."

"Whatever," Isabel relents. "How much do you think this will cost?"

"I don't know what restaurant they're going to. Could you give me fifty and I won't ask for any more the whole weekend?"

Isabel hates this part the most. Everything with Lauren since the age of nine has been a fierce negotiation. Her daughter's skills are being wasted. She might represent NFL players one day, although Isabel would prefer it if her daughter landed a job next week washing dishes.

"I'll give you twenty dollars and that's generous." Isabel hopes she's being firm enough. Twenty feels like a good counteroffer. *Damn it, I'm an attorney. I ought to be better at this.*

"Mom, c'mon, you know that's not enough for dinner; you don't want to embarrass me in front of these girls. I barely know them. With tip and all, it's gotta be at least thirty, and I have to chip in for gas, too."

"All right, thirty dollars and not another dime." In Isabel's own experience, no one ever paid her a fuel allowance for driving her friends around on a weekend night; but Isabel's relieved that the discussion is wrapping up.

"Okay, thirty, but I may need more later. I know you don't trust me, and that hurts. Can't you see I'm trying?" Lauren's just getting warmed up.

"Enough for now. This discussion is over!"

Isabel opens her purse ever so slightly and pulls out the cash. Lauren's right hand shoots out to pluck the bills from her mom's grasp as a lizard's tongue might capture an insect.

Deep down, Isabel knows that she ought to be stronger. The idea of "enabling" was drilled into her at the family session at Sutherland Farms in Florida. Perhaps it's her maternal instinct fighting against conventional wisdom; perhaps she's just weak. She's plainly out of practice. This seems all too familiar, reminiscent of Lauren living with her in Tucson as a teenager.

"God, Mom, what makes you such a tight-wad? You're so different from the way Grammy was."

Isabel ignores this zinger and dumps it into her "gunny sack of anxieties," spawned since her daughter's childhood. Lauren sees her mother sag under the burden.

"Sorry, Mom. I appreciate you. Gotta go. Tim will be here any minute!" and she heads for the door, jubilant.

"Tim?! I thought you were going with the girls!" Lauren's one-time boyfriend was never a good influence on her daughter. Lauren looks back over her shoulder without breaking stride.

"I am. Chill. He's just taking me to the meeting. Love you!"

One could easily mistake the immediacy of Lauren's response for the truth, for she's still a master at deception.

CHAPTER 5

The Invitation

Now that the interview is over, I'll focus on the nerve-wracking drive back home. Steinmetz turned out to be quite likable, and we hit it off. I'll consider his theories later. It's approaching ten, and I'm high atop a small mountain. I'm never keen on driving along a precipice, even midday. High places scare the crap out of me. My heart races, my mind disengages.

Cliffside driving requires me to white-knuckle the wheel at the perfect two and ten o'clock positions, center the vehicle over the double line and slow to a crawl. I imagine a little old blue-haired lady, in her Buick Road Master careening past me on my right side, within spitting distance from the ledge, glaring at me through her driver-side window as she hurtles by, flipping me the bird.

With that backdrop, the rules of the road at Kitt Peak are interesting. Most notable is the prohibition on the use of headlights after dark. Sure, no problem utilizing them during daylight hours; heck, go for the high beams; but when the sun sets, make sure you turn *off* your headlamps. We wouldn't want to inhibit any stargazing going on up here.

So, it may be tricky for me to find my way down the steep grade along the escarpment in the pitch black. I tend to be dramatic, for it's not all that bad. For one, it's only for the first mile or two. Second, at least parking lights are allowed; and there's nothing like the red-filtered glow from a thumb-sized LED to illuminate the thin-gauge aluminum guardrail that stands between my flimsy car and a 7,000 foot drop off.

It takes twenty-five minutes to serpentine my way down eight miles of hair-raising road to the bottom. I relax my grip and proceed another easy four miles until my right turn onto a flat Route 86. Here, I have no fear to drive ten miles per hour over the seventy mph speed limit. I'll be home in forty-five minutes. Mine is the only car on the road, and I feel free to utilize the full force of my high beams, and perhaps make up for some lost time back on the mountain.

Now that safety is no longer a concern, I reach for my cell phone and punch up my messages. I see three voice mails: one from an unknown caller, and the other two from Rafael, my younger brother by two years. I play the first and hear an automatic message from CVS, telling me that my renewal prescription for an anti-fungal that I thankfully no longer need will be ready for pickup. I move onto Raff.

"Bro, what are you doing next Saturday night? Probably nothing. Hah! Sorry. Anyway, I know how many times we've tried this sort of thing. Mare invited a woman over. Yes, an unattached woman; and I promised my darling wife that I would get you to come again. So, unless you want me living on your couch for the rest of my f'n life, you better be here. Okay? Call me."

I hear an urgent whisper in the background.

"Oh yeah, Marianne says she's cute. Call me."

I smile at my brother's whimsical solicitation, and I'm heartened by Mare's continued attempts at helping me to find happiness. I'm not terribly unhappy, as far as I know. I confess that I want to be with a good woman, someone that truly loves me without doubt or hesitation, someone that gets me. For this, she must be unusual.

As for the mystery woman being cute, I don't count on it. Every one of Marianne's setups has been represented as "cute." Must be the term "cute" has a much more profound meaning to a woman than to a man, whose broad view of life goes only as deep as sea level. I don't trust a woman's appraisal in this regard, and I lower my expectations. In any event, who am I kidding? I'm no Bradley Cooper either.

I look down momentarily at my phone to retrieve Raff's second message.

"Me again. I'm calling from the bathroom so the old bat can't hear this," he whispers. "Just had to say that I know that you're thinking that Mare always says they're cute. True, but don't forget there was that Sheila, and she was hot even though really bizarre. You ought to have at least fooled around with her. Moron. She wanted to. Christ, I wanted to. Messed up on that one, you did. Call me."

It's no coincidence that Rafael homed in on my very thoughts, as he knows me as well as I know myself. Of course, he was kidding about the bathroom thing as I hear Marianne still in the background lovingly berate him as the line goes silent. Theirs is the perfect relationship.

I switch the FM on low, and tune to my favorite pop channel at the start of "Believer."

> *First things first*
> *I'm a say all the words inside my head*
> *I'm fired up and tired of the way that things have*
> *been…*
> *The way that things have been….*

Oncoming headlights from what appears to be a small pickup truck, weaving over the rise at an insane speed, startle me. I hug the shoulder as my car kicks up gravel, and I curse the maniac in the truck that hurtles by. This was a close call.

I soon settle back down. The drive and the music are hypnotic. My thoughts go to the cosmos, my book, and the interview on the mountain.

While Steinmetz admits that his research is only half-baked, if correct, it may lead to a monumental change in the computation of how much dark energy is required to explain the accelerating expansion of the universe. That would be more than a mere footnote in my book. As Steinmetz reminded me, dark energy is something that we have conjured up as a countervailing force to gravity. We don't know what it is, we can't see it, and we can't detect it. Yet under current assumptions, the dark forces make up ninety-six percent of all the stuff that exists.

The rest, the four percent, is what we see and measure. It's the mass that is us here on Earth, the continents and the oceans, plants and animals, man-made infrastructure, even the atmosphere. Add to this the other planets, their moons, and other objects in our own solar system, including the sun. There's more: the billions upon billions of stars in our Milky Way galaxy, and all the planets and debris that revolve around them. Finally, include the mass of hundreds of billions of stars and their planets in each of some hundred billion galaxies in the universe that exist beyond our own. All of that, everything we know, everything we see, everything we measure, is the four percent!

And people are amazed when they look at Saturn through a little telescope. They cheer when simple geometry causes the moon to blot out the rays of the sun in totality, not to diminish the predictable wonderment of it all. Hell, even those who are lazing late in the day upon a west-facing beach, glancing up over the sand to where ocean meets sky, are filled with awe at the magnificent sight of an orange sun disappearing below the distant horizon.

Dark energy is the designated placeholder we created to answer one of the biggest mysteries of our time. Why is the universe coming apart when gravity should bring us closer together?

Truth be told, I love the cosmos. It's compelling in its science, joyous in its miracles, awe-inspiring in its vastness, fearsome in its bleak darkness yet captivating in its mysteries. The universe is unfathomable space with endless possibilities.

My preoccupation with it, however, gets in the way of a real love life, or so it's been suggested. Not that I'm some silly geek satirically portrayed in one very popular sitcom; for some unearthly reason, I do utterly resent that show. Yet, admittedly, there may be a few similarities that are often misunderstood by a would-be partner.

Ten minutes later, still doing about eighty, I'm surprised by a cluster of flashing red and blue lights coming at me from the distance. Soon enough, three Grand Prix police cruisers and two EMT rigs wail past in close succession.

"Holy shit, this is bad," I say out loud. I wonder if it's that ass in the pickup who got into some trouble.

I turn off the music. The balance of the ride home is uneventful. Once there, I check over my Google alerts, respond to a few emails, and pour some ginger ale into a short glass of Tito's and ice. I'm under the covers just after midnight, my usual bedtime. My mind's eye envisions the bright, white image of Saturn and its spectacular rings just before I nod off.

CHAPTER 6

Into the Desert

Tim is at the wheel of his 2012 Tacoma with three confederates squeezed beside him on the truck's only bench seat. They race west along Route 86 out of Tucson. This lonesome two-lane highway passes through limitless flats of beige, coarse sand. It's dotted with the low-lying green shoots of creosote and burro bush scrub. Roadside, there are dirt-poor dwellings and an occasional commercial structure: the inevitable self-storage unit, a dollar store, a single-pump gas station. These, like bacteria found in boiling springs, somehow exist despite the harsh isolation of their surroundings. Of course, the occupants of the vehicle are aware of none of this in the gloom of a moonless night and, for each, a giddy fog.

The radio blares out pop. Lauren is sandwiched like a slice of prosciutto between Tim, the driver, and Donovan, who sits on her right by the passenger window. A hard white plastic cooler filled with Bud Lights, and a large cylindrical flashlight, sit at Donovan's feet. Brittany, waif-like with thin, pale skin, who's close to voting age, and whom Lauren has known as long as she can remember as the timid little Johnson girl up the street, sits side-saddle on Donovan's lap.

She's wearing distressed jeans and, despite the briskness of the evening, a suggestively efficient halter top. Brittany's arms are around Donovan's head and she's kissing his long smooth neck, the easiest reach for her delicate mouth. Donovan, a strong-looking blonde of twenty, remains mute. His eyes are glassy.

Lauren should be physically uncomfortable but feels little. While she's aware of the familiarity of Tim's insane driving, and Brittany's attempts to arouse the interest of the reticent Donovan, Lauren is transfixed by the onrushing mix of illuminated solid and dashed lines on the road ahead, and as always, by the music.

Of course, there never was an AA meeting in Lauren's plans this evening, nor dinner out with a group of nonexistent girlfriends. Instead, Lauren and Tim met up for the first time since her homecoming, and then joined a bunch of twenty-somethings at a downtown club. There, Lauren was surprised to bump into little Brittany, now five years older than when Lauren saw her last. Lauren assumed that her young neighbor must have borrowed a very convincing ID, as Brittany could as easily pass for fourteen as for twenty-one.

At the club, Brittany introduced Tim and Lauren to Donovan, Brittany's new friend. Donovan was reserved, or stoned, or both. With a drink in her hand, Brittany explained that it was she who approached the tempting Donovan just a few minutes earlier.

"He's so hot; he was looking right at me. Why wait? I just went up to him to say 'hi'."

Lauren laughed inwardly at her one-time neighbor who seemed to have metamorphosed, like caterpillar into butterfly, from the all-too-quiet and bashful little girl to born-again nymphomaniac. Judging by his glazed look, Lauren assumed that while Donovan's unblinking eyes were pointed in Brittany's general direction, they weren't focused on much of anything.

"And I'm glad she did, I guess," said Donovan managing to express at least something.

At once, Lauren saw in Brittany a bit of herself as a teenager - on the surface, her cultivation of an over-sexed ego through personal visuals. Noticeable to Lauren are Brittany's designer clothes, a killer contour, and a supermodel's slenderness, in Lauren's own experience, brought about only by nonstop dieting and bulimia.

Even while mesmerized now by the small patch of ever-changing road ahead, Lauren considers that she might learn more about Brittany. Lauren thinks that maybe she should warn Brittany, tell her what she's been going through. Then, reality intrudes. *Who am I kidding? Even after Delray, I can't say no. Some cute guy offers a night out, and I throw it all away.*

Instead, Lauren turns to Tim.

"So, I forget, where are we heading, and why are we going so fucking fast to get there," Lauren says loudly, wondering about the seatbelts jammed in the crevice between the backrest and the bench.

"Huh? I told you. We're heading into the desert," asserts Tim, ignoring her apparent plea to slow down.

"A desert? I don't see a desert." Lauren pretends to peer into the sandy darkness to spot an oil sheik on top of a camel hump, or maybe behind the wheel of a Land Rover.

Tim, who tends to withdraw into himself when coming down, is solemn.

"Lauren, I told you. It's the Sonoran Desert."

Lauren laughs. "I must still be messed up. The Snorin' Desert?" baiting her former boyfriend. "That's it! By the time we get there, we'll *all* be snorin'."

Tim doesn't react to the palpable banter. "So-Nor-Run," he enunciates. "So-Nor-Run Desert."

Yes, Tim, like you, I grew up in Tucson and know the name of the fucking desert, Lauren thinks. "I like 'Snorin' better," she says, dismayed.

"Whatever."

Lauren gives up on Tim, whose dim-wittedness proves sobering, and fixes her gaze back on the road. She chastises herself. *What am I doing here? I was getting my life back. This whole thing is like high school all over again. I hated high school! I would bail this ride, and Tim along with it, but we're in the middle of bumfuck nowhere.*

Lauren drank a beer at the club, ending a good stretch of sobriety. After one there was another, and so on. For a couple of hours, it was as though she never moved out of Tucson. *What now?* Lauren asks herself. *Why can't I stop?!*

Lauren looks over again at her nearly anorexic neighbor. Brittany pushes her stainless-steel tongue ring down Donovan's throat and subtly rubs at his groin. Donovan is still unresponsive, as if being examined by his internist. Brittany pulls her tongue back into her own mouth, looking unhappy.

Lauren is confident that Donovan downed too many zannies before getting to the club. *This guy won't remember any of this in the morning.*

Turning to Brittany, Lauren rolls her eyes in sympathy. Brittany backs off from the task at hand, and happily catches up with her one-time neighbor. Talking over the music, they ignore the two silent young men. Lauren asks Brittany about her family.

"Yeah, my dad left, like, two years ago," Brittany confides. "I guess I should've seen it coming. They were, like, all business. They never smiled."

Lauren sympathizes. "Yeah, been there."

Brittany talks over Lauren in rapid fire without missing a beat. "After that, everything changed. We couldn't afford to keep the house in the foothills, so we moved down into the city. It's not a bad place. Mom did the best she could decorating and all. It's just small, and the houses are close together. But I hang out with some of the neighborhood girls. They're so great. There's this Five-Guys up the street we go to. I *love* their fries. I just can't stop eating them, I'm so bad."

Brittany beams while taking a breath. Lauren, who understands excess, slowly nods her head. *She's so skinny, I bet it's four fries and done.* Brittany goes on.

"But it's just the two of us in this little place, and I guess we get on each other's nerves."

"What about your dad? Spend any time with him?" Lauren manages to squeeze in the question.

"Yeah, like, every other weekend, but sometimes he's got to work, so I never know. Mom's still really ticked off at him. They can't even talk to each other. They only email. Can you believe that? Mom got a job doing books, but I still don't know if I can afford to go to college, even if I do get in somewhere."

Lauren whose highest academic achievement is a GED, steers the conversation away from education. She leans over to talk into Brittany's tiny ear.

"So, Brit, you been seeing anyone other than mister excitement over here?"

Brittany laughs at that. She moves over toward Lauren to quietly respond. "Yeah, I know how to pick 'em, huh? I just thought he was the handsome, quiet type." She laughs out loud. "I didn't know he couldn't actually talk!"

The two girls giggle. Lauren likes Brittany. *She's adorable, like someone's kid sister.*

"I don't know, Brit," says Lauren leaning over again to tease her. "He probably couldn't get a word in even if he could speak."

"You're so mean!" Brittany says loudly for all to hear. "No, I got nobody now," the younger girl says, finally answering Lauren's question. "I *was* going out with this guy for, like, a year and found out he was cheating on me, so I ended it. That was, like, a month ago."

The two girls pause.

"You want a cigarette?" Lauren asks, lighting one up for herself. Brittany cracks the window.

"No, I don't smoke."

"Brit, you just hit the joint back at the club."

"Yeah, but that's different. I'll do weed and coke. But that's all."

Everyone has their own special rules, Lauren judges. *I had my boundaries, but lines are made to be crossed. No going back now.*

Brittany changes direction. "What about you? Your parents got divorced too, right?"

"Yeah, I was, like, fifteen. Turns out Jack – you know, my dad - is a real asshole. Didn't know it then, but when Mom kicked me out, I had to go live with him down in Florida. It was a total cluster. Didn't last a year. I was on my own for four years after that. That didn't turn out so well either. I just moved back."

"Yeah, not surprising. I haven't seen you, like, forever; but I haven't seen a lot of people. So, your mom kicked you out, huh?"

"Sure enough. I guess I had it coming. I was outta control," Lauren says with a watery smile.

Brittany is curious. "Like, what do you mean?"

"Well, I did about everything: weed, bars, coke. Then I started with some pills. Things got bad quick."

"Okay," Brittany interrupts. "Like, that's more than I......" but Lauren keeps on rolling.

"Me and some friends sort of partied too hard in Mom's house a few times. Trashed the place. Some stuff was taken. It put her over the edge. Listen..."

Brittany's distracted by an intermittent buzz in her pocket, and she reaches in.

"...not to sound like your mom, or anything, but it really fucked me up. It's been like this scary roller coaster that I can't..."

"Oh, hey, Mia!" Brittany holds up her index finger to Lauren. "Oh, sorry, I'm going for a ride...Yeah, right now...You did what? What did he say? No way..."

Brittany brings the phone close to her ear and covers her mouth with her other hand, ending further interaction with Lauren, now sullen and reflective. *I wouldn't have listened either.*

An Imagine Dragons song starts to play through Tim's Alpines. Without warning, Tim jerks the truck to the right to avoid a little sedan that seems to have come out of nowhere from the opposite direction.

"What the fuck," Tim mutters in surprise.

Lauren yells over the song to scold him. "Damn it, Tim! Do you always have to drive so fast?! I hate it!"

> *Second thing second*
> *Don't you tell me what you think that I can be*
> *I'm the one at the sail, I'm the master of my sea…*
> *The master of my sea…*

Tim ignores her. Instead, he glances at Donovan.
"Hey, Donovan, do you play PUBG?
Donovan is temporarily drawn back amongst the living.
"Yeah. I love that game," Donovan replies with some energy. I've won, like, thirty times. Add me on live."

> *I was broken from a young age*
> *Taking my sulking to the masses*
> *Write down my poems for the few*
> *That looked at me, took to me, shook to me, feeling me*

Brittany catches Donovan's reply and looks up from her iPhone with eyes wide in disbelief. She's ticked-off, now playing second fiddle to an Xbox. Lauren, who's accustomed to hanging out with other addicts for whom video games are child's play, feels like a babysitter to her former beau.

"So, what's your number? I'll text you my name," Tim says.

While the young men who would be boys continue their conversation, their voices are subsumed in Lauren's mind by an aimless resentment.

> *Singing from heartache from the pain*
> *Taking my message from the veins*
> *Speaking my lesson from the brain*
> *Seeing the beauty through the….*
> *Pain…!*

The track continues as the truck barrels toward the Three Points intersection. At eighty-eight mph and while texting Donovan, Tim realizes too late that he's about to miss his turn onto Route 286. All in one instant, instinctively, he slams the brakes and pulls the wheel hard left calling out "Fuck me!" over the song's bittersweet poetry.

The sound of tires squealing on the pavement blends with the piercing screams of the two young women and the music. The truck slides onto a sandy shoulder that's positioned in front of a white vinyl-sided restaurant. The Tacoma cannot hold the force of the turn, and pitches onto its right side, toward a brick pillar, about four feet high, standing at the edge of the restaurant's parking lot nearest to the road's shoulder. It supports a sign that in daylight reads "Good Eats - Breakfast - Lunch - Dinner."

Nothing can prevent the truck from continuing its roll until it slams down onto the pillar that smashes through the passenger window, instantly severing Brittany's head from her young milky-white shoulders. In a moment, everything is still, and all that can be heard are the bewitching harmonies in the song's full-throated chorus, back-dropped by the constant sound of the rustle of a cool desert wind.

You made me a, you made me a believer, believer
(Pain, pain)
You break me down, you build me up, believer, believer
(Pain)
Oh let the bullets fly, oh let them rain
My life, my love, my drive, it came from
(Pain)
You made me a, you made me a believer, believer

CHAPTER 7

Henry's Musings

A misty rain blanketed Tucson this morning while I scoured the internet for everything to do with killer asteroids. Having devoured an eggs-on-toast brunch, I peek out the window of my second-story condo in Los Castillos to see if the weather has improved, and it hasn't. But it's Saturday, and I'm not ready to get back to my research, so I flop onto my living-room recliner to listen to music.

I'm soon enveloped by Emerson, Lake and Palmer's Trilogy, by now, an ancient song, but one of their best. After a simple lyrical introduction, the instrumental begins. I jack up the volume just before Emerson's blistering downward arpeggio crashes into the thundering rhythm of a repetitive bassline. It's the same exhilaration each time, for me, like a full-gear plunge off the side of a dive-boat just after sunset into the blackness of a bottomless ocean. As much as I should get back to work, it's hard to tear myself away.

Other than by turning on my audio system, I was never any good at making music. In high school, I played a trombone that would make a moose cry, and Mom influenced me to take up classical piano for five futile years. Yet music is as vital to me as fresh water, and it continuously flows through my mind. It's progressive rock today, but it could easily be a Gregorian chant, Black Gospel or Chillstep tomorrow, Streisand or Mars, Chopin or Chronixx. Under the influence of a woman, I even took to some country music, which had always tormented these Connecticut-raised eardrums, and country is all that remains now from that last gone-south relationship.

It's the end of the queue and though the music stops, a song always plays in my mind. The divine Trilogy lingers there now, as do sad thoughts of its brilliant keyboard performer whose defiant depression led to his final performance.

Too much negativity, even for me. I queue up a Jackson Browne station on my iPad, bring the volume down and turn to Google news. Avoiding further melancholy found in the World and US sections, I click onto Science, which is always full of uplifting stories about chasing the truth.

I also get to check out the competition. One caption catches my eye: "Oldest Known Case of Dandruff Found in 125m Year-Old Dinosaur." It's right up my alley. Kudos go to the writer for his tongue-in-cheek attention-getting use of this head-and-shoulders human malady to describe the flakes of fossilized skin found near the bones of a crow-sized flying raptor. I sure wish I wrote this column.

After some science, I go to the local Tucson news and spot a report on an accident out in the desert last night. Much to my distress, two fatalities are reported with alcohol as a suspected cause. A pickup truck is mentioned, the same I'm now convinced that nearly ran me off the road. Chills run down my spine. A foot or two closer and I could easily have been the anonymous victim.

The bad news makes me restless. I move a few feet to the kitchen, reheat a cup of morning coffee in the microwave, and bring out a box of Vanilla Wafers. I sit at the kitchen table, electronics at hand. My mind wanders to last night's voicemails from Raff, and now I smile. I should respond but delay the inevitable.

While I've become desensitized to the hot coals of dating failure and I'm naive enough still to be hopeful, the usual doubts set in. As Raff predicted, however, I'm free next Saturday night. No excuses.

My last serious love affair was with Jenna, the country music gal, also an x-ray technician. It ended after eight months. I was sitting across from her in a Starbucks sipping an iced tea, when she told me we had to talk. It was almost three years ago, yet I remember her words like it was yesterday.

"Henry, you're a really nice guy."

The kiss of death.

"Henry," she repeated. "You're really nice and even funny sometimes, you know, in that quirky sort of way. I enjoy being with you, and I care a lot for you, but you don't seem to have the same feelings for me. Or you can't show them. I don't know where this is going. I don't think it's going anywhere, Henry. Do you?"

I wasn't sure what to say. Even after eight months, we never used the L-word, although I'm pretty sure she would have reciprocated had I gone first. After a moment of awkward silence that lingered like a cough, a teary-eyed Jenna pushed her chair back, grabbed what was left of her blueberry scone and walked out the glass door. If anything, once her red line was crossed, Jenna was decisive.

She was right, seeing through me. I didn't love her, and to this day I don't know why. Was it me? She was cute and smart enough and had friends and interests of her own. We never argued, and money didn't come between us. While we weren't exactly passionate in bed, it seemed to work well for both parties. She even got along with my family, except maybe for Dad, who makes a point of disliking any woman I bring around. One might have believed she was a good catch for me, but come to think of it, no one ever said so.

Jenna deserved better. Deep down, I knew I couldn't love her. I should've stopped it myself much earlier. But then again, there was being alone once more.

I dunk a wafer into the coffee and continue to ponder. Since

Jenna, Marianne fixed me up three or four times, and I got about a dozen other dates through my overuse of Bumble, Match, Zoosk, Our Time, Christian Mingle and JDate. I usually took the lucky lady for drinks at Sullivan's. One of those from Marianne's efforts agreed to go all the way with me, to Casa Vincente for tapas. That's it, and each failure might have caused me to recoil into further desolation, but I'm not so depressed as I could be. I was actually married once, not that this is cause for merriment either.

They say that there is someone for everyone, to which my parents were a testament. My dad loved my mother deeply, and I believe was completely faithful during their fifty years together. Dad was devastated when we learned of her cancer, and her death destroyed him. It was during this awful period five years ago that I first grasped Dad's capacity for emotion and his facility for suffering. Dad's still around, but not the same.

So why the hesitation? Being honest with myself, for one, I'm still a little insecure about how I look. I suppose I should be less shallow at forty-four. I blame my mother, whom I resemble, and who is not here to defend herself, may she rest in peace. Can a person be both so insecure yet so vain at the same time? It's a rhetorical question.

Not that my dad was such a looker, but sometimes when I gaze into the mirror, I see the large rectangular face of Mom: a spacious forehead atop a large, sloping nose. The rest of her wasn't particularly appealing either. She was big boned, as one might politely describe a Brachiosaurus, and more angular than curvaceous.

It should be noted that none of this hindered my mother from being the most loving, encouraging, and consistent parent on the planet. Perhaps I've exaggerated her homeliness. In any case, she didn't light up a room. Too often has it been said that it's more important for the woman to be attractive. Regardless, it sure hasn't made my finding one any easier; and indeed, there surely is more to it than just my looks.

I do have a couple of things going for me. I'm smart in certain areas, and I can be funny. But to appreciate my subtle and sardonic humor, one must be of a certain type, and such people seem to come around as often as the alignment of the planets.

I decide to stop stalling, dump my coffee into the sink, and toss out the empty box of Vanilla Wafers. There's one more thing I must do before I get back to work.

Rafael answers on the first ring. My brother, who's rehearsed and ready, and possibly reading from notes, launches into a dramatic soliloquy with which I am deliberately patient.

"Hello bro… let me guess. You're calling to respond "yes" to our invitation because A, you haven't been with a woman in like ten years? Or is it B, because I'm your only friend in life, and you want to make sure my wife doesn't divorce me?"

In high school, Raff, a big ham, thought he would become an actor. At the age of sixteen, he played a pretty good Willy Loman in one of our drama department's more serious productions; although regardless of all the makeup, it was hard to be convincing as a sixty-something delusional and defeated salesman when in real life one was a pimple-faced teenager plotting to lose one's virginity.

I note that my brother didn't even consider the possibility of my declining their offer. I reply.

"Well, it feels more like twenty years, to be honest, and I'm not worried about your freaking marriage, which is awesome, no thanks to you."

"So, it's A! I knew it, you selfish bastard!" I hear the sounds of college football and the kids screaming and laughing in the background.

"What time?" I ask Raff.

"Hold on, commercial's over. Talk to Mare."

My call must have timed the SUV and failure-to-launch ads perfectly. His little performance complete, Raff's attention is drawn back to the game, and Marianne takes the handoff.

"Hello," she sings.

"Hey, Mare. Henry here. How are ya?"

"Yes, Henry, I know. So, I hear you're coming for dinner next week?"

"Yeah, Mare, I already told your husband that I would; but haven't I embarrassed you enough with these set-ups yet?" giving her an opening to be supportive.

"Embarrassed, me? No honey, sorry. If anyone's to be embarrassed it would be you, love." Marianne is not one to pull punches. "Listen, Henry, this woman is great: she's smart, funny, and so pretty. I have a good feeling. Trust me, and don't screw it up," she implores.

I'm thinking that I've heard this all before. I'm also hopeful that I didn't get quite as strong an endorsement.

"Mare," I said, responding on the upbeat, "if you say so, I'm down with this, and regardless, I promise to bring my A-game, and no cosmic revelations this time. What's her name, anyway?"

I look outside. It's stopped raining. The sun peeks through the clouds.

"Isabel. Isabel Dalton. You two don't know each other, do you?"

There's little chance of that. I will Google her when time permits. I'm then instructed to show up at 5:30, spend at least fifteen dollars on a bottle of red, and to dress appropriately. I agree without really knowing why she felt the need to mention that last part. I say goodbye to Marianne, but Raff, who's focused on the game, refuses the phone back. I imagine him on the sofa, arm around Rachel, twelve, or Adam, eight. Bella, their seventy-five pound brown hound-like mutt that Marianne rescued from a shelter, has likely nuzzled her way up onto the couch, and now lies on top of everyone sitting there. My brother has it good.

Raff is and always will be a man's man, and I accept that I'm something else. So, once again I dare to fall in with optimism, hoping that one Isabel Dalton figures me out to her liking. Thank goodness, it's not for another week.

CHAPTER 8

The Aftermath

First responders came upon Tim's pickup just past midnight. It was upended onto the brick pillar. They found Lauren in the cab, unconscious, between Tim, on top of her, and Donovan, beneath. The medics dragged Lauren's limp body from the truck, onto a gurney, and into a waiting ambulance that whisked her off to the closest level-one trauma facility. She opened her eyes and moved her head side to side in the rig but failed to respond to questions put to her by an EMT.

Lauren was transferred from the ER to a bed in the ICU at the Banner University Medical Center, Tucson. It's early afternoon on Saturday. She's connected to an IV and machines that monitor her heart, blood pressure and oxygenation, breathing and brain functions. She's got a big purple bruise on her forehead. Lauren's eyes are open, and she blinks intermittently. Isabel sits in a vinyl chair by her side.

A slight Asian woman in a white lab coat, carrying a clipboard, enters Lauren's private room.

"Hello, I'm Doctor Lee," she announces to Lauren. "And you must be her mother," turning to Isabel.

"Yes," Isabel responds, standing up from the chair.

"I'm going to ask your daughter some questions," the doctor says. Isabel nods. Lauren only blinks.

"Lauren, can you hear me?"

No response.

"I've been trying to get her to speak to me all morning," Isabel tells the doctor.

"Lauren, I need to know if you can hear me," says Dr. Lee.

Still, no response.

The doctor snaps her fingers in front of Lauren's face, and alongside her ears. Lauren blinks but doesn't respond.

"Okay, Lauren. You've been in a serious accident. While your vital signs are normal, perhaps you're in shock, so you can't hear me. Maybe it's something else. Or it may be voluntary. So, I'm going to have to stick you with a long needle to see your reaction."

Dr. Lee turns her back to Lauren as if to prepare the test.

"You keep your fucking hands off me!" Lauren yells, leaning forward onto her elbows.

"Ah. You *can* hear me. That's good. Now please, listen," Dr. Lee says in a serious tone. "I'm a psychiatrist, specializing in trauma. You've been involved in a terrible accident. You were found unconscious. You're lucky to be alive. I'm sorry to have to tell you this, but two people in the truck didn't make it."

Lauren and Isabel wince. The doctor looks down at her clipboard.

"A girl named Brittany died at the scene, and a young man named Donovan died here in the hospital not long ago."

Tears well up in Lauren's eyes. She starts to quiver, and she sobs. Isabel reaches out to take her daughter's hand, but Lauren turns her shaking body away. Isabel sits back down in the chair.

The psychiatrist pauses while her patient absorbs the news.

In a minute, Lauren whispers to Dr. Lee.

"What about Tim?"

"I'm not permitted to discuss the medical situation of the other man in the vehicle," the Doctor responds softly. "But I *will* say this. Like you, he will probably make a full recovery, but it will take time."

Dr. Lee again glances down at the clipboard. "Lauren, it says that you're scheduled to see a neurologist. He'll coordinate your tests, including an MRI. We need to determine if you've suffered any injury to your brain. I'm not sure yet but seeing that you're able to respond to me now, I believe the worst of it for you will be psychological. So, you might seek out a psychiatric social worker who specializes in trauma. We can refer you to one. I'll also prescribe a sedative for your anxiety."

"That may not be a good idea," Isabel informs Dr. Lee.

"Oh?"

"I'm in AA!" Lauren blurts out.

"Ah. Thank you for telling me. I'll put it on your chart. You can continue the Tylenol for the pain. Do you have any questions?"

"Is that it?!" Lauren exclaims. "They died!! And you tell me to take some Tylenol?! Are you kidding?! Brittany's dead! What's your prescription for that?!!"

"Lauren, I am truly sorry for your loss," the doctor responds. "There's nothing we can do for them now."

"You're sorry?!! I'm sorry it was Brittany sitting there and not me!!"

"Lauren, honey, try to calm down," Isabel says in a low voice, almost a whisper, her teary eyes glistening. "This is hard for all of us. It's not the doctor's fault."

"It's okay," Dr. Lee replies, but Lauren's rage continues.

"Yeah, whose fault is it?! Mine? Did they die because of me?!"

The room is silent for a few moments while its occupants consider the question. The doctor answers but not before Lauren starts to shudder and cry again.

"At this stage, it's best to consider it an accident and not to think about who, if anyone, was at fault."

"Thank you, Doctor," Isabel says.

"Lauren, I'll check in with you later in the day."

The psychiatrist leaves the room.

Lauren pushes the back of her head into the pillow and weeps.

Isabel leans forward in her chair and lowers her head. She closes her eyes, yet tears fall from them onto the floor.

CHAPTER 9

The Text

Marianne and Rafael are on the sofa in their living room, in front of the TV. The game is at half-time and Raff, who's not interested in hearing from the football pundits, mutes the volume. Bella's tail-end rests on Marianne's lap, with the bulk of her sprawled on top of Raff. The kids were car-pooled during the second quarter to their own sports endeavors: Adam to soccer, Rachel to dance.

Marianne, thirty-eight, is about five-seven and mostly slender. Her dark hair is in a ponytail. She's cute, even without any makeup.

Mare turns to her husband.

"You know, this is *absolutely* the last time I'm fixing your brother up. Isabel's perfect for him. If he doesn't get on with her, I'm done."

Raff, with dark hair and pale skin, and a receding hair line, is only slightly taller than his wife. Slouched down into the sofa, he scratches Bella behind her ear.

"I agree, hon. If he doesn't get *it* on with her, he's an idiot," Raff responds with a grin. "He's an idiot anyway. He should've slept with that Sheila."

"Yes, I've heard that before."

Raff shrugs.

"I'm thinking about a sandwich," he says. "You want something?"

"No, thanks. Seriously, Raff. Isabel is the total deal. You have to meet her."

"I think I've heard all *that* before," Rafael says with a smile.

"This time's different. She's different. You'll see."

"Saved the best for last, huh?" Raff quips.

A cell phone sounds a ping somewhere away from the sofa.

"Is that yours or mine?" Marianne asks.

"Yours. Mine's here under the dog somewhere."

Marianne heaves Bella toward Raff and launches herself from the couch. The mutt grumbles as Raff forces her onto the floor. He finds his phone and heads for the kitchen. Marianne grabs her own iPhone from a shelf in the TV console. There's a message from Isabel.

> *R u there? I'm at Banner hospital. ICU.*
> *Lauren in car accident in desert.*

Marianne gasps. She sits back down on the sofa, phone in hand, to respond.

> *Oh my goodness. So sorry. Is she OK?*

> *Possible concussion.*
> *Mentally IDK. 2 people dead!*
> *Don't tell anyone pls.*

Marianne gasps again, louder.

"Everything okay, hon?!" Raff yells from the kitchen.

"Yeah! No worries!" she responds and shifts back to the text.

> *Oh Shit!! Understood. So terrible!!! What can I do?*

Nothing now. Just need to talk.
Trying to hold together.

Call me when you can. I'm here for you!

Thx. Will do.

Marianne places the phone down onto the sofa cushion, bends over to rest her elbows on her knees, and with her head in her hands, imagines their pain. She wonders what happened out in the desert, and it crosses her mind that dinner with Isabel and Henry may have to wait.

CHAPTER 10

Call to a Friend

I t's Saturday evening. Isabel steps out of Lauren's hospital room to make a few calls. One is to Marianne.

"Hello, Mare? Is this a good time?"

"Yes. We're home. How's Lauren?"

"Her tests were all negative. She'll be fine, physically. Mentally, she's a basket case."

"What about you?"

"I'm exhausted."

"To be expected," Marianne responds. "What happened, Iz?"

"A girl who used to live up the block from us was with them. She died instantly. The boy sitting next to her died here in the hospital. I saw the families, Mare. It was so horrible!" Isabel starts to cry.

"Oh my God. Do you want me to come down there? Is anyone with you?"

Isabel tries to compose herself.

"No, I'm alone. It's okay. It's getting late. They're discharging her tomorrow morning. I'll go home soon, although I can't imagine I'll get much sleep."

"You should try. Can you tell me what happened? Where were they?"

"I'll tell you what I know. Her old boyfriend, Tim, came to my house last night in his pickup to take Lauren to an AA meeting." Isabel speaks slowly. "She was supposed to meet some girls there and go for dinner afterward. She was late getting home. I called her a half-dozen times, but she never answered. So, I phoned the police. That was around midnight." Isabel pauses.

"Iz? You there?"

"Sorry. It's hard to focus. The police didn't know anything, but twenty minutes later they called me back with the news. Turns out, there was no AA meeting. She and Tim went clubbing instead. Then, four of them went for a drive together in his pickup. They drove way out on Route 86, and Tim overturned his truck onto some brick pillar. There were no other vehicles; he just flipped over! They say he was speeding. They got a warrant on him at the hospital, and he was DUI. Lauren admitted to drinking, too. Two kids die, and Tim's life is ruined. I don't know if Lauren can handle this. I can't believe it myself. I'm in a real fog."

There's a moment of silence before Marianne responds.

"I don't know what to say, Iz. I'm here to help you anyway I can."

"I don't even know what I need, what to do."

"What *can* you do? Take it day by day," Marianne advises. "At some point, the two of you will need to talk to a professional."

"Right. Thanks, Mare. I should go now."

"Please stay in touch. Take care of yourself."

The call ends, and Isabel lets out a sigh before tears again stream down her cheeks.

CHAPTER 11

Back Home

Isabel picks Lauren up at the hospital on Sunday morning. They say little to each other until they're in Isabel's blue A4 and on the way home.

Lauren is somber and detached when she starts a conversation.

"My life is over," she says quietly.

"No! Brittany's life is over. And the boy. Your life goes on. You have to deal with this!"

Isabel intended to be sympathetic. She tells herself to be calm. Too late. Lauren withdraws. They ride in silence for a few minutes until Isabel regroups herself.

"Lauren. I don't mean to be angry. I'm sorry. Let's talk. We've got to get through this."

Lauren waits a moment to respond.

"I don't know," she says without emotion. "I've never felt this way. I'm numb. I don't care… about anything."

"I can't imagine how you feel, but you've got to change things. You can't go on like this. Neither can I. We'll look for professional help, one-on-one, when you're ready."

Lauren fails to react, and mother and daughter are again silent.

They reach Isabel's house in Catalina Foothills, an upscale suburb just outside of Tucson. Once inside, Lauren declares that she's going back to sleep, plods to her room, and shuts the door behind her.

It's at this moment, for Isabel, when the emergency of the accident ends, and when the process of acceptance begins. All at once, this new reality comes crashing down onto Isabel like an unexpected ocean wave at the beach.

Oh my God! That poor girl! What could I possibly say to her mother?

Isabel is now desperate to be alone, and away from her daughter.

What was I thinking, bringing her back?! She's worse than ever; and now she doesn't care; unable to care.

Isabel calls out to Lauren.

"I'm going to the market! I won't be long."

Keys still in her hand, she heads back to her car on the driveway.

Perhaps Lauren's outlook will change after some rest.

Isabel reaches the main road and commands Siri to call Marianne. When her friend answers, Isabel pulls her car onto a patch of sand off to the side.

"Isabel. I'm glad you called. How are things?"

"She's home, depressed. I'm trying to be supportive, but I'm angry. She brought this upon herself, and me. The whole AA meeting, going out with her new girlfriends, all a big lie! Right away, she's back at it, drinking with that dumbass, Tim. God knows what other drugs she's been doing. And like an idiot, I give her money. I feel like some of it's my fault."

"You can't believe that. It was the driver, although you could say they all had a hand in it."

"I guess. I just feel horrible."

Isabel starts to weep. "How can I show my face at the funeral?"

"I'm here for you, Iz."

Marianne holds on until Isabel composes herself.

"Sorry, Mare."

"Don't be silly. You're going through a lot. But do you have to go to the funerals?"

"I knew the girl and her mother. I have to be at hers."

"Got it. I'll go with you."

"No, you don't have to," Isabel says.

"I'm not asking you, Iz. I'll be with you at the funeral. When is it?"

"Tomorrow."

"Fine. Raff will be at work. He knows nothing about your daughter, and he won't know about any of this unless you tell him yourself. Either way, I'll see you there. Just tell me where and what time."

Isabel answers her, then caps the conversation.

"You're really a good friend. I can't thank you enough."

"You're right about that. I'll let it go for now," Marianne says, trying her best to lighten the air.

The phone call ends, and Isabel, somewhat more optimistic, contemplates her next move. While she's not directly responsible for the tragedy, she's guilty of enabling her daughter. It's tough love from now on! Time for a little chat. Lauren will have three weeks to get a job. She'll go to therapy. She'll move into a decent half-way house. She'll act like an adult, and no more bullshit. *I'll tell her in a calm tone, but I'm telling her now.*

Isabel turns the car around for home.

Isabel knocks on Lauren's door.

"Lauren, can I come in, we need to talk." No response.

"Lauren, are you asleep? I want to speak with you." She knocks with greater force.

"Lauren, really, enough is enough. Do I have to stick you with a needle?!" Isabel tries the door. The little hook-and-eye lock is engaged on the other side.

"Damn it, Lauren! I'm coming in if I have to break this fucking door down, you hear me?!" All quiet.

After a brief hesitation, Isabel takes two steps back and hurls herself at the door, instantly tearing the eye out of the opposite frame. She bursts into the room and finds her daughter sprawled on her bed. Lauren's on her back and her face is bloodless; her sheets are covered in vomit.

"Lauren!" Isabel shouts.

Lauren doesn't move.

Isabel spots a partially crushed blue-colored pill surrounded by a gritty residue on the nightstand. She shakes her daughter. No reaction. Isabel's baffled. *What do I do?!* She runs to the bathroom, comes back with a cup of cold water and splashes Lauren's face. Nothing. Isabel slaps her cheek.

"Lauren!"

No response. She slaps her again, harder.

"Lauren!! Wake up!!"

Still nothing. Finally, Isabel calls for help.

"911. What is your emergency?" asks the female dispatcher, serious and proficient.

"My daughter's unconscious! I think she's taken some pills! She's an addict!!"

"Okay, ma'am. What's your address there?"

Isabel quickly replies to this and to other identifying questions.

"Help is on the way. Is she breathing?"

Isabel listens to her daughter's intermittent gurgling gasps for air, sounding much like a death rattle.

"Barely."

"Okay. You'll do mouth-to-mouth if necessary. Tell me each time she takes a breath."

Isabel reports back to the dispatcher about every eight seconds.

Seven minutes later, Isabel hears the approaching sirens. An EMT rig and a police cruiser pull into her driveway. She runs to open the front door.

Three male medical responders are the first to enter. Two are EMTs; the third, the one in charge, has a paramedic badge on his chest. A policeman follows. Isabel ushers them into Lauren's room, which suddenly is congested with four, bulky, uniformed men. Each of the three medics carries a large trauma bag, and the fourth man is armed with a Glock 22 in his black holster.

Isabel is shaking. One of the EMTs, holding a clipboard, takes her aside.

"Are you the mother?"

"Yes," she gulps.

"What's your daughter's name?" he asks.

All hear her answer, while the first EMT makes notes.

Meanwhile, the Paramedic, with the second EMT at his side, leans over the bed.

"Lauren. Can you hear me? Lauren!" shouts the Paramedic.

No response.

"She is breathing! I have a slow pulse. Let's get the oxygen going," the Paramedic orders the second EMT, who goes into action.

"Looks like oxies, Al," the first EMT announces, pointing to the blue powder on the nightstand.

The Paramedic leans closer to Lauren, puts his thumb on her left eyelid and lifts it open.

"Okay, I've got a pinpoint pupil." He looks up at Isabel.

"You say your daughter's an addict?"

Isabel nods, quivering.

"Opiates?"

"Yes," Isabel replies, ashen.

"Narcan, Rob," the Paramedic directs the first EMT.

"On it."

In a few seconds, Rob hands a fully loaded syringe to the Paramedic who, without hesitation, shoots the naloxone into Lauren's arm.

Isabel watches all of this unfold before her, as if from some distant place. While she's aware of the gravity of the situation, it doesn't seem real. Strangely, her thoughts go to the ocean. She's underwater caught in an unmanageable current, drift-diving along a gray wall of coral. She grabs onto an exposed piece of substrate but loses her grip and is propelled forward into a gloomy translucence. The only thing she can do is let the current take her, and watch.

Within twenty seconds, Lauren's eyes jerk open.

"Oh my God!" Isabel exclaims, seeing her daughter awaken.

The Paramedic puts his muscular arm behind Lauren's back and hoists her into a sitting position on the bed.

"Lauren!" shouts the paramedic. "Wake up!"

Lauren mumbles something unintelligible.

"She's breathing. Taking off the mask," says the paramedic to the EMTs. "Lauren," he continues loudly. "Do you know where you are?"

"Mom's house?" Lauren answers, slurring the words, while her head moves like a bobble-head doll.

"Good, Lauren. What's your last name?"

"Dalton," Lauren answers, with more clarity.

"When's your birthday, Lauren?"

"February 26."

With this, Isabel is back in the room, and all her emotions crash in on her. At once, she feels everything, and breaks down, sobbing.

"Who's our President today, Lauren?" the paramedic continues.

"George Bush?"

"No. George Bush was a while ago, but you're not the only one that flubbed that question." The paramedic stands and, with a trace of a smile, looks over to Isabel. While the two EMTs go outside to retrieve a gurney, the paramedic has a few last words with the patient's mother, who tries to compose herself.

"Your daughter may be pretty agitated over the next few hours. It's the Narcan. She'll be nauseated, too. But she's okay, now. How about you? Are you okay?"

Isabel nods.

"Good. We'll meet you at the hospital."

Twenty minutes after that, Lauren is back in the Banner ER. The doctor who attended to her there the day before, looks down at Lauren's gurney and shakes his head. She peers up at him with despair in her eyes but says nothing.

CHAPTER 12

Road to Rehab

It's late morning, Tuesday. It's a two-hour drive north from Tucson to the female campus of the Dusty Palms rehab, just twenty miles northwest of Phoenix proper, in a small, safe middle-class community. For Isabel, it's just far enough away to ensure her privacy. She's at the wheel of her car. Lauren at her side, soulfully stares out the window. There's no conversation.

Ordinarily, the most striking of Isabel's features are her eyes: large emerald-green crystals that glisten and glow with a sweet intelligence not subject to deception. Yet today they show the stress from dreams of parenthood gone awry, underscored by dark circles. With a furrowed brow and hunched shoulders, she's almost unrecognizable.

Isabel has often heard that addicts must hit bottom before rounding the corner on their addiction. After the accident, and now with Lauren's oxycodone use, Isabel, who's normally disciplined and methodical in life, is at her own low point.

This whole thing has gotten way out of control.

Isabel speeds in a hypnotic state while she contemplates the road that led her here, and a way forward. She recalls someone telling her that addicts need a full year of sobriety before brain patterns change. *Why the hell have I been putting so much faith in those thirty-day programs? She'd be dead but for the Narcan, the EMTs and those ER docs.* It's all or nothing now. Isabel decides she will dip into savings, once more, this time for a six-month stint at rehab, as suggested by the Dusty Palms' administrator. If Lauren screws up, Isabel will cut her off for good.

Health insurance will cover Lauren's first twenty-eight days at Dusty Palms. Isabel negotiated with its controller about her out-of-pocket costs after the four weeks - down from $18,000 to $11,500 per month. That'll be about $60,000 if Lauren stays the course. *Thank goodness I can afford this, even write some of it off.*

Considering Lauren's overdose, her psychiatrist at Banner, Dr. Lee, kept her patient an extra two days in the hospital as a precaution. During this time, with her mother at her bedside, Lauren rebuffed any suggestions about rehabilitation, long-term or otherwise. Mother cajoled and insisted, while daughter whined and whimpered. Finally, Lauren weakened this morning, if only from exhaustion, and Isabel, with the doctor's approval, wasted no time to get Lauren discharged and on the road.

Isabel assumes that Lauren doubts her mother's resolve about the length of Lauren's stay at Dusty Palms. Isabel knows that, all too often, she's allowed herself to be manipulated by her daughter in these types of situations. This time, Isabel is determined to hold the line. *If Lauren leaves before completing her program, she'll be on the street, and she'll never survive.* Isabel concludes that she'll have done everything possible for her daughter. If she dies, Isabel will grieve, but she won't be responsible. For a mother, this is just about rock bottom.

Lauren looks out her side window down at the blur of the road. She figures she'll be out of Dusty Palms in two months, three tops. *It would cost Mom a fortune for six months.* But deep in her heart, Lauren knows she can't handle this alone.

Lauren's out of cigarettes and desperate for one now, but she's afraid to ask her mother for a pack. *She's driving like a maniac. She hates me.*

"Mom," Lauren breaks the silence. "Would you slow down please?"

Lauren feels the car decelerate but hears nothing from her mother. In a moment, Lauren again reflects on the accident. It's a horror-filled video loop in her mind.

It starts out like so many times in high school: scam money out of Mom, and hang out with Tim. The impetuous couple joins other partyers on a metaphorical raft, riding down a river of suds. The beer is amplified by shooters or drugs. For some, drunken abandon leads to sex.

Lauren watches the pavement move past her, still pondering her fuckup. Why did she go out with him again? He's like a stupid child, at twenty-two, still living with his parents. *He can't bring girls home, so he takes them to the desert. Really?! And I went?!*

Tim noticed Lauren when he was a junior in high school, she a sophomore. Lauren is classically beautiful, a trait upon which rests her entire dignity. She stands five-eight, her slender figure in perfect proportion. With glowing ivory skin, radiant pale blue eyes sheltered by rich lashes, and long, dark, shimmering hair, she could be of Spanish or Black Irish descent. Lauren is stunning and always turns heads.

She thinks back. What was so attractive about him? Sure, he was hot, and all the sneaking around was fun. But he's just boring now, and stupid. *Yes, he's as stupid as I am, going to that club, getting wasted. What was I thinking? Now Brittany's dead, and there's not a fucking thing in the world I can do about it.*

Lauren now considers the overdose. The oxies came with her

from Florida. How could she expect to stay sober with a handful of pills stashed in her purse? Another idiotic move. She wonders why she overdosed. A miscalculation? Were they laced with Fentanyl? She doesn't know.

Lauren faces forward and speaks softly. "Mom, I'm sorry."

With this, Isabel grips the wheel with force. Her face turns red.

"Sorry? I'll give you sorry!!" Isabel shouts while trying to stay on the road. "You don't know what sorry is! How sorry do you think I felt at Brittany's funeral where my friends and clients looked at me like it was my fault?! You're sorry?! I'm sorry...I ever met your father. I'm sorry... I ever wanted a child!"

The words are as hurtful as they are shocking to both mother and daughter alike. As she withdraws to her inner mind, Lauren repositions her gaze back to the asphalt. She tries to bury her feelings, but tears well up, and she sobs uncontrollably.

In a minute, Isabel composes herself and attempts to repair the damage.

"I didn't mean what I said, you know that, right? I apologize."

A momentary silence, then, "I just can't do this anymore, Laur," Isabel pleads.

Lauren seems to ignore her mother and stops crying, but her mind seethes with a disorienting blend of feelings and experiences and she thinks *this is just so not fair.*

CHAPTER 13

Dinner at the Spinozas

The week went quickly for me. I submitted a short article about gravitational lensing to *Science*, and collected the money owed me by a different periodical for my series on the bleaching effects of chemical runoff and rising ocean temperatures on coral reefs. It's late afternoon on Saturday. I'm temporarily flush and feeling accomplished, in my Ford Fiesta, heading over to Raff's house for dinner.

Raff left me a voicemail on Wednesday. He told me that dinner might have to be rescheduled but insisted that I keep this evening open. He didn't have any details beyond that, which was no surprise. Raff's on a need-to-know basis with Marianne, and that suits him just fine. Part of me met this news with some relief; but now that dinner's been confirmed, and I've bought the wine, I'm happy to give it another go.

Raff and Mare live in Casas Adobes, a lovely, quiet, well-healed unincorporated suburb just north of the city. I'm at the town center in twenty minutes and near to the Safeway parking lot, famous as the scene of an attempted assassination of a congresswoman, and the murder of six people. It's impossible to visit my brother without thinking of the tragedy.

I soon wind my way through Raff's thirty year-old subdivision of gray-and-tan adobe-mud homes that stand on flat acre lots of brown gravel and smoky sands. Parcels are minimally landscaped, Zen like, laced with sporadic desert trees, grasses, and cacti. Overhead, the sky is a cloudless blue, yet it's that time of day when the angled light is soft and diffuse, and the Indian rosewoods and blue palo verdes that I pass cast long shadows.

I'm casually dressed, as if there's a choice. I'm as good as I get in my jeans, leather boots and black tee-shirt (my favorite, which displays a swirling Milky Way with the words atop "I Need My Space").

Despite my wardrobe selection, I remind myself of my vow not to talk shop. I won't mention the cosmos unless someone else brings it up. There's a snow-ball's chance in hell that anyone will ask me about NASA's latest exploits on Mars, or the ocean of water suspected to exist below the icy surface of Pluto. Nor will we deliberate about discoveries made at the Hadron Collider or the inconsistencies between quantum field theory and relativity. All of this can wait for an intimate date with Isabel if I get that far.

Tonight, I will focus on her and the mundane: events of the day, movies, restaurants come and gone, politics if we dare, but nothing too dark or ambitious. Kids will be an allowable topic especially if she has her own. I will be polite and inquisitive. I will possess energy. I will be funny. I will drink.

I swing the Ford into Raff's driveway. There's no sign of any unfamiliar cars. I walk up a stone path to the front door, bottle in left hand, and ring the bell to their mid-sized Spanish ranch home with my right. I'm on time at 5:30, virtually to the second. I didn't dare arrive later than Isabel, but with Raff's penchant for teasing, better not to be too early, either. His daughter Rachel answers the door; she's out of breath. Bella's right behind, wagging her tail.

"Hello, Uncle Henry!" Rachel is a fan and always excited to see me. I love Raff's kids.

"Giving it the ole college try again?" she asks with a mischievous grin. The precocious little snot is just like her dad. Clearly, they've been practicing the whole week. All right, so long as they get this out of their system now, before *she* arrives.

"Yes, I love you too, Ray. Just wait until *you* start dating, you little munchkin. I'll have my revenge on you and your father both."

I feel I have a chance to best this twelve year-old girl.

"Well, Dad says I can't date until I'm twenty-one, so you might have to wait a long time, Uncle Henry."

Rachel, who's cute as a button and physically her mom in miniature, giggles, and darts back to some recess of the house as quickly as she arrived. I'm wondering now if the kids will be eating with us; should have thought that through before.

I head to the kitchen via the front hall. The dog is at my heels and demands my attention. As I stop to grab Bella by the snout and lovingly growl at her, little Adam charges into me to say a quick hello. Adam is in between video games with four online friends, and after a quick fist pump, he bolts back to his iPad and pals.

I continue to the kitchen where I find Marianne over the stove, wooden spoon in hand, her thick, mostly dark-brown hair in a bun, stirring the sausages and meatballs that struggle to stay afloat in a huge pot of red magma-like gravy. Her apron, which protects a simple gray pencil skirt and blue button-down, announces on its front that "Your Opinion Was Not in the Recipe."

Marianne is adorable. If Raff were in some terrible accident, God forbid, and Marianne became available, I would wait until after an appropriate mourning period before proposing, not that a right-thinking individual would harbor such saturnine thoughts. Anyway, my bet is that she would sooner be alone with the kids.

I hand Marianne the wine.

"You shouldn't have," she quips. Then she notices the tee-shirt and rolls her eyes big-time.

"Are you relaxed, Enrico?" Marianne likes her nicknames.

I'm somewhat relaxed. Should I be nervous? I'm hopeful, for sure, but a realist.

"No worries here, Mare."

"She may be late," Marianne continues. "Something about her daughter."

"Oh, how old's her daughter?" I'm happy to hear that Isabel has at least one child. I always wanted children; I think. I get sucked in by kids like Adam and Rachel who seem to easily adore me, with whom they have no real vested interest. I ignore that half the time they're giving their parents agita. Nevertheless, I always hoped that I would be a better father figure than mine was for Raff and me. Dad, a cardboard sales rep, seemed to have just enough energy to get his job done.

Jumping a thousand steps ahead, if Isabel and I become an item, her kids might be a diversion and free me from the rigors of a full-blown relationship, unless she expects me to shoulder some of the responsibility. Nah.

I may be overthinking this.

"I guess she's about twenty," Marianne responds.

That might make sense. I found Isabel online. She's a smart woman who got a BA in economics at the University of Arizona before attending its law school. I figure she's about my age, so she must have been a young mother.

"How do the two of you know each other, Mare?"

My sister-in-law turns to me. "Listen, hon, I'm sort of busy here right now. Why don't you go find your brother? He's out back." Marianne suggests this to me as if speaking to Rachel.

"I'm sorry, Mare, can I help with something?"

"Yes, clear out. That would be a great help, and don't worry."

She turns back to her cauldron of meat and gravy which in and of itself is always worth the trip over.

I head from the kitchen through the backdoor. I see Rafael, in the weakening twilight on his desert-landscaped patio, staking out another improvement project. While he leans over a low-lying rock wall, I try to gauge if he's lost weight. This has been Marianne's own improvement project since Raff popped his knee in a local triathlon last April, to then put on an extra twenty pounds. It shows on his five-nine frame.

While it's not in her blood to eliminate the home-made pastas and meat-rich gravies, Marianne, for Raff's own good mind you, has been sweetly encouraging him to get to the gym. If I didn't know any better, I would think of her as something of a delicious culinary sadist. But in June, Raff made partner in his engineering firm which means even more work and less time to stay slim. To be honest, it gives me more than an ounce of pleasure to see that my brother is human and remains just a little pudgy.

The table on the terrace is candlelit and gracefully set for four. I'm relieved that the kids will be eating elsewhere. Near the table is a rolling liquor cart with several bottles of the hard stuff and mixers, along with a bucket of ice and some cheese and crackers. Raff spots me coming out through the sliding screen door.

"Hey bro, are you psyched?"

"I am indeed," I lie. "Are you?"

"Not really. This is Mare's idea. For some reason she wants to do you a solid again." A pause, and some tentative probing with his trowel around an immovable boulder, another stake placement as he earnestly ponders his next remark. "She also likes to take in abandoned dogs who dig the crap out of my yard, so who knows?"

Raff cannot help but smile.

I complain to him about his conspiracy with Rachel and her greeting at the door. With a glint in his eyes, he disavows knowledge of this, but he does ease up on the needling. Raff puts aside his little hardscape plan, and we sit on the stone wall to chat about this and that, starting with sports, of which I know little; his business, which is doing well; my book, which is slow to progress; and a bit of politics, by Raff's instigation.

Rafael, who throws it right down the middle, is infuriated by the upsurge of anti-immigrant sentiment that has surfaced locally, the situation exacerbated with Mexico only an hour to the south. I'm more noncommittal about politics, some would say apathetic, and would make a good technocrat if someone would just pay me.

Overall, my conversation with Raff is easy-going, honest and free-flowing. I always appreciate the rarity of having such a good friend in a close relative.

Isabel arrives well after six. Mare and Bella usher her out back, where Raff and I are still schmoozing. Introductions are made. Rafael has never met her either. The four of us stand awkwardly on the patio, near the back door to the kitchen. The dog paws at Isabel's bare legs as the new arrival apologizes for her tardiness.

Still in my own head, I see Marianne banish Bella into the house.

"I bet you were late second-guessing dinner with those crazy Spinozas," Raff says, as I cringe. Maybe that's not so far from the truth, except Isabel's doubts would be about just this one Spinoza, and probably why dinner was almost cancelled. Meanwhile, I see Rachel out of the corner of my eye, jamming her nose up against the window screen in the family room at the end of the house, her ears perked up to catch any romantic sound waves.

I forcibly inject myself into the conversation with some correct pleasantries about her being fashionably late, and not to pay too much attention to my brother, I figure, a safe foil for the evening. Marianne has water boiling and excuses herself, declining an offer for help from Isabel. Without wasting any time, Raff also takes his leave, and the setup is afoot.

"Duty calls," Raff announces. "Why don't you get our guest a drink, Henry?" He disappears into the kitchen. A good idea, my brother.

"Of course, Isabel. What can I get for you?" The two of us are alone, and I feel the need for one myself.

"Well, what do you have?" Isabel speaks in a reserved tone and seems a bit on edge. I pray that it is not I who is off-putting, for I'm totally drawn to the dazzle of the two green jewels that are her eyes. They exude a warmth and clarity that I would love to wrap my arms around. Although I tend to get carried away early on, I'm typically not one to notice such details. To overlook these gems, however, would be like missing a blood-orange harvest moon on a clear night in September, and I wonder if I would ever have the audacity to tell her this.

"Well, let's see what Raff put out for us. There's vodka, gin, tequila. Take your pick, or all three if you like. Also, there's a bottle of red wine in the kitchen, but maybe that's being reserved for dinner. What do you normally drink?"

It's hard to say, but I fear that I'm speaking too loudly. Talking too much in such situations is standard.

"Uhm," she's thinking. "The tequila sounds great, thank you."

"Sure, do you want something in there besides tequila, then?"

"Actually, over ice and a little bit of that pineapple juice, if you don't mind."

"No problema, señorita; uno momento." I'm quick to show off my international flair. While Isabel waits, I pour the same drink for myself, being too distracted to create something different. We clink glasses.

"Cheers," I say as she quickly downs half of the tumbler's contents.

"Oh my God," she sighs. "I so needed this. I had no idea."

"Rough week?" I ask.

"Sure, you could say that." She starts to smile.

"Troubles at work?" I stupidly press.

The smile fades. "No, something else."

This path is heading over a cliff. I switch the subject.

"So, Marianne tells me you have a daughter."

Isabel coughs violently as if the spiked pineapple juice went down her trachea. It seems that my declaration hasn't lightened the air.

"Yes, I do. She's twenty-one and quite a handful."

Isabel tries to fake a smile but is about to weep. Three strikes you're out. I have one more stab at this.

"So how about them Wildcats?" Admittedly pat, but it elicits a smile. I'm back on track, averting disaster, unless she's an Arizona Wildcats fan, in which case my ignorance will be found out and game over.

"Yeah, how *about* them Wildcats?" She plays along. "In actual fact, I don't follow sports at all. Not a bit. Do you?"

"No, me? Not really," I say in truth. "I would rather play sports than watch. I guess I'm too busy with my own thing. Raff is the sports aficionado of the family."

"I agree," Isabel nods. "Watching sports bores the heck out of me; and like you say, who has time? So, what do you like to play at, Henry?"

I ignore the suggestive nature of this question (not that she intended such innuendo, but *my* mind goes there) and explain that I get my exercise from lap swimming and tennis. I learn that she's a runner, a biker and part-time gym rat, and that it was at her health club where she and Marianne met. She's toying with the idea of training for a duathlon in the spring. I encourage her. We stay on this subject for a few minutes.

I pour her another drink. We nibble on cheddar and fancy crackers. She brings us back to the topic of swimming. I hesitantly confide that I wear a mask and snorkel in the pool to facilitate breathing and to keep chlorine out of my big nose, lest I sneeze non-stop for a week. I also admit to how much flak I take from Raff and the kids, who laugh hysterically at the sight of Diver Dan in his Speedo jammers. Pardon me for saying, but this makes a big splash with Isabel, well into her second tequila, and she again nearly chokes on an ice cube. This is starting to feel good.

The minutes fly by. Shouts from inside inform us that the mother of Rachel's friend has arrived to pick Rachel up for a planned sleepover. We see Adam in his pajamas through the kitchen window gobble up a bit of pasta and a cookie in front of a small TV, then get ushered to bed.

Finally, I hear my brother's announcement through the screen door.

"Dinner is served!"

Raff who brings out the greens in a gigantic wooden bowl, and the open bottle of wine, is stunned to come upon Isabel and me guffawing about our experiences with online dating. I can't say how, but we moved seamlessly from sports, grocery shopping and cooking for one, and our favorite national parks, to internet mingling. I must say, she's come across some real losers. I'm starting to feel my oats.

Marianne follows Raff outside with a large ceramic casserole filled with squiggly pasta that cradles the meatballs and sausages. She sets the food down in the center of the table and we take our seats. I'm between Raff and Isabel. Marianne dishes out the fusilli and grates some fresh parmesan as we help ourselves to salad, home-made bread, Spanish olive oil and wine. Mare, who can multitask with the best of them, has no trouble joining in the conversation, leaving Rafael still somewhat astonished and speechless, a first for me, and I relish it.

At this point Isabel is flying. She's all loose and giddy. I'm not too far behind. I'm quite taken with her, aware of the fun that I'm having and how much I miss feeling funny and appreciated. I'm worried about only one thing. What happens when we're sober?

Somewhere toward the end of dinner, Isabel lets on as to the reason she arrived late. Directing her attention mostly to me, she explains.

"I have to say, I almost didn't show up at all tonight and finally decided to come, well, pretty much just before I came. I had some horrendous goings-on with my daughter earlier in the week; don't want to get into that now," she says wagging her finger. "But I'm so happy I made the right choice. This has been so much fun, and of course," now turning toward Marianne, "delicious too. Thank you so much."

I believe she touches my knee with her hand under the table. Am I misreading this, or is there a future here? At least one date? And would you look at those eyes!

My mouth must be open in amazement, or I have a piece of fusilli hanging from my chin, I don't know which, because Raff just then jolts my other leg with his knee. Mechanically, I take my napkin to my face, and just to be safe, wipe my teeth with my tongue should I have any spinach caught in a crevice. Shaking his head and grabbing me at my elbow to pull me in, Rafael whispers.

"God, you're stupid. I'm trying to say, 'nice job'."

I guess, for me, immediate success with a woman is hard to fathom.

Dessert, an intense French roast with Marianne's scratch chocolate-chip cookies, is concluded, and I walk Isabel to her car.

"You're sure you're okay to drive?" I inquire.

"Yes, I'm sure. Marianne's coffee was strong enough to rouse the dead. Thank you for your concern."

I then have the clearheaded courage to ask if I could call her.

"Of course," she smiles. "Why not? I had a really nice time tonight. Thank you so much."

Her sweet sincerity is as appealing to me right then as anything I can remember. In fact, my only mild disappointment about the entire evening is that she never took an interest in my tee-shirt. I put this thought aside when at that moment she leans over and kisses me on the cheek. This man-child is in love once again.

CHAPTER 14

Isabel's Musings

I sabel smiles as she pulls away in her A4 leaving Henry at curbside. She's unhurried while she weighs Henry's pros and cons in her mind. He's a nice guy, for sure, and smart enough. He may not be so attractive, but he does keep in shape. Isabel remembers how handsome Jack Dalton was when they got married. She grimaces as she calls to mind their last days together. He's not so cute anymore.

Isabel's smile returns as she thinks back on some of the things Henry said to make her laugh. The self-deprecating image of him in the Speedos with the snorkel was funny enough. After what happened that last week, it amazes Isabel that she could laugh at all.

Even his tee-shirt's so geeky it's kind of adorable. How odd Marianne warned me not to mention it as we were stepping out onto the patio. What's that about?

Isabel's thoughts stay with Mare, a real friend. Isabel was impressed with Marianne's good judgment and integrity from the start. She was especially taken with, even envious of, the way in which Mare described her relationship with Raff. Isabel quickly confided in Marianne about Lauren's issues, which Mare kept to herself.

Mare was a star last week, comforting and counseling, genuinely concerned. Isabel's not sure how she would have fared at the funeral without Marianne at her side.

It was Mare who finally convinced Isabel to keep their dinner plans this evening. Isabel could easily have stayed home, giving in to her grief, her guilt. Turns out, having dinner with those crazy Spinozas was the best thing she could have done for herself.

There must be something to this Henry if Marianne brought us together. We can all at least be friends.

Staying positive, Isabel thinks about the opportunity she'll have, while Lauren is away, to make adjustments in her own life. Henry was right. She'll enter that race. She'll eat well and, God, no more drinking like tonight! She'll delegate better at work and leave at a normal time. And she'll try to have some fun. Yes, fun! She deserves that. *If Henry calls, we'll go out.*

Above all, she thinks, she must remain calm. No more outbursts like the one in the car. That was unforgivable. She'll get back into her Nalanon group. *I need to stay balanced.*

Isabel's thinking shifts to her daughter, as it was bound to do. *This week must be a low point for her. Will it stick? It's got to.*

At that moment, her cell phone rings. The number displayed on the Audi console is unfamiliar, but she presses the control knob to accept the call.

"Hello, Mom?" Isabel hears her daughter through the car's speakers. She sounds like she's in distress.

"What is it, Lauren?" Isabel's annoyed. It's 9:30 Saturday night. Why is she getting this call?

"Mom, you have to get me out of here! This place is crazy. The people are mean. I haven't even seen a therapist yet. They don't know what they're doing. The staff is so unhappy. I think some of them might be using. They're totally badmouthing the owners. Someone was taken out in a straitjacket tonight in an ambulance. Where'd you find this place? It's a fucking shit-show, Mom. You have to come up here and get me out!"

Isabel immediately feels the tension rise in her body, but she's desperate to hold on to tonight's sense of well-being. She tells Lauren to make the best of it for now. She'll call the facility tomorrow.

"You can't call them tomorrow. It's Sunday. They won't be around. You have to just come get me." Lauren speaks in double time.

"Well, honey, that's not happening. I'll get with the facility on Monday if they don't answer tomorrow." What she doesn't say is *why the hell do you even have access to a phone at this hour? With no supervision. Maybe it is a shit-show!*

"In the meantime, you're there, and that's where you'll stay," Isabel says, agitated.

"If I stay here, I'll end up using."

In the midst of a verbal rampage, it takes a focused mind to sort the manipulative bullshit from the truth. Lauren set this one up nicely, but Isabel figures that it's unlikely that Lauren will have access to drugs. The straitjacket thing was also over the top. Instead of calling her out on the lies, about which there's no certainty, Isabel calls her bluff.

"That will be your choice, Lauren," she replies. "I have to go now, honey. Good luck." With that Isabel terminates the connection.

The phone rings again and again, but Isabel ignores all of Lauren's frenzied attempts to reconnect. Eventually her daughter gives up.

Generally, Isabel allows her tightly-wound emotions to get the better of her; but tonight, she feels competent. She thinks of how nicely those tequilas went down, and then of the ironic relationship of her drinks to Lauren's own choices about self-medication.

"Good God, I'm so ready for bed," Isabel pronounces out loud, as she completes the drive home.

CHAPTER 15

The Day After

I t's the day after I met my newly beloved. I'm up early and feel as fresh and alive as a newborn colt frolicking in a soft meadow. I'm at my four-square butcher-block table, still in my boxers and NASA tee-shirt, enjoying a quick bowl of Honey Bunches and blueberries. After breakfast, I sip my coffee and send out a few emails to schedule tennis. My Sonos is tuned to smooth jazz on 92.9, which serendipitously plays a Miles Davis piece, "I Thought About You." The coffee is as hot as the music is cool. A perfect start to a Sunday morning.

Alas, I must take my leave of this pleasure for there is much to do. I've decided to call Isabel later to give her time to feel the emptiness without me; more likely, I want to avoid the appearance of a stalker.

My writer's goal is to start the outline for my book. I've advanced my research sufficiently to make some hard and costly commitments. My coffee mug in hand, I move from the kitchen twenty feet into the living room where my laptop sits on a sleek metallic work-station. I lay the mug on my Star Trek ceramic coaster (the farthest my geekiness will boldly go) and rouse my computer with a touch of the keyboard.

My book will be a piece of non-fiction on the universe, suited to the average reader and unlike any of my more technical articles which are never found on your typical news stand. I'm no Hawking, so I need a hook. There will be absolutely no math. My vision is to seduce the masses about a huge cosmic question. Ergo, the book must be a perfect balance of enlightenment, entertainment, and perspective. It shall create lots of "aha" moments and some chuckles, and it will fly off the shelves.

My hook isn't baited yet. I'm inept when it comes to self-promotion, so I'm thinking that I should get some outside advice, starting with Raff.

Writing this thing will be on spec. It's way outside the scope of interest of any of my ordinary sponsors, and it's surely beyond anything I've done. Yet, at forty-four, I'm in a bit of a professional rut, so I'm willing to assume the risk. It's been nearly twenty years that I've been writing articles on science for consumption by an atypical subset of readers. While I have a blog and did manage to complete a short text on Pterosaurs, basically flying dinosaurs, I'm tired and bored, and, I fear, boring.

It's not the science; I love the science. It's the process: the painstaking research, the sucking up to big scientific egos, a lack of appreciation, more sucking up to bottom-line sponsors, the competition from younger, smarter and more techno-savvy writers, the selling and the schmoozing and such other crap that comes with not having a huge trust fund.

What's worse, as an independent, the compensation and absence of a corporate health plan are demoralizing. Sure, I have put away enough over the years so as not to live payday to payday. In fact, I've managed to scrape together a bit of a nest egg, and I do own more of my condo than the bank does. But this was accomplished more through thrifty management of overhead and not top line success.

More to the point, I have been forced to be frugal. Bored, boring, and budget conscious; the trifecta of gloom. If this book gets written, I'm dreaming of dollars, and if possible, a mini-series.

There's more to my ennui than just repetition and thrift, but it's hard to pinpoint. I do know what it's not. It's not some Brando-esque regret about what I could-a-been. I quit grad school a long time ago, with some dismay, but with my eyes open as to where I might fit into a professional world.

Nor does it stem from an underlying impulse to make a notable contribution to a broader society, for I'm confident that even the best of us quickly come and go. Most so-called great men and women, on a geological scale, have but a few seconds of planetary influence; and really, where have they left us? In the face of cataclysmic incongruities: a giant ice-melt juxtaposed with a growing scarcity of fresh water; religious jihad against those of the same faith; wars waged by rulers intent upon killing their own population in order to control it; and high-tech globalization that advances the lives of some while destroying those of others - against all these discordant realities, there's worldwide intransigence and polarization leading to a chilling effect on the political process, finger-pointing, disinformation and deceit.

More simply perhaps, the numbers of criminals and crazies in the world, some of whom actually run entire countries with atomic arsenals, and regardless, who always have a hugely disproportionate impact, are growing every day with a world population that is expected to reach nine billion by 2040. This is a world gone out of control.

But, while I do pay attention, I remain decidedly apolitical. And yes, there's something wrong with that too, as I may be compared to an atheist who reads scripture only to debunk it in confirmation of his own lack of faith. But what can one simple man do to hold back the surge?

Regardless of the elemental reason for my restlessness, this book can be the start of something fresh, my own personal Big Bang. But what if I fail? What if I don't get it written? What if it's the sound of the vacuum of space that I hear and not a big boom? Then what? Oh fear, the enemy of all things.

Laying aside my interminable doubts, I set about putting the plan for my great opus into motion. Somewhere in the back of my mind, also, I'm thinking about what to have for lunch.

CHAPTER 16

That Same Day

Isabel's Sunday is in keeping with her resolutions from the night before. She's up at six and on the road in twenty minutes. Donned in her cushioned black bike shorts and Pearl Izumi jersey, she steers her Audi with one hand, while she rips open the plastic around a protein bar with her teeth. With her bicycle hanging from its rack on the trunk, and helmet and bike shoes on the floor in the back, she drives the thirteen miles to the Julian Wash Greenway just off I-10. Here she meets up with a dozen other similarly ambitious women.

This group and its thirty-mile ride were organized by the bike shop where she bought her pricey Cervélo. At sixteen mph, the ride is over in just under two heart-pounding hours. Afterward, still drenched in sweat, she and another enthusiast, a divorce attorney, sit outside of Whole Foods for a few minutes to rehydrate on a juice smoothie.

Now, back at her tastefully appointed home, and out of the shower, Isabel's first thoughts are of her daughter. While it's unlikely that the rehab is as bad as Lauren claims, or that Isabel will reach anyone there with authority on a Sunday, she tries.

A therapy assistant, who just came on duty this morning, answers the call. She informs Isabel that her questions about her daughter's treatment or living conditions would have to wait until the office opens Monday morning. The TA reassures Isabel that, presently, "everything's normal."

Yet Isabel is uncertain. She found the rehab through a second-hand recommendation and, due to the exigency of the situation, didn't employ her usual due diligence. *I've put more effort into buying a new computer.* But, she thinks, she can always move Lauren out if it proves to be a bust.

Now that she's made the call, Isabel focuses on food. She stands in her granite kitchen and contemplates her breakfast options. This is the marital home that she received as part of her settlement with Jack, some five years ago. She realizes that she doesn't need 3,800 square feet but saw no reason to endure the pain of moving. The house is free and clear.

Isabel decides on a gruyere and spinach omelet and toast. She breaks two eggs, chops some pre-washed greens, and shreds the cheese. During the prep, she glances out at her kidney bean swimming pool and the brown highlands beyond. Today, the pool is merely decorative, but Isabel reminisces about Lauren in grade school with her friends gleefully splashing about. Despite the stress surrounding their daughter's issues, the little family did have some good times together.

In less than ten minutes, after a pinch of salt and a swirl of the pepper grinder, her plate is ready to run. She sits on a fluffy white sofa in the family room with the dish carefully in her lap, a cup of Morning Thunder on the coffee table in front of the large wall-mounted TV. She goes to her favorite Sunday morning news show, *Meet the Press.* Chuck Todd interviews a Colorado congressman about a mass shooting that occurred last Tuesday at a middle school in his district, just outside of Denver. It was the day that Isabel took Lauren to Dusty Palms.

The congressman decries the violence. He calls for background checks and better access to mental health care. Isabel shakes her head and, out loud, scolds the politician.

"If only it were that simple!"

Appalled by the violence, and disgusted with the reaction, she grabs the remote and switches to a local PBS show reporting on a food literacy program - kids growing vegetables in school gardens. At the end of the segment, Isabel wipes her plate clean with a last bit of toast.

She brings her dish and cup to the sink and grasps a plastic wrapped chocolate chip cookie that Marianne sent home with her the night before. *I so deserve this.* PBS shifts to a piece on the Tucson economy, and Isabel polishes off the treat with a sigh. By 11:00, she closes her eyes and dozes off on the sofa while *Arizona Week* presents follow-up coverage on the slayings.

In a half-hour, she forces herself awake and turns the TV off. There's catch-up work from the office, and time is money.

Elder law is a busy and growing field, especially in Arizona. She reads up on recent state regulations that control caregiving. She reviews a Medicaid application completed by her paralegal. She cuts and pastes a trust for an older couple, to shelter their assets for the day that one of them must enter a nursing home, and Arizona Medicaid, if it's still around, will look at their net worth to determine eligibility.

Isabel is committed to her clients and loves her independence. She's respected amongst her peers, and even by Agency staff against whom she often argues about Medicaid dispositions. On top of it all, she's doing quite well.

Her success mitigates the sting of Jack's infidelity and the anger she felt on that tumultuous day when she confronted him and told him to leave. Isabel is happy with her work. If only she could find a good man. Then there's Lauren.

It's 4:30. She's at her desk in the study when the phone rings.

"Hello."

"Isabel?" It's Henry on the line.

"Yes, hi!" She's surprised by her own enthusiasm, recognizing him at once.

"Oh hey, it's Henry, you know, from last night."

He's so cute in an awkward sort of way. I know who you are. I wasn't that drunk, was I?

"Henry, how nice of you to call," she replies. "Perfect timing. I'm ready for a break, and thanks, dinner was wonderful. How was your day today?"

Isabel feels in herself the pleasant feistiness from last night. Henry seems guarded, at first.

"Well, I was supposed to be working all day, but found myself at the fridge more than my desk. What about you?"

Her day was great, she says, and provides him with some of the details of her bike ride. She's animated and happy to be on the phone with him. For a few minutes, she does most of the talking. He starts to relax and moves the conversation along.

"Anyway," he says, "I had a really good time last night; hope I didn't pour too much alcohol into you."

"You did, you absolutely did. It was all your fault," she teases. "One would think that you were trying to take advantage of me."

There's a noticeable lull in the conversation as Henry takes his time to respond.

"Oh, you're a fast one, aren't you? Even if I were to try something, which I wouldn't, at least not at my brother's house, I'm not sure you would've noticed."

"Are you saying that your skills at this are such that I wouldn't even notice?" she asks, sounding a bit like a trial lawyer.

"Well, you know, I don't want to make any claims," he responds, seemingly cautious again. "We haven't even had dinner together."

"Are you asking me out, Henry?" Henry cannot see it, but

Isabel's smiling from ear to ear. *It took you long enough, but it was a nice segue.*

"Yes, as I said, you are quick." Isabel thinks that she can hear Henry sigh into his mouthpiece.

"Well, I don't know. What did you have in mind?" Isabel continues her taunt.

"How do you feel about sushi?"

Isabel, in fact, adores sushi. They make plans for Henry to pick her up on Thursday at seven.

The call ends. Isabel is still smiling.

On the other end of the line, Henry, who may as well be in high school, puts his cell phone down and gives himself a quick fist pump. "Yes!"

CHAPTER 17

Dusty Palms

After being discharged from detox, Lauren's upper back ordinarily hurts like the devil. The pain is a residual of withdrawal. This time she spent only three days there, not the usual six, and there's no pain.

It's Monday morning, and Lauren faces the familiar task of assimilating into rehab life. She exits Dusty Palm's primary conference room with a frown on her face.

That was the stupidest group she ever attended. *The therapist was lost. I could lead group a hell of a lot better. She's not even any older than me.* Maybe the techs lead groups at this rehab.

Lauren keeps her head down while walking back to her room through the sterile halls of this new one-story brick building.

She never should have gotten to that phone. Why did they leave an office door open? She could've called a dealer and arranged a drop-off. The place is a disaster. And who put that asshole, Don, in charge? *He was definitely coming on to me. And he's the weekend supervisor?*

Lauren's convincing herself into panic mode.

The rest of the staff seems sleepy. The place is three-quarters empty. She has not been assigned a therapist yet. That normally happens before group. No one seems to care. *But did Mom believe a fucking word? When the hell will she trust me?*

Lauren takes a deep breath. She's full of regret. She was getting back on track. Then she meets up with Tim, again. It was the mistake of her life. That poor girl! Right next to her. Lauren feels sick thinking about it; but she can't stop thinking about it. Why did *she* survive? *I'm so stupid! I should be dead. What the fuck do I have to do to get out of here. I've got to get out!*

Lauren returns to her room and launches onto her bed, in a room with four beds in all, three of which remain unassigned. Totally alone, Lauren buries her head in a flat pillow trying not to breathe.

CHAPTER 18

Date Night

With so much anticipation, I accomplished little, and the week went slowly. Rafael, my thespian brother, called Tuesday to encourage me.

"Look," he said, dramatically, sounding a bit like a young Clint Eastwood on horseback. "You've roped a beauty, and all you have to do is pull her in, hand over hand, slow-like. Just relax, and whatever you do, don't screw it up!"

This last part seems to be a common theme within the family.

Symptomatically, while asleep last night, I dreamed that I took Isabel to a Michael Jackson concert. We were told at the arena's gate that Michael Jackson had died, but that Michael Bolton would be standing in for him. I demanded our money back, but they refused, suggesting that we go to Reno where Michael Jackson would be making an appearance. The date having gone awry, Isabel dropped me at Raff's house where I was confronted at the door by little Rachel in an oversized apron wagging an angry wooden spoon at me saying, "I told you, Uncle Henry, to go slow, and what did you do? You screwed it up!" Then she giggled and ran away. Invariably, I recall the dreams that I would just as soon forget.

Now, Thursday evening is upon me.

It's 6:25. I hop into my car and proceed to the Dalton residence. I'm hoping that she took notice of the little Ford in Raff's driveway last week and has no higher expectations. Perhaps I should've met her at the restaurant and parked some distance away.

The Town of Catalina Foothills is thirty minutes from my condo. It's nestled between Casas Adobes to the northwest, the desolate Santa Catalina Mountains to the northeast, and densely-developed Tucson to the south. It's luxury in the desert and, if you can afford it, the place to live in Pima County. Despite its proximity, I've never had a reason to go there, until now.

It's dark out. I'd be totally lost without a GPS. As I make the gradual climb to Isabel's neighborhood, my headlights reveal asphalt roads cracked from annual temperature cycles, and sandy lanes, entwined like the veins in an acacia leaf. Here and there I'm able to see overbuilt earthen villas, lit up like Christmas trees, close to the street. I imagine that many of the dirt driveways I pass lead to more secluded, but no less palatial estates. Of course, gas stations, mini-marts and roadside malls are nowhere to be found amongst the opulence.

I arrive right on time. Isabel's house is situated on a small cul-de-sac, and I'm relieved that hers is modest compared to the mini-mansions that I passed along the way. I knock at the front door. It opens immediately, and Isabel stands there, smiling. She leans over and pecks me on the cheek.

'Hiya, Henry. Good to see you again," she says.

I'm nonplussed by her casual cheeriness. She looks good in jeans and a sweater, nothing fancy. I focus on her eyes and pearly-white grin, lit up by the front porch light.

"You look great," I say, astounding myself with this unfiltered sentiment.

"Why, thank you," she says, beaming.

"Are you hungry?" getting down to business.

"Most definitely. Do you want me to drive?"

"No, I got it, it's fine, as long as you're okay being seen in a Ford Fiesta."

"No, I meant only in case you want to drink. I can be our designated driver, at least until we get back here, and I don't give a fig about what we drive in, so long as we get there, and the food and the company's good."

Is she for real?

"Well, I may drink, but not enough to be dangerous," I say as a note to myself, "and the food is good, although your sushi standards may be higher than mine. They don't let me out too often."

"And it's a good thing. Imagine how many middle-aged inebriated women would be running around Tucson if you were out *all* the time."

I boldly retort. "You don't look a day older than thirty, and a few drinks seemed to do you some good."

Who am I, Sigmund Freud? Why do I say these things?

She responds. "Thanks for that first part. Maybe we'll talk about the rest of it over a Dragon Roll."

"You're on, except you'll have to fight me for it. I'm pretty good with my chop sticks."

I start to relax, and the banter goes on like this until we arrive at Yamato. I'm impressed by her wit, which I believe is *my* only saving grace in such nervous situations. I'm reminded that my relationship with Jenna was devoid of this delectable repartee.

We enter Yamato, and a very aloof Asian hostess shows us to our seats, handing us each a twelve-page menu. Isabel looks it over. I leave it face-down on the table.

"So, what are *you* having then?" seeing me ignore the prospectus.

"I'll just have what you're having," I tell her. "I can't tell one roll from the other once they're on my plate. I just avoid octopus."

"Why, what do you have against octopus?" she inquires. I explain that octopi are solitary and intelligent creatures, different than your average fish of the sea. Staying on this course, we soon learn that both of us are certified divers. I got my license in the pool at Penn (at least I got a degree in something there) and took my open-water test in a freezing rock quarry somewhere in the Lehigh Valley. She's the more experienced, with a PADI course in Bonaire, and trips to places like Australia, that I only can afford as an idea.

She goes back to the menu.

"Hey," she declares. "Don't think I'm doing all this work for both of us. That's not the way this relationship's going to progress." I like the sound of that. A relationship.

I relent and pick up my menu.

"By the way," she adds, "I understand that the octopi and squids of the world are taking over the oceans, so maybe we should be eating more of them and less tuna."

Well-said in a sushi restaurant.

A Latino waiter who wears a "George" name tag comes over. I guess all the genuine Japanese servers never made it east of Torrance. The waiter introduces himself as Jorge. We order some rolls and a Sapporo for each of us. I'm ignored then for a few minutes while Isabel and Jorge speak rapidly in Spanish. I catch a few key words like "Columbia" and "Architecto." I'm not sure whether he's an architect from Columbia, or he hopes to attend the School of Architecture at Columbia University. At long last, Jorge bows to Isabel and takes his leave.

My date turns to me.

"I'm sorry," she says cheerily. "I can't miss an opportunity to practice my Spanish."

"Sounds like you don't need any practice. I'm impressed."

"Thanks. It's just enough to get by with my Latino clients." She changes the subject.

"So, there was something I wanted to ask you."

I nod for her to continue.

"Let me preface this by saying that I'm only asking because I feel comfortable with you. Otherwise, I wouldn't say a thing."

I'm overcome with a sinking feeling.

"It's about your tee-shirt, the one with the galaxy and something about your space. Marianne told me not to say anything at dinner the other night. What did she mean?"

"Did my darling little sister-in-law say that?"

Now Isabel nods.

"Well, here's why. Like the tee-shirt says, I'm kind of enthralled with all matters of space. I'm no expert, but I've written a lot about it. Of all the scientific fields, I find this one fascinating on many levels. But it's been my experience that when I talk about it, I sometimes cause the woman I'm with to become," I pause for effect, "a little bleary-eyed."

"You mean bored," she says.

I pretend to ignore her.

"Marianne seems to care about me," I say with a shoulder shrug. "So, she set us up, and even though I swore not to talk a peep about space, when she saw the shirt, she flipped out figuring I couldn't keep my mouth shut. Come to think of it, I *was* wondering why you didn't mention it at all that evening."

Isabel laughs.

"But I *was* interested, especially after she told me not to say anything. I guess after my second drink, I just got used to it on you. So, what is it about space that's so interesting, in five minutes or less? I promise not to be bored, at least until the sushi comes," she teases. "Seriously, I'm interested."

"Are you sure, on our first official date? I've been told by more than one family member not to screw this up, and the last thing they would counsel me to do would be to run off at the mouth on this subject."

"No, really," she implores with sincerity.

"Okay then," I say, "but only if you promise to tell me about your daughter."

"Sure, I can do that," she responds in a quiet voice.

So, while looking across the table into the utter softness of her eyes, I begin to describe the universe in its appeal and significance to me, wondering if this familiar path will for once lead me to a better place.

CHAPTER 19

Date Night Continues

Isabel enjoys herself thoroughly at dinner. She's warmed and relaxed by this man. Sure, there are downsides to Henry. He's not rich, but Marianne had warned her. She's content with her own financial success and she's not marrying the guy. Jack was successful for a time, but that didn't stop him from being a jerk, or his philandering with that blond spinning instructor. *No, here is a good man. He's smart and sweet, and he doesn't seem full of himself; and good God, he makes me laugh. I've hardly even thought about Lauren all evening. I wonder what he's like in bed. Did I really just go there?!*

Fearing that she's getting ahead of herself, Isabel drives her attention back to Henry, who's at the point of expounding upon his cosmic passion and so has taken on a more serious air.

"Isabel, did you know that I'm a science writer?" Henry asks.

"Yes, I know, but we never talked about it," Isabel responds. "I found you on LinkedIn. Marianne also mentioned something about a book you're writing."

"She did?" Henry queries. "Well, I'm not sure where it's all heading. I wrote one book already on the dinosaurs. It was well-received in the science community, and maybe it's sitting on a shelf in some college library somewhere. You can also get it on Amazon. You might be the ninth buyer if you hurry. Never mind that. I'm trying to do something a bit different now, a little more generic and entertaining, trained at a larger audience."

"That sounds good," says Isabel. "What's it about?"

At this moment, Jorge returns with the Sapporos, pours them out into tall glasses and, seeing the couple engrossed in a frothy conversation, moves on. Henry takes a big swallow of beer then replies earnestly, but without a high degree of gravity.

"It's about the end of all things."

Isabel is briefly stunned, but quickly answers back. "Some light science for the average reader then?"

Henry smiles gently but stays on track.

"Cute, but I'm serious. There are several scenarios where things come to an end, which depend on whether we're talking about just Earth, our solar system, the Milky Way, or the entire cosmos. Of course, you've seen a movie about a huge asteroid about to collide with our planet. It's almost become mundane, but I'll include it. I might even have to debunk that famous drilling expedition. Then there's the sun running out of energy one day, expanding as a red giant and enveloping us in a big ball of fire. There are other hazards too. But the most mind-blowing thing for me is occurring right now as we sit here, the ever-expanding universe. I'll explain this to you roughly in the sequence in which I might write this section of the book. I intend the whole thing to be partly historical narrative, and like I said, partly just fun reading, at least that's my intention."

"Sure," she replies. "That sounds sensible." Isabel is more attentive now, savoring his authoritative manner. But impulsively, Henry digresses.

"Before I go on, I want to ask for your opinion about something." Isabel nods as if to say, "Lay it on me."

"I want the book to be an enjoyable read and something that

people will want to buy. So, I thought I would also add a little twist. It's not so scientific. It's even a little gimmicky."

"Sounds like what they call a hook."

"Yes, in a word."

Isabel encourages him to go on.

"Well, most observatories are located in really cool places," Henry continues. "Take the one in Hawaii at Mauna Kea on the Big Island. It's right on top of a volcano 14,000 feet up. There's a dozen in northern Chile, in the Atacama, the driest desert on the planet. I was thinking of combining the end-of-the-world thing with something of a travel guide around places where the big research gets done. What do you think?"

She pauses to consider his idea.

"I think that I like it. It could work, depending upon execution."

"Really. Good. I'll have to give it some more thought." Then Henry turns back to the science. "So, let me tell you a bit about the substance, at least how it starts off. The earlier history is more for context. Are you still with me, Iz? Do people call you Iz?"

"Yes, I'm listening," she replies. "Iz is fine. Some people also call me Izzy; my folks did."

"I like that, too. I take it your folks aren't around anymore?"

"No, it's just me and my older sister. But we can talk about that another time."

"Okay, sorry. Should I go on then, Izzy?" Henry asks.

"By all means, Enrico," she says, picking up on the moniker that Marianne created for him. At that, he smiles again but quickly jumps back to his explanation.

"So, if you allow?"

She nods.

"Do you remember Copernicus?

Isabel nods again. She remembers the name, she tells him, but not the significance.

"So, he was this Polish scientist back in the 1500s. He was

brilliant. He developed the concept of the universe in which the sun is at the center of all the planets, the heliocentric model: 'helio' being Greek for 'sun'."

This now sounds utterly familiar to Isabel.

"Prior to that, everyone believed that the sun and planets all revolved around the Earth, while the stars were stationary in the sky. Well not everyone; some of the ancient Greeks had other ideas, but Aristotle was not among them. Aristotle was no dummy, and it's totally counterintuitive to believe that it's the Earth that's moving. When you throw a rock straight up into the air, it doesn't land behind you, does it? There is no perpetual wind caused by the constant movement of the Earth. People are not being hurled into space by the Earth's centrifugal force. So, if the Earth's not moving, the planets, which we clearly see move in the sky every night, and the sun too, must be revolving around us. Are you with me?"

"Yes, go on."

"This was also the Church's view, the biblical view. At least the writers of the Bible, whoever they were, adopted Aristotle's logical view."

Then Henry declares, sounding a bit like James Earl Jones reciting *Hamlet*, "'Sun, stand still at Gibeon, and the moon, in the Valley of Aijalon. And the sun stood still, and the moon stopped.'[1] Those are Joshua's lines right out of the Old Testament before he took down the Amorites. Have you ever heard that before?"

"No, never like that, I'm sure."

Isabel thinks Henry's dramatization a bit overdone but is drawn in by his depth of knowledge. He goes on.

"Obviously, Joshua's words indicate that the sun was moving before it stopped. Anyway, for fear of being excommunicated as a heretic, Copernicus refused to publish his work until he was about to die, at least that's the way the legend goes. That was in 1543, the

---

[1] Joshua 10:12-13

very year that historians say was the start of the scientific revolution. When you read his thesis, you can see how apologetic Copernicus was to the Pope, to whom he dedicated it. I think he wanted to subtly stick it to the Holy Father, but that's just me. In any case, science ultimately adopts his view as he was mostly spot on, and others would corroborate his theories soon enough."

Henry takes a swig of beer. Isabel now definitely recalls the story that she learned in middle school, which is also the last time she gave it any thought.

"Copernicus was skilled in medicine, and in law, but I suppose his real passion was astronomy. Late in life he studied the night sky from an observatory where he lived in Poland. How he had access to an observatory is beyond me. I guess I should find out. But he looked at the sky for years, and one thing he noticed was that the planets progressed in one direction, then sometimes seemed to move in the reverse direction. This is what we call 'retrograde motion'." Henry speaks as if he coined the phrase himself. He continues apace.

"He also saw that each of the planets exhibited changes in brightness depending upon the time of year. Others before him came up with far-fetched explanations that kept the Earth at the center of things. But Copernicus pretty much nailed it, except for the fact that he said the planets all went around the sun in perfect circles, which of course they don't. Anyway, he figured out that it was the Earth's rotation that causes night and day, and that a planet wouldn't get brighter or dimmer if it's circling around us always from the same distance. Copernicus also determined that the planets' apparent reversal in direction was on account of the Earth's revolution around the sun, and its movement and speed in space relative to the other planets.

"Do you realize what an astoundingly bizarre construct this would have been back then? It flies in the face of our senses, and common sense: Earth spinning like a top, hurtling through space while our feet remain firmly on the ground. I think Copernicus got it and decided to leave this Earth before the shit hit the fan. Mind you, his model was technical, with geometric diagrams and such, but I want to explain it in depth without the need of a mathematician or a white board."

Isabel responds. "No, Henry, you do an excellent job, even over sushi. I do find it more interesting now as an adult."

At that, Henry is exuberant, but is perhaps cognizant of being excessive.

"Well, there's more, but I don't want to overwhelm you. My family would also have my head. Maybe I should stop here?"

Isabel smiles appreciatively. After a full day at the office, it's wearisome to concentrate on even this summary, especially with a beer in hand.

"Yes, that's a good idea," she admits. "We can discuss the rest some other time. I must say, I'm a bit embarrassed to admit that I hardly look up at the stars at all anymore."

Henry gives her an out. "Yes, around here you can hardly see anything. Too many lights. Isabel, have you ever looked at the night sky far away from the city through a telescope?"

"Well, no, I guess I never saw the night sky through a telescope," she responds.

"Just like Copernicus then. He did it all without a telescope. He died some sixty years before Galileo even picked up a telescope. He did it all just with the naked eye. Can you believe that?"

Henry pauses, and then speaks softly. "Well, Iz, have you ever seen the ocean then? We are in Arizona, after all, not very close to the ocean. Maybe you haven't seen the ocean yet?"

"You know I've been to the ocean," she says, recalling for him her scuba diving trips.

Henry drives the point home. "Of course, I know; but let's say you were on the beach on Bonaire, looking only at the ocean's surface. Wouldn't you want to see what beauty lies beneath?"

"Yes, of course I would. I get it. You want me to look through a telescope. You want me to look at the sky from someplace very dark, through a telescope."

"Yes, I want to take you to see the most unimaginable and wondrous ocean there is," he says purposefully, looking directly into her green beacons, now slightly melting with a dewy wistfulness. For as much as Henry's proposition might have been cynically viewed as being pretentious, Isabel is charmed.

She considers his proposal. He could almost be a caricature of a middle-aged geek, but he's perfectly genuine, quite intelligent, and sweet. With so many men, it's all about them. *No, this man's different. Marianne is right once again. I do like him, so long as he's able to shut it off from time to time.*

Responding tenderly, Isabel says, "I cannot think of anything nicer than to go with you to see what lies within this wondrous ocean."

With a grin on his face, Henry manages to finally change course.

"Okay, I will call you on it. So, now it's your turn," he says, gently prodding her about her daughter, without any real notion of what's to come.

CHAPTER 20

Wrapping Up Date Night

M y date with Isabel is going swimmingly. The more we sit here the better she looks; and she seemed to appreciate even Copernicus, who's just the tip of the iceberg. Not so easy with Hubble or Perlmutter. While I'm patting myself on the back, how smooth was that segue into the next date? I can't wait to tell Raff. On second thought, that might not be a good idea.

Jorge delivered our sushi toward the end of my Copernicus report, and so Iz is ahead of me by two or three rolls. Not to worry, I'm sure to catch up while she tells me about her kid. I hope whatever it is, is not too downbeat.

As Isabel begins, she seems to deliberately lower her voice.

"Well, as I told you, I have a twenty-one year-old daughter. She's as intuitive as she is beautiful. But she's had learning and emotional issues since the age of three and was recently diagnosed as being bipolar." Isabel pauses. "On top of all that, she's a drug addict."

With those last two words, the wind is unmistakably taken out of my sails.

"Wow," I hear myself say. "So sorry to learn this. What's she addicted to, then?" I sound as pathetic as an ignorant passerby at a fatal car crash asking, "Was anyone hurt?"

"Opiates. Heroin. As they say, her drug of choice."

"Okay, that sounds awful. So, do you want to talk about it?" a roundabout way to suggest my possible incapacity to *hear* about it. I'm a complete dolt for not considering something like this. Being bipolar is hard enough. Drug abuse has surged like an epidemic. It just never came so close to me. In my heart, I feel for her, for them both, and selfishly for me, as well.

Isabel responds. "Sure, I'm fine talking about it if you are. If we're to be friends, you should know about this, yes?"

In an instant, both she and I just took several cautionary steps backward in a possible relationship. I admire her for the intelligent way in which she phrased this, in effect not raising the stakes. My acceptance here binds me to nothing more than friendship. So, I agree without apparent hesitation, but at this unanticipated juncture, I suddenly feel ready for nothing more than friendship. How curious, the influence on me of circumstantial change in the shifting winds of commitment and desire.

"Of course, I'm all ears. I'm no expert in such things, but I should at least be a good sounding board." I lack confidence in even this, and wince at my own insipid indecision. To make matters worse, her eyes start to well up with tears. How quickly her mood changed; too quickly are things proceeding, says my inner coward.

"I'm so sorry," Isabel says, dabbing her eyes with a linen napkin.

"Don't be silly. It's okay," I reply, and she composes herself.

"Her name is Lauren." Isabel begins by telling me what Lauren was like growing up: the constancy and severity of her anxiety, her physical awkwardness, her lies. When she was three, Lauren would unpredictably come unglued over simple things: the feel of her socks on her feet, the presentation of the food on her plate, the speed of the car on the road. Isabel describes how she provided her daughter with an array of therapists to help her with a myriad of issues: motor skills, speech, learning, impulsivity, and defiant behaviors. This was even before drugs or alcohol were added to the mix.

Isabel recounts the additional strain all of this inflicted on her marriage.

"My relationship with Jack was star-crossed from the start. I was a junior at Michigan. We were reckless, and I became pregnant. I wanted that baby so much, probably for all the wrong reasons. I don't know what I was thinking, but I quit school, and we eloped. We moved here when he got a real estate job. He became obsessed with work and paid little attention to us. I was essentially alone with the baby."

"How did you become a lawyer?"

"When the real estate market fell apart, Jack lost his job and then his spirit. He found work, but it wasn't the same. Neither was he. He started to drink more. I saw the writing on the wall. I forced myself to finish college at U of A, and luckily got into law school there. It was about the only smart thing I've done. I took the Bar just about the time Lauren was getting through middle school. It was really stressful."

She pauses.

"It sounds like a rough period."

"Yes. Between Lauren's problems, my studying, his depression, and a lot less money, I thought I would go crazy. Things grew very tense between Jack and me."

"Understandable."

"We split up just after Lauren started high school."

Isabel continues her description of a fifteen year-old girl's evolving use of alcohol and drugs. She paints a dark portrait of her daughter: the substance abuse in juxtaposition with Lauren's wayward cunning, deceptive manipulation, and her cognizance of her developing beauty.

But as Isabel explains all this, an invisible pressure on her appears to be lifted. She speaks unhurriedly, yet fluidly with little concern for privacy. Any nervousness about divulging her confidential problems seems to be lightened by their possible transference to me. She confesses with unrestrained trust, and it's this that is to me both alluring and disquieting at the same moment.

At last, my rational thought prevails over my ambiguous discomfort. Even though I'm not inclined to drive so near to the rocky bluffs of intimacy, my hands grip the wheel, and I maintain control. It's not been more than a few minutes since I had this woman upon a pedestal, adoring her. Did I expect a flawless gem? Is there perhaps a nexus between my hesitation and perpetual aloneness? Get real, man! This is life, and you really like this woman. Familiar words resonate in my mind. Don't screw it up!

Such realization could not have been timed better, as Isabel recounts Lauren's return to Tucson and her part in the fatal accident. I immediately recognize that my near collision with the speeding pickup that Friday night was a precursor to the incident she describes.

"Oh my God, I know of this tragedy, Iz! I was driving back in the opposite direction that very night on 86 when I saw the truck fly by me. He was going way too fast, even weaving; and it wasn't long after that that I saw those emergency vehicles pass me by, heading into the desert. I read about it the next day. I can't believe it. So that was your daughter in that very truck! Damn! I'm so sorry, Isabel. What a disaster for you all."

The coincidence is more than Isabel can immediately absorb. At first, she seems quite perplexed, as if I had invented the story solely to flirt with her mind's inner anguish. Then, eventually accepting the truth, she presses me for further details, as if I hold the key to some essential puzzle. Of course, there wasn't much more to it, unless one believes in providence.

During the entire discussion, I've grasped my chop sticks forcefully, but haven't touched the food: not a single roll, not a grain of sticky rice, not a shaving of horseradish. My glass is still full of lager.

Iz concludes her somber narrative with her disclosure of the most recent events: bringing Lauren to the rehab and Isabel's doubts about its selection.

"Do you know, Lauren called me the night you and I first met? I was on my way home from Marianne's. She said how awful the rehab is, how she hadn't been assigned a therapist, and that some of the staff were using drugs. Would you believe patients were taken out in straitjackets? What could I say? Some of it seemed plausible. Some of it was outlandish."

"I guess I would have checked it out with the facility."

"Thank you. I spoke with a supervisor on Monday. I was on hold five minutes before they found her file. They had a consent from her, so at least they care about HIPAA. They told me she was assigned a therapist, but she wasn't scheduled until Friday. That's tomorrow. Fine. I mentioned the straitjacket thing. She laughed and told me how addicts will do or say anything. It was pointless to bring up the staff's drug usage, but I did ask how Lauren had access to a phone to call me unsupervised on a Saturday night. They had to investigate that one. The supervisor called me the next day. Apparently, Lauren broke into a locked office."

"Quite a talent."

Isabel scowls.

"I'm sorry."

"Oh, it's all right. I don't know what to believe," she says, shaking her head.

I naturally could be of little practical use to Isabel.

"Give it time. See how it goes." In this, my admittedly selfish goal is to bring the discussion to a close. Isabel seems to brighten, and we move on. But before we do, she apologizes for all of this possibly getting in the way of her being present, that is for me; while conversely, I realize that, but for Lauren, a point of great vulnerability for Isabel, I may not have even had a chance.

CHAPTER 21

Darkness

*I*t *was late at night, yet the air was still infused with a hot stickiness leftover from the sun's glare on that southern summer day. The hazy light from the half-moon was just enough for Lauren to make out his lumbering advance. She saw no others on the beach to whom she might call for help. Given his drunken state, Lauren thought she could outrun him, and tried; but she was equally unsteady, and he was soon to catch up to her.*

Looking back, she yelled, "Stay away from me, asshole!"

The man was tall and muscular. She saw that his leather belt had been undone, and its buckle dangled from his waist as he closed in on her. He grabbed her slender arm and easily pushed her face-first into the ground. She was still wearing a scant bikini, and upon impact, the coarse sand scraped her sunburned breasts.

The pursuer, holding her down, knelt to bring his face close to hers.

"Stop gaming me, you goddamn shit!" he warned, breathing hard. She could smell the bourbon on his breath. She tried to turn her head up to see his face, but he pushed her down again; her mouth tasted the grit. Then he was gone.

As she struggled to get up, three different men appeared out of no-where in the moonlight, surrounded her, and pushed her back into the sand. Lauren heard their drunken laughter and angry obscenities. One of them, the stockiest of the three, jumped onto her back and rubbed his stubbled face against her own, whispering threats of unspeakable violence.

Someone grabbed at the straps and pulled her top down toward her waist.

Lifting her head from the sand, Lauren shrieked.

"Stop!! Let me go!!"

The muscular one pressed his body against hers as he continued to swear at her up close. His companions tore at her bottoms and brought them down to her knees. She struggled to free herself but was pinned and powerless.

"Stop! You've got to stop!!"

They ignored her plea and pressed her face against the sand.

The pain that followed was unbearable. It ran through her like a sharpened lance.

Lauren lets out a horrifying scream and awakens. She bolts up in her bed.

Shit. Where am I?

Now she remembers. Alone in a room at Dusty Palms.

No one reacts to her scream. No one rushes in to check on her. Lauren wipes her forehead with the top of her sheet. She lies back down on her side. Her pillow is cold and damp from her sweat.

It's dark, and she's frightened.

CHAPTER 22

Sandy

It's Friday, ten days since Lauren's arrival at Dusty Palms. Sitting in an armless wooden chair in front of a small desk in a drab office, she waits for her therapist to arrive. She gazes at the one interesting visual before her.

Hanging on the wall behind the desk is an eleven by fourteen photo of a middle-aged couple, standing austere and erect on brown earth in front of a wooden corral fence. The two of them are separated by a foot of daylight; both have dark-skin and high cheek bones. In the background, there are two sheep that stand in a pen. The man, tall, brawny, and weathered, is wearing dusty blue jeans, a black tee, leather boots and a white wrinkled cowboy hat. The woman, a foot shorter and plump, is wearing a yellow dress with multiple layers of blue fringe and a white headband that supports one long brown and white feather. Lauren is only a bit curious.

She continues to wait. She hates waiting. *This whole thing is bullshit. They're so fucking disorganized. I'm wasting my life here. For what?*

A woman suddenly bursts in, shutting the door behind her.

"Sorry I'm late, hon. Get used to it, I guess."

Lauren turns, and before she can deliver a spiteful comment, sets her eyes on a tall and stocky, brown-skinned, mahogany-eyed woman in her early thirties who makes her presence known as much with her physicality as with a big, toothy grin. In a sleeveless white blouse and black jeans, she's attractive in an athletic way.

"Hello, Lauren. My name is Sandy Ortega, and I'm the therapist you've been waiting for."

Mexican, Lauren assumes. *But she's so big. No accent. Must've been born here. Cool eyes. Gorgeous hair!*

The tall woman's glossy jet-black strands are done in double braids that fall to the middle of her back. Lauren continues to stare.

"What? You never seen a Papago woman before?" Sandy asks as she takes her seat behind the desk.

"A what? What are you?"

Sandy towers over most other members of the Tohono O'odham Nation. She gets attention everywhere she goes.

"Look at you. You're so pretty," Sandy says to her new patient, elongating that last word, and ignoring Lauren's impertinent question. "Too pretty to be messing around with drugs, don't you think?"

Lauren's still dumbfounded.

"Thanks, I guess."

"Okay, in case they didn't tell you, which is a good bet, we're going take a look at a bit of your history today, to see how you came to be with us at lovely Dusty Palms."

"Yeah, been there, done that," Lauren sneers, finally reverting to her typical defensive posture.

"Okay, if you're so smart, pretty one, you tell me how the hell you ended up here."

"Who said I was smart?" Lauren retorts, feeling attacked.

"Well, *I* certainly didn't," Sandy quickly comes back. "I can see you're cute just by lookin' at you, but as far as what's up here," Sandy taps at her own temple, "I assume you're like most of my patients, a bit stupid and more than a bit crazy."

Lauren cannot help herself, and smiles. "Yeah, that about covers it," she admits.

"So, where did you fuck up to land yourself in here?" Sandy asks, steering the conversation back onto the road.

No therapist ever spoke to Lauren so directly, so aggressively. In her mind, Lauren questions. *Do I like this woman? Or do I hate her? How to respond?* In the past, Lauren's been fine with saying anything if only to be discharged one day. Understanding full well the depth of Sandy's question, Lauren opts to act the fool.

"Because I relapsed?" Lauren responds.

Sandy has no way of knowing for sure that she's being played. Had she spoken to Lauren's mother, she would have learned that the person sitting across from her is an innately intelligent girl who, even in the world of addicts, has taken the art of manipulation to a new level. But she only learned earlier today that Lauren had been assigned to her, so no chance to make the call.

"Well, Lauren, I mean in the big picture. I know you re-lapsed. Why?"

"Well," Lauren replies, "Like, I must've freaked out when I woke up in the hospital with this vision of our truck flipping over and the dude and girl sitting next to me getting crushed like two soda cans. I was sober before that," Lauren lies.

Sandy's unfazed. "Yes, I scanned your file. I'm sorry about the accident. We'll get into that later. But can you tell me how *you* might have had any responsibility for getting yourself in here?"

Uncharacteristically Lauren is quickly tiring of her own game and switches to angry honesty.

"Listen. Why don't you ask me how many times I've done this before? Eight! This is my eighth rehab! Ask me how many times I've OD'd and should have died! Four! I stopped breathing four times. Each time, someone pumped me with Narcan to save my fucking life. Then I should have died a fifth time in that damn truck! Why didn't I die?! Brittany's head got taken off. Why not mine? Can you tell me that!? So, now I'm here at lovely Dusty Hands, or whatever. You get that, Sandy? Like I said, been here before! What makes this any different? Just another day in paradise!"

Sandy senses a logjam breaking, and pounces.

"I don't *know* if it'll be any different! That's up to you! So, what do you want to talk about then? You seem to have all the answers."

There's a lull while Lauren considers her next move.

"Okay, here's what I want to talk about! What do *you* think about this place? It seems like a bit of a cluster to me!"

"Oh? Why do you say that?"

Lauren explains her reasoning: the phone call, the weekend supervisor, the staff, and a bunch of empty beds.

"Okay. Fair enough. I'll be honest, Lauren. There are things here I don't like either. But empty beds? The place is new. Give it time. As for the call, do you think you might also have had a hand in that? But sure, there's room for improvement. I hear you. Is that going stop you?"

"Huh?"

Sandy leans forward and gazes into Lauren's eyes.

"Is that going stop you from getting out of this what you can? Don't you think *you* could stand a bit of improvement? Or do you want to do this the rest of your *fucking* life?!"

The question hits Lauren like a slap in the face.

"Okay, you're right, I guess."

"You guess?!" Sandy lets this linger for a moment, then continues. "Listen, hon. Let me tell you about myself. I'm fifty percent Tohono O'odham. Who knows what the rest of me is? That means I'm native. I grew up on a goddamn reservation. My older brother was a mule for the cartel. He did trips mostly on foot from Nogales through our desert toward Phoenix. Six years ago, he fucked up and they shot him. We found his body on the Mexican side of our lands, just over the border. My younger brother is like you, a heroin addict. We got him some help. He's doing okay. Like you, still alive. But my folks are a mess. I went into this to make some kind of difference. I learned what I could learn and got a degree. I've been living through this shit myself, so I get where you're at, and I'm here to get you through. Okay?"

"Okay," Lauren responds quietly.

"Okay. So, were you going to any meetings before this last relapse?"

"No, not really. Not enough."

"When you go, is it NA?"

"No. AA"

"Gee, I figured you for an NA kind of gal." Sandy smiles.

"No. I like the people more at AA. They're older. More spiritual."

"Spiritual? You're talking my language, girl," says the Papago woman. "So, I take it you didn't have a chance to get into the community down in Tucson, did you?"

"No," her patient answers.

Why do I always screw up?! Lauren thinks. She was going to get a sponsor with lots of sober time and find new friends who had their shit together. She could have asked around for a job. *Instead, I ended up where I started, with that dumbass Tim. I'm such an idiot! Fuck!*

"I'm so stupid," Lauren continues. "I should've reached out right away when I moved back with Mom. I lied to her about that too. I screwed up, once again."

"Yes, I saw in your file that you moved back from Florida. Listen to me. Shit happens. Knocking yourself down now doesn't help. Let's try to understand it, though. We'll have time to talk about meetings and your step work later. But now, tell me, what is it that you want? What is it out of life that you want?"

"Like, I don't know."

"Any dreams?"

"No. Just nightmares." Lauren is surprised at her own honesty, and her eyes tear up. "I'm so messed up."

"Listen, Lauren, you know the drill. Let's review and figure out what you want to do and how to get you there. By the way, you've a whole life ahead of you to fuck-up and learn from your mistakes. Don't give up. You're young, and you might not be as dumb as you think."

This elicits the patient's sad smile.

The two of them speak about Lauren's history for almost ninety minutes. Sandy is impressed with what her patient understands about her own disease. Lauren describes her predisposition to addictive behaviors: drugs, men, food. She admits to being impulsive and obsessed with her appearance. She confides in Sandy about her desperate need for acceptance and her inability to put the brakes on. She talks of her fear of uncertainty, her panic attacks, and a perpetual anxiety.

They discuss her parents and the divorce.

"I hated Mom in middle school. She was always on my case about something. She didn't like the boy I was with. Whatever I did wasn't good enough. Jack was hardly around. It was ugly when they split up."

Sandy quickly interrupts. "Wait, Jack? Is that your father?"

"Yeah."

"And you call him Jack?"

"Yeah."

"Why?"

"I don't know. Maybe because he's just a jackass."

"Okay, sorry. Go on."

"Then *Jack* moved to Florida, he said for some kind of business deal. I think just to get away from us. So, he leaves me with her. That's when things got out of control."

"Things, meaning you, yes?"

"Yeah."

"You eventually moved to be with Jack down in Florida? Was that any better?"

"Better? No. Just different. I suppose he tried at first. He sent me to a psychiatrist right when I got down there. He always thought all my problems could be cured by a pill. I heard him fight with Mom about it. Anyway, the dumbass shrink wrote me a script for Xanax for the anxiety; and I was already using. I sold the shit on the street instead of mixing it. One of the smarter things I've done. Pretty soon, he just lost interest."

"You mean, your father lost interest in you?"

"Yeah, in me and everything. I don't know what he did all day. He drank, although I'm not sure how bad, I was so looped half the time myself. He let me get away with so much, until I had to go."

As the session finally ends, Sandy says to her new patient, "Well, we got off to a rocky start, but this was good, Lauren. Nice job. I'm glad you're my patient. I think I can help you."

They schedule a meeting in a week. Sandy will arrange an appointment for Lauren with a nurse practitioner on the outside to get her evaluated for meds to help with her anxiety.

As Lauren leaves the office, she considers her new therapist. *She couldn't be more different, but she's real. No bullshit about her. Doesn't let me get by with anything. I do like her.*

Meanwhile, Sandy still sits at the desk recording a few notes on an iPad.

Severe/Mult. trauma w/ things undisclosed (?)
Actions –

1. *push on history*
2. *consider alt. modalities*
3. *talk to mom*

CHAPTER 23

The Script

In keeping with her therapist's treatment plan, Lauren has an appointment today with an RNP at the office of Albert Larson, M.D. Dusty Palms hooked up with Larson to satisfy the medicinal needs of its patients. Doctor Larson, who already serves the burgeoning community of dual-diagnosis addicts, is happy for the expanded case load.

Larson's office is just two miles from the DP facility in downtown Surprise, Arizona, a fast-growing middle-income suburb of Phoenix. A DP tech, who was directed to drop Lauren off, stops her car in front of a low-rise white and brown cement block professional complex on West Bell Boulevard, about a mile from City Hall Plaza. Disembarking, Lauren finds a door to A. Larson MD & Associates, PLLC, and enters an unpretentious office setting in need of a facelift.

Instantly sizing the place up, Lauren fears that the services here will match Dusty Palm's shoddiness. *Sandy arranged for this, so I'll go with it. Regardless, whoever is behind this cheesy operation, must be struggling.*

Lauren is asked by the lone receptionist parked behind the

Plexiglas partition to take a seat with a large and diverse group of patients, complete the standard intake form, and wait. After the paperwork, Lauren sits back down and leans over the coffee table in front of her to peruse stacks of leaflets with captions like: "Positive Parenting of Your Addict," "Science of Addiction," "Has Your Addict Relapsed?" None strike her fancy, and she reclines back into her seat. But for these materials and the medical sign out front, this melting pot of a workplace might be mistaken for a satellite DMV, where individuals eagerly line up for their worst-ever photos.

Lauren people-watches for a few minutes. There's plenty of turnover and patients move in and out like the ebb and flow of a shoal of anchovies in the shallows. Lauren assumes that many are addicts or alcoholics. *We could have an AA meeting right here in the waiting room.*

Lauren's forty-five minute appointment should start at 2:15 p.m. After silently suffering for eight minutes, Lauren walks to the receptionist, sitting in her protective shield, and prods her for an update.

"Do I really have to wait for all of these people to go ahead of me?"

Lauren's not the first clinically anxious and patently rude patient to vex this middle-aged, bleary-eyed woman, who responds with a shrug of the shoulders.

"Yeah, I guess so, honey. It's been like this all day. All month."

She suggests to Lauren, again, to take a seat and to be patient.

Instinctually, Lauren would sass the receptionist. *Is that why you call us patients?!! You bring us all in here to wait for hours to test how patient we can be?* Instead, she restrains herself and steps outside for a desperately-needed cigarette. There, she cannot help but interrogate a skinny acne-faced teenager she puts at sixteen, who bums a Camel menthol off her, and whose name she learns is Josh. By the time Lauren flicks her burnt-out butt between her thumb and forefinger onto the concrete sidewalk, a mass grave for a hundred such coffin nails, Lauren has gotten Josh to open up.

Josh has been Dr. Larson's patient for four years. He's ADHD and a bit OCD, is big into dirt-bikes, and may not pass this, his sophomore year. Josh tells Lauren that while the doctor seems like a whack-job himself, everyone in town goes to him.

"He must be worth millions," Josh concludes, and Lauren acknowledges this with a nod.

Gee, thanks Josh. I'm all full of confidence now.

Eventually, Lauren goes back inside. Finally, just before 3:00 p.m., one of the RNPs, Jennifer Taylor, a chunky yet attractive black woman of thirty-five, dressed in a light pants suit, and wearing funky blue Ray-Bans, sticks her head through a doorway and asks Lauren to step into her office. It's a tiny carton just large enough for a desk and two brown armless metal chairs. There's a window across from her with a direct view of the traffic. Lauren sits in front of Jennifer's desk and spies a poster of Van Gogh's Vase of (white) Roses on the taupe wall behind the NP. Lauren smiles to herself.

If I weren't already crazy, I would go nuts being cooped up here.

Jennifer is innately friendly but is visibly tired toward the end of a long day. Lauren herself is worn out from the ordeal in the waiting room and has too little energy to be feisty. She cuts Jennifer some slack.

Jennifer starts off by asking Lauren what she wants to accomplish.

"I want to be happy," Lauren declares in truth.

"You and me both, girl. So, what stops you from being happy then?"

"I guess, everything."

Now Jennifer must lead the conversation. There's not enough time to explore *everything*.

"Well, besides unhappy, how do you feel? Would you describe yourself as being moody, or anxious?"

"For sure. I tend to go into panic mode."

"I bet that can get in the way of things, huh? Well, I suspect that

I'll have something for you to take that might smooth out some of the edges."

The NP then starts a perfunctory chronological interview to preserve a history for the file. Together, in minutes, they cover some fourteen years, touching quickly upon common problems related to learning issues, impulsivity, and self-esteem. Then the NP asks Lauren about high school and her discovery of alcohol, drugs and sex, and problems within her family. Lauren answers with minimal detail, just enough to keep the conversation going. During all of this, Jennifer jots some notes down, but otherwise shows no special interest.

Then, the NP starts to wrap up the interview.

"Have you ever been prescribed medication at a psychiatrist's office before?"

"Yeah. Jack, I mean my father, always thought that meds would be an instant cure for me," Lauren recounts. "Mom wouldn't even take an Advil herself unless her arm was cut off, or something." Lauren then tells Jennifer about being prescribed Xanax after the psychiatrist appointment that Jack initiated. Jennifer just shakes her head.

"Later on, I guess, even Mom got desperate enough to push the idea of meds for me."

"So, I take it you were prescribed other meds after the Xanax, yes?" Jennifer inquires.

"Yeah. There was this other doctor." Lauren recalls how, at her mother's insistence, she went begrudgingly to a shrink referred by one of the rehabs in Boca Raton. In forty-five minutes, the psychiatrist, a specialist in addictions, diagnosed her with bipolar disorder and put her on a combo of two different medications.

"Did they help to calm you?"

"I don't know. They might have. I stopped taking them after a few weeks."

Jennifer had read through Lauren's DP intake file, which referred to the accident and the subsequent overdose. It also contained a psychiatrist's case notes, which documented his diagnosis of bipolar disorder and the two prescriptions.

"You know, Lauren, the doctor may have caught this in its early stages. But Bipolar disorder is a progressive disease. It tends to get worse over time, especially if it goes untreated. You might keep that in mind, if you ever start feeling like you don't need to be on the meds."

Lauren shrugs. In any case, Jennifer is running out of time for Lauren, and her decision to prescribe a mood stabilizer for the anxiety and a bipolar medication was almost final even before Lauren arrived.

Jennifer gives Lauren the usual instructions.

"These meds are safe if taken as directed, but each prescription is somewhat experimental as applied; that is, we never know with certainty how a patient will react to them until they report back to us. So, take notice. We're going to start you off with a low dosage for each, and we'll make changes as necessary in your follow ups. Understood?" Lauren nods.

Despite the sprinting nature of the conversation, the protocol is familiar to Lauren.

"Great. So, will you give these a shot, for real, Lauren?"

"Yeah. Sure."

The meeting ends, the two women say their goodbyes, and Lauren heads out of the medical office. Outside in the parking lot, as she waits for the tech to arrive, a smoldering cigarette in hand, Lauren is leaving with some optimism. Now that the appointment is behind her, she isn't so annoyed by the rules of the game. This time, she'll take those little pills, long enough, at least, to see if any good comes of it.

CHAPTER 24

Kitt Peak Revisited

Henry arrives at Isabel's house. Even before he has a chance to ring the bell, she's out the door, in a red batwing sweater, designer jeans and running shoes. She swings a Toto-type picnic basket with her left hand, dinner for three, as per Henry's request.

Henry arranged this outing with Isabel the Sunday after their first date a week ago. Looking at her now in the driveway, he chuckles at his good fortune to be with someone so charming and attractive, if only this once on their trip to see "the wondrous ocean."

They meet at the back of his car. She pecks him on the cheek. He takes the basket and lays it carefully into the trunk.

"Henry, if you don't mind, I decided that we *should* stop at Three Points. Is that okay?"

"No problem, we've got time. Are you sure you're up for it?"

"No, but we're passing right by. It would feel wrong not to stop. This isn't exactly what you had in mind, is it?"

"No, not exactly," he smiles. "But I can be flexible from time to time. Anyway, it's important." Henry had prepared for this contingency.

They make good time into the desert. At first, Henry asks about Lauren. Then, in anticipation of the evening's activities, he directs the conversation back to the cosmos.

Isabel only half listens, preoccupied with her problems on Earth. It does feel good to have this new companion at a critical moment. He's so supportive, she thinks. Can this continue? Lauren will be back one of these days. Wait 'til he meets her.

"You've heard of Galileo, of course," Henry begins. "He was born twenty years after Copernicus died. Contrary to popular belief, Galileo didn't invent the telescope, although he did improve upon it. The telescope was invented in 1608 by some Dutch guy who wanted to sell it to the military. It was Galileo that first used it to look at the stars."

Isabel nods, hoping that Henry can give this history lesson without driving off the road at eighty mph.

"Using his shiny new telescope, he saw four moons revolving around Jupiter, essentially little planets circling a bigger planet that's not Earth. This was contrary to Earth being at the center of all things.

"Then he looked at Venus and saw that it appears in phases, just like our moon. When Venus is full, that is, when the sun's rays hit it straight on, it's always the smallest, the farthest point away from us. This can't happen if Venus revolves around Earth, only if both Venus and Earth revolve around the sun. Here, let me show you. Assume the steering wheel is the sun, my right hand Earth, and my left hand Venus."

Then, maintaining speed, Henry takes both hands off the wheel which he steers with his lower thighs.

"Whoa, space cowboy!" Isabel commands. "What do you think you're doing? This can wait until after we land."

"Sorry," Henry responds sheepishly. "Anyway, there goes the geocentric model out the window," he says, jerking his left thumb outward. Meanwhile, Isabel gazes like a hawk at his right hand to ensure it doesn't come off the steering wheel. Henry goes on.

"The Church rewarded Galileo for his great work with a stint in prison, and then, benevolently gave him a reprieve, putting him under house arrest until he died."

"Yes, I remember the nasty part about the Church. That's probably a good stopping point then, Henry, yes?"

"Yeah," Henry agrees. "We're coming up on Three Points any second."

Isabel stands in front of a sign that reads "Good Eats - Breakfast - Lunch - Dinner." She's in somber awe of what she imagines occurred here nearly three weeks ago.

"I can't believe it; there isn't a clue to the violence. Are you sure this is the place, Henry?"

Henry's positive. This is the restaurant that was described in news accounts. The State Police put him in touch with the ranking officer at the scene. Henry called the sympathetic trooper, who described the brick pillar, and said it was all fixed up like new. Henry looks at that pillar now. The replacement bricks are slightly off-color.

"I'm certain," Henry responds. "Should we ask inside?"

"No, I trust you. Anyway, I think it's closed. Let's go."

Henry sees lights on in the restaurant but makes no comment. Isabel turns toward the car, but before she takes another step, spies a sliver of metal amongst gray pebbles on the ground. The shiny piece glistens against the late-day sun. She leans over and picks up a silver ornament.

"Oh my God, this is Lauren's earring. I'm sure of it!"

At that, she breaks down and sobs swollen tears. Henry, standing by her side at the time, puts his arm around her shoulders. Without warning, she turns and buries her face into his chest, continuing to cry.

Instinctively, he puts his arms around her and rubs her back. Isabel's heavy tears are caught by the fibers of his fleece. He catches her scent: flowery, delicate, sensuous. Despite the muffling of her words, Henry hears her despair.

"It was here," she murmurs. "Their lives ended here."

Henry hesitates, not sure of what to say.

"Yes, that's right," he whispers.

"I'm sorry." Isabel weeps. "So sorry."

Henry is tentative; awkward. Her remarks seem to be directed to someone else. With his arms still around her, they stand on a gravel parking lot in front of a remote eatery, its green awning flapping in the wind. There was risk in asking Isabel to Kitt Peak, bringing her to the desert. He knew this.

Her body starts to relax.

"Thank you. I'm okay," she says.

He releases her and not a moment too soon, lest she notice a growing hardness. *Great timing,* he thinks. Henry's motivated by empathy, but there's no controlling this. He turns away and starts back to his car, a crisis in humiliation averted.

Both travelers are happy to get back in the Ford and on the road. Ten minutes later, Henry goes left at the Kitt Peak turnoff and they soon find themselves at the bottom of a steep winding mountain drive. He tilts his head up for a better view of the impending ascent, straightens his posture, and takes a deep breath.

Isabel notices his vice-like grip of the wheel and his sudden silence, a first for this trip, a first since they met.

"Is anything the matter, Henry?"

"Well," he manages, "I'm a bit afraid of heights."

Isabel grimaces. *My God, driving with him is quite an adventure. We're taking my car next time.*

"Do you want me to drive? It's no problem."

"No, I can manage. It's not too far to the top. I've done it before. Sorry, just bear with me."

"Not at all. As long as we get there."

She says this while looking back to see an imposing black Ram 2500 four-door pickup coming up from behind. Henry stares into his rear-view mirror and sees it, too. He grips the wheel even tighter.

Perceiving his dread, Isabel worries that when the monster truck is upon them, Henry will be intimidated right over a cliff.

"Don't let him bother you," she warns. "He'll get there two minutes later."

The trip up the mountain is for Henry eight torturous miles. The first long stretch of the climb is cliff side. While Henry's Fiesta struggles to ascend, the two have a perfect view of the deepening chasm beyond the guard rail to the right. Isabel puts aside her thoughts about Henry pulling a Thelma and Louise to admire the landscape.

Toward the west, she spies irregular brown and green molded hills, randomly interrupted by taller rocky ranges. These are separated by flattish basins smoothed by erosion. Here, each rounded cordillera appears to Isabel as a huge dirt grave, freshly shoveled as if barely covering the spine of a monstrous invertebrate, lying face down in its final resting place.

Three miles into the ascent, the big-boned pickup flashes its headlights, signaling to Henry that its driver wants to do the impossible, and pass. With help from Isabel's calming voice, Henry holds his position.

"Don't you dare move over for him, Henry! He'll have to wait." Henry obeys without a thought.

Finally, two miles from the top, the road curves sharply left until it traverses north over a high point on the ridge, ending up on the opposite face. It's now the descending side of the road that is nearer to the guardrail and the 7,000 foot vertical drop beyond. Henry breathes a sigh of relief as he maneuvers the Ford to the right, hugging the wall of granite lay bare in the fifties by heavy equipment and dynamite.

At this juncture, Isabel sees a peculiar site: large all-white, mostly rounded, domes peeking out over the top of the ridge. As the car nears the summit, the entireties of these white silo-like structures, numbering two dozen or so, the largest being eighteen stories high off the ground, appear interspersed amongst scrubby trees and mounds of rock on the broad sloping mountaintop. These buildings house the great telescopes, portals through which history unfolds.

"There are so many of them, and they're so big," she says. "I had no idea!"

Isabel gets no response from her companion, whose fingers are wrapped around the wheel with the strength of an anaconda.

Finally, Henry's little Ford, the huge SUV, and four other vehicles lined up immediately behind them, get to the top of the mountain. One by one, they proceed past a sign that announces their arrival at the Kitt Peak Observatory. The parking lot is to the left, adjacent to the brick visitor center, and all six vehicles pull in, one right after the other.

CHAPTER 25

On the Mountain

I'm pretty sure I made it up the mountain in record time. The ass behind us must not be aware of my prior, more cautious, attempts, as he lacks this perspective when he glares daggers at me while getting down from his truck. I figure he's unsure of his manhood to be driving such a big-balled behemoth. Sure enough, out of the corner of my eye, I see with much satisfaction, his wife alight from the other side of the cab, frowning and fussing, while wagging an emasculating finger at him.

Iz grabs my hand, taking my heart with it, and suddenly I have a problem remembering why I was so anxious.

"Let it go. No one ever said you had to be a daredevil." She pauses. "I actually think it's kinda cute that you're such a chicken shit." She's way too happy saying this.

"Gee, was that supposed to be some sort of reassuring compliment? It just makes me warm all over." Then I add some hen-clucking for emphasis.

She talks over my antics. "Although, Henry, if you don't mind,

I might insist upon doing some of the driving next time we take a road trip into the mountains."

"Be my guest, but I'm not sure how much we'll be doing this sort of thing if you keep tossing out tributes like that last one."

"Oh, don't get all sensitive on me, mister. So, now that we're up here, where are you taking me?"

Iz holds my left hand with her right and, like Dorothy, swings the picnic basket with her left. This all feels way more comfortable than our brief relationship would suggest. Consoling her in my arms at Three Points may have crossed a pivotal threshold, although I fear that there are bigger sexual crevasses to leap over than one simple hug, as tender and awkward as it may have been.

Isabel's hand is cool to the touch. It's fifteen degrees colder up here than in Tucson. A constant wind rushes at us, playing havoc with her sweater, like a red flag fluttering at the beach. We'll have to don the two sweatshirts I carry, delicately stuffed into a Circle K plastic grocery bag. We hustle into the square visitor center, one large pine-floored room with posters of planets and galaxies covering the wood-paneled walls. All the other recent arrivals are bunched-up, standing in a corner in anticipation of this evening's tour. I can't help but notice that there, waiting once again, is the impatient Ram-driving fool and his wife. How could anyone with enough interest to come up here be such a jerk? Must be the influence of his better half.

I lead Isabel past the group and greet Kelly, a fetching twenty-something blond sitting behind a gray Formica desk on the far right side of the building. She's wearing a dark Kitt-Peak hoody dotted with images of the planets around a bright orange sun.

"Hello, Kelly," I say to the receptionist, whom I've met here several times before. "Love your sweatshirt."

Kelly is an astronomy student out of Australia.

"Thanks, Mr. Spinoza. It's our new uniform."

"It's smashing," I say with a British accent and an idiotic grin.

When I get no reaction, I introduce Isabel and then ask, "Is Dr. Steinmetz around? He's expecting us about now."

"Yes, he told me you'd be coming. I'll ring him up."

While we wait for Steinmetz, Isabel strikes up a conversation with Kelly about her life in Sydney, and Isabel's one-week excursion through the Outback some years ago. I've never dated a woman who's seemingly so sure of herself, accessible, and of course well-travelled. I just shake my head.

Steinmetz arrives in jeans, a flannel shirt, and the same open ski parka he wore the night we met. He's toting a green nylon backpack. I make the introductions.

"Thank you, Doctor Steinmetz, for arranging all this. It's way beyond the call."

"Nonsense, and one last time, it's Dan, for crying out loud." Smiling now at Isabel he continues with a slight Midwestern twang. "As I told your friend here when we met a few weeks ago, I love visitors, when time permits. We live outside of Chicago. My wife's a teacher. For my liking, she and I are apart all too often, although I don't think she minds quite as much." He laughs. "First trip up to Kitt Peak, Isabel?"

"Yes, in fact my first time ever at an observatory."

"Well, you're in for a treat tonight. It's clear, and the moon is in its last quarter, so visibility should be quite good."

He glances down at the picnic basket. "Is that for us?"

We nod.

"Super. Why don't we eat while we wait for the sun to set? Are you hungry? It's a tad early."

Before I can say anything, Isabel responds.

"Not for me, I'm always hungry."

I'm glad to see that she's gotten past our stop at Three Points.

"That's the idea. I love a woman with a good appetite," Steinmetz announces.

"And I'm not at all surprised," Isabel retorts, with a devilish smile on her face, referring to a plumpness which hangs slightly over his forty-two-inch leather belt. The doctor is quick to laugh back at himself.

"Oh my, Henry, you have yourself a lovely little spitfire here. I must say, good job."

The three of us pull up armless plastic chairs to a small wooden table. It's looking a little like lunch in elementary school. Isabel breaks out the goodies: fried chicken, potato salad, and green beans. Steinmetz and I express our appreciation. Dan surprises us when he removes three ice-cold Modelos from his backpack, now looking somewhat damp.

"Sweet, although I'm not sure if Isabel actually likes beer," I say, with mischief in my eyes.

Steinmetz who takes this seriously, turns to her, "I could get you a pop if you like."

"Oh no, after that ride up here, I think I deserve a beer, don't you agree?" She turns toward me. "In fact, maybe I should have yours too if you insist upon driving home."

"One each only, I'm afraid," Steinmetz jumps in. "It'll be hard enough to distinguish between a star and a nebula without the influence of alcohol. But what's this? Did you have some trouble getting here?"

Isabel is only too willing to explain, in exaggerated detail, my drive up the mountain. The two of them laugh heartily when she describes the guy in the Ram who kept flashing his lights at me.

"The funniest thing was," Iz points out, "each time he flashed his headlights, Henry would slow down even more. The guy must have thought Henry was provoking him."

This can't be true, and I object over their giggles, although it would explain his attitude at the top.

Now that the ice is broken, Isabel asks Dan about himself. She learns that he's a research professor at the University of Chicago. He and his wife have three grown children and two Bernese Mountain

Dogs, and Dan admits that he misses the dogs more than his kids. Iz brings up the question of his research.

"So, Henry's been schooling me on a bit of astronomical history, perhaps in preparation for this excursion. I think he's just a wannabe science teacher. But what is it exactly you're doing up here if you don't mind my asking?"

"Mind? I live for this stuff!" Dan responds. "The answer I'm afraid is a bit of a lecture."

"That's okay," she says.

"So, what has Henry learned you about so far?"

In two short sentences, she summarizes what she knows of Copernicus and Galileo.

"Is that all?" asks Steinmetz, giving me a scolding look. "That's pretty much junior high school stuff. No matter. You've come to the right place. There's so much history in science; in fact, science is history." Steinmetz takes a breath then dives right back in. "To understand anything of my work, Isabel, you must understand Hubble. You've heard of the Hubble Space Telescope, yes?"

"Yes, of course. It's taken some amazing photos," she replies.

"And its soon to be replaced by something even bigger," I add.

"I couldn't agree with you more, Isabel," Dan says, disregarding me and James Webb both. What you may not know is that it was named after Edwin Hubble, surely the most famous astronomer of the last century."

Isabel shrugs her shoulders.

"Hubble did his work in the 1920s on Mount Wilson, in the San Gabriel Mountains just outside of Pasadena. Mount Wilson had the largest telescope in the world at the time, the hundred-inch Hooker. Working with the Hooker…."

Isabel interrupts. "Excuse me, Professor, really? The Hooker?"

I butt in. "The guy who paid for the mirror, John Hooker, insisted that they name it after him. Unfortunate, actually."

"Yes, that he was so vain," Isabel agrees.

"Or that his name was Hooker," I say with a wry smile.

The professor titters at that but is eager to continue. The sun is setting.

"If I may, Hubble literally stunned the world. His work formed the basis of so much to come, including our theories on the Big Bang, occurring some 13.8 billion years ago. Hubble settled the great controversy of his time about the size and nature of the universe; and yet, today, we're left with even bigger unanswered questions that stem from his discoveries."

Steinmetz takes another deep breath. "First a little background. You see, in the early twentieth century, there was great interest amongst astronomers about some fuzzy clouds they saw through their telescopes. They called these clouds 'nebulae', plural for nebula. These objects didn't look like stars, which of course are well-defined points of light. Many were large, spiral-shaped phenomena."

Steinmetz's practiced teaching skills come through, as Isabel listens with rapt attention. Who knows, I might learn a few tricks myself.

"Many scientists at the time believed that the entire universe was no larger than what we know today as our own galaxy. Regardless of how large they thought it was, and believe me, there was a lot of disagreement on that, these guys were confident that all the nebulae were gaseous clouds located within the Milky Way. But others were not so convinced. They theorized that some of the nebulae might be so-called separate 'island universes.' So far, so good?" Steinmetz asks.

"Yes, I'm with you. Go on," Isabel coaxes.

"Okay. So, there were these two points of view. Of course, in fact, the truth lies somewhere in between. Regardless, a famous debate took place at the Academy of Science, in 1920, between two highly esteemed astronomers to settle the argument."

That's it, if he tells the story of the Great Debate, we'll be here all night. Then Steinmetz veers back on course. "But we shall leave that for another time. Bottom line, this debate was more about theory than observation." Steinmetz pauses and dramatically whispers, "They really didn't know, you see, until Hubble."

Isabel maintains her focus. To be honest, the professor even has me on the edge of my little white PVC chair.

"Forgive me now, Isabel, because I have to backtrack a bit. I have a sneaking suspicion, however, that you'll appreciate this little detour. The story of Hubble is a perfect example of how science is history, for without the prior work of others, he wouldn't have accomplished what he did. So, for you to grasp the basis for my work, you need to understand Hubble, and to understand Hubble, you need to hear about another great astronomer, a woman," Steinmetz says with genuine emphasis, "who never received the recognition she deserved for paving the way."

As anticipated, Isabel perks up at the mention of a woman playing a key role. Dan continues with his lecture fluidly as if in his Intro Astronomy class at Chicago.

"Her name was Henrietta Swan Leavitt. Leavitt was working at the Harvard Observatory in the mountains of Peru." Steinmetz shovels in some potato salad and takes a gulp of his Modelo. I notice a little glob of mayonnaise hanging from his cheek. "It's there in Peru, in 1912, where she studied a particular type of star that varies in brightness at regular intervals, for it pulsates."

Of course, I know of this. These are stars that are writhing and throbbing in the throes of death.

Steinmetz wipes away the mayo with a paper napkin. Then he picks up the pace.

"For simplicity's sake, I'll refer to these stars as Variables. Each Variable star would have its own repetitive interval of brightness: a pulsation toward greater and greater luminosity, climaxing once every day, or once every hundred days, or somewhere in between."

Isabel concentrates, but my somewhat twisted mind deviates as I cannot help but make a sexual connection to his use of that conspicuous word.

"Leavitt pointed her telescope up at a small and local cloud-like cluster and studied nearly 2,000 stars within that cloud. From these, she culled out about fifty, which she determined to be pulsating Variables. She made the logical assumption that since all these Variables were in the same cluster, they were all about the same distance from Earth.

"Then, she catalogued each of the Variables in terms of their overall luminosity and the number of days between surges in brightness. She plotted this information on a graph."

My mind wanders, as Dan seizes a notepad and black Sharpie from his bag to illustrate Leavitt's graph to Isabel. As important as Leavitt is to astronomical history, I've heard it all before. Isabel, on the other hand, gazes at the graph sitting on the table in between her and Steinmetz, trying hard to assimilate the data, as if sucking on a new-flavor milk shake through a narrow plastic straw. I look at her in total admiration.

I hear Dan describe the logarithmic relationship Leavitt found between a Variable's maximum luminosity and the number of days it took the star to reach the peak of its brightness.

"This was an awesome discovery, the importance of which was almost overlooked!" Dan exclaims. I'm shocked to see excitement in Isabel's eyes. I have to say, her apparent enthusiasm for all this cosmological history is something of a turn-on.

She says, "I think I get it! So, we have blinking stars…"

"No, not blinking," the professor cuts her off. "Pulsating: where each pulse is like a florescent lamp that starts off dim and then gets brighter over time."

"Ah, got it," she says. "So, pulsating stars, where the longer the cycle was between peaks in brightness, the brighter it finally appeared to her."

"Exactly!" he responds. Dan goes on to explain in technical detail the differences between the *apparent brightness* of a star, as Leavitt saw it through her telescope, and its *actual brightness*. "The actual brightness," he says, "depends upon its size and the energy it produces. It's this distinction that necessitated the calibration of Leavitt's graph." At this point, her eyes glaze over, and Dan takes notice.

"Shall I go on, then?" Dan asks.

"Please; but frankly, Professor, you're losing me on this calibration stuff," she admits.

"Understandable. It's a difficult concept."

I'm not surprised, either. As I recall, the geometric model used to calibrate Leavitt's numbers on apparent brightness was extremely complex. It was because of stuff like this that I left Penn and my dream of becoming an astrophysicist behind. Consequently, my belief in the science often necessitates a bit of blind faith.

Dan skips over the calibration issue.

"Okay. Let's just assume it got done."

Easy for him to say. He then explains how Hubble used Leavitt's graph to determine the distance from Earth of certain Variable stars he saw through the telescope looking at Andromeda.

"To the extent the star appeared dim through the Hooker eyepiece compared to its actual brightness shown on the graph, it would have to have been far away. To the extent that it appeared bright, let's say almost as bright as its actual brightness, it must have been very close to Earth. Of course, the actual distance was computed by precise formulaic calculations. Thus, Hubble determined the Variables' distance from Earth."

Isabel and I are both pretty numb. Nevertheless, our professor rushes to his finale before the imaginary bell rings.

"This is why Variable stars are called 'standard candles'. One cannot use just any random star to do this, for if it's not a pulsating Variable, one will not be able to apply Leavitt's graph to determine its actual brightness. With any normal star, one will not be able to ascertain if the star appears bright to us because it's near or bright to us because it's very large."

Now Isabel interrupts. "I think I'm getting most of this, Professor. It's very interesting, standard candles and all. But how come I've never heard of this Henrietta..." Isabel sounds indignant. "What's her name again?"

"Swan Leavitt. Henrietta Swan Leavitt. Like I said, she never got much recognition. Without her, who knows, it might have been decades longer before we comprehended the vastness of the universe."

"So how does a woman become an astronomer in the early 1900s?" asks Isabel, who now wants to champion this female pioneer. Not surprising, as I can envision Isabel herself, in about the same period, driving a Conestoga across the prairie, red bandana about her head, a shotgun across her lap.

"I'm not sure we even had the right to vote yet," she adds.

Steinmetz scratches his head. "If I'm not mistaken, that was in 1920 as well. I should know, my wife teaches history. Well, you will not like the answer, I'm afraid, but she just came cheap. That's all there was to it. In fact, Harvard's head astronomer hired a half-dozen or so women, a group that was referred to as 'the Computers'. They were just old-fashioned data processors at first, and Harvard got away with paying them peanuts."

"Really? Who would have guessed?" Isabel responds with sarcasm.

"Actually, if you like, I have a photo of the group," Steinmetz offers.

"Sure, I would love to see that."

While I finish off a drumstick and the beer, Steinmetz wipes his hands, takes out an iPad from his backpack and in a minute retrieves images from what's labelled Lesson 5.

"Here are the Computers." Dan points to the grainy, black and white, group photo of ten women, looking like the staff at a Christian boarding school for girls back then. Steinmetz swipes to the next image. "Here's Henrietta. She was the Computers' team leader before she became an astronomer."

While the three of us gaze at the iPad, an eerie chill runs down my spine. Leavitt's photo reminds me so much of my mother in her wedding picture. Leavitt could easily have been Mom's somewhat thinner and more delicate kid sister. I decide to keep this to myself.

"Well, good for Henrietta. She showed those guys," Isabel cheers, and by this is revitalized.

Through a small window, we see that dusk is upon us. Dan quickly describes to Isabel how Hubble found Variables within Andromeda, which prior to Hubble's work was believed to be just another gaseous spiral nebula within our own Milky Way. He used Leavitt's scale to determine actual distances to the Variables within Andromeda.

"What he discovered was mind blowing. He determined that Andromeda was about a million light years from Earth. This was three times farther than the largest estimates at that time for the size of the entire Milky Way. It put Andromeda firmly outside of it, as an entirely separate galaxy, then estimated to hold within it millions upon millions of stars. Andromeda is the closest galaxy to our own. Of course, we know today that it's 2.5 million light years away, and that it contains billions, not just millions, of stars. That takes nothing away from Hubble. Today, when we see a galaxy at the farthest reaches of the universe through the telescope that bears his name, we're looking back in time, some thirteen billion years ago, when the light waves from that galaxy started on their journey here for us to see now."

Steinmetz pauses to take a few more bites from a crispy breast. Isabel is quiet, trying to wrap her mind around the infinite.

Still chewing on the chicken, Dan finishes up. "Hubble opened our eyes to the vastness of space and to vital questions yet unanswered, one of which I'm working on up here. But I'm afraid I've gone on too long. We really ought to spend some time upstairs with the telescope before the tour group comes around. I'll have to finish my long-winded explanation another time."

In any event, Isabel has reached her limit. "That's fine, Dan. My head is about ready to burst, and this beer isn't helping any."

"Lightweight," I add. She looks in my direction with admiring, yet whimsical eyes, perhaps in acknowledgement that she's here with me and not just attending a free lecture and public tour.

With that, Steinmetz downs his beer, and we find our way outside and up the stairs to the observation platform, where I first met him three weeks ago. It's dark by now, and a solitary bright-white quarter moon appears low over the eastern horizon. We sit for a while to allow our eyes to adjust.

The heavens above are an awesome sight, even before we make use of the telescope. The Milky Way's stunning galactic disk appears as a creamy pale cascade, streaming down from the heavens, largely obscured by opposing patches of darkness, an arched column of fiery ash and sulfuric dust, as if erupting from a monstrous Earthbound caldera. Isabel shivers, I assume from the cold. She soaks up the image of the night sky, silently in awe.

We spend a good hour outside on the platform with Dan, our capable tour leader. Iz is astonished when she views Saturn and its rings, the Orion Nebula, Andromeda, and a close-up shot of the moon, all through the telescope. With our naked eyes, we see dozens of iridescent satellites glide past us on high, carrying out unknown feats of communication or surveillance. Isabel thinks that one or two meteors, ablaze in their blistering descent, passed through her field of vision in an immeasurable instant.

Finally, when the public group arrives, we say our goodbyes to Dr. Steinmetz. He insists that we return for a private tour of the research telescopes and control room. Likewise, Isabel invites Dan to dinner with us at her home.

"You must finish your lecture, Professor. We haven't heard anything yet about your own work."

It comes as no surprise to me that Dan doesn't hesitate to accept.

Iz and I make it down the mountain, thankfully without much fanfare, and with some guidance from the light of the moon. Strangely perhaps, Isabel is quiet for most of the ride home. She seems contented and at ease. We pass Three Points without comment.

When we finally reach her house an hour later, I walk her to her front door. There, she places her picnic basket on the terra cotta walkway, softly illuminated by her porch light.

She turns to me and says with untroubled sincerity, "Henry, thank you so much for taking me to see the wondrous ocean for the very first time. Without you, I would never have known it was there."

At that, she leans forward and gently pulls my hands around her waist. Letting go, she brings her arms around me in an all-out embrace, and we kiss as if it were written in the stars.

CHAPTER 26

Session Two

S andy sits with Carla, another of her cases, in the same colorless room where Sandy meets all her patients. The two have been reviewing Carla's after-care plan. This patient arrived just three weeks prior and will be discharged in six days. The session ends, and as Carla closes the door behind her, her stocky counselor bites at her lower lip and contemplates the all-too-familiar scenario.

What can be done in just three meetings? She's withdrawn. She needs more time. Even sixty days is a drop in the bucket with what she's got going on. But no, kick her off the island to see if she can swim. Who's the idiot who came up with this system?

Sandy turns her thoughts to Lauren, who should arrive any minute.

I can work with that one. She's smart; too smart, maybe; and what a mouth?! An interesting case. Her mother's good to keep her here so long. Must be rich, and desperate. She might've found a better place though. *I wonder if I'll still be here when Lauren gets discharged.*

Lauren barges through the door without knocking.

"Yes, please do come in," Sandy says, as Lauren takes a seat.

"Oops," Lauren giggles. "I assumed you were alone." She pauses. "Guess I was right," Lauren says, pretending to look around the tiny room.

Sandy lets it go. Lauren has bigger problems than just being ill-mannered.

The meeting starts. Sandy first checks in with Lauren about her visit the day before to Doctor Larson's office. All seems in order. Lauren had started on both prescriptions earlier this morning.

Sandy presents her treatment plan for Lauren. Lauren had already been included in a six-woman group focused on "relapse prevention", a catch-all strategy. In past rehabs, Lauren had been assigned to other treatment options, including groups focused on trauma.

"Whatever." One word saying it all for Lauren.

"Fine, whatever. So, how are you doing otherwise?" the therapist asks.

"I hate it here! I can't believe you work for them."

"You want to give it some more thought? Because you don't seem very certain." Sandy's mockery sails over Lauren's head.

"Yes, I'm sure. I hate it."

"Listen. We don't have all that much time today; let's make this about you, and not me or Dusty Palms, okay? Let's get back to your life in Florida, starting with your father."

"What do you want to know?"

"Why don't you just tell me what stands out for you?"

"Well, I was only with him a year, when I was a junior. There isn't much to say. Like I said, he tried for the first few weeks; but I got pretty fucked up, so he stopped trying. After a while, he didn't care much about anything, least of all me. So, I left."

"Did he tell you to leave, or did you decide that on your own?"

"Let's say it was mutual."

Sandy urges Lauren to provide details about that first year.

Lauren describes a rudderless teenager interested in three things: the beach, boys, and beer.

"Just beer, or was there harder stuff, too?" Sandy asks.

"You mean drugs?"

"Yep," Sandy says.

"No, not at first," Lauren responds. "The beer did a number on me when I had too much, which was always." Lauren laughs at herself. "Honestly, I felt best with weed, you know, just chill, but it was hard to smoke on the beach. Anyway, I had already been into some pills back in Arizona, before Mom packed me up. I guess it was a couple of months in Florida when I started doing other stuff again."

"Like what?"

"Some dope, this time."

"Heroin," Sandy confirms.

"Yeah. It was too easy to get."

"IV?"

"Snorting, too."

"When did you develop a tolerance?"

"Late in the school year, I guess. March, maybe? I never went back."

"To school."

"Yeah. I was pretty much hooked by then. I never gave school a second thought."

"How'd you get the money?"

"Well, at first, I took it from Jack. But he caught on; he didn't have enough himself. Mostly, Mom sent me money."

"She did? Why?"

"I had to eat, for one. Jack wouldn't even keep food in the house."

"Is that the only reason?"

"No. I made up shit."

"Like what?"

"Oh, I don't know. Anything. Needed stuff for school. Needed clothes. Needed stuff at CVS. It was easy. Mom wasn't there, and they didn't talk. He didn't care. I didn't need so much at first either. She gave me a debit card."

"Okay, so when did you move out from your father's house?"

"Must've been in the summer. It was hot."

"Anything going on? Anything happen that caused you to split?"

"No. Not really."

"Well, something must've happened, or did you just wake up one morning and say, 'Gee, I think I'll leave today'."

"We had a fight, okay? He was a real asshole, you know, yelling about how bad I was. I couldn't take it anymore."

"Okay. Where did you end up after that?"

"I went to a friend's."

"Boy?"

"Yeah. Kyle. Sort of a boyfriend."

"You were sleeping together."

"Yes."

"Was that the fight with your dad?"

"Hah! At that point, Jack wouldn't give a shit if I was sleeping with the Miami Dolphins."

"So, what was the fight about?"

"I don't remember. We had so many fights. Does it matter?"

"Maybe not." Sandy pauses.

"Okay, Lauren, what's the next thing that stands out?"

"That's easy. I OD'd."

"How soon after you moved out of your dad's?"

"Pretty soon. A few days maybe. A week tops."

"You were with Kyle still?"

"Yes. He was the one who found me. He got me to the ER. Then he got me into detox at a rehab. He worked it out with Mom. I was there sixty days. It was a nice place. A lot better than this shithole."

"Yes, I'm sure it was. Where did you end up after that?"

"They put me in their sober home. I did intensive outpatient therapy for another couple of months with that same rehab."

They discuss Lauren's experience at her first rehab, Sutherland Farms. Lauren describes a facility that was well-managed, with a happy and caring staff, effective classroom and group sessions, pretty grounds, and a soothing atmosphere. Even the food was decent. There was also a five-day family component which Lauren's mother attended.

"I admit, it sounds idyllic," Sandy says. "How long were you sober after that?"

"After IOP? About a month, or so."

"Not very long, huh? And Kyle?"

"What about him?"

"Did you get back with him?"

"No, he dumped me right after I got into the rehab. He was, like, older and four years sober. Couldn't be hanging around with me."

"Yeah, he should've avoided you like the Ebola."

"What?"

"Never mind. Guess you were lucky he was there."

Lauren leers at Sandy. "Yeah. I'm just so lucky all the time. Maybe they should just call me Lucky Lauren."

The two women become silent as the air in the room takes on a gloomy heaviness.

"I think this is a good point to stop," Sandy says.

"Yeah. Let's stop."

CHAPTER 27

Step Class

"**O**kay, let's calm down ladies. We're scheduled for ninety minutes, and we're gonna do step review this morning."

Some good-hearted grumbling is heard from the eleven mostly young women seated in a large oval. Among them is Lauren, who remains silent.

Each of the women holds a Big Book in hand, the gospel of AA as written down in 1939 by its famous founder, referred to by members as Bill W.

"Okay, please turn to Chapter Five. Michelle, why don't you start, and we'll go around the circle from there?"

Lauren isn't thrilled. *Shit! I've heard this a million times.*

Michelle reads the first step.

"One. We admitted that we were powerless over alcohol – that our lives had become unmanageable...."

Lauren disengages. Been there, done that. *Sure, "a Power greater than ourselves could restore us to sanity." Was it the same Power that made me crazy in the first place? Turn my life over to God as I understand him? But I don't understand him!*

Lauren drifts in and out of awareness as the recitation progresses around the room.

"Four. Made a searching and fearless moral inventory of ourselves."

Hah! Inventory? I couldn't even do the inventory at that thrift store that fired me.

Now it's Lauren's turn. She reads slowly, barely audible. "Eight. Made a list of all persons we had harmed and became willing to make amends to them all."

Right back into her head, Lauren broods. *Bad luck to be on my list. You're dead, and no amount of apology will bring you back either.*

"Eleven. Sought through prayer and meditation to improve our conscious contact with God..."

Lauren fades to her inner self. *God? I don't know God, and I'm damn sure he doesn't know me either.*

Her thoughts are trapped in the eternal web of her mind's eye, which now shamefully recalls the violent image of Brittany's last moments on Earth.

Fuck! Why am I here?

CHAPTER 28

Reflections

As much as I would like to understand them, women bewilder me, like complex math. I mention this with reference to Isabel's reaction to the goings-on at Kitt Peak: Steinmetz's unending historical discourse and our time spent atop the mini-observatory. I have to say that even I appreciated Dan's enthusiastic description of Henrietta Leavitt and her foundational work. It must be this that first aroused Isabel's cosmic interest, and she never looked back from there.

Isabel was filled with eager wonderment at the vision of the night sky, its thousands of jewels of light and most of all, the Milky Way's galactic plane. She was spellbound by the telescope's meandering revelations, the planets and their orbital specks, gaseous nebulae that serve as nurseries to the stars, and the grim and disfigured surface of our own moon.

Her pleasure in all of this is nothing less than stunning. I've failed on innumerable occasions in my use of, what I refer to as, the "scientific seduction". Likewise, I've been cautioned a thousand times by family to not give in to my instinctive mating rituals. But now, in contravention of all of this, a woman, a lovely and vivacious woman mind you, an intelligent woman, a woman of means, seems to find me fascinating, science and all. It was all too easy. She bit at the bait and got hook, line, and sinker.

Something is askew, for I'm not accustomed to such success. In the field of romance, normal for me is defined in terms of the struggle.

Perhaps it was something done differently. Could it be as simple as eliciting the assistance of an expert? I generally work alone. Is that to be my take-away? I note that it was me that she kissed, and not *le Professeur,* and I think I might have achieved the same effect as he, just by reading to her passionately from Wikipedia on those same topics.

Could it be something amiss in her? This remains a distinct possibility.

By the way, it might have been the nicest, sweetest, and most breathtaking kiss of my life. So, of course, this bemusement is moot. How could I possibly return this unforeseen gift? Any doubts will be filed under "exigent exit strategies".

As of this moment, I'm sitting outside on Raff's patio, again, sipping at my second cup of coffee of the day, at the very place where I first encountered Ms. Dalton two weeks back. Raff and I were out here chatting when he had to go in, to answer a call from a senior partner. Of course, he was prodding me about Isabel, and I gave him just enough positive news to discourage the customary brotherly advice. I didn't share the details of our adventures with Steinmetz atop the mountain. Why would I? He wouldn't treat it seriously. I hardly believe it myself.

I want so much to crow to Raff about the notion of the wondrous ocean with which I tantalized Isabel. I dare not. Knowing him this would only lead to flagrant mockery.

I'm even more concerned about Marianne's reaction, for she as broker has the greater stake in this relational outcome. My brother's in it only for sport. Marianne would be quite displeased with my violation of her prime directive of avoiding all things geeky, and I took Isabel to an observatory, of all places!

Raff returns. Of course, I can't speak openly of Isabel's plight with her daughter either. So, I have nothing more to share that's of any consequence. It's unusually awkward, so I decide to leave, and drain my coffee.

"Well, I just came to say hello. I'm anxious to get back to my book. I've started to write." I lie. My outline is not quite finished, and I have yet to put down a word that may one day be read.

Rafael is too astute to be hoodwinked. While he doesn't push the topic, he knows that I'm being purposely aloof. He'll talk this over with his wife. She'll get to the bottom of it through her girl-friend. To be honest, I'm hoping that I can be kept in that loop as well, despite its multiple levels of hearsay, if only to validate what occurred before my own eyes.

"Well, that's great, bro. I don't want to hold up progress. Glad you came by." He's no less transparent than I. He can't wait for me to leave so he can run back to Mare. Let's face it, it was she who sent her husband out on this fact-finding mission in the first place.

I say my goodbyes to them both as they walk me to my car. I can only wonder how Isabel will describe what it is that we have, or what she feels. As I pull away, I look in my rearview mirror and see Marianne pretending to pound Raff's chest with both her fists, screaming at him good naturedly, as if saying "You idiot, you didn't get anything out of him? Leave it to me! Leave it to me!"

I have to laugh. I love them so.

CHAPTER 29

Spin Class

Afternoon spin class is over, and Isabel and Marianne, soaked and shiny from their arduous workout, relax with iced cappuccinos at a corner table in their health club's café, delightfully renamed "Fit Bite". The two haven't seen each other since the night on the patio.

"So, first tell me about Lauren."

"I *assume* things are okay." Isabel describes the unexpected call from her daughter that Saturday night and her own doubts about the choice of a facility.

"I finally spoke with one of the managers who told me, 'You know how addicts say anything to get what they want.' It appears that my darling daughter forced her way into a locked office."

Marianne shakes her head.

"It's simmered down since then. They're forbidden any outside contact for the first ten days. After that, we had one very short supervised phone call. Can't say I learned much. We're scheduled for another phone session soon. They're discouraging any visits yet. To be honest, and it's terrible to say, I'm fine with that."

"Understandable, Izzy. Anyway, she's their problem for now; why not just go with it?"

Isabel agrees. Marianne inquires about Henry.

"So, my sources tell me that you and my brother-in-law have been in touch."

"Yes, your sources probably told you that we went out a couple of times already. He's very nice." Isabel isn't certain how much she can discuss with Marianne, who senses her hesitation.

"C'mon Iz, you know I won't discuss anything with either of the boys if you don't want me to."

"You sure?"

"Of course, I'm sure. You'd be surprised how much I forget to tell Raff. Why do you think we have such a good marriage?" Marianne asks, with an impish smile.

"And that's why I like you so much. Under those conditions, I'll tell all. Just don't judge me too harshly."

"Why do you say that?"

"You'll see. Just be kind."

Now that the bucket is tipped, Isabel describes everything to the last detail: from sushi to Three Points to the trip up the mountain and the visit with Steinmetz. She excitedly summarizes what she remembers about Henrietta Swan Leavitt and admits how the professor's lecture and the views from the mountaintop tantalized her. Marianne is as shocked as she is thrilled.

"Oh my God, Isabel. What have I done? I can't believe it. You're turning into Henry! Can we still be friends? I totally blame myself. Will you be wearing those terrible shirts he always has on?" The two of them guffaw at this remark, causing other exercise enthusiasts in the café to turn their heads. Speaking softly, Isabel responds.

"No, no, not the shirts; but I have to admit, and don't say a thing to Raff, I was into it. Believe me, I surprised myself."

"Okay fine. I forgive you, hon. But tell me more about Henry. Did you get into him, too?"

"Well, everything you told me about Henry is true, and he's obviously a bit of a geek, but he's so sweet and funny, and we do have a good time together. I've decided to ignore the negatives and just go with it, like you said. I like him a lot, but you better not breathe a word."

"Your secret is safe with me, love. I'm not sure Raff would believe me anyway," Mare says, still grinning. "Frankly, I'm not sure how much Henry would believe." They laugh again.

"'Take you to the most wondrous ocean for the first time'. Did Henry really say that?"

"Yes, those were pretty much his exact words."

"And it worked?!"

"Yes," Isabel says. "Yes, it worked; it really worked."

"I'll be damned! There's more to Henry than meets the eye. I guess there's only one solution to this horrible dilemma."

Isabel says nothing, waiting for the other shoe to drop.

"We'll have to double date!" Marianne announces with a big grin while raising her fist for the reciprocal pump, with which Isabel tentatively complies.

"Oh God, sure," Isabel says with a shrug of resignation. "Just not yet."

CHAPTER 30

Family Call

I sabel's at her office. It's been just over two weeks since she carted Lauren off to Dusty Palms. An over-the-phone family session is scheduled today at 10:30. It would be an exaggeration to say that Isabel dreads this call, but neither is she looking forward to it.

It's something of a paradox that Lauren's past rehab stays have been the most relaxing times in Isabel's recent life, and so it is today. Gone are the obligations of parenting a young troubled addict, with all its spontaneous eruptions. No calls from total strangers in the middle of the night, or reports of accidents, crimes, or disappearances. No lost, stolen, or damaged items to deal with: a purse, a debit card, car keys, a driver's license, a cell phone, cash. No discussions with police, doctors, hospitals, or jail keepers. No more need for emergent decisions based upon uncertain truths. Granted is a reprieve from the guilt of not doing more, of not being with her, for casting her out. Isabel is well aware of the paradox.

So, when Isabel's cell phone rings at 10:35 a.m. and displays an unknown number, her heart skips a beat in anticipation of the intrusion into the calm.

"Hello, this is Isabel Dalton."

"Hello, Mrs. Dalton, this is Sandy Ortega, Lauren's therapist at Dusty Palms. Is this a good time for you?"

"Yes. I've been expecting your call. Is Lauren with you?"

"Yeah, hi Mom," Isabel hears a subdued voice through the speaker on the other end.

"Hi, hon. How are you feeling?"

"Okay, I guess."

Isabel tries to be positive. "Okay's a good start."

"So, Mrs. Dalton, we're just calling to check in with you, especially to see how *you're* doing, and to bring you up to speed on Lauren's progress here."

"Yes, I appreciate that. I'm doing much better, thank you."

"Mom, I'm sorry. I know I'm an utter failure. I know you can't stand me," Lauren blurts out. "I want you to know that I don't blame you for feeling that way."

Isabel grimaces. *Is this real or just more manipulative BS?* Either way, Isabel responds with sincerity.

"Lauren, you know I don't feel that way. I'll always love you, no matter what."

Sandy cuts them off. This talk is just scratching the surface.

"Since Lauren will be here for a good while, I'm hoping you can come up for a family weekend; for you, that should be after a couple of months. There's obviously a lot going on and dealing with it face-to-face will be more effective. I'll send you details if that's all right."

"Sounds good," Isabel responds.

For several minutes, Sandy summarizes Lauren's activities, while Lauren remains mostly silent. Sandy exaggerates the benefits of Group, and she describes her individual sessions with Lauren in broad brush strokes. Then she asks Lauren if there's anything she would like to tell her mom. Lauren seems ready for this question, as if it was pre-arranged.

"Oh yeah, I wanted you to know that I am taking meds for my anxiety. It's too early to say if it's helping, but I wanted to tell you I would try it."

Isabel had already been alerted by DP staff about covering the copays for the recent psychiatric visit and the scripts.

"Thank you for telling me," Isabel replies. "I hope the medicine helps you."

Plans are made for another call in two weeks, and the short conversation ends.

Five minutes later, Isabel's phone rings again. It's Sandy back on the line.

"Mrs. Dalton, I wanted to talk to you privately."

"Good idea. I was planning on calling you myself. I thought you should be aware of her history, and what brought her back to Tucson."

"Yes. I agree. I'm sorry for the delay in this. It's the first reason for my call."

Sandy listens intently as Isabel provides an account of Lauren from childhood through the recent series of events.

Isabel describes a smart and intuitive youngster with a hypo-manic personality. Lauren manifested an air of defiance, amazing fits of impulsivity, and a consistent propensity to lie. She lied about anything and everything. The deceptions were so rampant and so broad in scope that Isabel wondered whether Lauren could even recognize the truth.

Things only worsened in Lauren's adolescence. Isabel perused everything there was on personality disorders, trying to pigeonhole her daughter into one category or another. After a while, she gave up on labels and focused only on the symptoms.

One evening, when she was fifteen, Lauren disappeared from

the house without a word. It was sometime after Isabel and Jack separated. Isabel had cruised for hours to finally find Lauren with friends in the center of their normally respectable town. The kids had been drinking in the park, they later admitted, but Lauren was incoherently inebriated; a fall-down drunk. The others, who seemed only happily buzzed, were themselves confused by Lauren's bizarre display.

Lauren's reaction to the alcohol was hypersensitive; allergic. Not that this impeded her enthusiasm. She, like all her friends, would drink often and plenty, but her apparent alcohol-induced lunacy, and her pattern of continuous lying even to her companions, fueled a reputation amongst them that she was in fact crazy.

Isabel tells Sandy that Lauren's emotional problems may have a genetic origin. Isabel's aunt was bipolar, and Jack's dad was an alcoholic.

"Mrs. Dalton, I'll be honest. I don't find it helpful to try to solve the nature versus nurture problem. From what I can see, it's always some combination of both."

"Of course. I'm not trying to deny my responsibility in this. Sure, I had a hand in it. I was angry, half the time at Lauren, the other half at Jack. He could have been more helpful. I felt trapped with her, and what's worse, incompetent. I resented her, and she must have sensed it."

"I didn't mean to put you on the spot," Sandy remarks.

"It's okay. I want to tell you about what happened in Florida."

"Go ahead."

"It's best you get the details from her if she even talks about it. Basically, she was at a bar drinking one night and got smashed. I guess she mouthed off or something. I don't know. It doesn't matter. Three men grabbed her and took her someplace and raped her."

"Oh my God, that's terrible."

Isabel starts to whimper. Sandy waits while Isabel regains her composure.

"Tell me, what does a mother do in this situation?" Isabel asks. "It makes me sick to think what she's endured, and not just this. She's like an abused dog. She suffers but seems to have no control over it, and she doesn't understand why her life's so miserable. That's the saddest part. It just keeps happening, and she doesn't know how to stop it." Isabel chokes back the tears. "I feel so bad for her, and helpless." Isabel weeps out loud.

Sandy says nothing and waits.

"Sorry. I'm okay."

"I understand your pain, Mrs. Dalton. You're not helpless. You're doing a lot for her. You took her back. That was a big step. You didn't have to do that. You got her here, and for six months. Do you know how many patients I've had with that kind of support? None! I can really help Lauren in that time."

Isabel pauses before answering.

"Do you really think things can change? She doesn't seem any more mature now than when she was fifteen."

"But she's here. Alive. Sometimes the only thing a parent can do for an addicted child is to keep her alive until the day she figures it out for herself. As you said, your daughter is intuitive. I saw that right off. She's sassy. Even funny. Her personality seems to be kicking like hell to get to the surface to take a deep breath, if you know what I mean."

"Yes, well put."

"Okay. Now tell me please, did she use after the rape?"

"Yes." Isabel takes a deep breath. "She overdosed on heroin and was saved in the ER. She was that close to death. It wasn't the first time."

Sandy waits for Isabel to continue.

"Anyway, I got her into a rehab for thirty days. She had legal troubles, so when she got out, we decided she'd come back to Arizona. Then this accident, and *another* overdose."

Sandy remains silent.

"I'm so stupid," Isabel says. "I should've seen it coming. I left her alone in my house when we got back from the hospital. She must have brought the pills back from Florida. She looked like death when I found her."

Sandy consoles Isabel. "It's not your fault. Whether she had the drugs or not, whether you left her alone then or some other time, she'd find a way."

"I suppose."

"I'd like to get back to the incident in Florida. Her father lives there, right? Did he help her at all?"

"Yes, he lives there. No, he wasn't any help. They weren't getting along at that point. I called him. He said she was making the whole rape thing up, but he could offer no proof. He was angry at her. I tell you I don't know the man anymore. The odd thing is that the police couldn't corroborate her story, either. I got mixed messages from the hospital. But she spoke about it in such detail. It's got to be real."

"You'd be surprised how elaborate their lies can be. But I always assume a patient's being honest unless there's a reason not to."

"Of course."

Sandy moves on to the second reason for her call.

"Mrs. Dalton, I need to ask you a question. Let me rephrase that. Based on what Lauren's said to me, I'm *required* to ask you a question. Have there been any instances where Lauren has threatened or attempted suicide?"

"Why, what did she say?"

"She talks about death a lot. She questions why she didn't die. She doesn't seem sure if life is worth the effort. Is this a reaction to the accident in the desert? Maybe. I'd like to get your perspective."

"Yes, I would say it's natural that she'd talk about death with what she went through in the desert. Death surrounds her. Here's my answer. Sure, she's threatened suicide many times. She becomes hysterical and irrational, and I told you how manipulative she can be. She's never slit her wrists or jumped off a bridge. Does an over-dose count as attempted suicide?"

"It's a great question," Sandy replies. "Lots of PhDs are writing papers about it. It's hard to know what's in someone's mind, especially after they're gone. I don't get the sense that she's manipulating me on this. To be clear, she hasn't threatened directly, and it hasn't risen to the level of confining her. But she does talk about death a lot. Let's just be aware of it."

"Of course."

"Do you have any questions," Sandy asks.

"No, I think we've covered it. Thank you."

"Don't give up on your daughter, Mrs. Dalton. And do come to family weekend. I think it'll do you both some good. And most importantly, take care of yourself. You can't be any good to Lauren if you're so stressed out. We've got her now. Try to relax."

"Yes, thanks Sandy. I'll try."

"And trust me. You can get to the other side. Lauren can too. I think I can help."

Sandy and Isabel agree to stay in touch, and the call ends.

Isabel thinks. *Relax, yes. A vacation sounds good. Someplace far away.* But the notion of her daughter's possible suicide returns to tug at her heartstrings. If Lauren's life stays on its current path, maybe she *would* be better off dead. Isabel attempts to shake off this appalling idea, but in a vanishing moment, she feels both a horrible sadness and a sense of relief at the thought of Lauren's death, and she shudders.

CHAPTER 31

Friends

Christmas is around the corner. It's been a month since our excursion to Kitt Peak, and Isabel and I have become good friends. I would say that we are more than just friends, but we're not yet lovers, and I'm not pushing it.

For one, work is busy for us both. Isabel's firm always ramps up in mid-October, when her would-be clients have moved on from the illusory command of summer down-time and are ready to plan for a short, but incalculable, future. For my part, I've been asked to coordinate with the Lowell Observatory, up in Flagstaff, on an article about galaxy alignment. While I'd like to devote all my working time to my book, I'm instead commuting virtually to the highlands. I do feel good, however, that my local reputation as a science writer creates value for me.

Meanwhile, my relationship with Iz may best be described as fun and relaxed. We meet for drinks or dinner a few times each week, and we do a lot of talking. Unmistakably, both of us like to talk, and we constantly interrupt the other, but we joke about this too, ready to warm-heartedly take great offense at the other's infraction.

We've been busy telling each other the best stories of our lives, the ones that might be told and re-told over turkey and other holiday accoutrements. Isabel's travels and her elder clients are her favorite topics, while I often rely on my extended family for anecdotal fodder.

I do try to temper my exuberance in this with her, lest I become my father, famous for spinning never-ending yarns that sapped the energy out of any polite listener. Some of our closest relatives were suspected to have clandestinely re-arranged seating charts at family weddings to avoid his table, for those in adjacent chairs were not the only ones at risk. His mind-numbing stories were often heard between the clearing of the salad plates and the cutting of the cake. Indifferent to civil society, he shouted tedious tales across expanses of white linen, around towering centerpieces and over the din of yet another rendition of YMCA.

Contrary to those of my father, I hope, my stories are refined like flour and neatly packaged to be of unusual interest and amusement. For me, they are the comfort-food of conversation, as my best ones are no less pleasurable than a warm bowl of mac 'n cheese. These are the stories that may one day be met by the groans and backward eye rolls from the one who has heard them all before, and I imagine that it is Isabel who is the one grumbling. Perhaps she should lap it in now before gangrenous repetition sets in.

No matter the subject, our discussions are always peppered with little disses and sasses, and bits of self-deprecation thrown in from time to time, all of which keeps us grounded. If we agree on anything, it's the importance of not taking ourselves too seriously. There's one notable exception to this rule for Isabel, and that is Lauren.

Nor are there any bounds to the scope of our conversations. The subject of sex, for instance, has been broached purely in a frivolous manner, but with an undercurrent of recognition and acceptance. We will be making love to one another one day, of that I'm almost certain, and hence my composure and restraint. I respect Isabel too much to be aggressive, and being truthful, so far it is she who made all the right moves. Why change the formula? What I'm saying in a roundabout way is that our kiss of passion that night after Kitt Peak was the last of its kind.

Sitting on her sofa, we do cuddle and even peck at each other, a bit like ninth graders, often while watching a movie on her big screen. Regrettably, her one-time fascination with the cosmos hasn't also extended to the movies I like: savage battles between comic super-heroes, or the nuking of plummeting asteroids or alien mother-ships. She doesn't even like my most favorite alien horror film ever: a sweaty and seductive long-legged actress in a military style wife-beater en-cased in a high-tech forklift, wrestling to the death with a green, slimy metallic creature that resembles an erect hissing crocodile in a giant oval bike helmet, which breeds in human chest cavities and bleeds acid. She thinks this movie, and all the others, are "stupid!"

I don't get it, especially when she'd rather watch a re-run con-cerning the heir to an Alaskan family's fortune, who's as handsome as they come, who could be dating an underwear model, and who, by the way, was incongruously cast as a green superhero in one of my own movie choices. The guy tells no one about his inheritance, instead opts to live in New York, work as an assistant book editor for a measly fifty-five a year for an older bitchy woman, who's cer-tainly attractive but who likely has had work done. The guy refuses the family fortune, puts up with his boss's crustiness, only to fall in love with her before she gets deported to Canada. And *my* movies are stupid?

Getting to know each other also requires a further exposure of one's dirty laundry and some complaining about prior lives. In truth, Isabel seems to present a balanced picture of her life with Jack, and her difficulties as a young mother in the unfamiliarity of Tucson. While she homes in on her own poor choices, the story is also laced with a bit of vitriol relative to Jack's obsession with work and his not being there for her early on. He drank more after losing his job, and of course, his infidelity put an end to it all.

Isabel may disagree, but I tend to be more flippant where my failed marriage is concerned. I was in my mid-twenties when I wedded Nancy, a kindly, plain-looking nurse. It was a terrible idea, as our relationship from the start was one of lustful disharmony. I imagine, however, that each of us took the lead from the other and went ahead with the nuptials despite never having been introduced to the term "self-awareness". Our sentence was finally commuted after three and a half years, and we were both set free to reoffend. It all seems like ancient history now. We didn't have any kids.

On this note, it's funny how many would-be Monday morning marital quarterbacks told me afterward how they always believed Nancy and me to be incompatible, but never breathed a word of this during our engagement. Among these was Raff, but because of an immature pride, I know in my heart that I would've discounted even his opinion had he spoken up. I needn't worry about this now, as Isabel has already been referred over to me by someone much smarter in life than I.

So, our young relationship is evolving, and I couldn't be any happier or more hopeful, nor more in love in my own way. Oddly enough, however, I've heard nothing lately through the family grape-vine in corroboration of my sentiments, and this gives me pause. I've been disappointed before.

CHAPTER 32

Isabel's Quandary

"Oh, hi honey, so good to hear from you. How are things with your daughter?"

It's mid-day one week before Christmas. Marianne, in her front hallway, cradles her cell phone against her shoulder while she leans down to lace up her running shoes. Bella, at her side, wagging her tail, licks Marianne in the ear.

"Lauren's doing fine, I suppose. Thanks. I don't have much time, and I was hoping to ask a quick question, if that's okay."

Marianne gently pushes the dog away and heads toward the kitchen, with Bella close behind.

"Sure, love, the kids are in school. I was about to take the dog for a walk, but she can wait."

"Are you sure?"

"I'm sure. What's up?" Marianne asks, taking a seat at the kitchen table.

Isabel lowers her voice.

"I realize how awkward this might be for you, but I have something to ask about Henry."

"Enrico? Uh oh; something wrong? I didn't hear anything from you lately. *He* seems to be in seventh heaven, but he doesn't let on to any of the gory details. What's he done now?"

"Well, nothing. That's the problem."

After a moment of quiet, Mare responds.

"Okay, I'm listening."

"Well, bottom line, we've been seeing each other for what, almost two months now, and we haven't, you know, gone to bed yet."

Marianne bites her lip to stop from chuckling at the thought of having sex with Henry.

"So, go on."

"I was fine with it until recently. We always have a great time together and I like him a lot. He's so considerate, and we are always teasing and laughing. That part of it couldn't be better. But we haven't gotten past just cuddling and a few kisses. That's what we used to call first base, right?"

Now Marianne let's out a big laugh.

"Yes, I think that's correct."

Isabel continues. "Seriously, Mare, I'm wondering if you think he's ...gay ...or something else."

Now Marianne stops laughing. *Damn! Could this be the issue? Like Raff said, he should've had sex with that crazy Sheila. She was into it; why wasn't he? Oh... my... God. We're family; he must know we'd be okay with it, whatever it is.*

"Well, if he's gay, honey, he sure hasn't come out with us."

Marianne's known him too long not to pick up on it. Nancy never said anything to her. Jenna didn't seem unhappy about their sex life; she was all over him. But was he all over her? *I don't remember.*

"Maybe you should just ask him, dear," Marianne suggests.

Now it's Isabel's turn to laugh. "I thought I would ask you first."

"Listen, hon, you took me by surprise on this. But I gotta tell you, I think I would know if he were gay, and I don't. Henry's different, but not in that way. I've known him for years. It never even crossed my mind. I think it's more likely that he's shy, or afraid, or, sorry, just dopey."

"Well, that's a relief," Isabel is laughing once again. "I guess I can put up with dopey for a while longer."

The two talk of getting together, say their goodbyes and the conversation ends.

Marianne puts her cell phone down on the table and thinks to herself. *I wonder if I should have Raff say something to him. Oh Lord!*

CHAPTER 33

Dinner with Steinmetz

It's Saturday eve. Isabel hurriedly bastes her pork loin and returns it to the oven. She's about done with her southwest potato casserole: a mélange of corn, shredded mozzarella, pinto beans, and serrano peppers. I could do without the beans but say nothing. She slides the glass casserole dish into the oven next to the pork. I'm working on a salad. I arrived thirty minutes ago. So far, Isabel seems to be a bit off.

"I don't know, do you think this was a good idea?"

"What," I reply. "Cooking the dinner? I think we should cook it, don't you? Well, technically not the salad. I could stop working on the salad if you just want me to relax." My obnoxious teasing misses the mark.

"You know what I'm saying." She's not her jovial self. "Having Dan over."

At least she wasn't referring to our relationship. As for Dan, it's a little late to ask me now, especially as it was she who did the arranging, and he's due to arrive within minutes.

"Well, you and the professor were buds that night up on the mountain. If anything, I'll be the third wheel around here."

"Don't be silly. He's old, chubby and balding, and happily married by the way."

"Exactly the ones you have to look out for." I get no reaction. I wonder what's eating at her.

"Hey, are you okay? You were so interested in Dan's lecture last time. You don't seem yourself tonight."

"Yes, I'm fine. Sorry." She puts on a watery smile, and I drop it.

"So, what's the story? He's leaving from here to fly back to Chicago on the red-eye?"

"Yes, that's what he said," she answers.

"I guess scientists get off for Christmas too, even the Jewish ones."

"Jewish! Oh my God. I didn't think of that. Yes, he's probably Jewish. And I'm making pork. I didn't even ask him. How stupid!"

I cut her off. "I wouldn't worry. If he was so concerned, he should've said something. Anyway, there's plenty of that potato stuff with all those beans. He can have my beans; I'll eat his pork."

Isabel remains mostly quiet, and my jabbering, which ordinarily has a comfortable home in this relationship, now seems out of place. Thankfully, the doorbell rings.

Steinmetz has flowers *and* a bottle of wine, way over-the-top per my standards. Isabel seems rejuvenated with his arrival. Dan and I loiter in the kitchen as she plants the flowers in a crystal vase and attends to dinner. As I pop the cork and pour out the wine, she needlessly apologizes for the pork.

Steinmetz, it turns out, far from being an observant Jew, is married to a good Catholic girl, and they raised their children in both traditions. Dan laughs as he describes their past Christmases as the family hanging around the tree, doling out gifts while eating potato latkes.

Isabel brings out a chilled platter of cooked shrimp from the fridge neatly placed around a small bowl of cocktail sauce. Dan is unfazed about these equally-taboo crustaceans, and he dives right in, as do I.

"Dan, so this might be a personal question," Isabel says going deeper, "but how do you feel about God, as a scientist that is."

I pose the logical albeit annoying question. "So, does God also have a PhD?" My doltish remark is ignored, and I'm back on the mountaintop.

The professor responds. "Well, there's nothing incompatible between the belief in scientific principals and faith in God. I'm not talking about organized religion, mind you, as I don't participate; but to me the belief in God and the practice of science both involve the unending search for the truth, and I'm all for that."

"I am the way, and the truth, and the life," I say hypnotically in a deep and celestial tone. This is one of those catchy phrases one might pick up during one's K-through-eight years at Catholic school in Simsbury, Connecticut, near to Canton, which is where I grew up. It astonishes them both, for different reasons, and they turn to me open-mouthed.

"John fourteen, verse six. Just something Jesus said to his disciples at the Last Supper," I explain, with a shrug.

"Ah, New Testament stuff. Out of my league," says Steinmetz.

"Yes, Henry, I've heard it before," Isabel remarks, with a bit of an eye roll. "Though, I wonder, Dan, how does one even recognize the truth."

"In actual fact," Steinmetz responds without hesitation, "whether you're talking about space or more earthly matters, getting at the truth involves an understanding of the details, then testing things out in relation to what's already known to be true. Hence, truth is foundational. It builds upon itself."

Isabel smiles. "You put that so well. Easier said than done."

"Who said it was easy? It's why I became a scientist in the first place."

He might have said the same thing about becoming a philosopher, a poet, a journalist, maybe a shrink, or even a man of the cloth.

Dan continues after a big gulp of his wine. "It's the truth that protects us, from outside risks, even from ourselves. If you don't know there are alligators in the river, you just might go for a quick dip.

"The truth gives meaning to life. When you see things for what they are, you start to see yourself for who *you* are. If you can't measure and understand your surroundings, you start to have a warped view of yourself, as well. Hubble proved that to us in a big way."

Dan takes another slurp of his wine. Clearly, he's a man who likes to hear himself talk, especially with a drink in his hand. Yet, at the same time, he's unpretentious, and I find his soliloquy endearing.

"If you want to understand something, you must look at it up close. Take the dandelion. An ordinary weed, but when you pay attention, you'll learn that it's edible. In fact, it's good for you. It's got antioxidants, for crying out loud! It's been used in Chinese medicine for thousands of years. It came over on the Mayflower, so it's even deep-rooted in this country, pardon the pun." Dan laughs out loud. "And if you look at them without prejudice, they're very pretty wildflowers. But if you don't know any of this, you won't think twice before picking up some broadleaf herbicide at Lowes to kill them off."

Dan takes a breath and another sip of wine. The pause is short term.

"Isabel, did Henry tell you that he may be descended from a very famous Dutch philosopher, someone who made a real mark on the world?"

Uh, oh.

"No, he didn't." Isabel turns to me, lips pursed, and her head cocked to one side.

"Yes, Baruch Spinoza, who came from a family of Portuguese Jews. That would make Henry and me distant cousins." Dan again laughs at his own remark.

"Very distant," I reply. Dan chuckles and continues.

"Spinoza lived in the seventeenth century. He was inspired by the radical philosophy of a contemporary, René Descartes. This was at the very beginning of the Enlightenment. Spinoza told us that everything in the universe fundamentally is of the same substance, a unified reality, governed by a singular set of rules. To him, God and nature were one and the same."

"Sounds like something I would say," I joke, but no one laughs. Isabel interrupts.

"You *would* say that. You worship the universe. If there was some sort of cosmic church, you'd be there every Sunday."

"Or Saturday," Steinmetz chimes in. "Sounds like you've inherited some ancestral genes, Henry," he says, quickly returning to his mini-lecture.

"So, Spinoza, the philosopher, was shunned by Jews and Christians alike – they thought him an atheist. And while he certainly questioned the tenets and teachings of organized religion of that period, he never refuted the existence of God.

"But what I find most intriguing in its pure irony is that, to eke out a living, Spinoza was a lens grinder. He made lenses for telescopes, for crying out loud."

Wow. I didn't know that. That *is* ironic.

Isabel and Dan continue with this all-too serious discussion of truth, God, and the universe for a few minutes longer. It's a bit heavy, and I refill my glass. Finally, Isabel moves off-topic.

"Dan, let's not forget that you promised to tell us more about what *you* do in your own search for the truth."

"You betcha! I have some time before I have to get to the airport. We shall discuss it over the ceremonial......swine," says Dan, lifting his wine glass, and eliciting a giggle from Iz. I suppose it was a tad clever.

Dan turns the conversation toward me and asks about my book. I'm on the spot. I admit that progress is slow.

"Does the professor know what your book is about, Henry?"

"Yes, it's about how it all comes to an end," Dan quickly answers. "We discussed it the first time we met. It's an important topic even for the average layperson; no, especially for the layperson. Death is the ultimate truth, and unlike other species, we know that it's coming. I like Henry's historical approach to it, too. If he can give it some good context, it'll be a fascinating read."

"Thanks," I say. "If it ever does get written."

"Did Henry tell you about his other idea?" Isabel asks.

"No, another book, then?"

"No, in the same book," she says. I cringe. Why are we talking about this?

"He wants to add a travel element to it - a guide to places where the observatories are located."

"A travel guide? Interesting. I'm not sure anyone did a guide-book like that, at least not in conjunction with the science. I like it. You've got all those beautiful places in Chile, and in Hawaii. There's ORM in the Canaries. Even here, you've got Apache in New Mexico, and our very own Kitt Peak. Plenty more. I'm not sure how you join the two concepts, but that's your problem, my young friend." Dan laughs easily, looking at me.

Yes, and still a problem at that.

"I appreciate your encouragement, Professor," I say, adding, "and if you can send me on a few of those excursions, maybe it'll get written one day."

Dan smiles. "You betcha! We'll squeeze you in under one of our NSF grants, if we get any more of them. Who knows?"

Dinner is ready and we all serve ourselves in the kitchen. We take our plates and wine glasses into the separate dining room, pulling up to Isabel's massive gray granite table, over which hangs a silver-metal and glass chandelier, slightly dimmed for the occasion. The table is set in minimalist style, with elegant blue-cloth place mats and napkins, polished silverware, and tall water glasses. I'm happy I wore a collared polo shirt this evening with my nicest khakis.

Inviting Dan was in fact a very good idea. Isabel's dinner is delectable and her mood much improved. Dan, who charms us with conversation on a host of non-technical topics, is fascinating in his acuity. While Isabel's law background peeks through in her willingness to consider opposing sides of an issue, Dan is dogmatic, and his opinions are singular. Any rare indecision on his part, it seems to me, is only temporary, pending a complete investigation. I see myself more as a cautious observer, at the ready to satirically poke holes through any proposition.

It's clear that our professor's mind is capable of things that neither Isabel nor I can fathom. Even she, who was born into intelligence (unlike some of us who must work hard at it) and passed at least one bar exam, could not begin to grasp the mathematics required of Dan's vocation. Putting it simply, the discipline of elder law ain't rocket science, while astrophysics is a close relative.

There is one odd thing, however, about our professor's manner, juxtaposed with his intellect. He's a bit of a slob. It's not that he likes to eat, although he did power down two full portions of pork and potatoes, and he picked through my spinach and endive salad on the hunt for itinerant pecans and craisins. Nor would I complain about his fondness for alcohol, as he is in good company.

No, he's just sloppy. If I had to guess, it's the mahogany-colored Italian wine that Dan brought with the flowers that ends up on his pink-and-white checked button-down, which, as the evening wears on, increasingly resembles a tablecloth. Also, I'm pretty sure that some of the casserole will fall to the floor when he stands up to leave.

Despite his brilliance, Dan's a regular guy. Maybe I shouldn't be so surprised that he was drawn to me at our first meeting. I took to him easily because of his humility. Scientists, like surgeons, can be quite full of themselves, and I've come across many just like that. If

Hubble himself had but one character flaw, it was his inability to be *humble,* and such was his reputation. Dan's nature, on the contrary, may ironically be described as down-to-earth. To me, he's just your typical easy-going, hard-working, Midwesterner who wouldn't speak ill of a soul and who would give you the shirt off his back, stains, and all. The fact that he's also brilliant is happenstance. Even his sloppiness may not detract from his charm, as such older men are more easily forgiven for uncorrected flaws from their youth.

So, our time together this evening flows quickly, and after a while my natural reticence falls away, and I find myself magnificently buoyant in the mix of drink and conversation. Ultimately, as I mop up some gravy with a chunk of French white bread, Isabel insists upon finally hearing about Steinmetz's research.

"Dan, do you think you could pry yourself away from the casserole a minute and tell me quickly about what you do on the mountain?"

I add, "Yeah, I'm beginning to think that maybe you've just got a big satellite dish up there with a Chicago sports channel, a keg, and a lazy boy."

Finally, this evokes the desired effect. "Yes, we have that too!" Dan responds laughing. "But okay, I think maybe it's a good idea to cover this before I get totally shnookered."

Too late for that, my old friend.

"Oh my, I'll have to make this quick; I do have a plane to catch. You know one of the benefits of our odd hours is that these cheap night-flights are no big deal for us. Be that as it may, where did we leave off last time?"

I respond. "As I recall, you covered the size of the universe, that is all of Leavitt and part of Hubble."

"Yes, spot on Henry. Onto Doppler. So, Iz, I'm not sure if I told you, but my research involves dark energy, or DE. To understand DE, you must first understand another DE, the Doppler Effect. Has Henry mentioned Doppler to you yet?"

She and I have not spoken of any such things since our outing at Kitt Peak. Isabel knew little of Copernicus, I wonder if it's the same with Doppler.

Isabel responds. "Not yet, Doctor, but I have heard of the Doppler Effect as it relates to sound, yes?"

Okay, there's no wagering real money against her.

"Precisely, my dear. Go to the head of the class. In 1840 something…."

It's amazing how the professor himself jumps behind the wheel and flicks on his instructional cruise-control with complete competence, despite five glasses of wine and being mostly shitfaced. Yet, he may need a cup of java before driving to the airport.

The professor goes on to explain Doppler's theories on sound waves, using the example of an observer on the tracks waiting for an oncoming train. The train's whistle increases in pitch as it approaches yet goes lower when it passes the observer.

"Why is this?" he asks Isabel.

She shrugs her shoulders. At least she's no Einstein. Steinmetz continues to tell her how the sound waves get bunched up while the train heads into the very noise it creates. These shorter waves are higher in pitch. Conversely, after the train passes the observer, the waves get stretched out. Here, the sound goes lower. Dan takes another slurp of the merlot.

"Clear?"

It could not have been explained better in a brightly lit classroom, mid-morning, by a teetotaler.

"I get it, Dan. But what does this have to do with space?" she asks.

"Excellent question." Dan instinctively reaches for his wine glass, but wisely switches to water.

"Well, instead of sound waves, think of waves of light. Waves are waves for the most part. When an object, like a galaxy, is moving toward you, the waves of light you see from that object are shorter in length. On the other hand, if this object is moving away from you, the waves of light behind it seem longer to you, that is farther apart. In simple terms, in the visible spectrum of light, the shorter waves we see more as blue, the longer waves we see more as red. Got it?"

"I suppose so," she replies.

While Isabel is captivated by Steinmetz, I can only think of her. Look how she's lapping up this Doppler stuff. The only effect that Doppler might have had on Jenna would've been a catatonic trance. Iz looks so good, too. Will Dan ever stop talking? And they say *I* can be long-winded. What time did he say that flight was?

"Back in the early 1900s, an astronomer at the Lowell Observatory up in Flagstaff, a man named Slipher, was the first to attach a spectroscope to a telescope. A spectroscope is a prism, an instrument that separates out light into its various bands of color by wavelength. Remember, ROYGBIV? Slipher captured images of the light, separated into wavelengths, given off by galaxies. In other words, he took photographs of the rainbow images emitted by those galaxies. These images are called spectra.

"By comparing the spectra of these galaxies to spectra made using light here on Earth, Slipher determined that the galactic images always shifted toward the red-end of the spectrum, where the light waves are longer. This is what's called a 'redshift'. The longer, reddish waves mean that the galaxy, like that noisy train, is moving away from the observer - in other words, from Earth.

"Hubble performed similar observations for many galaxies and obtained the same results. But it was Hubble who determined that the *farther* the galaxy was from Earth, the *faster* it moves away from us. This is called Hubble's Law. So, what do you think it all means?"

I yawn uncontrollably as the wine and the lecture have a

common effect on me. This might have been taken as an insult had anyone noticed.

In but a few seconds, Isabel responds. "The universe is expanding?"

"Yes! I'm thinking you're too smart for this guy." He gestures to me.

C'mon, where's your filter, man? That hurts. I was thinking the same thing.

"I knew that as soon as I met her," I reply.

Isabel reaches for my hand.

"Actually, guys, I didn't know the answer," she admits. "I just heard you mention it before."

"And an honest girl, at that," Steinmetz remarks with a grin. "Okay, in the interest of moving along, the universe is expanding, yes, but there's more to it."

Iz listens eagerly. I start to clear the table for I know what's coming.

Looking at Isabel, Steinmetz asks, "Do you have a large rubber band, a ruler and some scissors? As they say, a picture is worth a thousand words."

Iz returns in a minute with the requested props. Dan continues his lecture.

"So, again, Hubble's law says that the *farther* a galaxy is away from Earth, the *faster* it moves away from us. What Hubble *didn't* find were galaxies of varying distances moving away from us at the same rate, or even at random velocities. That might have suggested that only the outer edges of the universe are moving away from us. Instead, what he saw was what Einstein's theory of general relativity predicted."

Isabel looks bewildered. Steinmetz continues; he has a plane to catch.

"It's not the outer edges of the universe that are expanding, it's the fabric of space itself that's expanding!" Dan picks up the scissors and cuts the rubber band into a single strand. He takes out a Sharpie from his pants pocket and marks the strand of rubber with four large evenly-spaced dots.

"Look. The rubber represents space, and the dots on it are the galaxies." He holds the strand firmly with his left hand and stretches it out with his right. "As space gets stretched out, these dots, the galaxies, which sit passively in the fabric of space, go for a very fast ride. And the farther out they are, the faster they go. Reverse engineer this going backwards in time, some 13.8 billion years, and what you get is the Big Bang."

Despite the visuals, I suspect that Iz is having problems wrapping her head around all of it. If only for the sake of completion, Dan finishes up now with Perlmutter, Schmidt and Riess.

"Isabel, I know this was a lot to take in, but let's get to the punchline. I should get going. A few scientists were awarded the Nobel for their work in 1998 that reached an astounding conclusion. These scientists employed the large telescopes and advanced computer simulations to research the universe's expansion using exploding supernovae as their standard candles. Let me preface this by saying that all our knowledge leads us to the conclusion that *if* the universe is made up of only normal matter, that is the stuff that we see and measure, then gravity should ultimately reign in the expansion of the universe. *If* it were just normal matter we are dealing with, the expansion would at some point be expected to slow down, even reverse. But what these guys determined was that not only is the universe expanding, its expansion is accelerating; it's expanding faster and faster over time. It will not slow down! Hence, we believe that there's a force at work that counteracts gravity and promotes the expansion of space. We don't know what it is, we don't understand it, we can't see or measure it directly, but we believe strongly that it is there; and we call it… dark energy!"

Talk about the dramatic. I wish my brother could've heard this. Trying to stay positive, however, after loading up the dishwasher and fully focusing on this last part, I must admire the professor's way with words. I only hope it sticks with me when I start to write about some of it myself.

"Wrapping up, what I'm doing on the mountain is tweaking their work, for I've found that the type of supernovae they used as standard candles actually come in various subsets, and their conclusions as to the acceleration may have to be slowed down. Regardless, the universe will still be accelerating outward, and we will still need dark energy to explain it, just not as much perhaps."

Isabel brews a single paper cup of strong coffee for our professor as he heads out the door. He takes his leave with wishes for a merry Christmas and a hug for both of us. As his arms are around me, he whispers in my ear.

"You got yourself a wonderful girl, Henry. Don't screw it up." At that, coffee in hand, he heads out the door for the airport.

Together, the two of us clean up the mess that is Isabel's kitchen, the last thing on Earth I would choose to do now. Iz heads to the dining room with her Dust Buster to suck up remnants from the meal beneath the table, particularly where Dan was sitting.

"Gosh, he's brilliant, and the conversation was interesting, again, but he's a bit sloppy, right?" she says, as she re-enters the kitchen.

I respond. "I would say worse than that, but yes."

Isabel, who didn't drink much tonight, seems more animated than she should be at 10:30. Whatever bothered her prior to Dan's arrival has resolved itself. She continues to talk about dark energy and the expansion of space.

"So, I think I get most of it, but Dan didn't say how fast space is expanding, did he?"

"No," I reply. "I don't think he got to that."

"So, how fast is it?"

"It depends upon where you are. If you go out about a million light years away, you'd be talking about speeds of like 150,000 miles per hour."

"What?!" Of course, Isabel is incredulous. Who wouldn't be?

"Yeah, I know." Normally this type of discussion would be thrilling, but I'm weary.

"What's worse," I continue, "is that this is fairly close to us. Theoretically, if you go out real far, space could be expanding close to the speed of light."

"How fast is that?"

"About 186,000 miles per second, give or take."

At this point, Isabel doesn't bother to respond.

"I guess that's enough of this for now," she says. "The whole thing doesn't even seem real." She pauses. "You look tired."

"Yes, I'm worn out. I think I drank too much."

"D'ya think? You guys polished off two bottles. Well, don't take this the wrong way, but why don't you stay over. You don't have to drive home like this."

An hour ago, I couldn't keep my eyes off her. Now, I can't keep them open. But what does she mean, "don't take this the wrong way"? Which way would she like me to take it?

"Sure, that sounds like a plan. But to be honest, maybe I better just take the couch." I face facts. My body is crying out for only one thing, and it's not that. Although, God knows what she's thinking, and if I had any energy, I might even be concerned.

We finish up in the kitchen, and Isabel shows me to a spare bedroom, complete with a full bath, and kisses me lightly on the forehead, as if I were Lauren's brother.

"Sleep well, Henry," she says with a funny gleam in her eye.

I find everything I need in the bathroom, strip down to my boxers, and crawl between crisp queen-size sheets. I lean over to my phone, which is on the nightstand, set my alarm, and within thirty seconds, I feel sleep overtake me.

CHAPTER 34

Awakening

It's 7:15 on Sunday morning, and Isabel is awakened by a noise. *Shit! Another raccoon in the attic! I thought I got rid of them.* She bolts up and only then remembers that she has a house guest. In a few minutes she emerges from the bathroom in her master suite wearing a white terry cloth robe.

She finds Henry in the kitchen, sitting at the table reading the weekend paper. His hair is damp from a shower, and he's clean-shaven, barefoot, but otherwise fully dressed. The kitchen table is set for breakfast, and Iz sees two glasses of juice, bread, sliced cheese, and boiled eggs in their shells all artfully laid out, with Steinmetz's flowers positioned in the center. There's a smell of freshly-brewed coffee in the air.

Henry touches his iPhone in front of him on the table. A famous keyboard intro starts to play through the phone's miniaturized speakers. It's an old Burt Bacharach tune that reached the top of the charts. Isabel recognizes it at once - *This Guy's in Love with You.*

Her face lights up into a big smile as she turns to Henry.

"I haven't heard this one in a long time," she says.

"Not too corny?"

"No, it's lovely. Who sings it?"

Henry stands up from his seat at the table.

"Would you believe, Herb Albert?" he responds.

"The trumpet player?"

"The same."

Henry moves closer to Isabel. He reaches out for her right hand with his left, and draws her in. He places his right hand on the small of her back, and he leads her into a gentle rocking motion side to side.

"He's good," Isabel remarks, as they slow-dance.

"Who?"

"Herb Albert."

"I suppose."

Henry pulls her in close until their cheeks almost touch. Isabel feels the warmth of his breath on her face. They move to and fro on the kitchen's stone floor. Each of them looks into the eyes of the other as if to know the other's thoughts and feelings. Henry moves his head forward and brushes her lips with his own. She presses herself against him and leans into his tender kiss.

"This is such a nice surprise," she whispers. "You're so full of surprises."

"I've been waiting for the right moment," Henry says.

"I *was* beginning to wonder."

They rock back and forth to the music.

"I was making up excuses for myself, but I was just scared," Henry explains. "I guess, it's been a while."

They kiss again, mouths open slightly, tongues delicately searching.

"You've nothing to be nervous about," Isabel assures.

Another kiss.

"I'm just glad you find me attractive," she adds.

"Attractive? You're beautiful. I'm in love with you," he whispers as their lips and tongues intertwine.

"I love you, too, Henry," she avows in a soft voice.

As the song plays out, Henry, shaking slightly, undoes the belt of Isabel's robe, which he removes from around her shoulders to reveal her in a blue negligée. She wriggles free of the robe and he unceremoniously flings it into a heap on a chair. Her eyes are closed as he continues to kiss her softly, on her lips, on the side of her neck. He gently moves his hands up and down her bare back.

"Why don't we take this to the bedroom?" she suggests in a whisper.

"What about breakfast?" he quietly quips.

"Later."

"Okay, your place, or mine?" he murmurs.

She giggles quietly. "I was thinking about my place."

They move away from the kitchen toward her bedroom.

"Should we turn the coffee pot off?" Henry asks.

"My God, you're so annoying," she responds. "Just keep moving."

CHAPTER 35

Coffee with Marianne

Isabel and Marianne are at the Fit Bite café, seated at the same table they sat at just over a month ago, glistening now as then.

As always, Marianne inquires after Lauren.

"I heard from her on Monday. We did another call with her therapist. Things seem okay. I'm going up there for a little visit right after Christmas, but why don't we talk about something else, if you don't mind?"

"Sure, of course, what should we talk about? I'd ask you about Henry, but since our last call, I'm afraid what I'll hear."

Isabel's serious. "You didn't say anything about that to Raff, did you?"

"No, absolutely not. You know I wouldn't, as much as I thought about it." Marianne gently smiles. "Why, did anything happen?" she asks slyly.

Without answering directly, Isabel recounts their evening with Steinmetz.

"Mare, I was such a bitch to Henry when he first came over."

"You were? To my poor defenseless Henry?"

"Yes, Henry. I felt so sorry."

"Ah, he probably deserved it, acting like a dope."

"Yeah, maybe. With all that stuff about the wondrous ocean, it was all so romantic, only to fizzle out. I admit, I was disappointed. But as the evening wore on, I realized how childish I was acting. He never held himself out as some great lover, or even interested in me that way. Maybe he's just naturally poetic." Mare rolls her eyes. Isabel goes on.

"God, when I first met him, I was thinking it would be nice if we were all just good friends. I wasn't attracted to him that way at all. But when I suspected that he didn't find *me* attractive, I became indignant."

"Yeah, the nerve of some guys." They laugh.

"Anyway, toward the end of the evening, I said to myself, even if he is gay, it's not my business. He's become a good friend, and we laugh a lot. Why not just take that for what it is?"

"Really, Iz? I still don't believe any of this!" Marianne says loudly enough to attract attention. "Could I be so wrong about Henry all these years? This isn't right."

Isabel ignores her and continues.

"So, the two of them got pretty buzzed on the wine. By the end of the evening, Henry couldn't keep his eyes open. So, after Steinmetz left, I insisted that he stay over."

"Oh?"

"Oh, nothing." Isabel speaks softly. "He agreed, so long as he could sleep on the couch. So, I put him in the guest bedroom, and gave him a little peck on the forehead and said goodnight."

"OH... MY... GOD!" Mare responds. "Did you read him a bed-time story, too?!" Some heads turn toward the sound of Marianne's voice. "So, nothing happened. I don't believe it. Here I think I'm such a good judge of character. Not that this is a character issue, it's just that, well, not what I expected. I wish he'd just come out with it. I wonder if Raff knows and won't tell me. Nah, Raff's not that good."

Mare is flushed and flummoxed.

"Wait, there's more," says Isabel, chuckling; but Marianne talks right over her.

"I can't keep this from Raff. I don't know how *he'll* handle it. Shit, I can't believe Henry's been able to keep this from us for so long; and why? We don't care if he's gay, but do you know how many times I've tried setting him up? No wonder!"

Isabel laughs harder. A few patrons sitting close to them peer at the two women, wanting in on the joke. "You mean I'm not the first one? Hold on, Mare. Let me finish," Isabel pleads, tears rolling down her cheek.

"There's more?!"

"Yes, there's more," Isabel responds, still laughing.

Marianne crosses her arms and waits.

"So, it's I don't know, 7:30 the next morning, and I hear rustling in the kitchen. I was so afraid it was those awful raccoons again. Did I ever tell you my raccoon story, Mare?"

"Stop it! I don't care about your fucking raccoons, Iz. Just tell me what happened!"

"Okay, calm down." Isabel slows the pace. "So, I threw on a robe and went into the kitchen to see what was going on, and there's Henry."

"In the kitchen."

"Right, he's in the kitchen. He's been up for who knows how long, showered, dressed. He's made coffee and breakfast, you know, eggs, cheese, toast..."

"Yeah, I get it, breakfast, that's nice. So, get to the fucking punchline already," Mare says in an emphatic whisper.

"Okay. So, he puts on some music."

"Yeah. Go on."

"It's this song, *This Guy's in Love with You.* Do you know it? Herb Albert the trumpet..."

"Stop it! You're doing this purposely," Marianne demands. Isabel guffaws.

"Okay. We start to dance to the music, a very slow dance, and we hold each other tight; and then he kisses me, right there in the kitchen, a gentle, sensual kiss." Marianne nods with her mouth slightly open. "And we kiss some more," Isabel continues. "I'll tell you, he's a good kisser. So, he says something like he's been waiting for the right moment, maybe he was a bit afraid, and I told him how I was beginning to have my doubts. That's when he told me that he loves me. He said it right there while we were dancing in the kitchen. So, we went into my boudoir and, as they say, the rest is history."

Mare's arm makes a big arc as she slams the table with her right palm with full force. "I knew it, he's not gay! Way to go, Enrico!!" she yells out.

Now everyone in Fit Bite looks over, annoyed.

"He's removed all doubt," Isabel adds. "It felt so good, and he's so sweet and gentle. I couldn't believe it. I'm very happy," she says with a big smile.

"You can't believe it?!! I can't believe it! How can you be so cruel to me? You had me going. Here I thought I made a terrible mistake. But I didn't. I nailed it! Damn, I'm good!" Marianne says with a little fist pump of her own. "But watch out, Iz, 'cause I owe you one," Marianne says, wagging a forefinger, grinning.

"No, it is I who owe you, Mare, for so much," Isabel says as she reaches across the table and clasps her friend's still-clammy hands in her own.

CHAPTER 36

AWOL

Lauren and five other patients pile into the back of the rehab's white Chevy van with two V-shaped brown and green palm trees stenciled on each side. The driver, a tech, spins the wheels out of the facility's gravel lot and drives to Surprise's Word of God Church, on the outer edge of the greater Phoenix metro area. They're going to an open 3 p.m. AA meeting. In preparation, the women primped and preened for hours, for men will be there.

Lauren, the least made up, and the prettiest among them, is restless. She's been at Dusty Palms for seven weeks and stays mostly to herself. While the other five yammer on about their prospects, Lauren's silent.

They arrive at the church and mingle with some thirty other addicts and alcoholics in the entryway of the large gray stucco and stone building. The crowd meanders into a large conference room alongside the sanctuary. Rows of metal chairs fill the room. They're separated by a center aisle leading to a lectern.

The meeting starts. There's the usual reading of the tools from the Big Book, after which a seventeen-year-sober African-American woman, a manager at a local shelter, is called upon to present her own story.

"I was born in Crenshaw, in South LA. My mom was an addict, and my dad drank. So, really, I'm not sure how we made it those first six years." A few in the crowd shake their head and voice an amen.

"My younger brother and me eventually moved in with my grandma. She was nice. She loved us like a mother should, and things were good until I was twelve; that's when she got sick. I took care of her as best I could, but she passed. After that, we had no place to go, so..."

Lauren might have been empathetic had she been listening. Only one thing on her mind: escape. *It's fucking hot in here. I'm going to suffocate if I don't get out.* She feels her heart beating against her chest. Her breathing is labored, like she's just been running full out.

Jon, a tall, kinky-haired alcoholic, early thirties, mixed race, who relapsed six months prior, makes eye contact. He holds a pack of Camels, her brand. He motions to her, bringing thumb and forefinger to his lips. Smoke?

She launches from her chair, causing a stir in her row. She meets him outside in the parking lot. It's late in the day. The sun is low in the December desert sky. It's getting chilly, but she breathes easier.

Lauren knows Jon from a three-minute conversation at a meeting four weeks ago. He does his best at small talk while she drags on a cigarette. He lives nearby.

"Hey, how about a cup of coffee at my place?"

Lauren needs no time to think.

"Yeah, let's get outta here."

The two get into Jon's 2004 red Wrangler and travel a quarter mile to his trailer home across West Bell Road. His AA house-mate is out working a shift at a pizza joint.

There's more small talk while Jon fills his four-cup coffee maker. He coaxes her onto a small sofa in front of a huge screen TV. They pretend to talk some more while a re-run of The Americans plays on the wall.

Before Mr. Coffee has cycled out, they're naked and humping on Jon's double bed. She fucks with a vengeful fury, without concern for safety or feelings. She's got no past, sees no future. Lust rides over emotion, instinct over intellect.

She possesses and controls him; owns him. It's only this that soothes and softens.

He's released, and it ends. Withdrawing, he opens his eyes, looks at her and shakes his head, startled and stupefied by the aggression. Nevertheless, he's asleep within minutes.

She dresses, grabs his pack of Camels and a dollar lighter, stuffs them in her purse, and leaves the trailer. She's got almost nothing. No phone. No cash. Just a Florida driver's license in a wallet along-side some cigarettes.

Where now? Meeting's over. Can't get back to the rehab, even if I knew where it was. Could call an Uber. Fuck it, I'm done with that place.

She walks on a cracked asphalt drive in a direction that she thinks takes her out of the trailer park. Her path arcs around and in five minutes she finds herself back where she started. *Typical.*

Heading in a different direction, she cuts through tiny back-yards of concrete. She passes a portly balding man sitting on an alu-minum folding lawn chair. He's drinking bottled beer and watching four Ball Park Franks sizzle on a portable three-legged charcoal grill.

Damn. Smells good. Too awkward to ask for one.

Lauren comes to a four-foot cinder block wall. She turns her head to see if anyone's looking, scales it, and lands in a 200-vehicle parking lot on the other side. It's mostly empty. She sees a tattered fairway abutting the lot, perhaps the eighteenth hole of a second-rate golf club. Sure enough, she walks past a pro shop and a real estate office on her way to the street.

West Bell Road is a newly paved black asphalt six-lane boulevard with a wide median of green zoysia and evenly spaced palms. She turns right onto the road's concrete sidewalk, hoping to get to Surprise's town center. She has no plan, but if something positive is to happen, it won't be in a trailer park or the links next door.

She spots the church on the left, across the avenue. It's far enough away that she won't be recognized if anyone from the meeting's still around.

Lauren walks west toward the sun that's setting behind distant foothills. There's a six-foot brown stone wall on her right. A Latino, wearing long-sleeves and a canvas backpack, pedals his single-gear bicycle on the pavement past her from the opposite direction.

She spies another fairway beyond the wall: this one opulent and well-groomed, a more upscale golf course, literally, where the grass is greener. Walking a minute more, Lauren reaches the end of the stone wall. A black aluminum fence supported by intermittent stout brick pillars takes its place.

Newish two-story homes sit behind the fence, with their sky-lighted front halls, two-car front-facing garages, second-floor bonus rooms, and pristine concrete-and-brick yards. All the homes are crammed in with the efficiency of a submarine, each onto its own one-eighth acre lot. There's just enough space between neighbors to plant a single privacy palm or hedge.

There are tens of thousands of these homes in Surprise, and adjacent communities, in subdivisions with regal names like Sedgewick Manor, Desert View, Sierra Madre, or Regal Ranch. Many are fifty-five-and-over communities, that purposely exclude those rowdy and annoying fifty-four-year-olds, and younger. All the construction required few trees to be cut. This all sprung out of the stark emptiness of the Sonoran Desert.

Ten minutes down the road, the subdivision ends, and to the right, Lauren sees a flat, white, two-tiered building with two great cylindrical chimneys, and a porte-cochere made to resemble a ship's bowsprit. It's surrounded by a gigantic pebbled parking lot, muddy brown like the mighty Mississippi after a turbulent rainstorm. The sign atop the building reads "Riverboat Bingo".

What the hell is Bingo? I should know this. A game? Lauren recalls something about a dog. There was an old lady in her mom's waiting room. The old woman went on and on about it.

Do you like to play Bingo, little girl? Do you? Was at the Indians last week. Won a thousand dollars!

It's strange that she remembers this bizarre woman, but where do dogs and Indians come into it? *Shit! Must be the drugs really screwed with my mind.*

Lauren passes the riverboat building and comes upon a small pumping station adjacent to a narrow waterway. She continues onto a bridge, sees a small sign for the Beardsley Canal. Looking down, she sees a concrete channel of greenish water. It appears to Lauren like a long moat, that winds its way along the edge of the town in defense against an encroaching desert.

The sidewalk ends, and West Bell Road turns into the sun Valley Parkway. Cars speed past her going seventy mph. She continues along the highway's shoulder and looks ahead into a dry, vast wilderness. No more crowded subdivisions, fairways and sand traps, gambling halls, and trailer parks. It's the end of civilization. Instead, there's a scattering of Mesquite and Ironwood trees, distant powerlines, and the dry, tan earth as far as the eye can see.

Damn! I should've gone the other way.

Lauren is chilled and feels a terrible soreness within her.

What happened back there? I don't even remember his name.

Why do I do this? Why can't I stop?

The walking is hypnotic. Lauren goes deep to the one thing that's always there, the music. It's a haunting sound that she can't shake from the back of her mind, stirring voices that have lingered since that fateful night in the desert. It's *Believer*, and along with the pain, it causes her to stop in midstride, and to question.

What do I do now?

CHAPTER 37

Just Letting Go

I was good. I think I was at my best. She was into it. Unless she was faking. She's so nice, she might've done that for me. Especially the first time. No, she's got too much integrity for that. I was just good. She said, I was really good.

Actually, she didn't use the word *good*. What she said was that I was *gentle*. *So gentle*. What did she expect? Rough? I'm not into contact sports. I'm afraid to stand at the net in tennis. Maybe I wasn't very good. It's been a while; it was our first time. I can be better.

One thing I do know. *She* was good; and she loves me. She said that she loves me! Wow!

It's Thursday evening, and it's been four days since we crossed that bridge. I'm still ruminating on it as if my thoughts will alter the experience. I try to recall her light scent of lavender and sweet breath against my face. I imagine seeing her caring soul again through the limpid portals that are her dazzling green eyes. I want so much to be with her again. I'm on my way to meet her, and my mind is filled with song.

Love I get so lost, sometimes
Days pass and this emptiness fills my heart
When I want to run away
I drive off in my car
But whichever way I go
I come back to the place you are

I called her afterward, that Sunday evening, just to touch base and reassure, as if it weren't I who needed confirmation. We spoke every day since. She invited me to go to a Nalanon meeting, of all things. We're joining up there this evening. It's only for an hour, and we'll grab dinner downtown afterward. I'm already a bit hungry, and I have a serious proposal for her.

All my instincts, they return
And the grand facade, so soon will burn
Without a noise, without my pride
I reach out from the inside

I pull up to a traffic light and glance to the right. It's a gorgeous woman driving a white Camaro in the next lane over. I do a double-take and verify that it's a hot late-twenty something blond in the driver's seat, all alone, bee-bopping to her own song. The blond looks over at me in my Fiesta, and smiles. I can imagine a half-dozen reasons why she smiled, most of them unfavorable. Nevertheless, I courageously smile back before the light turns, and she accelerates away from me as fast as Elon Musk's Falcon 9. Normally there are no such exchanges before launch, but I'm feeling too good not to smile.

In your eyes
The light the heat
In your eyes
I am complete

In your eyes
I see the doorway to a thousand churches
In your eyes
The resolution of all the fruitless searches
In your eyes
I see the light and the heat
In your eyes
Oh, I want to be that complete
I want to touch the light
The heat I see in your eyes

It's perhaps no coincidence that the Nalanon meeting is being held at Banner University Medical Center. Isabel's coming directly from the office. I find the venue, a dining room off the cafeteria. I'm fifteen minutes early. Some twenty chairs have been neatly arranged in an oval, presumably by the middle-aged couple standing in its center. They chat quietly, despite being the only ones in the room. They turn to me as I enter.

"Welcome. I'm Daphne, and this is Chuck." Both extend their hands.

"Oh, hello. My name is Henry. I'm meeting a friend here if that's okay."

"Sure, Henry. Of course. It's so good of you to come," Daphne says sounding a bit like a Stepford wife.

I take a seat, and they go back to their discussion, which seems to surround the plan for tonight's meeting. In all, I count about fifteen more attendees filtering in over the next ten minutes: people of all ages, races and, I suppose, walks of life. There are middle-aged and older white couples, casually dressed; a solitary tall and handsome fifty-something African-American man with a shaved head sporting an elegant tan suit and power tie; two young, skinny Asian girls in their late teens with tattoos on their necks and arms and who knows where else; an older Hispanic man, in worn jeans and work boots and a blue denim work shirt with a Diamondbacks' cap covering jet black hair; he's accompanied by a younger, somewhat muscular Latina, similarly dressed, except for the hat. She takes a seat next to mine. It seems to me that everyone is talking to everyone else in the room, which soon becomes a raucous cocktail party without the booze. Many say hello to me, or just smile. I look around for my date, feeling uncomfortable.

Finally, a lovely professional woman with dark coloring and beautiful eyes takes the empty seat, which I've been saving, next to mine. She leans over and unabashedly kisses me on the lips. I daresay, everyone in the room takes notice; some smile; some even nod and cluck in approval, like they're part of some attentive Sicilian family, duty-bound to chaperone Isabel and me, as if she's my beautiful Apollonia. In my eyes, she may as well be, as I too have been struck by a bolt of lightning.

Daphne calls for order a few minutes after the hour.

"Okay folks, let's get started. Please take your seats." Daphne volunteered to lead the meeting this week. It's obviously not her first gig. She addresses some unresolved administrative issues.

"We haven't decided what to do with the surplus in our account. We paid for the literature, and there's still, how much did you say, Chuck?" I figure Chuck for the Treasurer.

"We have a balance of $183," Chuck replies. "I think we were deciding if we're going to donate some of it back to the head office, or more locally."

"Any discussion on this?" Daphne urges.

After some back and forth between, at most, four of the attendees, the group votes by a decidedly unenthusiastic show of hands, to give it all to a local church that sponsors a soup kitchen frequented by the homeless addict population.

"Does anyone have any announcements?" Daphne asks. No one

responds. At this point, the meeting gets its official start. Daphne continues reading from a well-worn script in her hand.

"Is there anyone here at a Nalanon meeting for the first time?" I reluctantly raise my hand.

"Welcome. It's customary for you to tell us your first name and what person in your life brings you here."

"Okay. I'm Henry...."

At that, I hear a chorus of voices almost in perfect unison sing out, "Hi, Henry!"

"...oh, hey, I'm here... with my friend Isabel."

"Welcome to our meeting, Henry," Daphne says, taking a solo. "At this point, we'll go around the room to introduce ourselves, first names only please, and who brings you here. Chuck, why don't you start?"

"Hi, I'm Chuck."

"Hi, Chuck," sings the chorus.

"I'm here for Emily, my daughter, an addict."

And so on, until everyone in the oval makes a similar introduction.

I'm hypnotized by this monotonous droning and go within myself. My skeptical side reflexively excoriates this gathering as being sweetly slick and artificial. Yet, I also sense something of an ongoing substance. The beautiful melody that only recently played in my nomadic brain is inexplicably replaced by the most irritating tune ever composed since music itself was invented, since Adam crooned his first love song to Eve. Like many of the world's most annoying television ads, I could never shake it. "It's a Small World After All" just pops into my head like the million bad ideas and unspeakable thoughts I've had these past forty-four years; and its chorus now resonates in my mind, over, and over, and over again.

Turns out, "It's a Small World After All" is well suited to the moment. Of course, it's known as the song that was perfectly chosen as the repetitive accompaniment to the sugary ride at Disney World that bears the same name. But what was once a pathetically mawkish melody, has in a way, over time, transformed into prophecy.

In this instant of my meandering reflection, all those adorable robotic characters, which by now are past their fiftieth birthdays, decked out in their fading native costumes, lip syncing off-rhythm to those tedious lyrics, in fact might be viewed as the bygone representatives of the best of our Judeo-Christian ideals: civility, equality, respect, truth and love. Yes, it hits me like a snowball in the face. It's a small world, and we're all in this together; it's a small world, and it's not ours to keep; it's a small world, and we all better get along. Despite my innate negativity, I realize now that it cannot be said or sung any better than that.

As the tune in my head fades, I grasp its relationship to the present. Despite the all-too-scripted nature of this gathering, and in the same way the song is performed by those sweet little droids in a dark and dank tunnel, there is great community here, and commonality of purpose. It's on their faces, in their eyes, and on their lips: my son the addict, my husband, my daughter, my father the addict, my sister the alcoholic, my mom, my brother, my partner. They're all condemned to the same life sentence.

Here, their bond is their bewilderment, their determination, their love; and something else. Something powerful. You can feel it in the room: an undercurrent masked by participation in ritual, as if in church singing from the hymnal. Their mutual connections are made solid by a manifest congeniality, and initially at least, the awkwardness in which they all find themselves. I imagine that, just by showing up every week, they've become trusted friends. It's a small world, indeed.

The meeting's just getting started. Someone hands me a weathered blue book that is falling apart at the seams, and a similarly colored skimpy pamphlet. Skimming through the book, I see that it's a compilation of personal accounts, reflections, and mini-essays from anonymous contributors on dozens of spiritual subjects ranging anywhere from procrastination and expectations, to forgiveness, courage, or living in the moment.

A cardboard box is passed around for a small contribution from everyone but me, the novice. Now Daphne directs us to the pamphlet and asks someone to read the Newcomer's Welcome. The handsome black man volunteers. His name is Isaiah, and he's built like an NBA star one might find on a box of Wheaties.

I feel all eyes upon me, the only newcomer among us. Isaiah reads that I'm in a safe place where privacy is sacrosanct; that by coming to this family group, I am now amongst others who understand my plight; that I am no longer alone. I am told that with the help of a Higher Power as I understand Him, I will learn to release my addict in love, instead of trying to change him. Yet I'm told that this is not a religious program, more a spiritual way of life. In contrast to the author's intent, I hear all of this with a deep sense of foreboding, but I can't say exactly why.

Then going around the oval, each takes a turn reading aloud, paragraph by paragraph, one of the twelve steps, the cornerstone to the impending revelations that have been promised. Despite being immersed in all this good will, I'm still not sold, as this faith-based sobriety to-do list seems in need of an atheist's manual. Not to get ahead of myself, perhaps the blue book I'm holding contains those very instructions. But then, reference is twice made to "God as we understand Him", and this presumptuousness is for me a deal-killer. I stay silent.

After the twelve steps, we continue to read consecutively about Nalanon's guidelines relating to the meeting and group structure. Once these introductory recitations are complete, Daphne directs us to this evening's topic.

"I had a hard time deciding on the theme for tonight's readings. I thought we might focus on a subject related to the holiday. But then," she smiles, "something pointed me to the thought of just... letting go."

She describes her life as a single mother of two addicted sons and how emotionally hard things were prior to coming to her first meeting. It was here that she learned about acceptance, and her release to God. "So, that's the one. Letting go. Can I have a volunteer to read in the blue book on page…."

We read various passages on tonight's subject. In one, a woman tells us that by letting go to a Higher Power, she no longer feels the urge to cruise her neighborhood late at night looking for her addicted sister. Another describes how letting go allows her to be much calmer and soft-spoken when dealing with her addict, even in the face of crisis. The scientific cynic in me reflects. *I understand your conclusions, but where's your methodology?*

Daphne encourages our participation, and Isabel is the first to raise her hand.

"The idea of letting go certainly resonates with me, but I'm afraid I've got more work to do." Isabel briefly describes her doubts about Dusty Palms, and Lauren's grievances. Most here seem already aware of what precipitated Lauren's return to rehab.

"I ignore all her complaints, figuring she's just manipulating me again, but I feel guilty. I try to let go, but something doesn't feel right. Her therapist said some things privately to me that I found disturbing. I have so many doubts, and they just get in the way." To my surprise, she starts to quietly sob, and I put my arm around her, hoping not to violate a group norm.

Others chime in. Gossip and so-called cross-talking are discouraged according to the guidelines, yet a few offer direct advice and encouragement. One tells Isabel to stick to her guns and not let Lauren get the better of her. Daphne gently admonishes him for not staying with his own feelings and experiences; but it's too late, not unlike a judge's instructions to jury members to disregard inadmissible testimony after it was already elicited.

Someone hands Isabel a tissue box. Another woman takes the floor. The readings remind her of her husband's dishonesty about his drinking, and her obsession to catch him in his lies, even to the point of tailing him in his car. "Letting go" told her to either accept him at his word or not, but to move on. "Letting go" gave her control over her own life. She says that the truth will eventually be revealed. She didn't say what that truth was for her, and I'm pretty sure I'm in no position to raise my hand to ask.

A portly, fifty-something, white man, with his graying and sullen wife, I presume, sitting next to him, talks of his addicted teenage son's recent deceptions and legal entanglements. The frustrated father reminds everyone about his son's failures in treatment and the insanity he brings to their home.

"I'm finally ready to let it all go and to kick him out once and for all, but his mother won't let me." With a distorted face and angry tears in her eyes, the gray-haired woman interrupts him and pleads with the group.

"We can't kick him out! Where will he go? What will he do? He will die on the street, I'm sure of it! He needs more time."

The bulky Latina next to me, Lucinda, reflects upon her brother, a great athlete, who became an opiate addict after having surgery for a broken ankle and being prescribed oxycodone. Now he's a heroin addict in recovery.

"I would love to let it all go, but my parents don't understand how this happened, and can't deal with it. So, my brother relies on me for so much, and my parents rely on me to deal with *him*. How do you let *that* go?" The older man to her left shakes his head, exasperated.

What I only felt before as an undercurrent has now reared its head with a visible fury. It's their suffering. Each one in the oval endures it. More than anything, it's the power of their torment that ultimately binds them. It overcomes any of their superficial differences. They stand together against a common foe, just as a divided nation unites at times of war. It's sad on so many different levels yet uplifting at the same time. I quickly wipe my eyes lest anyone see *me* cry.

At the end of the meeting, we all stand and hold hands to recite the famous Serenity Prayer.

"God, grant me the serenity to accept the things I cannot change, the courage to change the things I can, and the wisdom to know the difference." As much as I would like to pigeonhole this little invocation with the rest of the meeting's synthetic convention, it hits home. It's an acknowledgment of contrast. It's a call for reason, logic, and balance. In but a few words, it encapsulates a spiritual theory of everything. If I had my own prayer, this might be it.

Regardless, I'm happy to release Lucinda's grasp. The meeting over, most remain for the after-party, and they huddle in small groups. I follow Isabel to where Daphne and Chuck are standing with Isaiah. They all greet Isabel anew with big hugs, and I'm formally introduced to the imposing African-American who, standing a head taller than I, grips my hand with the force of a bull dog's clench around his favorite rubber toy.

Isaiah is a litigation attorney, whose wife couldn't be here this evening, and whose nineteen-year-old son is a meth addict. Free from any Nalanon guidelines, they talk openly about their problems, consoling, validating, and giving advice. As Chuck and Daphne chat with Isabel about Lauren, Isaiah turns to me for a semi-private conversation.

"So, Henry, we all love Isabel so much here; she's a beautiful lady."

I do my best not to take this as, *Henry, if you hurt her, I will break you.*

"Yes, I can feel that in just this one meeting, and believe me, I understand the sentiment."

"So, Henry, do you have any children of your own?"

"Me? No, I was married for a short time, but thankfully, no kids from that union."

Isaiah continues with his line of questioning. "Did ya' get a good sense this evening of what sorts of issues you might be dealing with through Isabel?"

"Yes, for sure, it was something of an eye-opener." I'm thinking at this point of getting my own lawyer.

Isaiah smiles broadly. "Well, in the immortal words of James Brown, 'you ain't seen nothin' yet', brother."

Now I relax a little and smile. "Yeah, that's 'Gravity', right? I'm a fan too."

"Yes sir, that's 'Gravity'. It'll bring you right down to Earth every time, unless by some miracle you can defy it. Get ready."

"I sure will, Isaiah." I reply, a bit unsettled again by his warning. "I sure will."

Thankfully, after a few minutes more, the gathering breaks. Isabel and I go our separate ways to the restaurant. I'm looking forward to being with her; I'm just not as hungry.

CHAPTER 38

The Proposal

In a small Italian bistro, Henry lazily sits forward with his elbows on the red and white checkered tablecloth, gazing into Isabel's eyes. She's sipping on a Pinot Grigio and he on a vodka martini.

"So aside from my little melt down, what did you think of the meeting?" she asks.

They discuss Henry's mixed views. She understands.

"Did you get what you wanted out of it?" Henry inquires.

"Not entirely. But it's my own fault."

"Because you skirted over something."

"Yes. It's good of you to notice."

"But what was it? I can't recall."

"I didn't disclose what her therapist said to me privately on the phone."

"Exactly. That was it. So, what *did* she say?"

"You know, no one even asked me about that at the meeting. Not even after the meeting."

"Yeah, including me. You can't blame *them*. If you want them to know, you should have spoken up."

"Of course, you're right. The fact is, I wasn't sure I wanted to talk about it."

"Seems like you're not so keen on talking about it now," Henry cajoles.

So, Isabel describes her phone call with Sandy, and Lauren's preoccupation with her own survival.

"It may be something, or it may be nothing. Anyway, there isn't anything you can do about it that you aren't already doing," Henry says, trying to put a positive spin on it. "At least she's talking about it."

Switching subjects, Henry asks about Isaiah.

"I've known Isaiah forever," Isabel explains. "His wife was a year behind me in law school. We're both active in the alumni society. She can be very sweet. She's a family lawyer. He was an assistant DA. Now he's doing criminal defense. He's a champ. I had no idea about their troubles with Cameron until we ran into each other at my first meeting. Thank goodness they were there; so supportive."

"When was that?" Henry asks.

"Oh, I guess it's been almost six years. I was a lost soul, not that I'm so grounded today," Isabel says, with a frail smile.

A dish of fried calamari with a side of marinara is set between Iz and Henry, and not a moment too soon, as his appetite has returned. Henry, who already downed most of his drink, decides against a second round, prioritizing this evening's intended purpose.

"Iz," Henry says, getting her attention. "I want to ask you something very important," he announces with great drama. Henry reaches into his pants' pocket with his right hand and grabs something very small, hiding it in his closed fist.

He has her attention now. *Oh my God, he seems like he's about to propose. Has he lost his mind?*

"What's up, Enrico?" she says studying his right hand.

"I realize this may be a little premature, but life is short, isn't it?"

Yeah, its short, but not that short; and what's that in your hand, man?!

"Henry, there's no need to rush things. I'm very…"

But Henry cuts her off. "No, this cannot wait! I'm sorry, but I have to ask this before I lose my nerve."

"No, Henry, really…."

He turns his palm upward and opens his hand to her, exposing a small black USB flash drive.

"I've decided to take a trip to advance my book. It's got to happen soon, and I want you to come with me." He hands her the memory stick. "Everything's on here: maps, photos, possible accommodations, itinerary; you name it. I thought it would be more romantic this way than just sharing a folder on my Dropbox."

He pauses as Isabel exhales.

"You didn't think it was a ring, did you?" Henry asks with mock seriousness.

"A ring? Of course not," she lies. "You may be a bit of a nerd, but you're not a lunatic."

"A nerd, huh? Possibly. I've been called worse. So, what do you think?"

"About what? You haven't even told me where you're going."

"Where *we're* going, you mean."

"Whatever! Talking to you is like pulling teeth. What is the destination, Henry?"

"The Atacama."

"The Atacama? Where is that again?"

"Northern Chile. The driest desert in the world. In the high country. The Atacama Desert."

"You want to take me to a desert? The first trip you propose, and it's to a desert?"

"For God's sake, Isabel, you've been everywhere else. Anyway, that's why I brought you the flash drive. See for yourself. The Atacama's a cool place, even aside from all the observatories. I'm going to line up some interviews; you can come along to those, or not. After Kitt Peak though, I thought you'd really be into it."

She's silent. *I would love to get away. I've never been to South America, and it sounds like an adventure. It may be exactly what I need.*

"How long would we be down there, and when would we leave?"

"That's more like it! I figure about twelve days, in late March, toward the end of their summer when the Milky Way appears high in the sky. I would go earlier, but it can be cloudy. Clear skies will be guaranteed by the end of March, and the moon won't be full during those two weeks."

"You've certainly done your homework. Well, the end of March might be okay. Lauren's due to come out of rehab the end of April, so that shouldn't interfere, and I'll have plenty of time to plan out my work."

"So, that's a yes, then?" Henry asks eagerly.

"Maybe. Let me look at your research. Are you sure I can't interest you in a scuba trip to Fiji instead?"

Henry responds without hesitation. "Once my book becomes a best seller, I promise, I'll take *you* to Fiji."

"I like the sound of that. We'll talk again about the desert once I look at this," referring to the flash drive which she stows in a zippered compartment in her purse.

Henry is animated right through his Rigatoni Bolognese, and he's so carefree that he insists upon picking up the tab, instead of the usual Dutch treat. Isabel doesn't fuss. They leave the restaurant for their cars, and Henry follows her back to her house, where the two lovers will spend the night entwined.

CHAPTER 39

Out of the Desert

"So, what the hell happened yesterday?" Sandy demands, as Lauren takes her weekly seat in front of her.

"You don't waste any time, do you?" Lauren lashes back.

"I thought we were making progress here, and then you go missing!"

"This is progress? What makes you think this is progress? I told you how much I hate this place!"

Sandy pauses.

"Okay. Why don't we take it down a notch? I'm sorry I started off like that."

Another pause.

"I was worried about you."

"You were? You'd be the only one, then. They didn't exactly panic when they couldn't find me."

Sandy tilts her head and rolls her eyes back.

"They did send Kat back out to look for you, but I admit, they should've called the police."

"Why didn't they, then? What, are they afraid for their reputation?"

"Maybe. I don't know. At least they called your mom."

"Oh shit. Did she flip out?"

"What'd you expect? Of course, she did. She was probably asleep by the time they reached her. By the way, she wasn't excited about having the police involved either."

"Well, they found me anyway."

"Listen. Can we slow down please and put aside the attitude? I've apologized for the bad start. Let's do it over."

"Yeah. Sorry," Lauren quietly responds.

"Tell me about it. Take your time. I rescheduled my next session for you."

"There's not much to tell, actually. We all got into the druggie buggy and headed over to the church."

"The one on West Bell?"

"Yeah, that's the one."

"So, who was with you."

"Kat drove; and let's see, Kim, Paula, Monique, Bert. I'm blanking on the last one. Oh, how can I forget? Good ole Sarah."

"Were you all getting along pretty much?"

"No, you know they all hate me."

"Lauren, we've been through this already. You have your supporters and would probably have a few friends if you cared."

"Which I don't."

"Like I said, we've been through this. Let's move on if we can."

"Well, that's the point isn't it? *They* all move on. I'm stuck here for six months. Who gets the full sentence here, besides me?"

"Fine. We've been through that too. This seems to be your M.O. You see the light, at least you convince me you do, and then you rehash it all over again the next week. What gets in the way? Why do you keep testing me like this? Why can't we take this to the next level?"

"Slow learner, I guess."

"That's bull shit."

"Forgetful?"

"Yes, you are, but that's not it either. Anger?"

"Maybe?"

A pause.

"What makes you so angry, then?" Sandy asks, probing.

Now Lauren pauses, but Sandy jumps on her.

"Don't think about it! What makes you angry?!!"

"I do! I'm stupid! I do stupid things! Okay? I can't stop it! I was born stupid, and people suffer!"

"Thank you, I had to hear that. Yes, they do suffer. We all suffer at some point. Who did you cause to suffer?"

"Brittany. Donovan. Others."

"Yes. We've talked through this, but let's do it again. It's important. Do you think you were responsible for that accident?"

"Yes, I do."

"Do you think there was something that you could've done to prevent it?"

"Yes, maybe."

"Fair enough. If anything, you're consistent. Were others responsible as well?"

"Sure, we were all responsible."

"Including Brittany and Donovan, yes?"

"Yes, I suppose so."

Sandy pauses to let Lauren wrestle with this, again.

"So, who else suffers?"

Lauren thinks.

"Mom. She suffers."

"Yes, she does. Why does she suffer?"

"Because she cares about me?"

"Is that a question?"

"She cares."

"Yes, without a doubt. Who else?"

"Suffers?"

"Yes."

"I do. I suffer, too," Lauren whispers.

"Yes, you do; and just to drive the point home, who causes you to suffer?"

"Mostly me. I cause my own suffering."

"Right again! So, here's a question for you. Why the fuck do you keep doing this to yourself?"

"I don't know. Like I said, I'm stupid."

"No, no, before stupid, came what?" asks Sandy.

"What?" Lauren is confused.

"When we first got onto this tangent, I said how you just won't accept things as they are; how you rehash them, don't let them go. It's your M.O., the way you operate, at least with me. What came right after that? Do you recall?"

"Anger?"

"Yes, and who are you angry at?"

"Me."

"Right. Don't you see what's happening here? You're so angry, you keep punishing yourself, and others, by doing, as you call it, stupid things; and people suffer. But these actions only fuel your anger further. It's a vicious cycle, a self-fulfilling prophecy. Do you get it? Do you see that, Lauren?"

"I guess so."

"No. Let's be clear. This is critical. Tell me what we just said. I need to know that you understand this."

Lauren repeats it back to Sandy, and it's understood.

"You know what you have to do? You have to break the cycle."

"Yeah, how?"

"You've got to believe. You've got to at least believe in yourself. You're an intelligent and beautiful young woman. You need to see that; believe that."

"Yeah, working on it."

"Good enough. Let's get back to yesterday. What happened at the meeting?"

"Like I said, not much. I had a cigarette outside with this guy, then we ditched the meeting and went out for coffee. That's all."

"Really? And the police picked you up for what, violating the coffee laws? Do you want to start over now and tell me what really happened?"

"Okay, sure. After coffee, he just left me there. I didn't know what to do. I didn't have a phone on me, so I couldn't call you guys. So, I took a long walk, figuring someone would find me."

"Oh? You could have asked someone for a phone. You could have asked the police for help."

"I didn't want them involved. I was embarrassed to ask anyone else."

"All right. Let's say I accept that for now. Where'd you walk to?"

"I didn't know where I was going." Lauren giggles. "I just went up the big street that the church is on."

"West Bell. Which way?"

"Why? What's the difference? I went for a walk. I didn't have a clue where I was going."

"No big deal. Just curious. What did you see?"

"A bunch of golf courses. Some houses. I did see this weird bingo place."

"Riverboat Bingo?"

"Yep."

"I know it. You ever play bingo, Lauren?"

"No. Can't say I have, but I did hear about it."

Lauren recounts her strange memory of the old lady in her mother's law office and her confusion about the dogs and Indians. Sandy laughs loudly.

"Oh my God. That's too funny. You ever hear this one?" Sandy sings a quick verse.

There was a farmer, had a dog...
And Bingo was his name-o.

"There's your dog, honey!"

"Oh no, really? Oh my God. I remember it now. I'm mortified." Lauren laughs, too, at herself.

"Yes, that's so funny. As for the so-called Indians, coincidentally, it's my people that own a few casinos. One's in Tucson. There's bingo there; the game, not the dog," Sandy says, still laughing. "I guess that's where your old lady friend may have gotten lucky."

"Okay, how would I know that?" says Lauren, back on the defense.

"Relax. You wouldn't. I'm just saying. So, where'd you have coffee with this young fella? I bet it was that West Bell Diner up the block. All the AAs hang out there."

"Yes, that's the one. The diner."

"Well, Lauren, that's odd. That diner went out a business four years ago. Why don't you tell me what really happened? Did you make it with this guy? What's his name, anyway?"

Lauren is red-faced with embarrassment and anger.

"Yeah, we made it all right! In his creepy trailer across the street. Okay? What of it?"

Sandy takes her time to answer.

"Oh nothing. Tell me, was it a beautiful thing?"

"Sure. It was beautiful. Fuck you!"

Again, Sandy pauses. "Lauren, I'm sorry. I'm sorry I caught you in a lie. But really, whose fault was that? Second, I didn't mean to goad you. That was wrong. Not what I was taught. I apologize."

"Yeah. That was nasty!"

"Yes. I guess I didn't like being lied to. Hey, I'm human," Sandy snaps back.

Lauren nods in acceptance, mutters her own apology for her outburst, and the lie.

"Thank you, Lauren, I appreciate that. Back to business. Let me rephrase my question. Was it worth it?"

"No. I don't know. I can hardly remember. It was like a bad dream. I don't even remember his name."

"Could it be Jon?"

"Yes. Jon."

"Kat told me. Apparently, he's had his eye on you, like a few other guys, I'm sure. Jon has a bit of a reputation, though. It's interesting to me that you can't remember. Anything strange happen on your walk? Where did you go after the riverboat?"

Lauren describes her walk toward the desert.

"I was in a short skirt, flimsy blouse and heels. It was freaking cold. I was hurting. I stood there for a bit, finally turned around. I walked for another hour maybe. I don't remember walking so much since Mom sent me out to Wyoming for that ridiculous wilderness program. I've got huge blisters on my feet now. I finally made it to town."

"Go on."

"I got offered drugs. Twice. I just kept walking."

"Good girl."

"Some guy in a car pulls over and asks me where I'm going. I tell him none of his business. He follows me slowly. He propositions me."

"Really? What did he say?"

"He said, like, 'What's a pretty girl like you doing here?' I asked him what he would like me to be doing. That's all I said. He said, 'Oh, there's a lot of things you could do.' I said, like, 'Okay, but we've got to have dinner first.' I was hungry. I figured I could just ditch him after we ate. Anyway, that's when he arrested me. I think it was entrapment. I didn't do anything wrong."

"Okay, I believe you now. You're lucky they let you go. Your mother put up quite a fuss."

"So, what happens now?"

"You'll lose some privileges. That's about all. They should be sending you somewhere else, but I have a sneaking suspicion that won't be happening, unless your mother insists."

"Yeah, I don't think she will. I'd have to start all over."

The two decide to take a three-minute stretch. Lauren goes out for a quick cigarette. When they resume, it's on a different topic.

"I've been speaking to your mom, you know. She mentioned one trauma that triggered your move back to Arizona. Do you want to get into that? I think it would be a good time for this now."

"Okay. If you want."

"I want. So, I take it you were living in a sober home at the time?"

"Yes, it was one halfway house after another. I might hold the record for how many I got kicked out of." Lauren smiles.

"They caught you using?"

"No, mostly I just didn't follow the rules: you know, the curfew and hooking up. They would always look the other way, at first, but after a while they had enough of me."

"Did you like getting kicked out?"

"I didn't mind. There were always other houses, as long as I was three days sober, and those were the legit places. You could always get in somewhere if you had the money, and Mom kept paying the rent. She gave me a hundred last chances. So yeah, at first it was fine. I did what I wanted."

Sandy jots some notes. "Sounds like something changed."

"I guess so."

"Tell me about it."

"Sure," Lauren says without a trace of emotion. "Will you believe me?"

"I wonder why you ask. You've already lost some credibility today. But I'm your therapist, and I'll always give you the benefit of the doubt, unless you give me cause not to. Should I believe you?"

"Yeah. No bullshit now."

"Fine. So, tell me."

"I was at this sober home in Delray. I must've skipped out after curfew two or three times without getting caught. They had no resident counselor, and my roommate didn't give a shit. This time was no different. It was around 10:30, and this guy Chris picked me up out front. I met him a few days before. He was in his truck, and I was walking in town heading toward the beach. I guess, like, I wasn't wearing much: a bikini and flip-flops. So, he rolls down the window and starts talking to me. He was cute. I remember I was almost ninety days sober then. I even had a part-time job."

Sandy nods her head. *Go on.*

"We went to the beach together. He seemed okay. Later, I met him at this bar. We drank beers. I thought I could control it only drinking beer. Anyway, a few days later he texted me to ask me out that night. I had already relapsed, so it was easy to say yes. In half an hour he picked me up, and we went back to that same bar. I drank way too much this time. Vodka, who knows what else. I got wild. Said a few things. Before I knew it, Chris and two of his buddies took me outside, tossed me into the back of a truck, and we drove onto some deserted beach. It was dark. There was no one around. They grabbed me from the truck and threw me onto the sand, face first, and they held me there, while one of them pulled down my skirt, my underwear. They fucked me right there in the sand. It was probably all three of them, one after the other. I'm not sure. I only remember the pain. It was everywhere. There was sand in my mouth, up my nose. I wanted to scream, but I was choking. I was still so wasted; it was like a horrible nightmare. I remember Chris's voice. He was angry. I don't know what he said. I can't remember the other two guys. I was so in my head at the time; everything was outa control. It didn't seem real, except for the pain."

Sandy makes notes. "I'm so sorry this happened, Lauren. Go on if you can."

"Someone must've heard us. One of the guys threatened to kill me if I went to the cops. Then they split, left me on the ground. I stumbled out to some path, into a parking lot. The police came first, then an ambulance. They took me to the hospital."

Lauren stops here for a second, then finishes her account. "They called Jack."

"Your father." Sandy interrupts.

"Yeah, he was the last person on Earth I wanted to see. But they didn't know who else to call. The cops must've had his number, I don't know. Anyway, he finally shows up. It was late, and he was pissed. Can you believe it? He was angry at me! He was even angry at the cops. There I was. The evidence was right there. I could've been killed. And he's angry at me! Not at these three assholes. He's angry at me!"

Tears well up in Lauren's eyes and roll down her face, red and contorted. Sandy hands her a tall box of tissues, then gives her a moment.

"What happened after that? Was any legal action taken?"

"No. I don't think so. The police asked me for information: you know, names, descriptions. I didn't have much. I was texting with that Chris, so I had his number, and I remembered the bar. I don't know if the Police ever went there, or if they even tried to find him. Probably not. To be honest, I was scared. I wasn't anxious to press charges." Lauren takes a breath.

"Jack sure didn't push it, either." Lauren is seething. "I told him what happened, and he said, 'How can you be sure of anything? You were high as a kite.' He said, 'For all I know, you could be making this whole thing up.' I ask him, 'Why on Earth would I make this shit up?!' He said, 'Because you're an addict!' His exact words!"

Again, another tissue and a momentary pause.

"Have you been in touch with your father since that evening?"

Lauren is apoplectic. She replies as more tears flow down her cheeks. "Hell no! I am so done with him. I was already done with him!"

"I believe you, Lauren. This is a serious trauma." Sandy is aware of how hackneyed that sounds but goes on as trained. "I'm glad you're talking about it. Is there anything else you want to add?"

Lauren takes a second to compose herself. "No, I think I've said enough."

"Okay, then. How did you deal with things afterward?"

"Not well." Lauren attempts to smile. "I stayed at a girlfriend's for a few nights. She was good to me. Mom asked if she should come down. I don't know if she believed me or not. I guess she did. But I'm sure the two of them spoke."

"Your parents."

"Yeah. Anyway, I convinced her to stay in Tucson. I don't think she wanted to come, and I thought I could get through it. I was so ashamed. I didn't want her to see me. I felt bad about asking her for help again. Stupid! I already relapsed, and I couldn't stop thinking about it, and crying. I called my dealer in a couple of days. He came in a flash."

"Heroin?" Sandy asks.

"Yeah. It was cut with Fentanyl this time; anyway, that's what they found out later. I didn't have enough to pay him, so he gave me credit. He was "nice" like that." Lauren sneers. "They don't have to find you. They figure you'll be back."

Sandy nods her head. "Yes, I know."

"Well, I suppose it was the Fentanyl, plus I hadn't done opiates in months. I OD'd right away. My girlfriend found me lying on the floor in her apartment. She dialed 911. I guess I got lucky, again; if you want to call it that."

"My God, girl. You've been through hell, haven't you? What happened next? How did you end up back in Arizona?"

"I was in the ER and got them to call Mom, and she put me back into a rehab in Boca. I detoxed and felt better. I was there for twenty-eight days. The insurance ran out, so I had to go."

Lauren takes a breath and continues.

"Mom sort of offered me to stay longer, but I refused. She didn't fight me on it. So, the police had me on a second possession charge now. I was already in drug court and had done a few stints in jail, the last one for forty-five days. So, when I got out of rehab, I had to deal with that. My attorney told us that I should stop fighting the charges. If I insisted on sticking it out in drug court, I was bound to do some time in a real prison. He said at least a year, maybe more. He told me to plead guilty to the original possession charge, and they would let me go on time served, that I should get the hell out of Dodge. That's when Mom told me to come back."

"Oh, I see. So, you left the state for good. Does it stay on your record?"

"Yeah, it's a felony in Florida. Doesn't exactly look good on the ole resume, does it?"

"No, I guess not."

There's a short pause in the conversation. Sandy waits for Lauren to speak again.

"Then there's this fucking accident, and Brittany." Lauren weeps as her mind goes back to her most recent calamity. "Why am I the one that survives? I shouldn't even be here."

Alarm bells ring in Sandy's head again.

"Yes, I can appreciate those feelings, Lauren. We should discuss that sometime soon." Lauren nods without conviction, wiping her face with a fresh tissue.

"Is there anything else you want to say?"

"No, that's pretty much how it's been these last few months," Lauren replies, pausing to blow her nose. "Have you ever heard such a fucked up deal in your life?"

Sandy needs no extra time to respond.

"Actually, I have."

CHAPTER 40

The Feast

It's Christmas eve at the Spinozas', and there's a wafting of an untold variety of delectable aromas throughout. It's the Feast of the Seven Fishes, and Mare honors her Crocetti family tradition by setting seven as a minimum, not a hard stop. In her menu tonight are chunks of fresh cod casserole with onions, garlic, and tomatoes; shrimps and scallops, deep-fried until crispy and golden; home-made linguini covered with open littlenecks bathed in butter; and insalata de mare. There are raw oysters with horseradish and lemons on a tray of ice; mushrooms stuffed with crabmeat; and, as a special non-marine-like request from little Adam, his favorite: pigs in blankets. The front of Adam's navy and red Wildcats sweat-shirt is already stained with big yellow blotches of mustard.

Isabel and Henry are the last to arrive. They find Rafael pouring drinks from behind a makeshift bar set up in the living room.

"Hey, toss your coats in the guest bedroom, but don't let the dog out," Raff directs.

Easier said than done. Afterward, Isabel motions to Henry.

"Look how nicely they decorated the tree."

"Yeah, lovely," Henry tepidly admits.

"I guess we should put our gifts with the others," Isabel says, pointing to the carefully wrapped presents under the pine.

Marianne arranged a Secret Santa between only the adults; the children will have to wait for the real thing on Christmas morning. She set a twenty-dollar limit and gave each participant the name of the recipient with a quick description of likes and interests.

"To whom did you say you are giving this?" Henry asks, pointing to a carefully wrapped box that Isabel carries under her arm.

"I didn't. It's a secret." Isabel smiles.

"Whatever," Henry says, pretending to be annoyed. "I got a climate-change coffee mug for my person, with a map of the world on it showing all the lowlands underwater. Like, most of Florida has disappeared."

"Like, you told me already, Henry."

"Oh, I did?"

"Yes, but I don't remember who *you're* giving it to."

"You mean, to whom I am giving it?" he chides lovingly.

"Yes, excuse me….to *whooom* you are giving it. So, to *whooom are* you giving it?"

"I cannot say. It's a secret. I would have to kill you if I told you."

"Never mind, then. I'm sure whooomever it is will love it; as long as it is not I," Isabel answers back with increasing sarcasm.

"You mean, as long as it's not *me*," retorts the science writer to the attorney.

"Oh my God!" Isabel says, on the verge of genuine irritation.

The two place their gifts with the others and head off to mingle amongst the dozen or so adults in attendance.

Henry recognizes two couples from the neighborhood. Their kids are in Rachel's class, and the children are all noisily running about the house with Adam, the youngest, trying to keep up. The adults greet Henry approvingly as he introduces them to Isabel. She soon excuses herself, though, to see if Marianne needs help.

Henry, who's engrossed in conversation with one couple about the new Walmart going up too near their subdivision, acknowledges her with a nod.

Isabel makes her way to the kitchen, where she sees her friend flitting about between stove and center island, breading shrimp while sautéing the littlenecks, all with the focused skill of a circus juggler. The aroma of sizzling mushrooms and garlic in heaps of melting butter and cheap white wine is overwhelmingly seductive.

An elderly couple face each other across the pine kitchen table. Isabel enters just in time to hear the gray and bent man declare in a crackly fortissimo how he never trusted his former business partner.

"He moved to Florida, without so much as a word. But the son-of-a-bitch got what he deserved. His first week there, his car was swallowed up by a sink hole!"

The frail and gray-haired woman nods, apparently in agreement.

Mare sees Isabel and greets her with a grin while patting her on the back with a scorched oven mitt. She's careful to keep her bare right hand, smothered with Panko and olive oil, away from Isabel's holiday garb. Mare herself is wearing a dress of scarlet velour protected by a new solid-blue apron, an early Christmas gift from Raff.

"Don't you look lovely, my dear," remarks Isabel. "Can I help?"

"Yes, I could use a hand," answers Mare. "Things back to normal with Lauren?"

"I don't know. Define normal. But if you're referring to her extracurricular activities, yes, she's back at the rehab."

"You still going up there?"

"Yeah, on Tuesday, just for a quick visit. To be honest, it's with mixed emotions."

"Who wouldn't feel that way? Relax. It'll be good for both of you," Marianne says, guiding Isabel toward the kitchen table. "Let me introduce you to someone, Izzy."

The two women stand behind the old man who's sitting across

from his female companion. "Rudy, I want you to meet my good friend, Isabel."

The man, who's wearing a hearing aide, turns to look at Isabel. He slowly stands to offer her a weak hand.

"Iz, Rudy is my father-in-law," Marianne says, returning to the stove.

Ah, I should have known. This could be Henry in another 35 years.

"Hello, Mr. Spinoza. It's good to meet you."

"Likewise; and this is my…lady friend, Deborah," pointing to her across the table. "Are you one of the neighbors?" Rudy speaks slowly and loudly and seems older to Isabel than he ought to in relation to his two sons.

As if on cue, Henry ambles in with a drink in each hand, giving one to Isabel.

"Hiya, Pop. Hello, Deborah." Henry says with good volume. "I see you've met Izzy."

"Oh, so you're the one with Henry now. It's about time he got a nice woman."

"Well, thank you, I guess," answers Isabel, not really knowing how to interpret Rudy's comment. "I suppose I came to the same conclusion."

"Yeah, Pop, thanks for that awesome compliment." The son's barb elicits no response from the father.

"You're a lawyer," Rudy says as if accusing her of being a felon. "So, what kind of lawyer are you?"

"Actually, I'm an elder attorney."

"A WHAT?"

"An ELDER attorney," Isabel shouts over the sound of fish frying.

"Oh, you mean like me. Let me ask you something. What you do, does it do any good?"

"Well, sure Mr. Spinoza, I think I do a lot of good."

Isabel is as defensive as she is loud. "I help my clients with their finances, so they can afford the care they need, or might need in the future. I help them protect what they have for themselves in retirement, or to pass something on to their family. Let's say I help them to get organized."

"Before they go, you mean." Rudy scowls. "Well, I don't really have much of anything anymore except for social security, and who knows when they'll take that away. I'm pretty organized already, wouldn't you say?" Deborah, who has been nothing but quiet, continues to bobble.

"I don't really know, Mr. Spinoza. It's hard to say without all the details," Isabel responds in CYA fashion.

"Hey, Pop, why don't we talk about something else. Any plans for New Years, you crazy kids?"

"No!" Rudy responds in a word that somehow conveys his son's awesome stupidity to even ask.

"Okay, then. Sorry," Henry sighs.

At this, Isabel puts down the glass that Henry handed her and politely excuses herself to help Mare. Henry signals to Izzy that he's going back to the living room to be with the others. Rudy resumes his one-sided discourse with Deborah.

The older couple departs just after dinner. The food was a big hit with everyone else. Raff's toast to his beautiful, intelligent, and talented wife goes on long enough to be awkward but is finally halted by a children's chorus of demands for dessert. After cookies and milk, the kids squeeze into a den off the living area, to watch *The Secret Life of Pets 2*. The adults, each grasping mugs of hot cider and rum, gather around the tree for the secret Santa.

Bending down for the first gift to be opened, Marianne grabs a thin flexible package. It has Joyce Walker's name on it. Joyce is a neighbor two doors down and a big animal lover. She tears the wrapping and delights in receiving the latest Original Sloth Calendar.

"It's perfect. It reminds me of Bob."

Everyone claps and laughs, including her husband Bob Walker, standing next to her.

As Marianne distributes the gifts, wrapping paper piles up beneath the tree as a variety of unusual presents are revealed: a disco light for the bathtub, a pistol-activated spider catcher, a paper-airplane propeller for longer duration flights, a set of stainless-steel straws, and a can of unicorn meat. One of the neighbors receives Henry's coffee mug with apparent confusion and dismay. Isabel also receives a well-chosen mug which states, "I'm not arguing, I'm simply explaining why I'm right."

Henry is the last to receive a gift. Marianne hands him the heavy box that he recognizes at once to be the one that Isabel placed beneath the tree.

"Hey, wait a minute. What's this? It's not supposed to work this way," says Henry. "We're supposed to exchange gifts tomorrow."

"Calm down, Enrico," Marianne directs. "My house, my rules." Now, looking on with curious amusement, the others encourage Henry to open his gift. He unceremoniously rips the wrapping from the box to expose a high-end pair of binoculars. Speechless, he turns to Isabel.

"They're stargazing binoculars," Isabel says.

Henry's so touched he can barely speak above a whisper. "Yeah, I know, and they're beauties. But why?"

"Well, I figure we can't take a telescope with us to the Atacama," Isabel explains, while Marianne provides background on this charming subterfuge to her other guests.

"Oh my God. You're going? We're going? That's fantastic! I was thinking that you decided against it but didn't know how to tell me."

"Ye of little faith. If I didn't want to go, I would come out with it. The trip will be awesome."

Suddenly, with both hands, Raff grabs Henry by the shoulders from behind while quietly speaking into his ear. "Good job, my brother. I hear you were that close to screwing it up, too. Have a great trip wherever the hell you're taking her."

This evening, the Spinoza home is filled with laughter and joy and that spirit of comradery that culminates but once every year. More than anyone, it's Henry, holding Isabel's left hand as if never to let go, who seems to be in euphoric delight, while Isabel, standing by his side and holding the binoculars with her other hand, contemplates the upcoming journey.

CHAPTER 41

The Visitation

"Your route is being calculated."

It's the day after Christmas and Isabel has found the address for Dusty Palms saved in her GPS. She's heading up to Surprise to visit Lauren and to meet her therapist.

Isabel gets on the road with mixed emotions. Trying to stay positive, she reminisces about the splendor of Christmas eve and the time with Henry the next day. With a big apology for not matching her generosity, he gave her a collection of Pink songs and an audio book of Pat Conroy's *South of Broad*, which she'll listen to now on her ride north. Yesterday, they cuddled in front of the TV, watching *It's a Wonderful Life* for the umpteenth time, munching on Tostitos and sipping beer. The topper for Isabel was when Henry teared up at the end of the movie. He blamed this on rubbing his eyes after eating the jalapeno-infused corn chips.

Isabel also cannot but dwell on Lauren's recent escapade in Surprise, and the late-night call she received from the rehab, the same night that Henry first suggested the trip to the Atacama. Shaken awake by the sound of her phone on her nightstand, her heart pounding, she grabbed the call in a whisper so as not to disturb her guest. She then slipped out of bed and went to the kitchen to hear DP's night manager describe the scant details of Lauren's disappearance.

The call was brief. Isabel's internal reaction was an inharmonious blend of concern and agitation. She sat alone in the kitchen worrying about the suffering that might befall her daughter, and she was angry: at Lauren, for being in this situation; at herself, for allowing these emotions to get the better of her.

The second call from the rehab came almost an hour later. Lauren had been arrested. At least she was safe. Isabel contacted the Surprise police department and, with a combination of effusive charm and subtle intimidation, convinced the on-duty desk sergeant to drop the charges and return Lauren to the rehab. In fact, it seemed to Isabel a surprisingly easy task, as she detected a sense of relief in his voice. "The Ransom of Red Chief" came to mind.

But it was Isabel who was most relieved. By one a.m., she was back in bed to find Henry face up, snoring like an elephant seal. She would tell him about these events in the morning.

Looking at Henry in her bed, Isabel couldn't help but smile. Despite his lack of involvement in Lauren's late-night drama, it was just nice to have him there. Isabel made up her mind at that very moment. She'd go with Henry to Chile. It's just what she needed: relaxation, a bit of adventure, and, of course, the romance. She purchased the binoculars the very next day.

Isabel pulls into the rehab's lot just as the sixth chapter of her audio-book ends. Inside, at the reception desk, she encounters Kat, who leads her to Sandy's simple office.

"Hello, Mrs. Dalton," says Sandy Ortega, shaking Isabel's cool hand. "Nice to meet you. Hope you had a good trip up. Lauren will be here in a minute."

Isabel looks up at Sandy, a virtual stone tower, like a lighthouse, adorned at the top by a shining white smile. *She's so big; unusual and beautiful, in such a natural way. Indigenous, I bet. I wonder what Nation.*

Lauren enters and gives her mother a tentative hug. Isabel pats her daughter on the back.

"Hi, Mom. Thanks for coming to visit me," she whispers. "I love you."

"Yes. I love you, too, Lauren," Isabel responds instinctively. "How are you doing?"

"Okay, I guess. I'm sorry about the other night, with the police, and all."

"Thanks for saying that, but I don't know what to think," Isabel replies. "You scare me, Lauren."

"Entirely understandable, Mrs. Dalton," Sandy quickly inter-jects. She turns to her patient, who looks deflated.

"Relax, Lauren. We'll have plenty of time to get beyond this."

Sandy sits behind her desk, and the other two each take a seat in front of her. Isabel spies the photo on the wall, and pointing to it asks, "Family?"

"Yes, my parents. They're Tohono-O'odham in case you were wondering."

"I was. What a great photograph."

"Thanks," says Sandy, who moves the conversation along. "It's good of you to come up, Mrs. Dalton. May I assume that you're still planning on being here in February for family weekend?"

"Yes. I'm planning on it."

"Great. We don't have much time today, but we can revisit any issues next time. Let me start off by saying that your daughter and I have been exploring some serious trauma that she's experienced recently. I think you're aware of much of it, although perhaps not in great detail. Not to excuse her conduct, I think some of her harmful actions might be related to the trauma."

"I wouldn't be surprised. She's been through a lot. We all have. But I'm a practical sort, Sandy. Should I be concerned that she'll disappear and get arrested again?"

"I don't know. Let's ask her." They both look to Lauren.

Lauren at once is defensive, blaming the arrest on a trap sprung by the undercover officer. She makes a good case, and this doesn't go unnoticed by the attorney in the room.

They go to Lauren's impulsivity behind her disappearance with Jon and subsequent activities. Ultimately, what follows is exactly where Sandy steers them, a methodical airing of grievances between mother and daughter, and a lessening of tensions.

Despite the stressful conversation, Lauren's recent AWOL and her resentment toward Dusty Palms, Isabel also senses a positive difference in her, especially in the way she expresses herself.

"It's weird to say this, Lauren, after your disappearing act, but you seem more controlled when you speak; more reasoned, more mature."

"No, I agree. It could be the meds, Mom. They calm me down. They also make me fat. I look horrible, but I don't care as much." Lauren giggles at her own remark.

"You look good, honey. A little more weight suits you fine."

Isabel is impressed with Sandy. *She's young, but self-assured, and real. She talks straight and doesn't pull any punches. Maybe this place isn't so horrible.*

They all discuss a possible future. Lauren asks Isabel for another chance.

"When I returned home, I just fell into my old ways. I didn't think. It was just easy to hook up with Tim. I forgot what he was like. I promise, Mom, that I'll be better. But if it's okay, we decided that I may need some support when I get back."

"Yes, Mrs. Dalton. If you do allow Lauren back, I would suggest an intensive outpatient program for two months, at least. They'll also do drug testing, so you'll know where things stand. It goes without saying, she's got to stick with the meetings."

"Okay, I'm open to it. I have to say, Lauren, this is all conditioned upon your staying here the full six months, and no more escapes or police. One final thing. This will be the last time I intervene on your behalf. If you screw up again after all this, you'll be on your own. Sandy's my witness. I will cut you off like I did in Florida, but this time there'll be no rehab. Is that understood?" Isabel presents this without acrimony, as if dealing with a recalcitrant client.

"Yes, Mom, I agree. I hear you loud and clear. No more screw-ups."

"Having said that, my prior offer stands. If you keep this going for a year, I'll support you with a salon school, or some other vocational training."

"How about college? Is that a possibility?" Lauren asks.

"College?" *Since when does she want to go to college?*

"I don't know, dear. Maybe you will have to send yourself to college."

"Okay, but will you at least think about it?"

Always negotiating. "Sure, but let's remember how much you applied yourself in high school."

"Of course, I fucked up high school. Never mind college. Salon school sounds fine. One more thing. I just want to make sure that the six months I do here are part of the one year. This rehab is jail. It wouldn't be fair if I don't get credit for time served." Lauren delivers this with a subtle smile, selling her position as would a shrewd politician.

"Okay, honey," Isabel replies. "I can see your point. Six months more after completing your sentence here."

After the short session, mother and daughter have a simple buffet lunch in the rehab's cafeteria. They sit across from one another at a long metal table covered with a paper cloth. They discuss the aftermath of the accident, the funerals, news reports, and Tim's legal fate. Then, Lauren moves them off topic.

"Listen, Mom, I've been thinking. Is there something I can do to get out of here, I mean earlier? I can't stay here six months. I won't make it. It's crazy here. They're awful. The girls hate me. The staff doesn't care. They're always complaining about their salary, talking trash about the owners. It all seems so sleazy. Something's wrong here, Mom. I'm not sure…."

"Enough!" Isabel says, loud enough to attract attention from others sitting nearby. She lowers her voice. "This place seems okay to me. Not the fanciest rehab I've sent you to. Not the most organized maybe. But Sandy seems competent. She's so interesting, too. I'm quite impressed by her. In fact, you and she seem to have a good rapport."

"Yes, Sandy's great, I agree. She might be the best therapist I've had. She's the only thing keeping me sane, but this place sucks, Mom. Trust me. I don't know where you found it, but it's the worst. I don't feel safe."

"I *don't* trust you, Lauren. Why should I, after everything?"

"I'm telling you the truth on this. I'm afraid to be here."

"I don't get you, Laur. You agreed to the full six months in Sandy's office not ten minutes ago."

"She won't talk about it. She tells me it's fine here, but I don't believe her."

"I'm not ready for you to come home. I want you here the full six."

Lauren doesn't let up.

"I don't have to come home. I don't even want to come home. I can stay in Surprise. There's a good recovery community right here. I could get a job. I just need you to help me with rent to start out."

"And utilities? What about food? Oh, and a phone? Will you need that too? A car? Insurance, maybe?" Isabel whispers with angry sarcasm.

"I'll get a job. I can cover most of it."

"No, I told you its six months here, or nothing. Then you can come back."

"I don't want to go back. I don't have any friends in Tucson, and I won't be able to make any. They'll all hate me."

Suddenly, Isabel sees the problem. It's what she herself has had to deal with, but worse for her daughter. The stigma from the accident will stand out on Lauren like a facial tattoo. Many will blame her: her boyfriend's accomplice; the older one who should have known better; a drug addict, whose relapse ended in the death of innocents. She will be shunned. It won't be easy.

Isabel breathes deeply while thinking it through. *Too bad. I had to deal with it myself; you will too. No more running away like a child. Face your problems, head on.*

"Sorry, Lauren, it might be difficult for you to return after the accident, but that's what I had to do. It's where I live, and I'll be damned if I'm going to deal with you from far away again. This is your last hurrah. We can talk about your finding a sober house after making your way into the community, but it's going to be in Tucson, or it will be without my support. You got that?"

Lauren leaps from her chair, crying out barely intelligible words between convulsive sobs. "I can't live with that!"

Many nearby turn to look as Lauren bolts from the cafeteria, leaving her mother there open-mouthed. In a minute, Isabel, with a silent scowl, busses their dishes, signs out of the rehab, and heads home.

CHAPTER 42

One Week and Counting

The last few months have been unremarkable, if being in the most delectable relationship possible could be considered ordinary. Tucson is fantastic in winter. In our free time, we took long hikes in the surrounding brown hills. I taught Iz how to hit a forehand. We ate out and we cooked at home. I slept over often, but we maintained a healthy independence. We talked, and we talked; and we laughed; and we spoke of our love, even though I seemed to declare it more than she.

We leave for Chile in a week, and I'm already prepping for it. It's so unlike me. What does one really need in the driest spot on Earth? I'll leave the poncho and umbrella at home. Not even the astronomers with whom I arranged interviews will be wearing anything but tee-shirts over jeans or khakis.

I'll need my hiking boots, so I scrape the mud that's caked to their bottoms into the kitchen sink with my best paring knife. Don't forget the sunglasses or dorky beige safari hat. I put them with my passport on the counter.

Mostly, it's the mental prep that has me going. There are certain aspects of flight that unsettle me, and this one will be long and dark. I get jittery in turbulence, regardless of explanations from overconfident aviators on the science of lift, changes in atmospheric pressure, the jet stream, and topographical effects on wind. The fact that wings are engineered to flex ninety degrees provides little comfort. All I know is that if the world's topflight engineers and contractors can jointly screw up the Hubble Telescope's precision mirror the first time around, a mere billion-dollar error, there's nothing to say that either an Airbus or Boeing grease monkey won't forget to add enough rubberizer, or whatever, to an airplane wing.

I can't tell you how many times I've been told that it's safer to fly than to drive to the airport. Yet, when I'm driving, it's my own self behind the wheel, as in self-preservation. God knows who's up in that cockpit - likely some one-time top-gun maverick who flew Super Hornets for the Navy over Kuwait in '91, and who now looks for creative ways to alleviate his boredom while flying big limos for United.

That's just the half of it. Aside from the turbulence, and control issues, there are lightning strikes (the most severe risk), wind shear, missiles, on-board acts of terrorism, mid-air collisions or just running out of gas.

I've got two answers to the turbulence. One, looking out the window, I must see a clear object in the distance: the ground, a white fluffy cloud, the moon, a ship on the ocean, even just the tiniest star in the night sky, just enough to prove that up is up and down is down, and we're going straight ahead. It's called *perspective.*

Perspective is possibly the most important element of a good flight. Without it, who's to say that we're not just a bunch of seatbelted extras, all crammed into a giant cigar tube suspended in mid-air by a ten-story movie-lot crane that vibrates us like an off-balance washing machine, only to be dropped to the ground while cameras roll to capture the final crash sequence. I imagine the director's announcement: "One take only, people. Let's nail this." And who's to say it's not me in the leading role of this flop of a B-action movie? Perspective is the reality check that keeps my mind out of the dark clouds.

My second answer to turbulence, and all, is what I must include in the outer pocket of my carry-on backpack: five clear one-shot mini bottles, saved from prior flights, refilled with my own brand of vodka. Pills don't work as well or as quickly. Placing the bottles in a clear zip-top baggie gets them legally through TSA. It's drinking them on-board that's the tricky part; unlawful unless they're served by a flight attendant, an unlikely event during moderate turbulence when the crew take their jump seats and when swilling the booze is most needed.

Although alcohol consumption on the upcoming flight may be less of a challenge. We're going first class most of the way. Isabel wanted to go all out on this, her "first romantic vacation in a dog's age". Given how much I love her, and, after a bit of a back and forth about how to share expenses, I relented. Regardless, I'll have my five mini-bottles with me just in case.

We're staying in San Pedro de Atacama, billed online as a stunning desert oasis in the middle of hundreds of square miles of barren landscape. Isabel retained a travel consultant specializing in South America, who booked us at the four-star Cañón de Atacama Desert Hotel & Spa. To be sure, this was not one of the options on my flash drive. It'll be our hub, from which we'll do day trips to locally famous destinations. It'll also be where Isabel will luxuriate while I'm away two nights on a research mission near to the Pacific coast.

Leaving aside my usual trepidations, this is going to be the best trip of my life. Of course, Isabel's swamped at work this week, so, we only have dinner on Thursday, two days before departure, to finalize any last-minute details. I can hardly wait.

CHAPTER 43

Isabel's Dilemma

I sabel is at her desk, holding her phone close. She speaks clearly and loudly into the mouthpiece.

"Mrs. Lehman, I assure you that Jane is quite capable to file your Medicaid application. I'll be back in two weeks."

Isabel listens to her elderly client's worried response.

"No, Mrs. Lehman. She's not an attorney; she's a paralegal. But she's been doing this for four years. Jane is excellent. She's better than I am with this sort of thing."

Isabel's client isn't appeased.

"Of course, Mrs. Lehman, you're always free to find another attorney. We'll calculate the unused portion of your retainer and return it to you."

Isabel puts the call on speaker, rolls her chair back from the desk, and folds her arms.

"No, no, I don't want to make any changes," Dorothy Lehman responds. "You came highly recommended, and you're very nice. But I'm worried. I'm too old to take care of him anymore."

Isabel quickly picks the phone back up.

"Yes, I understand. I promise, you're in good hands. I don't know what Medicaid will say, but we're doing everything possible to qualify him. I'll be back soon. We'll talk then. Yes, thank you. Goodbye."

Isabel hangs up the phone and sighs. *Four down, three to go. Here's the reason I don't take long vacations.*

Other than some last-minute work adjustments and a final call to Dusty Palms, Isabel's ready for this trip. Just two and a half more days until Saturday's flights: a hop-skip to Houston where they'll connect to the long-jump, a red-eye to Santiago. She imagines herself relaxing on board in that extra-wide comfy seat which, with a push of a button, transforms into a tiny bed. A glass or two of wine, a romantic movie, and it's off to la la land.

I only hope Henry's not as bad on a plane as he warned. No one's getting in the way of my nirvana, not even Henry. One anxious child is enough. At this, she smiles.

Isabel tries the rehab but only reaches voicemail. This has happened before, not a concern. Someone will call her back within the hour.

The past few months have been surprisingly calm. Her relationship with Henry is perfect for today, and there's no worry about tomorrow.

As for Lauren, Isabel's been on the phone with her and Sandy every week. She also drove up to Surprise in late February for a Family Weekend that coincided with Lauren's birthday. In comparison with the recovery work she did with Lauren at Sutherland Farms, Isabel was unimpressed.

Nevertheless, Lauren's been on an even keel, acquiescing to her six-month term. There have been no new angry outbursts or unhinged stunts. Yet, her attitude is one of dispirited acceptance. Sandy privately voices concern to Isabel, but places hope in her patient's resumption of a quasi-normal life, free from her self-described captivity. Only one month to go.

Isabel eats a sandwich at her desk. It's early afternoon, and it's been two hours since her call to DP. She tries again, and, as before, is directed to voicemail. She dials Sandy's cell phone and leaves a message. In ten minutes, her own cell phone rings.

"Mrs. Dalton, it's Sandy up at Dusty Palms."

"How are you, Sandy? I was beginning to worry."

"To be honest, not good. Your daughter's fine, that's not it. It's the rehab. It's closing."

"What?!!"

"Yes. They arrested the owners and the Director this morning; they took them away in handcuffs. We lost our license. Everyone's got to go. The patients. The staff. Everyone."

"No, that's not possible! I've never heard of such a thing. What am I going to do? Where's everyone going?"

"Mostly home. Lauren got five months of sobriety out of this, Mrs. Dalton, and we did some good work. It could be worse."

"No, the timing couldn't be worse! I'm leaving for South America on Saturday," Isabel says, before realizing how privileged this sounds. "What can I do with her? Can't you put her somewhere else, Sandy, at least for the two weeks we're gone?"

"I'm afraid not. By now, all the facilities around here are full up. Some of the girls got placed, but Lauren was a low priority."

"Wonderful!" Isabel tries to think. "Why were they arrested?"

"Supposedly, they overcharged insurance thousands every week for drug tests that never happened. They also paid people to bring in patients with good insurance coverage. That's gotta be illegal."

The first crime is easy, Isabel thinks. *That's insurance fraud.* Isabel was taught the meaning of fraud in first-year torts; and she knows that a good drug test is as simple as a supervised pee into a cup plus a fifty dollar lab fee.

As to the second allegation, Congress made patient brokering a federal crime.

Isabel recalls how Lauren, then living on her own in Florida, told her about shady individuals lurking outside her AA meetings to tempt young addicts, still on their parents' health plans, with a free high, then a ride to the rehab that initiated the conspiracy. The finder collects a pre-arranged kickback as the addict is entering detox. Sometimes, the payoff is later split with the addict himself. Of course, the rehab collects the insurance.

Lauren once described a facility that was "vertically integrated": a rehab that owns its own sober home listed under a different name. After thirty days, the rehab's patient steps down to the affiliated house, at a steep discount, where he's encouraged to relapse. He then gets sent back up to that same rehab, which collects the big bucks from insurance all over again.

Isabel wanted to disbelieve Lauren about these loathsome scams, but her daughter emailed her links to news articles covering the stories. In one article, it was reported that the Delray Beach Police were so successful in uncovering such activities that illicit rehabs were moving out-of-state on their own accord. *Damn! Could Lauren have been correct about Dusty Palms?*

"I'm afraid you'll have to come get Lauren tomorrow, Mrs. Dalton."

This sinks in, and Isabel becomes desperate.

"Oh my God. Sandy, I know this is a lot to ask and sounds entitled, but is it possible for you to put her up for the two weeks? I could pay you."

A slight pause.

"Honestly, I love your daughter, and would do anything for her. She's troubled, but terrific. I just can't. I'm going home myself, and we have enough trouble there. It wouldn't be right. And I've got to find a job quick, so I'll be pounding the pavement. Sorry."

"I understand."

"I have to say, Mrs. Dalton, I wouldn't leave her alone in a new situation just yet. I'm concerned. She hasn't bounced back from the accident, even after so long. She's been through so much. I think you need to be with her, at least for a month to see how things go in Tucson. Maybe the change in scenery will do her good."

"I hope so."

"I spent a lot of time with your daughter, sometimes more than just our weekly session. We went over a lot of difficult stuff. At times, she was surprisingly mature and carefree. Other times, she was anxious and afraid. Then there were days she was just going through the motions. Life didn't fully open-up for her the way I hoped. You know, she's been out of contact for so long: great for her sobriety, but isolated. She wasn't on her cell phone twenty-four-seven, but she's also had little contact with the outside."

Isabel remains quiet.

"Normally, I would say live your own life, but in good conscience, I can't. She needs your support to transition back. Until she does that, she's got no one else."

With these words, Isabel cannot help but cry. It's just one more crisis on top of everything.

"I'm so sorry," Sandy continues. "I wish I had better news. This must be awful on you."

"I'll be okay," Isabel says, regaining some composure. She promises to be at the rehab before noon the next day and ends the call. Isabel shuts the door to her office, sits back in her chair and closes her eyes. *This is so unfair.*

CHAPTER 44

Change in Plans

"I'm afraid I have some bad news, Henry."

Isabel, dressed in her work attire, sits across from her sweetheart in Zinburger at a middle table for two. Drinks are coming: a Stella for Henry, a Cosmo for Isabel. She's been dreading this conversation.

This is going to be awful, but what choice do I have?

"Oh, I know, you're backing out on me last minute," says Henry, grinning.

"Yes, I'm afraid so," Isabel says, soberly. "I'm really sorry."

Henry cocks his head sideways and smiles halfway.

"You're joking."

"No. I'm serious. I'm not kidding. You know how we're always kidding? This is not one of those times."

Henry sits stone-faced and stops breathing. His eyes open wide but don't blink. He looks away as if into another universe.

Finally, he takes a breath and turns back toward her.

"I don't believe you," Henry says, testing her.

"I'm serious. Lauren's rehab shut down. The owners were

arrested. They lost their license. Everyone's got to leave. I'm driving up there tomorrow to get her."

"Arrested? What for?" Henry demands. Isabel explains.

"This can't be happening, Iz. We've been planning this since Christmas. This was going to be the trip of a lifetime. You can't tell me, just like that, you can't go. This trip's too important. There's got to be another way."

"Believe me, I'm as disappointed as you are; but she's my daughter. I can't just leave her alone, not the way she is."

"We have thousands invested in this trip. You more than me. You can't just walk away from it."

"You think I'm happy about any of this, Henry? But you're going. You've got to finish your research. You can't afford not to go, and you should try to enjoy yourself."

"Wait! We have trip insurance, don't we? We can go in a month."

"This isn't covered. I already thought of that. If Lauren died, God forbid, or even just overdosed, we'd get our money back. But not for this."

"Couldn't we say she got sick? After all, she *is* ill," Henry says.

Isabel frowns, as if he just crossed a line.

"Trust me, it's not covered, and we can't lie about it. That's insurance fraud. People get arrested for that kind of thing in case you haven't noticed."

"Fine, but why do *you* have to stay home? Can't she go to a friend's? Can't you put her someplace else? Another rehab? What about Isaiah? Maybe he can take her for two weeks. What about Marianne?"

"Really, Henry? Did you think I wouldn't look at alternatives?" Isabel says in an angry whisper. "There are no friends, and Isaiah has his own troubles. As for Marianne and your brother, it's too much to even ask, and don't you go making any requests from them either. Wednesday's the earliest any beds become available in the entire state. Even if there were openings, I can't just dump her in the first rehab I find."

"Why not? How much worse could it be than where she is now?"

Henry purses his lips. Isabel is irate.

"I'm sure *you* make perfect choices with your drug-addicted bipolar daughter. Oh! That's right, you've got no children. Maybe as a judge, you should recuse yourself."

"Hold on. I'm not judging. I didn't mean that."

"Well, that's how it sounded!" Isabel sits back with arms crossed.

The waiter sets their drinks down while other diners look their way. Isabel downs half the Cosmo in a few seconds.

"Iz, calm down. I'm sorry."

The two sit in silence for an eternity, lasting ten seconds.

"How about Jack? Would he take her the two weeks? We could put her on a plane tomorrow evening."

"Are you kidding me?! She hates him, and he doesn't give a shit about her. I wouldn't trust Jack with a goldfish! Where have you been, Henry?!"

Almost everyone in the restaurant turns to witness the noisy feud, as Isabel launches from her chair.

"I'm sorry, I've got to go," she says heading for the exit. Henry's at her heels.

"We'll be right back," he says to a passing waitress, who responds with a shrug.

Henry reaches Isabel in the lot just before she opens the door to her car.

"I don't know what I'm saying," he says. "I feel like the rug's been yanked out from under me. I can't imagine this trip without you! It's all I've been thinking about for so long. It's way more than disappointment. I feel awful! I might sound like an immature brat, but I just can't believe this is happening."

"Yes, you're right, you're a child. Grow up, Henry! Deep down I knew this day was coming. We've been living a fantasy these past months; a dream that had to end. In case you haven't been listening, my daughter's mentally-ill, and who knows, suicidal. You're not equipped to deal with her. *I'm* not equipped to deal with her; how can I expect *you* to?!"

She sees Henry stagger, as if the earth beneath him is giving way. He fights back.

"You're wrong! I've *been* listening, and I'm here for you. I was just so let down I became a fucking idiot! I'm sorry. Please, let's go back inside and discuss this like adults. We'll work it out; but no matter what, I'm not going to Chile without you!"

Isabel isn't persuaded. The Atacama was an empty promise, San Pedro a mirage. Life with Henry was a delightful illusion, the truth behind which would inevitably be revealed.

Isabel's deep-seated anxieties bubble to the surface, while her own troubled history sucks her out to sea, like a rip current taking hold of a small child in the shallows. Her past now flashes into her mind, blinding her like oncoming headlights over the rise.

Isabel and Jack, a young couple with stars in their eyes. *Sure. Let's keep the baby, elope, and move to Arizona.* A child is born; downhill from there. Lauren's issues become manifest and Isabel's struggles with them ever present. Jack's job loss, his drinking, his absence. He strays, and the marriage ends. During it all, Isabel gets a JD, by the force of necessity alone.

She becomes a competent attorney: intelligent, diligent, rational. Yet, with her daughter's escalating drug use, when the going gets rough, she banishes Lauren to be with the man she trusts the least. From there, Lauren flounders in Florida: in and out of rehabs and sober homes; she injects, snorts, and swallows enough of God knows what to require someone just at the right place and time to save her life.

Then, the inconceivable happens. Lauren is raped. For the victim, a nightmarish recollection, lacking in clarity but for the pain; for her mother, a perpetual image of Lauren, defenseless, being brutalized in the worst way possible. It's a vision that Isabel bears as punishment for her neglect, for not being there, for casting her daughter aside.

So, she brings Lauren back from Florida. Within ten days, Isabel overlooks the warning signs, and two die on her watch. That she leaves Lauren alone in the house at her daughter's most vulnerable moment, to inhale a toxic blue powder, almost seems peripheral to the violence in the desert.

With all that's gone wrong, it's almost predictable that Dusty Palms would be run by a bunch of thieves. It's only by Isabel's arrogance that she disbelieves what her daughter says about its conditions.

Finally, there's Henry, a good man; a loving soul. Isabel deceives him by dangling the prospect of happiness before him like a carrot in front of a horse.

I mapped out this route. Look where the road has taken us. The truth is, I'm a failure, as a mother, as a partner.

Isabel prepares for what must come next, as tears flow down her cheeks.

"This hasn't been real. You should be with someone else, someone without my kind of baggage. I'm a mess of a package deal, Henry. It's more than you can handle. It's more than I can handle. You deserve better."

Henry says nothing as he assimilates what's been said. Then, he takes her hand, looks directly into her eyes, and speaks slowly and deliberately, as if he has nothing to lose, with everything to lose.

"Listen. I love you. There will be no one else. It's you I want, with all your goddamn baggage: your old beat-up briefcase, that fancy Coach-leather backpack, even your hot pink rollaboard I would just as soon leave on the carousel." Henry forces a smile, and then continues. "We can end this any time you like. If I'm not man enough to take you and your daughter on, make you happy, and be there for the both of you, you can drop me like a hot potato."

Isabel tries to interrupt.

"No, I'm not done yet. While you blame yourself for Lauren's choices, you don't give me a chance. I haven't even met your daughter yet, and you've already written me off, just because of a few dumbass remarks I made in the heat of the moment. You don't know; she may really like me. Right away. I might even be of help to you two. Is that so impossible?"

Isabel pauses to take this in. *He never ceases to surprise me.*

"No, it's not *impossible,*" Isabel says with a hint of a smile, as she wipes away her tears. She allows Henry to guide her back inside the restaurant. Her eyes swollen, Isabel's a reluctant jumble of confused emotions. *I don't know where this is going. Nothing's been resolved; but I do love him, that much I know.*

They sit, and Henry takes a big gulp from his bottle of warm beer.

"Isabel," he says. "We're going on this trip. You, me, and Lauren. We're *all* going!"

"Don't be ridiculous! You don't know what you're saying."

Henry ignores her and continues.

"I guess she and I will have to get to know one another while we're there. That part's going to be weird, but we have no choice. And you'll have to come up with the money for her; I can't. But it'll probably be cheaper than putting her into another rehab last minute for two weeks. I'm guessing she doesn't have to fly first class, either."

"You're crazy! What makes you think I can even get her to go?"

"Listen. She's been cooped up in a rehab for what? Five months? You give her the choice of another rehab or a twelve-day vacation to northern Chile, at a first-class hotel and spa in eighty-degrees without a chance of rain, and what choice do you think she's going make?"

"You're good to suggest this," she replies. "I admit, it even crossed my mind; but I thought it over, and it's a terrible idea! You don't know what she's capable of, what's she's done, what she'll do in Chile. She'll run away with the first hot Latino guy that lays eyes on her. She'll shoot up. She'll get into another accident, or worse. I don't know. You've never experienced any of this. You have no clue what I've been through!"

"No, you're wrong, love. This is an excellent idea! It might be the best fucking idea I ever came up with. And I'm not looking at this with rose-colored glasses, either. Will she put a damper on things? You bet. Will she be unpredictable? Yeah, maybe. Will we have to keep an eye on her? Yeah, so what? Do I have a lot to learn? Without a doubt. But think of the positives. We get to go to the Atacama! We don't lose our money, and the change of scenery might do her some good. She might actually learn something down there."

Isabel pauses, thinking of something Sandy said. *A change of scenery.*

"What kind of vacation is that?" she counters. "Always on the look-out for the next calamity? And in a foreign country, no less. It's not what I had in mind, baby-sitting a twenty-two-year-old, with what we're paying. Oh, yeah, and add another room to that."

"Forgive me but look who's being unrealistic now. This is the way it is. The sooner you accept that and adjust, the sooner you and I can get on with our lives together."

Isabel says nothing while she absorbs this.

"Your daughter is alive after going through so much shit. You always say she's intuitive, beautiful, witty; not a surprise, knowing her mother. You have no idea what the future holds. Why don't you just let loose and give this a try?"

"I don't know, there are so many risks. I'm worried."

"Hey, I worry enough for the both of us. But I'll be there with you and I swear, Iz, I'll have your back."

Isabel pauses again.

"Well, I suppose she can find trouble just as easy here in Tucson. At least it's not Columbia. Holy crap. Okay, if you're willing to be open-minded, and flexible if things get hairy, we can try."

"Yes. I promise. No expectations." Then Henry winces. "Oh shit! Does she even have a passport? I just thought of that."

"Yes, as a matter of fact, she does. I was planning on taking her to Italy after Jack and I separated, but that idea got nixed once she started to act out."

They both fall silent to think about what may lie ahead.

"God, I hope this works," she says. "I do want to see Chile. I suppose they have hospitals down there."

Henry nods, grimacing.

"I always wanted to go with you to the desert, Henry. You know that don't you?"

"Yes. I know, hon. C'mon, let's order. We've got a shitload to do."

Isabel sighs, having made the difficult choice between flawed options, but worrisome doubt lingers. Advice given to her recently by a friend comes to mind. *Just let it go.*

CHAPTER 45

The Pickup

"**I** told you how awful this place was! Why didn't you believe me?" Lauren whines, as she gets into the passenger side of her mom's A4.

"Okay, let's go. It's bedlam here. Did you find Sandy?"

"Yes. We said goodbye. But don't ignore me. Can you just admit it?"

Isabel wants the ride back home to be calm. She's got to get Lauren on board with Chile. But first, there's Henry. *Shit, why didn't I mention him before?*

"Yes, honey, you were right," Isabel says, as she maneuvers the car out of the parking lot, and onto the road.

"You didn't believe me from the start, when I called you that night!"

"They said you broke into the office. Why should I believe you?"

"That's a lie! The door was wide open!"

"Oh, and they dragged someone out in a straitjacket, I suppose?"

"Okay, maybe I exaggerated some of it, to make a point, but I didn't break in anywhere."

"Fine. Let's move on. You're five-months sober, and you did some good work. Let's look on the bright side, shall we?"

"Sure Mom, let's."

Hopefully, this isn't just sarcasm talking.

"Thanks, honey, I appreciate that."

"Are you kidding?! It was fucking torture! They were assholes! Now they're going to jail!"

"I hear you," Isabel says softly, "but the good news is that it's shutting down, I rushed up to get you, and justice will be done."

Justice will be done? That might be a bit much. Isabel directs the car onto the expressway. She quickly glances over at her daughter in the passenger seat.

"Oh my God," Lauren replies. "Can't you stop being a lawyer for a minute? I saw you twice in five months. I was all alone up there. Why didn't you visit more?"

Now may not be the time to jump in with Henry.

"I thought it would be better for both of us. Frankly, I was afraid of more scenes like we had at Christmas."

"Yeah, I panicked that first time you visited. Maybe now you understand why. My rehab was being run by criminals."

"I admit, your doubts were justified. I'm surprised how things turned out. I made a mistake, and you're right. I didn't listen to you, even a little. I apologize."

There's a long moment of silence, as Lauren takes this in.

"Wow. First time for everything," she responds.

Another pause, and she moves on.

"So now what, Mom? What do I do now?"

"Funny that you ask." Isabel turns again to Lauren, then focuses back on the road. "I've got a great answer for you, at least for the next two weeks."

Lauren looks on in silent disbelief.

"We had a trip planned, and we'd like you to join us."

"We?"

"I've been seeing a gentleman."

"You have?!"

"Yes, he's very sweet, and funny. He's anxious to meet you."

"I'm anxious too, but not to meet him. You got any other surprises you want to tell me about?"

"Aren't you the least bit interested in where we're going?"

"You keep saying we. Who's this we? You and me? You and this guy? You're not seriously suggesting that the three of us go wherever. I haven't even met him. I'll stay home, thanks. You two have a good time."

"That's not an option." Isabel turns her head to face her daughter for an instant. "If you don't join us, you can go back into rehab. I have a nice one picked out just for you," Isabel lies, thinking back on what Henry said.

"No fucking way! I'm not going on vacation with you and your new boyfriend. I can stay home. I've been sober for five months, and I'm not about to do anything stupid."

"I wish I could believe that. Maybe soon, but not right away. You've got no choice. It's rehab or the trip. There's no place else for you, and you sure as shit aren't staying in my house by yourself."

"Well, I'm definitely not going to another rehab. Not after what you put me through. Where are you going?"

It wasn't easy, but Henry was right. Lucky United still had a few seats and the hotel had a cancellation. I'll firm it up later if I can close this.

"Chile," Isabel responds, spoon feeding the answer.

"What's Chile. Is that in Mexico, or something?"

"Get serious. You know very well where Chile is."

"Well, not exactly," Lauren replies. "So, what's in Chile, anyway?"

"Glad you asked. We'll be up north, close to the mountains. It's very dry. Blue skies are guaranteed. It'll be in the seventies and eighties. We're staying in an oasis. Our hotel is first-class and has a spa, and there's lot's to do all around."

"It sounds like you're taking a vacation in the desert."

Isabel nods, glancing at her daughter. "It's the driest spot on Earth."

"I don't want to go to a desert. We live in a fucking desert! Whose brilliant idea was this? Your new man?"

"Yes, as a matter of fact, and stop with the f-bombs, will you? He has business down there, so he'll be taking off without us for a couple of days."

"Ooh. Sounds mysterious. Secret business in South America. What is he, a drug smuggler?"

Isabel can't help but giggle at the thought.

"No, when you meet him, you'll understand why that's funny. He's a science writer. He mostly writes articles about astronomy and nature. He's doing research for a book."

"He sounds like a huge geek, Mom. Does the geek have a name?"

"Henry, and yes, he's a bit of a nerd. But a lovable one."

"Oh. How adorable. You're in love," Lauren teases, with attitude.

"If you must know, I am. He's a good man."

"Better than Jack, I hope." Lauren is serious now.

"Let's not even go there; but yes, since you asked, better than your dad."

"You're right. Let's not go there."

After a pause, Isabel prods her daughter.

"So, Lauren, what do you think?"

"About what? A trip to the desert with you and the nerd? It sounds like I'll be interfering with a budding romance, is what I think, Mother. You guys can't really want a depressed drug addict around."

"We do. I mean, we want you to come. It was Henry's idea."

Lauren thinks a second before asking her next question.

"Are you two sleeping together?"

"None of your business, child," Isabel says, with a glint in her eyes.

"Oh my God, you've slept with him. A nerdy old man. How disgusting!" Lauren razzes her again.

"Are you going, or not?!"

"Do I get my own room?"

"Well you're not staying in the same room with a nerdy old man and his girlfriend," Isabel says, evoking a little smile from Lauren.

"Okay, fine. I'm in," she says, sounding defeated. "When do we leave?"

"Tomorrow afternoon. We fly to Houston first; we'll catch a red-eye from there."

"Really?! That doesn't give me much time to shop."

"Shop?" Iz asks. "Shop for what?"

"A bathing suit, for one. I'm still on the meds, you know. I've put on weight."

Isabel turns to her, and back again. "You look great."

"Yeah, thanks, but nothing fits me. I just need a few things. Underwear, bras, jeans. A few tops, maybe. Flip flops. Don't worry, after you pay for this trip, you won't even notice what I spend."

She has a point there.

"Okay. We'll go this afternoon. Afterward, you won't leave the house until we get picked up for the airport."

"No problema, mamacita. The only person I know in Tucson is doing time."

"Yes, and it's very sad," Isabel replies.

"So, Mom, what do I do after this trip. I'm done with rehabs, so don't even think about it."

"I don't know, Lauren. We'll figure it out while we're down there. Let's enjoy ourselves for the two weeks, and please, just stay out of trouble. Yes?"

"Trouble? Moi? You know, trouble just has a habit of finding me, Mom."

"So, I've noticed."

CHAPTER 46

First Contact

M y condo's on the way to the airport from Catalina Foothills, so Isabel and Lauren are already in the back seat when the Uber pulls up. I roll my blue Costco bag toward the trunk, wave-off the driver's offer to help, toss in my stuff, and get in the passenger side up front.

The driver introduces himself as Jesús and confirms our destination. Isabel greets me and introduces Lauren, who grunts out hello from the back seat. Turning at an angle, I lean through the center arm rest to steal a quick kiss from Iz. I offer my hand to Lauren, who's reluctant to pause the fierce action of both thumbs on her cell phone. She gives me back a quick limp fish.

"A pleasure. I've heard a lot about you," I say.

"I bet you have," she sneers, and goes back to texting. Lots to make up after five months.

"No, mostly good stuff. Some not so good, maybe. I'm glad we'll have this opportunity to get to know one another." As rehearsed.

"Sure. What's your name, again?"

I see Isabel roll her eyes. "It's Henry! You know his name. Stop playing games," says Isabel, annoyed.

"No, it's okay," I respond while turning to face forward, buckling my seatbelt to mute the incessant chimes. "I've got a bad memory for names, too, Laura," I quip loudly into the wind shield. "Or is it Floren?"

"Oh my God," I hear Lauren say. "Is it too late for rehab?"

While Isabel's instinct is to admonish her (perhaps for referring to her addiction within earshot of Jesús, or just for being obnoxious) there's something about her that appeals to me. No doubt, she's quick-witted like her mother, so, she's bright. She's also remarkably pretty, noticeable in the few seconds that I contorted my body to face her: physical virtues much beyond merely the fresh beauty of youth. None of this is a surprise as Isabel forewarned me, but it's good to get a mother's biased judgment validated in the flesh.

It likely would have been a quiet ride after such initial pleasantries but for Jesús, who discovers we're travelling to Chile. Our driver lets on in almost-perfect English that he's a Bolivian who lost his job years back at a soybean trading desk in La Paz. Leaving behind his wife and son, he moved to Santiago to live with his cousin, who worked at the headquarters of Codelco, the Chilean national copper mining company.

Jesús is good humored, but he's as talkative as the guy who sold me my Fiesta at the Ford dealer. So, no surprise that he describes to us, in utter detail, how he landed a job with Codelco in sales. Then, without missing a beat, he takes us on a virtual tour of Chile's capital, describing too many not-to-miss attractions.

Thankfully, Isabel cuts him off.

"Jesús, we're only in Santiago for three hours. We're catching the first flight out to Calama."

"Calama! You must see Chuqui! I spent half my time there. The largest copper mine in the world. It's a giant oval excavation, in a hundred layers, like a fancy wedding cake."

"It's not in our plans, Jesús. Maybe on the way back," I say, being polite.

"Excuse me, Jesús, but how did you end up here, anyway?" Isabel asks.

The driver explains that he got a better job with Hudbay Minerals, a Canadian mining company, which had plans to reopen the Rosemont copper mine just outside of Tucson. Permits were withheld on account of environmental issues, and the project now faces a lawsuit brought by a triad of native American tribes. Jesús was laid off until the legal issues get settled, so he drives for Uber and Lyft to support his small family back in Bolivia, and himself.

Suddenly, Lauren pipes up out of nowhere. "Which tribe sued you?"

"There are three," Jesús replies. "The Hopi, the Tohono O'odham and.."

"Wait! That's Sandy's people," Lauren interrupts. "I would tell your boss not to mess with them. If they're anything like Sandy, he'll be sorry!"

This seems to do the impossible and silences Jesús until we get to the airport. He lets us off at the curb in front of the United sign, where I tip him generously.

CHAPTER 47

Heading South

The three get through security without incident. Henry's relieved that his five mini-bottles caused no fuss; Isabel, that Lauren wasn't found to have a stash of her own. They make their way to the gate.

Henry leans over to whisper in Isabel's ear, jamming his left foot onto her right heel, causing her blue Nike Zoom to peel off in mid-stride.

"Will you watch where you're going?" Isabel pleads, while quickly kneeling to get her shoe back on.

"Ooh, sorry about that, hon," he responds in a hushed voice. "I was going to say, she's just as you described: a real pistol; smart and pretty. Almost as pretty as her mother."

"Thank you, but you don't have to whisper," Isabel whispers back. "She can't hear you with those bloody things in her ears cranked up so loud. She'll be deaf before she's thirty."

Lauren walks two steps behind, with her backpack and head-phones on, oblivious to the world. Henry looks over his shoulder to see a self-absorbed, sassy, somewhat immature twenty-two year-old girl. It's hard to fathom the hardship she's endured.

"You're right. She wouldn't know if we were on the deck of the Titanic abandoning ship," Henry declares. At the same time, he tries to remember what he was like at that age, with his own self-centered passion for music.

In a minute they come upon a gate with an LED display:

Flight 4545 Houston Departs 3:50p Boarding 3:20p

"I guess this is us!" says Henry, with childlike enthusiasm, despite the presence of a third wheel.

They sit together, three across in coach on the two-hour flight to Houston, decompressing. As Henry munches on peanuts at his window seat, he gazes out upon the tan and russet earth tones of the Chihuahuan Desert below. The blue sky is cloudless, the air perfectly smooth, and he's carefree, savoring the 32,000-foot view.

Henry takes note at the back of the inflight magazine of the aircraft's linear flight path that crosses state and international boundaries as if they were just lines on a map. It takes them over Arizona and New Mexico, then above Jaurez, just across the border from El Paso, and back into US territory for a direct shot over Austin, and into George Bush.

Lauren, on the aisle, keeps to herself, and ignoring or ignorant of FCC regulations, continues texting. Isabel reads *Truman* by McCullough, and does a crossword, unaware of her daughter's ongoing infraction.

There's a two-hour layover in Houston where Lauren raises the question of the seating plan for the next flight. She wants the window but is confronted with a different dilemma.

"You mean I'm not sitting with you? Where are *you* sitting?" asks Lauren, disquieted.

"We'll be in the front of the plane, honey. You're farther back, but you do have a window seat. There wasn't any more room up front."

"You mean you're in first class, and I'm alone in the back of the bus? Oh, that's fair." Lauren crosses her arms. "I'm not going!"

"Technically, we're in business class, but fine, we'll leave you here in the airport in Houston," Isabel counters, raising the stakes.

"No problem. I have friends in Houston. That's in Texas, right?" Lauren knows that a pinch of detail always makes the stew of deceit taste a little more credible.

"Yes, we're in Texas."

"I tell you what," Henry says interrupting the squabble. "I'll share the seat with you, Lauren. You can come get me halfway through the flight. It's about nine hours, come see us in four and a half, and I'll move back."

While Henry's dismayed by Lauren's immature display, he sees the logic in giving in. *She'll have a harder time sticking her threats once she's down there. In any case, she'll have nothing to complain about. Maybe she'll use my upper-class bed-seat as intended. I know, I won't.*

Isabel nods, and Lauren relents, retreating to her music. The usual boarding announcements are made. Henry and Isabel, being polite and cautious, forego their business class privileges, and wait for Lauren's group to be called.

At the plane's entryway, a flight attendant directs Lauren to turn right at the second aisle toward the back, where she sees a 2x3x2 seating configuration. Finding her row toward the tail and sitting by the window, Lauren plugs into the plane's on-demand entertainment system and is content to be left alone.

As Henry comes aboard, he scrutinizes the cabin's condition, as if fine upholstery reflects an ability to stay aloft. He and Isabel turn left to business class with a much roomier 2x1x2 arrangement.

Henry moves toward the bulkhead to claim his left-side window seat. He stows his backpack on the floor in front of him. Then he tests out the lie-flat feature of his own seat, while Isabel arranges her things to his right.

"Wow, this is amazing," he says. "Not very wide, but at least a chance to stretch out."

"Do you think she'll be all right back there?" Isabel asks.

"Sure. What can she do? Open an emergency exit?"

Isabel grimaces.

"Never mind that," Henry continues. "Six-year-olds fly by themselves. She's fine."

He squeezes her hand, and she smiles.

"You're right. I should stop letting her get to me. I can be a little crazy sometimes."

"D'ya think?" Henry grins.

They're still parked at the gate when Isabel is served a Pinot Grigio, and Henry, a screwdriver.

"I don't know," Isabel says. "I feel a little funny drinking with Lauren on board."

"Hey, enjoy it while you can. I'm sure we won't be sampling Chile's great wines while eating dinner with her. I take it you cautioned your daughter about doing shots back there."

Isabel frowns.

"No. She'll have to make her own choices. But if she orders a drink, she won't be able to pay for it."

"Ah," Henry replies, and nods his head.

By the time the big jet rolls down the runway, Isabel is sedate. Henry, still on alert, peers out into the darkness.

When the plane reaches cruising altitude, the couple dine on filet and potatoes au gratin, with a mellow Chilean cabernet. They chuckle about the whirlwind of the last few days, and they discuss plans for the week ahead. Isabel passes on dessert, dons her noise-cancelling headphones, and goes back to her biography. Henry has another glass of wine with a wedge of New York cheesecake and looks out onto a brightly-lit waning moon.

A few minutes after dessert, the cabin lights are dimmed. Isabel stows the book, arranges her comforter, and transforms her seat.

"I'm going to sleep," she announces.

"Okay, hon. I'll be right here."

"Maybe you ought to try to get some rest, too. You'll be a zombie tomorrow," Isabel suggests, while covering her eyes with a black mask.

"I can't sleep. I'm going see about a movie."

Iz rolls onto her side and is breathing heavily within seconds.

Henry looks over at her and shakes his head with envy before covering her shoulders with the thick quilt. Browsing on his console through the list of action films, Henry is aghast when he comes across *Alive,* the true story of a Uruguayan rugby team's airplane crash into the Andes. *Whose bright idea was this? Showing* Alive *here is like showing* Jaws *to an adolescents' surfing class. Glad it's oceans we're flying over tonight and not 20,000 foot craggy peaks.* He switches genres and settles on *The Philadelphia Story,* a sentimental favorite.

Henry does his best to relax with the movie and another glass of wine. He tries to nap, but at 530 mph the jumbo jet bumps and vibrates with each occasional air pocket. Each time, his pulse quickens, and he focuses through the plexiglass to find an external frame of reference. Every so often, Isabel stirs, and reaches over blindly to touch his hand in a tender moment. For Henry, dog-tired, four hours pass slowly.

It's about three a.m. Houston time, when chimes ring and the seat belt sign comes on. The chief flight attendant announces that the captain requires everyone to buckle up as turbulence is expected. Flight service is suspended, and Henry sees their two attendants strap into their jump seats in the galley. Not a minute goes by before the chop starts. The captain gets on the PA, apologizes for some weather, and promises to look for a smoother ride.

Henry peers into the night toward the Ecuadorian coast and sees not-too-distant lightning bolts dance between clouds illuminated by the flashes. Otherwise, there's only blackness: the moon, the stars, obscured by a thick stratus layer above; a lightless, indistinct Pacific below. He reaches down to the floor and grabs the baggie of mini-bottles from his backpack. He rips open the self-sealed closure and unscrews the cap off one of the bottles to take a big prophylactic gulp. The aircraft bounces hard as it passes through a downdraft. Henry quietly curses, tightens his belt, grabs onto his armrest, and takes another swig. He looks over at Iz, who doesn't stir.

It's at this moment that Lauren bursts through the security curtain to consummate the deal for Henry's seat.

"Miss, the seat belt sign is on! You have to sit down," directs one very annoyed flight attendant from her jump seat, as Lauren approaches the bulkhead.

"I will!" Lauren retorts, indignant. She spots Isabel and Henry. "He's in my seat," pointing to Henry.

"Now?" Henry demands. "You want to switch now? Oh my God!"

"What time is it, Henry," Isabel asks, removing the mask, groggy from her slumber.

"It's been five hours, Mom."

Henry, irritated, undoes his seatbelt and leans up to respond to the flight attendant. "She's right. This is her seat. I'm moving back."

The flight attendant shakes her head, and shrugs to her teammate. Henry quickly grabs his baggie of vodka and stuffs it into his backpack. The plane bucks while he hoists himself up and tries to make it into the aisle without disturbing Isabel. With another jolting air current, he lands in her lap.

"For God sakes, Henry. I would've gotten up."

The plane lurches with more force, and Henry, finally in the aisle, holds onto Isabel's seatback to brace himself, while slinging his backpack over one shoulder.

"Holy crap!" he mutters.

As the jet bumps and shudders, he quickly heads aft with palms against the luggage compartments for support, softly swearing all the way. The voice of an agitated flight attendant, reminding passengers to stay in their seats, is heard over the PA.

Lauren easily slides over her mother's lap and takes her upgraded position.

"Mom," Lauren whispers, "Did you know your boyfriend's an alcoholic?"

"Relax, Lauren. He's not an alcoholic."

"Didn't you see him?" Lauren continues. "He snuck like ten little bottles into his backpack, and he could barely stand up."

"No, I know. He's afraid. He hates to fly. And it wasn't ten, it was five bottles."

"Okay, Mom, if you think it was five, it was five. All the same."

"Lauren, he's afraid of the turbulence. The vodka calms him down."

"Would you listen to yourself, Mom?" Lauren remains clinical. "Calms him down? That's what we all say. Did you learn anything at those family sessions?"

"Lauren, you're mistaken. Get to know him. You'll see."

"No, I was the one in all those rehabs, remember? The last time for five freaking months," Lauren whispers. "Don't you think I might have paid attention at least some of the time? You're in denial, Mother. You also seem to prefer alcoholic men. Seriously, what's that about? Did grandpa have a problem?"

"No, of course not," Isabel responds, incredulous. "Why do you say that? You think your dad's an alcoholic?"

"No, I don't know, forget that; but you really ought to reflect on this, Mom," Lauren counsels, and pauses. "By the way, these seats are awesome," she says, as she plugs her headphones into the console.

Isabel gives up and sighs. Meanwhile, Henry gropes his way toward the very back and finds Lauren's seat two rows from the lavatory. He manages to crawl over the hefty middle-aged Latina in the aisle seat, and buckles back in, pulling the strap tight.

The plane's rolls and yaws are exaggerated here, like the back end of a roller coaster. Henry seizes one of the vodka shots and drains it with a vengeance, feeling the burn all the way down. With each jolting loss of altitude, he squeezes his armrest, while his new neighbor crosses herself and pleads out loud.

"Dios mio!"

Henry couldn't agree more.

CHAPTER 48

Flight to Calama

We just deplaned in Santiago, customs was a nightmare in a foreign language, and I'm shot. My head is pounding like a kick drum in a heavy metal band. To think, all that vodka and wine and I still didn't sleep. I can't endure another flight. Maybe this whole desert trip thing was stupid. I bet Mauna Kea would have been a lot easier.

I must say, the two of them seem rather garrulous. Look at them, rushing to the next gate, like BFFs on their way to Vegas, engrossed in some serious conversation about what, a good facial foundation? My, that was nasty, and sexist. Why do I suddenly feel like the odd man out? I'm toast.

"Henry, are you keeping up? Look at you, you look awful," Isabel declares.

Thanks honey, but right now I don't give a fart. Did I just *say* that?

"Yeah, Mom, I'd be shaking too after what he drank."

All hail the expert.

"C'mon Henry, maybe you can sleep at the gate."

Now that's a good idea. Lead the way.

I almost feel human after slouching on a stainless-steel vinyl-cushioned chair for an hour, asleep. My neck hurts, and I see some spittle drying on my sweater. Overall, a vast improvement. I was slowly awakened by the gate agent's pre-boarding announcements in Spanish, then English, confirming for me that we're no longer in Kansas.

"Henry, are you up? We're boarding."

I wasn't sure until now whether Isabel was the type to be first in line to wait, or to wait first to be last. Personally, I fancy the latter, but may have to concede to her in this if we're to stay together.

"Yes, hon, I'm coming."

Isabel is well-rested and all smiles. Lauren, on the other hand, has a scowl on. Is this depression? Exhaustion? Maybe it's just Lauren. I've known her for all of twelve hours so I'm not sure of anything, but I'll keep an eye out.

"Oh, the dead one has arisen," says Isabel, in good humor.

How apropos, as I was convinced of an early demise on-board last night. It's almost unbelievable that a huge winged metallic, computer-controlled cylinder weighing nearly a half million pounds, can even fly through the thin atmosphere seven miles up, at two thirds the speed of sound. When, on top of that, the aircraft is dodging one-billion-volt energy flashes targeted at random, it's strange that a person, strapped into the comfort of the plane's interior, and shaken as if to be poured into a martini glass, could have so much faith as to fall asleep. I would think that there would be more people like me (and my Latina neighbor) preoccupied with falling from the sky. In all candor, I do understand the science of flight, but sometimes raw emotion clouds the truth.

The flight from Santiago to Calama, two unavoidable hours, heads north, back toward the States. Chile is 2,600 miles long but only one hundred miles wide, give or take, east to west. Santiago is located near the midpoint of this slenderest of nations and hangs there like a Texas belt buckle at the waistline of a lissome ballerina. The arid Atacama with its crystal-clear skies, so attractive to the professional star gazer, emerges five hundred miles north of the capital.

Chile's lengthy western border is a rocky shore along the Pacific. My guess is that most Chileans are unaware that it's only a tiny continental shelf that stands between them and a giant precipice concealed by the ocean's waters. Plate tectonics created a vast trench along most of the coastline. It plunges at its deepest 27,000 feet, nearly the height of Everest, off the shore at Antofagasta, the northern coastal city where I will stay overnight when I visit Paranal.

It's the oceanic plate that forces its way under the South American continental plate that has created this vast trench. It was in 1960, that the sudden breaking of rock and abrupt unsticking of those very same tectonic plates twenty miles beneath Chile's surface, caused the most powerful earthquake in recorded history, 9.5 on the Richter scale. This was a force equivalent to 1,200 megatons of TNT, or 80,000 times more powerful than Hiroshima's "Little Boy". This Great Chilean Earthquake was 5,000 times stronger than the 1989 San Francisco Bay Area quake that took out the Bay Bridge and the I-880 viaduct. The biggest one ever, killed thousands, and left two million people homeless.

The Chilean earthquake also initiated an awesome Tsunami, a wave that traveled 200 mph across the Pacific as far as Japan, where twenty-two hours later, 140 souls were lost. Another earthquake, like the one in 1960, and ten million Chileans that live on the edge of a great chasm may be in for a wild ride.

It was these same tectonics, that (in geologic time) recently formed the Andes, only forty-five million years ago. These are no foothills, standing somewhere between the height of the American Rockies and the Himalayas.

I see them now from my window seat looking toward the eastern horizon. In but ten minutes, our pilot announces that we're about to pass Aconcagua, just on the other side of the Argentinian border, at 23,000 feet, the highest peak in the Western Hemisphere. Viewing the profile of so many rugged snow-capped mountains chained together as if powerful gladiators in the arena, I spot the one most massive: a broad-based solid mound of volcanic rock, a head taller than its comrades, peering out over a delicate layer of clouds nestled up to its shoulders. Turns out that my imagery is not entirely unique as, our captain now informs, the indigenous meaning of Aconcagua is "sentinel of stone".

On the left side of the aircraft, my fellow passengers might look through their portals to see the lesser Chilean Coastal Range, that extends almost the entire length of Chile. The Atacama lies well north of here, between the rain shadows of these two mountain chains. Air and ocean currents combine with the northern Chilean topography to form the driest hot desert in the world; and since it's been this way for as long as forty million years, it's one of the oldest deserts on the planet.

As interesting as all this minutia is to me, even I know not to dangle such tidbits before Lauren, who sits next to me in the middle seat. I turn my head to the left and see her lazily flipping through a Spanish-language LATAM airlines in-flight magazine. Apparently Iz, asleep again to Lauren's left, didn't endow her daughter's cell phone with international service. I'm surprised that this alone didn't cause an uprising.

Lauren senses my intrusion and squarely returns my gaze with a squint of her eyes and an unmistakably fake smile. She may as well have told me to fuck off. I imitate her body language, pay back the sentiment, and return to my window.

Looking down at the land from on high through white wispy

puffs of vapor, I observe rich walnut and orange browns, deep pine and crocodile greens, and the white of the Andes' peaks, all mottled and vivid like the colors in Van Gogh's *Sunset at Montmajour*. But halfway through the flight, the sky is clear, and the earth takes on the colors of a muddy sand. With its muted grayish browns striated and patched with lighter shades of beige, it reminds me of a marbled steak that's been in the freezer too long. We've come upon the southern edge of the Atacama, a 40,000 square mile swath of parched, barren, and mostly lifeless earth.

I remove my new 15x binoculars from my backpack to have at the ready. Over the next hour, an empty paved road appears and disappears like an apparition. A few minutes later, we pass over a huge man-made crater, an open-pit copper mine, that when magnified through the lenses, looks like an ancient amphitheater in the land of the giants. These are the only signs of human influence I detect until we're within three minutes of the airport.

Our final descent into Calama is other-worldly. We fly past a solar farm, as isolated as an Antarctic weather station, and, a minute later, a dozen or so wind turbines. With some imagination, these small energy projects look to be part of phase-one of the colonization of Mars. Our pilot extends the flaps, deploys the landing gear, and we steadily drop into the flat desert valley of sand and rock.

I check on my two companions. I see Isabel waking from her slumber in time to adjust her seatbelt. Lauren who, as far as I can tell, hasn't peered past me out the window all flight, bites at a hangnail in total apathy. We hit the runway, and there's still no sign of life. Yet, I'm in the Atacama, full of anticipation of the beauty in the sky that will be unveiled tonight.

CHAPTER 49

Oasis

We collect our gear off a shiny metal carousel and follow signs out of baggage claim for "la salida". We're met by a skinny light-skinned Chilean in his twenties who holds up a home-made cardboard sign with the name "Dalton" in thick black letters. He's in jeans, a Scotch-plaid flannel shirt and work boots. We shake hands, as he struggles to welcome us in heavy-accented broken English.

"Hello. Señora y Señor Dalton, I am Miguel, your driver. Ah, uno más. Hello to you," acknowledging Lauren just behind me. She looks back at him, quizzically.

"No problema, I have espacio. If you please, I drive you to San Pedro de Atacama."

Miguel grabs the women's rolling luggage from them, and we make for the exit.

"Miguel," I say in my best raised-in-New-England accent, "esta airporto es nuvo, y mooey granday, si?"

"Si, si, nuevo. A few years, maybe. For the cobre."

"The copper. They built it for the mines," Isabel explains.

"Yeah, got it, Iz," I say, as if my comprehension was ever in doubt. Isabel's tongue sticks out at me.

We exit the airport and head across to the parking lot. It's sunny, the air is dry at a perfect room temperature. In a minute, Miguel points to a green dusty Nissan Pathfinder.

"Es mío," Miguel announces, as he opens the liftgate and loads our luggage.

Isabel takes the front passenger seat.

"Honey, you don't mind if I ride up front with Miguel, do you? I want to practice my Spanish."

Lauren and I reply simultaneously.

"Be my guest," Lauren says, with indifference.

"No problema, mi amor," I reply, exhausting my Spanish vocabulary.

We're on our way to the oasis, about an hour's drive.

Iz wastes no time engaging Miguel in quick conversation, impressive as it is unintelligible. Lauren, who's on the left side in the back with me, hugs her door handle and looks out her window, creating as much distance between us as she can.

"He has to stop for gas," Isabel translates over the noise of the SUV.

From this side of the airport, Calama, which I couldn't see from the plane, is now laid out before us. It's a small city of 150,000, Miguel explains through his interpreter; most of its residents are connected to the *cobre*. A big mining town.

To reach the cheapest gas, I think, we pass through row upon row of modest cinder block and corrugated metal dwellings, homes to the Chilean working class. This could be Scranton of the high desert, or perhaps Bakersfield, small blue-collar cities I passed through aimlessly in my youth. Calama, however, with its colorless cast, seems far less well-off than either.

We pull into a two-pump Copec gas station. While Miguel

fills up and Lauren excuses herself for a cigarette, Isabel turns to address me.

"This is so great. If only I had two months, I'd be fluent. He even said my accent was good."

"He's just looking for his tip."

She ignores me. "I'm getting most of it. It's so interesting. The city was founded here in the middle of the desert along a 'río' that originates at some huge volcano."

"Rio? I thought that was in Brazil," I tease. She ignores my witticism.

"The volcano is in the Andes. He said it's 6,000 meters high."

"About 20,000 feet. The size of Kilimanjaro," I add. "That's huge."

"He was born in Calama. He said the river is the city's 'alma', which I'm pretty sure means 'soul'."

"Did you say 'alma', Iz? A-L-M-A?"

"Yes, why?"

"That's interesting. I never knew that."

Iz gives me a puzzled look.

"You'll see," I reassure her.

Miguel hops back behind the wheel before Isabel can press me on it. Lauren flicks a smoldering butt onto the sidewalk far from the pumps, walks back to the car, and climbs in.

"Okay, lista?" Miguel asks Iz.

"Sí, como no. Vámonos, Miguel."

Isabel seems as happy as a Spanish flea on a Catalan Sheepdog. Her daughter not so much, and Iz takes notice. She swings her left arm over the seat and faces her.

"So, Laur, you're awfully quiet. What do you think?"

"About what?"

"I don't know, about anything. You've never been this far from the States. What do you think about Chile?"

"It's ugly? Poor?"

"Yes, you might see Calama that way. Makes you appreciate Tucson more, doesn't it?"

"Maybe."

"I bet the people are nice, though, and they work hard. Keep an open mind, honey," Isabel suggests. "I have a feeling that things will start to look different soon enough."

I do like Isabel's attitude. Nothing's getting in the way of her Spanish adventure, not even her sulking, depressed daughter.

We're soon on Route 23, a smooth two-lane highway with a posted speed limit of 100 km, or sixty mph. I figure Miguel's doing seventy-five, and on the flat, straight open road, he's passing five-axle tarp-covered dump trucks, hauling gravel or copper concentrate, as easily as powerful four-door pickups are passing us.

Miguel and Isabel chat non-stop. For me, it's become background noise, like Spanish talk radio. Every so often, Isabel feeds Lauren and me pieces of information she deems vital.

"Miguel is married and has two children, a boy and a girl."

"Lucky guy," I reply.

"Yeah, but the boy has Asperger's."

"That's too bad."

"His wife's a nurse for the mining company."

"That might be helpful." I try to conceal any sense of futility.

After a few minutes of radio silence, she starts up again.

"Miguel says we're travelling on a 'meseta'."

"A what?" I ask.

"I believe it's a plateau. We're at 2,500 meters right here."

"Really?" I reply. She has my attention now. "That's nearly 8,000 feet. You'd never know it. Everything's so flat."

Outside of Calama, the ribbon of the road is surrounded by dirty-white sand and small stones, a blended color of speckled gray wool, I would say in these parts, as from a llama. But it's best defined by what's absent: no animals, no vegetation, not a cactus or puff of desert grass in sight, not even a hungry vulture soaring overhead. I'd bet if I got down on hands and knees, I wouldn't see a spider.

Other than the road, which seems to have been laid out onto the ground as easily as a beach blanket, there's no other sign of humanity. The desert extends out for almost as far as the eye can see: a giant, empty dirt parking lot where one might hold, every Saturday, the largest swap-meet on Earth. There are distant hills to our right, and on our left, to the northeast, we see tall mountains on the horizon. It's hard to make out but some are snow-covered. These are the great Andes. If we're already at 8,000 feet, we could be viewing 20,000 foot titans, but at this distance, they're unimposing.

All is quiet for a few minutes until out of nowhere, Lauren speaks up.

"My God, there's nothing here. Absolutely nothing! I thought it would be like Tucson, but compared to this, the Snorin' desert looks more like Miami Beach. You didn't say we were going to the moon, Mom."

"Lauren, I'm just as amazed as you are, honey. I didn't know *what* it would be like."

"Actually," I butt in, "it's more like Mars than the moon."

Lauren turns to me. "I'm sure *you're* excited about going to Mars, Henry, but I didn't sign up for this."

Progress! She called me Henry.

"I admit," I reply, "It would be cool to see Mars up close, but I'm happy right here on Earth with you guys."

"Be honest," Isabel says, looking back at me. "You'd go in a minute if you didn't have to blast off into space for three months."

"More like six, but you might be right."

"Yeah, there isn't enough vodka in the world to get you through that one," Lauren chimes in, with a little gleam in her eyes.

Isabel and I laugh. A joke. She made a joke! We'll be buds in no time.

In an hour, the topography starts to change. We're still far from the Andes, now directly ahead, but close enough that they appear as mountains and not just bumps on the horizon. The road curves through somewhat hillier terrain. I'm alerted by an occasional roadside guardrail, and Lauren requests for Miguel to drive slower; he does.

We descend quite unexpectedly where the road was carved through brown craggy foothills. We pass by contiguous fifty-foot mounds of rock and sand on our left that appear like the bony plates on the back of a massive stegosaurus. The road then ascends, and over the rise we see a big swath of green in the distance, I judge a half mile away, and about a mile across. It's our oasis, San Pedro de Atacama.

Miguel announces through Isabel that we're almost there. When we cross over a muddy brown rivulet, the well-maintained and clearly-lined pavement of Route 23 is lost to that same rich brown mud that now covers the asphalt. Just ahead we can see the beginnings of a town, with street signs, and single-story flat-roofed adobe buildings fronted by simple stone and clay walls.

Miguel, however, takes a sharp left turn at the first corner, in front of a sign for a "Restaurante", and onto a narrow rutted dirt road that winds like a long-tailed snake through green mesquite. The SUV's suspension squeaks and groans with every bump and hole that Miguel targets. We pass two hungry collarless mutts, one black, one white. Our driver sounds his horn, and waves at a short Latina with a plastic grocery bag swinging from each hand, as she ambles roadside. A young man in shorts and a hooded sweatshirt rolls past us on a fat-tired bicycle from the opposite direction. There are clearings with sad-looking abodes of old brick, concrete and sheet metal, looking like small house trailers. With some irony, the residents on our right need only peek out a rear window to see the majesty of a great snow-capped volcano standing in near-perfect symmetry alone in the distance.

I must admit that I have some doubts about sipping mojitos on the veranda of a four-star luxury hotel and spa, that's been promised at the end of this expedition. The odds are better that we'll run into a band of swarthy desperados in faded ponchos, straw hats and bandoliers filled with large-shell cartridges for the menacing shotguns they'll cradle in their arms. But being politically correct, I keep this to myself. On the other hand, Lauren who has no filter, seems to agree.

"Where is he taking us, Mom? This can't be the way to our hotel. I've scored drugs in places that felt safer."

Isabel talks with Miguel, who laughs.

Iz comes back. "I'm told not to worry. It's very safe. He's done this before."

Things start to change. Soon, we find ourselves driving alongside a small river, perhaps the one we already crossed. The road leads us into a majestic gorge, some four hundred feet wide, surrounded by canyon walls of jagged clay-colored rock reaching up at least as high. We're surrounded by the striking beauty as we pass through a steel gate secured by an unarmed woman in a khaki hotel uniform, and head onto a smooth sand driveway. We three are looking up at sheer orange-red rock walls looming over us hundreds of feet, when the SUV pulls under a stone porte-cochere in front of what might pass for the Four Seasons in Scottsdale.

Even Lauren is stunned by it all.

"Oh my God!" she exclaims.

As Miguel helps us out of the Nissan, and a bell-hop attends to our luggage, we're greeted by two of the front-desk staff with big glasses of ice-cold red punch. We've arrived. It's delicious!

CHAPTER 50

Breakfast in the Gorge

H enry and Isabel sit side-by-side at their breakfast table on a
flowered banquette, under a wooden straw-roofed canopy, on
the hotel's outdoor stone patio. Looking ahead, and still in awe, they
gaze upon the chiseled beauty of the northeast side of the gorge. It's
8 a.m., and the rays of the early sun, now hanging just above the
canyon rim, shine upon them.

"It's stunning," Isabel declares.

"As are you, my love."

"Stop it. I'm serious."

"As am I, my love."

"Oh, forget it."

"Okay, it is amazing, and I can't believe we're here," Henry
concedes.

"Was last night up to your expectations?"

"If you're referring to the stargazing, yes."

"You didn't have any other expectations, did you?" she asks,
smiling.

"No, I know better by now. Seriously, Iz? The sky was outstanding!

I *was* hoping to see more of an arch to the galactic plane. I guess we're not at a steep enough angle. But that's the least of it. I've never seen so many stars! By the way, I think your binoculars are as good as their telescope."

"They're *your* binoculars," Isabel says. "The hotel does a nice job, though, don't you think? Putting the viewing area up on the hill, away from the lights. Lying on a soft platform wrapped up in a blanket. I remember getting a stiff neck and freezing my ass off on Kitt Peak. Of course, the guide here is no Steinmetz."

"No, but he was good. I think even Lauren got into it," Henry says.

"Really? I thought she fell asleep before he finished his little explanation of the Southern Cross."

"I don't think. I heard an ooh and an ah coming from her cot when we saw the meteor."

"When *you* saw it. I missed it. I'm sorry she isn't up yet. I'd like her to see this, the way the sun's just peeking over the ridge."

"Let her sleep," Henry says. "We don't leave until ten. They'll be plenty of other beautiful sights."

"Well, she better get up soon. She can't hang here alone," Iz replies.

"She seems to be doing well. You two are like best friends." Henry mentions Isabel's private conversation with Lauren at the airport.

"Henry, she was telling me how she felt funny about being here. At first, I assumed she was referring to Chile; but I think what she was saying was, *here.*" Iz makes an arch with both arms. "You know, like being alive."

"Sorry. I was pretty beat at the time."

"Yes, you were. It's okay. Who knows what she meant? I've decided to play it down and focus on having fun."

"Good idea. Speak of the devil." Henry motions to Isabel with his head toward Lauren, who saunters in as if on cue, her hair still wet from a morning shower. She pulls up a chair to the breakfast table to face the couple.

"Good morning, hon," says Isabel. "Did you see the sunrise over the ridge?" Isabel asks, pointing toward the canyon wall behind Lauren.

"Yes, Mom," Lauren replies, without turning around to look.

Isabel shakes her head. Henry interjects.

"Look at you, all ready to go. How'd you sleep?"

"Fine."

"And here we were concerned that you'd miss the trip to the salt flats," he adds.

"I'll have you know," Lauren says, "I've been getting up at 6:30 for the past five months."

"No, I'm actually impressed you made it up so early. 7:30 here is 3:30 in the morning in Arizona."

Lauren doesn't react.

"So, where *are* we going?" she asks, grabbing a croissant from the basket on the table, while a waiter pours cups of coffee from behind.

"We're going to see the flamingos," Isabel explains. "We thought we'd start off easy."

"What do you mean? What's *not* easy?"

"I don't think there's anything so difficult. There's a trip to the geysers that everyone recommends. But we'll have to leave in the wee hours to get there by sunrise. I'm thinking we'll do that tomorrow. There are also a few hikes we definitely should do."

"Yeah," Henry chimes in. "I'm sure you won't want to pass up on the Lunar Valley. NASA tested its Mars rover there."

"So why don't they call it the Mars Valley?" Lauren asks.

"It's funny you mention that. They have a Mars Valley here too," Henry replies. "But it's also known as Death Valley."

"You're confusing me," Lauren grumbles.

"Of course," Isabel remarks. "Marte for Mars, and Muerte for death. They probably got confused themselves."

"Well, Henry, maybe you should take a walk on Mars then," Lauren says with a guileful smirk.

"Only if you come with, Lauren." Henry smiles, enjoying the banter.

"We'll all get up early tomorrow and do the geysers," says Isabel, quickly moving the conversation along. "Henry's leaving for one of his interviews in the afternoon, right, darling? And you'll be back Thursday?"

"Yep."

"So, Lauren, when Henry leaves, you and I can pamper ourselves for a couple of days, sit by the pool, relax in the jacuzzi. We might borrow their bikes, explore the town, pick up a few souvenirs. We'll start the serious hiking on Friday. Okay?"

"Can I get a massage?" Lauren asks. "After five months at a rehab, I could use one."

"Sure, why not. I'll get one too."

"What about me?" Henry asks. "I could use a massage."

"You can have your massage, hon, when you finish your work down here and write that book."

"Slave driver," Henry says, grinning.

CHAPTER 51

Salt and Soul

W e're in the hotel's comfy VW van on the way to see the Andean flamingos in the Salar de Atacama, the largest salt flats in Chile. That's where these birds come once a year to mate.

Our driver knows the road and likes to speed. Iz and I sit behind him in the second row, Lauren shares the third row with a young couple, and there are two older women in the back.

Our guide sits in the bucket seat to the driver's right. His name is Enrico, which Isabel finds humorous. Enrico's black hair is combed over a white cherubic face. He's wearing a brown zip-up jacket with a Cañón de Atacama emblem on its front. Enrico explains to us in decent English what we're about to see.

"When you get there, the first thing to notice is some big volcans in the north. Licancabur is the most famous and the most beautiful because of its size and shape. It is the same you see from near the hotel. Part of it is in Bolivia. The cone is at 5,900 metros, or in feet, almost 20,000. A lake sits in the crater, the most high lake in the world. Los Atacameños believe this mountain to be sacred. Some ruins have been found on the other side, maybe 3,000 years old."

"The Atacameños? I ask.

"Yes, the indígena. We have 10,000 in San Pedro."

"Indigenous, Henry. 10,000 here," Isabel says.

"Yes, I caught that, hon."

"Do they live on reservations, too?" I look back at Lauren, who asked the question.

"No," Enrico replies. "No reservations in Chile. There are many different groups of the indígena. The big group is Mapuche in the south. Ten percent of the population in Chile is indígena. All of them have suffered."

I look back and see Lauren shake her head in acknowledgment. Enrico goes on.

"When we get there, you will walk on paths where you want to go. Please be careful in the flats. Stay on the path. The minerals are cakes on the land and are sharp in places. If you fall, you may cut yourself."

The van follows a sudden curve in the road, and our guide faces forward holding onto the door handle, then turns back to us.

"The surface water, the lagoons, are shallow and salty. Most water is from underground. The evaporation is much, it leaves the minerals and a little water. Also, this salar is the place of the largest production in the world for litio; they use this for your telephone, your laptop computers, and cameras."

"Oh, lithium," Iz says for all to hear.

"Sí, lo siento. Litium. For batteries and more. You cannot see this facility; it is farther on the salar. They say production here must double in ten years. There is much discussion from local people, los Atacameños also, who care about the land, the water. They are afraid.

"What do *you* think, Enrico?" I ask.

"Of course, more production is good for the economia, but I am also afraid. It is a story of money y corrupción. The family of Pinochet owns much of the company. The company owns the land,

and the law is the friend to the company. There is talk now that half of the salar will be bought by los Rusos."

Isabel translates. "Russians." I acknowledge this with a nod. It sounds a bit nefarious.

"What about the floods. Did they affect the salar?" A query shouted by one of the women in the back row.

"Floods? Here?" I ask.

"Sometimes we have rain in the mountains, in January or February," Enrico replies. "Last year, it was a very bad flood. Calama had no clean water to drink in four days. Many houses in San Pedro were lost. Five people dead. The salar was not hurt."

The woman in the back says that climate change was to blame.

"Sí, cambio climático," says Enrico, slipping into Spanish. "Perhaps. It was very dry in the south, en Patagonia. This is not normal. The south dry, the Atacama, so much water. Not good."

Enrico takes a breather. In a minute, he points out of the van's left side.

"We are now at the entrance to ALMA, the largest telescope in the world. The operations center is four miles on this road." Enrico refers to a wide, well-maintained, dirt driveway that winds its way up the Andean foothills. There's a modern concrete gate- house set back from the highway. Our driver speeds up as we pass.

Isabel turns to me with a stunned look. She leans over to talk in my ear.

"So, this is your *soul* that you wouldn't tell me about."

"Yes, ma'am. ALMA is the Atacama Large Millimeter Array, but I never knew about the other meaning." I add, "I didn't see it anywhere on their website either. By the way, it's not the largest telescope in the world, but it *is* the largest radio telescope array, at least until someone builds a bigger one."

"When is your interview?" Isabel inquires.

"Monday," I respond.

The young man next to Lauren asks Enrico where the telescope is located. I jump to provide the answer for all.

"Actually, it's a complex of sixty-six huge satellite-dishes; they're fixed to a flat plateau 17,000 feet high. That's way beyond the operations center."

As I speak, Isabel jabs my leg with her knee, and frowns as if to say, "Shut-up, Henry, this isn't your show."

But Enrico's unbothered by my interruption.

"Sí, señor. Perfecto. How do you know such things?"

"I'm a science writer, Enrico. I visit ALMA on Monday."

"Ah, a scientist. In astronomia?"

"No, not a scientist. Just a writer. Like a journalist. For a magazine."

"Como periodista," Isabel translates for Enrico.

"Sí, lo entiendo bién, señora," Enrico says with a polite smile, as I continue.

"Given the altitude, only a few are permitted to see the antennas firsthand. Regrettably, I'm not one of those."

Judging from photos, it's an unbelievable daytime sight. An alien outpost on some distant planet. Giant mushroom-like robotic beings huddled together on a reddish brown mesa, scanning the sky. They're surrounded by earthen waves, taller mounds, and grand volcanic mountaintops, some capped in snow, looming in the background. At night, it's even more spectacular in the photos. The same mechanized dishes point out over the silhouette of a transcendent landscape, into a never-ending ocean of stars: watching, listening, searching.

While Enrico moves on to enlighten us on the Andean flamingos' mating rituals, I'm lost in thought. My meeting on Monday is with Dr. Stephen Ralston, to whom I was introduced via email by Steinmetz, Ralston's former colleague in Chicago. Ralston just became involved with the most momentous advancement in astronomical research perhaps since Hubble himself, about which the science community is all abuzz; and it's on the cutting edge of dark energy research.

The salt flats are light years from the highway, but we finally get there over a bumpy and dusty sand road. The scene is as described, an extensive plain of clumps and chunks of what might be white ice crystals, mottled dirty over time. The speckled terrain is interspersed with immense blue puddles, randomly shaped like big amoebae. In these shallow brine-pools, a flock of lithe birds, a corps de ballet in matching pink tutus, perform the second act of *Swan Lake*, bobbing for algae and underwater insects. All of this is viewed against the Andean backdrop, which includes that one perfectly-formed immense cone of what was once magma spewed from the bowels of the Earth, then cooled, a million years ago; the volcano, Licancabur.

We explore the flats for ninety minutes and then pile back into the van for the hotel. Enrico answers a few questions but is otherwise done for the day. The two women in the back doze. The young couple takes an interest in Lauren, who manages to divert the conversation away from her life, to theirs.

We pass ALMA, to our right now, and Isabel is reminded of my upcoming interview.

"What's it about?" she asks.

I answer over the noise of the speeding van. I'm excited to just be connected in a small way to Ralston, and his involvement with recent discoveries that have shaken the world of astronomy.

"It concerns gravitational waves," I say. "Ripples in the space-time continuum."

"Really? Space-time continuum? It sounds like something you picked up from the Syfy Channel."

"Yes, love, you know how we like to joke all the time. Well, this is not one of those times." A familiar line that brings an instant smile to her lips, and she kisses me on mine.

I expound in detail about the discovery made by scientists in 2015. They detected gravitational waves by shooting lasers in remote locations just above the ground for two miles, and then back again.

"Before this, these disturbances in the fabric of space-time were only a prediction in Einstein's theory of relativity. Their first discovery was of waves created by the merger of two black holes. They won the Nobel Prize for this."

Isabel seems impressed.

"That's just the half of it," I go on. "In 2017, the same scientists used their lasers to detect gravitational waves from the collision of two neutron stars."

The man behind us pushes forward on his seat to eavesdrop, while the woman with him continues her chat with Lauren.

"The density of a neutron star is off the charts. A teaspoon of the stuff might weigh ten million tons."

"That's not even possible," Isabel proclaims.

"No, I've heard of these things," says the man leaning over from the third row. "They're like dying stars that collapse in on themselves, right?"

"Exactly. Thank you." I reply to him. He beams.

"Sorry, but I overheard your discussion. This stuff is so cool," he adds.

I continue. I explain how during this event, when the Nobel prize winners detected the gravity waves with their lasers, they immediately alerted the world's astronomers. Using their telescopes, many astronomers were able to see and record the explosive light show produced by the collision of the two neutron stars.

"This was the first time anything like this was pulled off in the history of astronomy. It was a whole new way of looking back in time at the same event through multiple windows. Putting it simply, the Nobel winners felt the vibe, while the folks with the scopes saw the light."

"Cute," Isabel says.

"That's good," says the young man.

"Thanks." I make a mental note to use it in my book. "Anyway, Ralston's in charge of ALMA's collaboration on future cosmic occurrences. There are literally dozens of observatories and research facilities throughout the globe that are ready to launch into action for the next event that's picked up by the lasers."

"It's pretty amazing. Why haven't I heard of this?" Isabel asks me.

"Maybe you're just watching too much cable news."

She shrugs, and the fellow behind us laughs, as we continue our ride through the empty wilderness back to luxury.

CHAPTER 52

The Geysers

It's 4:30 in the morning the following day. The three of us sip coffee in the lobby and nibble on mild sausage, cheese, and hard-boiled eggs, with slices of soft French bread. It's a quick breakfast supplied by the bleary-eyed line-cook who, in his stained white apron, stands away from us while attending to our needs. The van is warming up under the hotel's porte-cochere, a driver behind the wheel.

My iPhone tells me that it's fifty-four degrees with an expected high of seventy-one by this afternoon. So, it's anomalous that the duffle at my feet holds winter gear that was on the travel agent's what-to-bring list.

We feel a pleasant rush of dry cool air as Enrico and a tall and slender companion enter through the automatic glass doors. The two are clad in matching navy bomber jackets, embellished with the hotel's logo.

Enrico introduces us to his colleague, Mateo, who will be our official guide this morning. Mateo's in his late twenties and rather good-looking. Lauren instinctively, perhaps, primps.

"I go for a ride," Enrico explains, relaxed and smiling.

Apparently, we're the only guests to have signed up for the trek to the geysers.

The two guides quickly down some breakfast and pour coffee and lots of sugar into hot paper-cups for the road. Mateo checks in with us to make sure we have warm clothing. We exit the hotel and climb into the van: Enrico first, who takes the back seat and reclines against the window. The three of us resume our positions from yesterday. This time it's Mateo up front with the driver.

Our new guide speaks English fluently and with ease.

"Good morning. Again, I am Mateo, and our driver today is Juan. We are heading for El Tatio Geysers. To the Atacameños in their ancient language, this means "the old man that cries.""

So, it's amusing that Mateo pronounces *geysers*, sounding like a Brit, as *geezers;* as though we're travelling to see a few codgers on porch rockers, lamenting over glasses of foam about the old days, yelling at neighborhood kids speeding past on skateboards. Lauren chortles, and Mateo eyes her, but soon enough, we become accustomed to his Oxford-like pronunciation.

"It will take an hour and a half to reach the *geezers*. They are 4,200 meters in altitude, higher than 14,000 feet. So, we're heading up. It's a gradual and steady climb, 6,000 feet up from here, and we have to hurry if we're going to make it by sunrise."

Mateo gestures to the driver. Rotating tires spray sand, and the van lurches forward through the gorge. In a few minutes, we turn left onto a paved street into town, now silent and dark except for the pale glow from the waning half-moon. Civilization ends in four blocks, and we again hear the crunch of packed sand and gravel beneath our wheels, as the van begins its northern climb into the Andes.

Indeed, our driver is in a hurry. The gray road ahead, illuminated by the VW's high beams, passes beneath us as would the pristine tracks one might see riding at the front of a Japanese bullet train. I've never gone so fast on an unpaved surface, even in broad daylight, but Juan handles the VW like a Le Mans racer.

I look back and see Lauren grip the underside of her bench seat with both hands, too afraid to utter a word. It helps that most of the route is a straight shot, and red taillights in the distance show us the way. Even so, I'm not comforted by the relaxed Spanish chatter between guide and driver spoken as fast as we're traveling and, as it seems, beyond much of Isabel's comprehension. This doesn't stop her from joining in as best as she can.

It's pitch-black on either side of us. Daring to look out my window and up to the heavens, I see that the moon has made its way westward across the canvas of millions of brilliant celestial bodies: planets, stars, and nebulae, and I'm reminded why I'm here. Eventually, as we draw near to El Tatio, the sun starts its rise on our right, stars fade to complete the miraculous cycle, and we see the outline of the mountains that define this plateau. It's all so wonderful.

El Tatio Geysers are a genuine attraction, but Yellowstone they're not, so there's only a small parking lot, the size one would find at a roadside mini-mall. Despite our van's blistering pace, we're late, and sunrise has technically occurred. The parking lot is filled with other hotel vans, full-sized coach buses, and SUVs. Mateo reports that it's 28 degrees Fahrenheit. Anyone can see that it's windy.

"Please put on all your extra clothing," he instructs. "Also, at 14,000 feet, the air has a lot less oxygen. So, go slowly. Do not rush. Stay on the paths. We will meet back at the van in one hour."

I hear Lauren mutter from behind. "Go slowly, he says?"

After donning our parkas, ski hats and mittens, we alight from the vehicle and make a pit stop. I'm reminded of a restroom, jammed with fully-geared skiers, one might find on the unpretentious slopes near Flagstaff.

The three of us meet up and randomly choose a path through the geothermal field. As compared to Old Faithful, the geysers themselves are not impressive. If they spout hot water at all, it's just a foot or two high. Lauren, however, has never seen geothermal activity.

"That's amazing," she says, pointing to a bubbling pool.

We stop at a steam vent.

"Oh my God. Where's it all coming from?" she asks.

I explain that it's ground water hitting magma not too far from the surface; then I'm asked to explain magma.

We come to a thermal mud pot, and Lauren's still excited.

"These are so cool. They could have a great spa, right here."

"I'm pretty sure this mud will burn your face off, Laur," Isabel advises.

I do appreciate Lauren's enthusiasm for these individual features, but for me, it's the entire setting, taken together, that's uniquely enticing. These geysers are at the highest altitude of any found in the world, and they're encircled by some of the grandest volcanos of the Andes, a few of which are considered active. Each of the dozens of these small geysers in proximity spew a bubbling broth rich in multi-colored minerals that precipitate onto the landscape in exquisite artistry. The puddles and mists from each of these hot water fountains combine to suggest a giant cauldron of a Chilean cazuela, an eternal boiling stew.

"So, Henry, why did we have to do this so early?" Lauren inquires.

"I think it has to do with the steam. Later in the day, it won't be so cold, and hence, not so dramatic."

"*I* was always told to skip the drama," Lauren replies, with a cute smile.

Am I imagining things, or is she being pleasant this morning?

Our final stop in the geothermal field is a hot-springs swimming hole, complete with bathers in swimsuits.

"Darn, they should have said something," Iz laments. "I would have tried this."

"You won't see *me* jumping in this soup," Lauren announces. "God knows what's living in *there*."

"You might survive," I say. Turning to Iz. "Sure would've liked to see you sopping wet, half-naked in this freezing cold. Maybe we should come back tomorrow?"

Isabel grins at us. "You're just a bunch a wusses."

Lauren beats me to the punch.

"Wusses?! I'm not sure that's even a word anymore; and you can't be calling me names when I get up at four a.m. to take a spin with fast and furious over there," gesturing toward the parking lot, "without even a complaint."

I laugh hard and give Lauren a high five. Her mother smiles and concedes the point.

We finish meandering through the geothermal field, and head back to the parking lot, where we find the three amigos leaning against the van. It's just after seven, and it feels like half the day has elapsed.

It's daylight as we exit the geothermal field and begin our gradual descent. Low-lying bushy scrub and tufted grasses, yellowed from frost, dot the high plain. We pass small brine ponds with grazing flamingos.

Lower down, and out of the shadows of the tallest peaks, all flora and fauna disappear. We hit a long straight-a-way, about four miles, on the flat, gently sloping, plateau of bone-dry sand and dirt. The road is but a packed path through the earthen plain which it traverses. Tire tracks are visible at its outer edges, where beige sand has been pushed from the center into three-inch mounds along either side. We proceed at a good clip and leave behind the southern-most volcanic mountains of this part of the Andean range. They protrude, far behind us now, like giant, dark abscesses on an otherwise smooth surface.

Besides the six of us, and the VW rover, there's nothing else for miles. We're totally alone. There's so much beauty in desolation, and if anything on our planet resembles Mars, it's this.

We've been on the road over an hour when Mateo again turns to speak.

"We are almost at our next stop. It is a very small Atacameño village called Machuca. It is known for raising llamas. There are tourist shops and stands where you can try their food. I am always asked, so I will tell you: yes, the food is safe. In fact, I think it is very good!"

A not-so-subtle commercial, and we all giggle. It's Enrico in the back that laughs loudest.

Machuca is a quick right off the road. Indeed, it's small: three rows of seven or so adobe and stone rectangular huts, laid out on a long flat dirt lot. The village is nestled at the bottom of the surrounding Andean foothills, once again dotted with green low-lying scrub and grasses. A tiny white church, with sky-blue doors and a golden thatch roof, sits on a hill just above the village.

Iz and Lauren check out some weavings and trinkets for sale. Not much of a shopper, I hang with the guys at a smoky llama-kabob stand, a long charcoal grill manned by an older teenager. It turns out that it's Enrico's cousin. He cooks and serves up the cubes of meat on wooden skewers. He and Enrico are Atacameños.

A tiny old woman sits behind us on the stone floor against an adobe wall. She's wearing a red bandana under a straw hat, a tattered red sweater, and an old blue chiffon skirt. She's introduced to me as Enrico's aunt, and she gives me a broad smile lacking for nothing except a few teeth. Curiously, there's an immature llama tied from the neck to a door handle standing close to her, chewing on its leather leash.

While Iz continues to browse, Lauren saunters over. By this

time, I'm grazing on a llama-kabob. It's a bit gamy, although I could be convinced that I'm eating lamb. I offer Lauren a taste.

"What is it?"

I point to the little llama behind us.

"Seriously, Henry?! You're eating that cute, furry animal?"

"No, not that one."

Mateo and Enrico laugh; then Mateo encourages Lauren to take a bite. She refuses.

"I'm not much of a meat eater, especially when it's wagging its tail at me."

We all laugh.

"Stay in Chile a month, and you may change your mind," Mateo says. "Did you find something nice to buy?"

It doesn't surprise me to see our handsome guide hit on my girlfriend's lovely daughter. But the old woman, speaking through her nephew, Enrico, interrupts Mateo's advances.

"Que bonita esta chica. Americana?"

"Sí, tía," Enrico replies.

"My aunt says you are very pretty," Enrico says to Lauren.

"How sweet." She turns toward his aunt, "Muchas gracias, señora."

"You speak some Spanish?" Enrico asks Lauren.

"No, not really," she responds.

"Escuchame, preciosa," the old woman says. "Sola en el desierto es peligroso. Tenga cuidado."

"What did she say?" Lauren asks Enrico.

"My aunt is old and how do you say, a little crazy."

"Sí, vieja, pero no soy loca. Los jóvenes no saben nada."

"She knows some English too. Okay, Tía," Enrico continues, looking back at her. "She says, 'alone in the desert is dangerous and to be careful'."

"Please tell her, I'm not alone. My mother is here, and Henry," pointing to me. Tía doesn't wait for the reply.

"Escala la montaña! Ve todo desde las alturas."

"Okay, Tía." Enrico shrugs, and turns to Lauren. "She says, 'to climb the mountain and see things from there'."

Lauren's puzzled, but polite.

"Please tell her that I will; and thank you."

Mateo chimes in. "You know, the Atacameños believe some mountains to be sacred. For instance, the volcano Licancabur."

"Yes, we learned that yesterday," I reply. "So, she's a mountain worshipper?" I ask, while smiling at Tía.

"Yes, perhaps so, but they are also Catholic," Mateo says, pointing up the hill to the church, complete with a wooden cross atop a little bell tower. He turns back to Lauren.

"Can I show you a special shop before we go?" Lauren smiles, and Mateo shepherds her away.

I chat some more with Enrico until Isabel finds us. She looks worn out.

"Something wrong, hon?"

"I feel a bit woozy."

"I guess you don't want to have a bite of llama, then?"

"Oh my Lord, no."

"You're probably tired," I suggest. "You can take a nap when we get back. Wouldn't mind one myself."

"Where's Lauren?" she asks.

"She went shopping with our handsome guide."

"Well, would you mind finding her? I'd like to get going."

I look at Enrico who understands what's to be done. He jogs out of sight, brings back the young couple, and we're on the road again in a hot minute. Lauren switches rows with us, so she's closer to Mateo. He notices Isabel's fatigue.

"Is she feeling all right?" Mateo asks me.

"Yes, she'll be fine. She's just tired."

"I hope you are right."

Isabel's head leans against my shoulder all the way back.

CHAPTER 53

Figuring It Out

Henry waits outside his hotel room, a modern ground floor unit accessed from an outdoor walkway. Isabel's been throwing up since they returned from El Tatio. Henry didn't wait long before asking the hotel to summon a physician.

The doctor emerges from the couple's room carrying an old-fashioned black medical bag. Henry's at the threshold, concerned.

"Hello, doctor. I'm her friend. How is she?" Henry asks, assuming the doctor speaks English.

"Not well. You went to the geezers this morning, yes?"

"Yes."

"It is too high for some people. She has a bad case of altitude sickness. Of course, a big headache. She is dizzy. She vomits. I gave her something for the vomit. She must drink water. She must rest. She will be okay, but it will take two days, maybe three. She should eat, but lightly. Sopa is best. The hotel knows what to do. I will come back tomorrow to check."

"Oh, gosh. Does this happen often?"

"No, not often, but it happens. Everyone is different. Sometimes a patient feels better in three hours. But I think not with your friend."

"Oh boy. I understand. Okay. Thank you very much."

The two shake hands, and the doctor walks up the concrete path.

Henry knocks and peeks around the door as he enters. Isabel's on the king-sized bed atop the covers, in jeans from this morning, and wearing a fresh tee-shirt. There's a plastic-lined pail on the floor beside her. Her face is clammy and ashen.

"Hey, how do you feel?"

"Same as before," she whispers. "Like someone hit me on the head with a rock. I'm so nauseated. Dizzy. I just threw up again, while he was here."

"Wow, I'm so sorry, hon."

"Not your fault. Where's Lauren?"

"I think she's hanging with Mateo. She doesn't know you're this sick."

"Well, would you find her?" Isabel pleads. "Let her know."

"Of course. I'll cancel my trip."

"No, don't."

"I can't leave you like this."

"You can't help me either. I'll ride it out, sleep it off. I'll have a maid check on me; deliver soup. I can always call the front desk. You know how hard it was to schedule your meeting at Paranal."

"True, but I don't feel right about leaving."

"That's sweet. I'll be okay. The doctor promised," Isabel says, forcing a smile.

"Well, I suppose Lauren can look in on you."

"No, that's the thing. Who's going to watch her? I don't trust her here alone. I need to sleep, and I can't be worrying about what she's up to. You'll take her with you."

"Really? You think that's a good idea?" Henry asks, shaking his head. "She won't want to go with me. Can't say I blame her."

"Listen," Isabel says with quiet conviction. "I don't have the strength to argue. Lauren won't have a choice. You'll take her with you. You've got to finish your research. I need to rest. You promised to be flexible and do what's needed. You promised."

"Yes, but …"

"No buts. You talked me into this trip, remember? You've got to do this for me. Please." Isabel says this with as much force as she can muster, then closes her eyes.

"Okay! I'll figure it out." Henry tilts his head back, gazes up at the ceiling and takes a deep breath.

He finds Lauren near the lobby sitting with Mateo on a soft couch, sipping lemonade, and laughing.

Henry wastes no time. "I'm sorry to interrupt, Lauren, but we have to talk."

"Okay, señor, no problem, I am going home anyway," Mateo volunteers.

"Adios, Mateo. Call me later?" Lauren implores.

"Maybe. Dale suave, chica."

Mateo exits, and Henry sits in Mateo's spot.

"How's Mom?"

"Not good, actually. That's why I'm here."

"Oh my God, is she going to die?"

"No! It's not that serious."

"Well, you really scared me. What's wrong with her?"

Henry describes the altitude sickness and its symptoms, then continues.

"So, you know how I was supposed to go to the west coast this afternoon?"

"Huh, sure. I guess."

"Well, your mom is insisting that I still go to make my meeting at the observatory tomorrow. She's also expecting you to go with me."

"What?! Is she crazy?! I'm not going anywhere with anyone, especially with you. I'm fine. I can help take care of her."

"Lauren, relax. Believe me, I had the same reaction. Nothing personal, but I didn't plan on having you on this excursion either. Maybe she *is* a little off. Her head is killing her. I don't know."

"That's not it. She still doesn't trust me. She'll never trust me."

"To be honest, that's part of it, but I'm thinking the same thing. She has doubts about me, too. I think maybe she's testing me, even if it's subconscious."

Lauren pauses to let this sink in, while Henry thinks he said too much. She replies. "You don't know what you're talking about, Henry. This is about me, not you. She wouldn't send me with you if she didn't trust *you*. I thought you were smarter!"

"Ouch! You also thought I was an alcoholic!"

"Yes. I'm still not sure. I saw what I saw."

"Fine. Let's put that aside. We've got to deal with *this*."

"Yes, I'm going to speak with her right now, is how I'm gonna deal with *this*."

Lauren marches off, with Henry close behind.

Henry again waits at the door outside of his own hotel room, listening to the argument unfold. He hears Lauren's profanity and considers barging in to end the quarrel but stays put a little longer. Lauren emerges soon enough, tears flowing down her cheeks.

"Bitch!" she declares out loud, slamming the door behind her. "What a whack-job! I can't believe after what I went through, she still doesn't trust me. I'm almost six months sober!"

This is unexplored territory for Henry. He's angry that Lauren treats her mother with such contempt, especially now, but he restrains himself.

"So, what did you two decide?"

"*We* decided nothing. *She* told me that if I don't go with you, I won't have a place to live when we get back home. Talk about manipulation!"

"So, you're going with me, then?"

"Looks that way, Henry."

"Oh, God. Fine. It'll be okay," Henry says to convince himself as much as her. "We have to leave soon. Why don't you pack up for two days? I'll see about getting an extra room for you."

"Yes, you do that. I'm sure as hell not staying with you."

Right. The less said the better, he figures.

Lauren bolts to her room, three doors down. Henry heads to the lobby to get some help with tonight's hotel in Antofagasta. He hesitates along the way.

Shit! I didn't bank on this. Am I doing the right thing?

He stays the course. The Cañón de Atacama concierge reserves an extra room for Lauren at the hotel in Antofagasta; and while Henry doesn't request it, Lauren's assigned the room adjoining his. He's uncertain but says nothing. *Maybe it's best to keep a close eye on her.* The concierge also manages to secure Paranal's last tiny room, normally reserved for the Directors, for the next night.

Henry's cell phone reads 3 p.m. Time to get going. *If we're lucky, we'll make it to Antofagasta by 7:30.*

CHAPTER 54

Parts Unknown

Isabel's in a deep sleep. There's a big glass of water next to her on the nightstand. I kiss her on her warm and damp forehead as I take my leave. I slip from the room, close the door behind me, and sling my backpack over one shoulder.

I knock on Lauren's door but there's no answer. I knock again, louder. I go around the back of her unit, and standing on its cement patio, peek inside through a glass door. The lights are on, but no sign of Lauren. Maybe she's in the lobby, and so I head there.

A white Nissan Altima is parked in the circle under the porte-cochere. I figure it's my rental car and get the keys at the front desk. The clerk hasn't seen a pretty twenty-two year-old girl. I return to the car, toss my bag into the trunk and head back inside to continue my search.

Maybe she's getting something to eat before we go. Maybe she convinced Mateo to return, and they're sitting on that same sofa again, waiting for me to show up. Maybe, but I don't think so.

I cross paths with a small Latina housekeeper, about my age, who just entered the hotel through a side door. I get her attention.

"Excuse me, miss, do you speak English?"

"Sí, poquito."

"I look for a girl," I say, shading my eyes with my right hand pretending to scan the horizon, as if I'm the Lone Ranger explaining to Tonto that we're on a search mission.

"Sí?"

"She is twenty-two years old, very pretty, bonita, and tall," I say, now bringing my hand to the bridge of my nose. "Dark hair," I add, and grab a tuft of my own.

"Sí. La vi. Tomó una bicicleta."

"A bicycle?"

"Sí, una bicycle."

"Where? Donde?"

"Venga, te mostraré," and she motions me to follow her.

She takes me outside through the same side door and points to a bicycle rack with four hybrids standing unlocked within its grid.

"Holy shit!" I blurt out. "Oh God, lo siento. Which way?" I ask, now in full panic. "Donde?!"

She points toward the hotel's exit. I commandeer the largest of the bicycles, hoping that I'm not committing larceny. Soon enough, I realize that even this one's too small as, with each revolution of the pedal, my knee nearly knocks me in the chin. As my legs gyrate, I speed toward the hotel gate, hoping to head her off at the pass, without a clue as to where that might be.

CHAPTER 55

Licancabur

Lauren's been riding less than three minutes, but she's breathing hard: a smoker not accustomed to altitude or exercise. She nears the end of the sheer canyon wall. As a result of some ancient geological violence, the last few hundred feet of the gorge angle downward to the grade of the dry-earth road. Here, she sees a sign that reads *Monumento Arquelógico Pukará,* and she stops.

Behind the sign, people are snaking their way down a large hill of rock and red sand. It was likely part of the precipitous gorge at one time, but now, slanted and weathered, it's a more manageable climb. Her eyes follow the narrow path up the hill to see that it reaches the height of the ravine wall that extends back to the hotel.

I can do this. Fuck her.

Lauren swings her leg over the bicycle and parks it against the base of the hill. She climbs the twenty or so stone steps that lead to the winding dirt pathway upward.

She doesn't listen. She thinks she knows me. She has no idea! She only wants to control me. I should've never come back.

Now on the parched stone-lined pebbly trail, Lauren serpentines her way up the rugged mound, passes those she saw heading down, and leaves any vestige of an oasis below. A third of the way up and feeling her chest heave, she stops to catch her breath. She looks down to the road and sees Henry riding the ill-fitted hybrid, pumping his legs as would a three-year-old on his new Christmas tricycle. She can't help but giggle.

How adorkable! He and Mom sure make a strange couple together.

Henry stops, eyes the sign, and spots her bicycle ditched at the side of the road. He looks up, sees Lauren looking down at him. He frantically waves. She hears him call out to her in a faint voice, but she turns to continue her climb.

Lauren is at the top of the massive hill when her pursuer finally catches up to her. She's had a minute to recover and is absorbed by something other than Henry's pursuit. The snow-capped volcano Licancabur stands east and slightly north in all its grandeur, with the half-moon just starting its ascent, hanging behind the mountain like a fixture in the cloudless blue sky.

"It's beautiful, isn't it?" Henry gasps.

Lauren fails to respond. She just gazes at the awe-inspiring vista, a giant earthen cone that rises from the desert floor to the heavens.

"That's Licancabur," he says.

"It *is* beautiful," she says. "It's more than beautiful."

They pause together to take in the spectacle.

"And those are the ruins," Henry says pointing down and to the left to the stone foundations that are all that remain of what appears to have been a small village built into the hillside.

"Must have been prime real estate back then," he says. "It served as an Atacameño fort. We were going to do this hike together, the three of us, one afternoon."

Lauren's silent. The words of the old indigenous woman echo in her mind. *Alone in the desert is dangerous. Go to the mountaintop and see things from there.* She didn't climb this hill because of what the old woman said, but now grasps at her meaning.

"You could touch the moon from on top of that mountain," Lauren says with quiet emotion, continuing to focus on the volcano that stands in the distance.

"Are you all right?" Henry asks.

"Yes, Henry. I'm sorry I dragged you up here," she says turning to him. She's now at ease and introspective. Whatever anger she felt has abated like the wind at the end of a storm. She senses a new awareness and a power within.

"Do you think she will ever trust me?"

"I do. She needs time, and frankly, so do you. You may think you're different now, and maybe you are, but your mom hasn't seen that yet with her own eyes. Put yourself in her shoes."

"Yes, I know you're right. I was just angry."

"Well it's good that you can articulate that. If I may say, you suddenly seem calm, more mature than just an hour ago."

"Yeah, I blow hot and cold, huh?"

Henry smiles.

"So, will you come with me to Paranal, Lauren? It's not what we planned, for sure, but it'll be different. If you want to prove something to your mother, this would be a good opportunity."

"Fine. I'll go on your little road trip with you under one condition: you don't speed like that lunatic driver we had this morning."

"Gee, was that this morning? Seems like ages ago. Okay, you're on," and after another minute of reflection, the two start their trek together down the trail.

CHAPTER 56

Across the Desert

I peek in at Isabel from the doorway and see her asleep under the covers. I scribble her a sweet note and inch out of the room. Lauren's outside waiting for me with a duffle at her feet. In a few minutes, we buckle into the white Altima, still in the circle. Per my request to the staff, there are a couple of sandwiches, cookies, and bottles of Sprite in the front seat for the long ride. I set my rent-a-car navigation to the oceanside hotel in Antofagasta, and we're on the road for the Pacific coast.

First things first. Lauren dons her headphones and connects her iPhone to the Nissan's USB port to minimize battery drain. It's amazing, the survival skills a young woman must master in the desert. But I'm fine with her plugging into the car, and unplugging from the world, while I get comfortable with my bearings.

By the way, Lauren's wrong. No matter what Isabel had in mind when she cast me out into this wasteland, this *is* about me; it's my test too. Sure, it's a bit of a cliché to acknowledge while crossing the Atacama, that I've been wandering forty years in search of my own promised land. Yet, with metaphoric irony, it pretty much all comes down to this: can I make it through the desert with Isabel's daughter without major fireworks?

Lauren's just your average, somewhat immature, impulsive bi-polar twenty-two-year-old with a history of serious trauma, drugs, alcohol, and jail. Yet, she was so calm and thoughtful on top of that hill. She's savvy and sassy, and takes her meds religiously, we presume. How hard can this be? How easy it would have been for Moses had he just had a driver's license and credit card.

But why am I even doing this? Isabel exposes a different side when it comes to protecting and controlling her daughter, and I'm not sure I like it. Perhaps I should've resisted. When she treats Lauren like a child, *I* get the fuzzy end of the lollipop.

We're back on Route 23 heading west into the sun. At this pace, it'll be at least an hour before passing through Calama, and I'd love some music.

"Hey, Lauren?"

She turns her head.

"What are you listening to?"

"Fletcher," she says, with a purse of the lips and wrinkle of the brow.

I've got her now.

"'Wasted Youth'?" I ask.

She smiles broadly and removes the headphones.

"One would think," she says, nodding slowly. "Actually, it's 'Undrunk'."

"Equally fitting," I respond without hesitation. "The lyrics are a little out there for me, but I'm old."

"Yes, yes you are, Henry, and that's why it's so cool."

"So, you want to move it to the speakers so I can listen in on your playlist?"

"Sure, *Enrico*. It would be my pleasure."

With that, and as easy as falling off a log, she makes the connection. "Undrunk" is not my favorite Fletch song, but it's a start.

"What else you got," I ask when it's over.

"What do you like? I've got it all."

"Classical, too?"

"Classic *rock*."

"I was thinking along the lines of Chopin, or Saint-Saëns," I respond.

"Sorry, hundred year limit. You wanna try again?"

"Any jazz?"

"I have some jazz."

"Really, like what?"

"Lady Gaga?"

"Yeah, 'The Tramp'. She does great jazz. We can listen to that later. Any instrumentals?"

"You mean, without a singer?"

"Yes."

"No, I don't get those, especially when they play stuff as random as my hair in the morning."

She's cute, and I laugh.

"Ah, improvisation," I respond. "I love your comparison, but I thought you of all people would understand."

"Huh? No."

"Shall we move onto rock, then?" I ask.

"Yeah, that's easy."

"What kind of rock do you listen to?" I ask.

"All kinds, if it's good."

I glance in my rearview mirror and see headlights appear in the distance.

"What do *you* like best?" she asks.

"I don't get hung up on genres, either. I agree, it's all about quality."

"Okay. You drive and I'll DJ."

She starts with some Ariana Grande, a wonderfully-talented contemporary diva. I'm just thankful it's not "7 Rings". My parents were enthralled with Julie Andrews and would sit Raff and me in front of a TV, with Connecticut's first laser disc player. While I could watch Mary Poppins a thousand times, by the fifth go-round of the Sound of Music, it was *not* one of my favorite things.

I peer again into the mirror. It's an oversized gray pickup that edges closer, now on our tail on this two lane highway.

Lauren sees me looking up, and she looks back.

"Pay no mind. He'll pass me if he wants," I advise.

She turns to face forward as Christina Aguilera sings "Fall in Line". Lauren has a thing for female vocalists, as do I.

At this moment, on a straightaway, the pickup decides to make its move. There's some sort of truck barreling toward us in the opposite direction. I'm doing a hair above sixty, so the pickup has plenty of time to get around. I maintain our speed.

I can see now that the advancing truck is a huge tractor hauling a giant backhoe chained to a low-boy. The pickup is now by our side and for some odd reason, slows to match our pace. There's a young Latino in the passenger seat. His mouth moves as he gazes past me to check Lauren out. Jerk! I decelerate to let them pass. There's still time, but it's dicey.

It's when the pickup thrusts forward and makes for safety ahead of us in the appropriate lane, that I see a silver Mercedes sedan behind it, also intending to pass. Utter insanity! It's right beside me now, in the eastbound lane, but it's too late! All in an instant, the truck driver blasts his horn and brakes hard as the huge twenty-two wheeler skids off the road at breakneck speed. It slides over the narrow shoulder and into the flat desert sand, as the low-boy hurls stones and dust into our windshield. In the same moment, the Mercedes driver jams his brakes and swerves back into the right lane, inches behind us, missing the head-on collision with the truck by half a second.

But it's Lauren's spine chilling scream that causes me to lose control. We careen onto the shoulder, spin 180 degrees, and land to face east in soft sand. The Mercedes honks at us like an angry goose as it flies past and soon disappears. All that's heard are Lauren's loud unrestrained sobs, the end of the song, and the hum of the Altima's engine.

I shut off the music and, for a second, lower my head into the steering wheel. Then I take a deep breath and look over at Lauren, trembling, crying.

"You're okay. Relax. We're fine. Nothing happened."

"NOTHING HAPPENED?!" she retorts. "ARE YOU FUCKING OUT OF YOUR MIND?!!"

Still shaking, she clasps her purse and tries to grab a cigarette from the pack.

"No one got hit. Everyone's all right!"

"I'M NOT ALL RIGHT!" Tears fall onto her face like rain drops on a leaf. "You're an idiot! You weren't watching! You were all about the music and nearly got us killed!"

She finally manages to pinch on a cigarette and lights up.

"That's not true! It wasn't my fault! It was the asshole in the Mercedes! He should never have pulled that stunt!"

I see the tractor-trailer pulling out of the desert and back onto the road, final proof of this small miracle. Lauren sobs and trembles while she sucks on her Camel. I try a new tactic and take her hand in mine.

"That must have been a hell of a scare for you," I say.

We sit there like that for an awkward minute while she continues to whimper. Finally, she retracts her hand, opens her window to clear the air, and stops crying.

"Holy shit! I can't believe that just happened! I can't stop shaking. What the fuck!"

I see her whole body quiver, like she's just crawled out of a frozen lake after falling through the ice. She rebuffs me when I start to put my arm around her.

"I've been through this before, Henry. It turned out real bad!"

"Yes, I know."

"You know?"

"It was back near Tucson, in the desert."

"Mom told you?" She flicks out the butt through the window and looks into my eyes, like she's seeing me for the first time.

"Yes, she told me; and I was there."

"What?! What do you mean you were there?!"

I urge her to relax, like instructing a mixed martial arts fighter to lighten up before heading into the Octagon. We're still on the road's edge. I decide to stay put while I explain the circumstances of my trip back from Kitt Peak that night.

"Oh my God!" she exclaims. "I remember you! A little car we nearly ran off the road a minute before the accident. Your car? I'll never forget. The car and Imagine Dragons; then their fucking video games." She drags on the cigarette. "Game over for Brittany and Donovan. That was you in that car, Henry?" she asks; she accuses. "How is that possible?!"

"It was 'Believer'. I was listening to the same damn song, but I forgot it until now. How strange."

We're silent for a half minute, trying to distill what we can from our coincidental connection to the tragedy.

"Can we get going, Lauren? I'll be careful. Better to drive in the light."

"Sure."

I pull back onto an empty road.

"Are you all right?" I ask.

"I don't know."

"Do you want to listen to more music?"

"No. Not now."

We drive without a word for ten minutes. My cell phone rings. It's Isabel. She still sounds weak, but I'm heartened to hear her voice. She says she feels a bit better, but exhausted. My description of the ride is, for the most part, a fabrication. I motion to Lauren, offering her the phone, but she refuses. The call ends with expressions of love. Lauren and I ride in silence a minute longer. We pass through Calama and pick up Route 25 South toward Antofagasta.

Lauren's question comes out of the blue.

"Henry, what exactly are you doing down here?"

I'm glad to talk about something positive.

"I'm researching a book," I respond.

She encourages me to explain.

"Do you know anything about cosmology?" I ask.

"Sure, why? If I can keep it together, I'm going to salon school in about six months. People say I have a natural flair for it."

I bite my lip; she notes my reaction.

"What did I say? I can be good at it."

"I don't doubt that for a second, Laur. I apologize. If I said cosmetology, I meant to say cosmology. It's easy to confuse the two. Cosmology is the study of the universe; you know, space," I say, pointing my forefinger up at the sky.

"I'm so stupid."

"Simple mistake. I confuse those words all the time."

It's nice to hear her giggle.

"I should have just said astronomy. I love the stuff. My book is about different ways things might end."

"What do you mean, end?"

"You know, the science behind the end of the world. An asteroid the size of Manhattan collides with Earth at 50,000 miles per hour; or the sun gets brighter and turns the whole planet into a desert, like this one," I say, "but way hotter. Or the sun fizzles out instead and becomes a red giant that envelopes us in a blazing . . "

"STOP!"

"What?"

"STOP! Who do you think you're talking to, Henry?!"

Oh my God, what now?

"Do you know how hard this is? There isn't a day that goes by that I don't think about a bottle of beer, or doing shots, or getting high. Give me a half hour in any town back home, and I'll scrounge up a dealer hawking anything you want. Every time I go into a restaurant, the first thing they ask me is, 'can I get you something to drink?'" she says in a nasally voice. "You know, they're not talking about apple juice. And you're telling me the world's coming to an end? Doesn't exactly inspire me to stay on the straight and narrow."

Oh God. Am I the one who keeps stepping in it? How do I turn this ride around? I remain composed.

"I feel for you, Lauren," I say, hoping not to sound too patronizing, "but most of the things I'm talking about won't happen for a billion years. Even the asteroid strike is unlikely to occur in your lifetime, and they're tracking NEOs years in advance so we can avoid them."

She sighs, seemingly spent. It hasn't exactly been an easy ride for her either.

"NEOs?" she asks quietly.

"Near-Earth objects."

"You mean they can predict which ones will hit us, and like, we can punch a hole in it to nuke the thing?" she asks.

"Well, that wouldn't work. What they might do is crash a ship into it at 20,000 mph to throw it slightly off course. Easier than a weightless drilling expedition."

She takes a deep breath, and we go silent for a minute.

"Sorry," she says. "In case you haven't noticed, I tend to shoot first, and ask questions later."

"Indeed, I *have* noticed."

I look over at her. Her lips turn upward, creating star-quality dimples, perfectly symmetrical, on both cheeks.

"So, here's a question, Henry. Why are you writing about things that won't happen for a billion years, when there's all sorts of shit that I'm legit worried about that's happening right now?"

She grabs another Camel, cracks the window, lights up and

waits patiently for my answer. No one ever asked me *that*. I take a moment to ponder, while we continue down the desolate road. Out of the corner of my right eye, I see miles of flat rock and sand lying between us and a setting sun. I glance at her watching me, waiting, with perhaps something of a smug look on her face.

I could make up a logical answer. It's an economic decision. There's so much written already about topical issues. I don't have much of value to add. It's risky, but I stick with the truth.

"Honestly, it's the cosmos that I love, and to write about anything else now, would feel like a betrayal."

"Wow! It all sounds pretty gushy to me, even coming from a nerd."

"A nerd? Like mother, like daughter, I guess."

"Mother might be jealous the way you talk about the cosmos."

"It's 'A Different Kind of Love'," I quip.

"I know that song! Brendan James! He's cute, even though he's probably your age. I love piano players."

"Yes, he's got a sweet voice for an old timer like me."

She laughs, finally.

"So, tell me about your cosmic love. Where's the romance in it, the mystique?"

That's easy. I tell her to sit back and relax, for it's a long story. She has a lemon cookie and then unfurls the aluminum foil around a chicken salad sandwich. She eats as my narrative unfolds.

I tell her about Copernicus, Galileo, Hubble, and more. I describe Hubble's quest to measure the size of the expanding universe and follow up with the recent discovery that the expansion is accelerating, not slowing, as expected. Gravity ought to have slowed the expansion, I tell her; even reverse it, drawing the cosmos in closer together. Why is this happening?! So, scientists created a place-holder for the elusive answer: an unknown force that counteracts gravity, and they named it - *dark energy*.

She wrestles with the concept.

"That's cheating!" she concludes.

"That's theory," I say. "It's the way science progresses."

Yet, I admit to myself that dark energy is unlike most hypotheses that are grounded in a series of gradual intellectual advances, one small step after another. This theory seems to necessitate more a colossal leap.

"It's even more incredible," I continue, "when one considers that, according to our best calculations, the dark forces make up ninety-six percent of the mass of everything in the universe, and that the other four percent is what we can see or measure. It's a fantastic gap in knowledge and the greatest scientific mystery of our time. There's your mystique, Lauren."

"But that's ridiculous," she says. "Last week, they figured it all out. Then, this week, they realize that they only figured out four percent of it? So, they make up an answer for what's missing, hoping to fill in the blank next week, so they can go on believing what they thought they knew last week. How do they get away with this shit?!"

She's quite intuitive for someone with just a GED. I don't answer. I'm sure of one thing, and maybe only one thing. We know a lot more today than we did five hundred years ago. It may take another five hundred years to get this answer, or we may never get it.

She doesn't wait for my response.

"Anyway, why are we going to the observatory tomorrow?"

A leading question that takes me to a brief discourse on gravitational waves. My meetings with Ralston at ALMA on Monday, and Jose Hernandez-Navarro at Paranal, tomorrow, concern their collaborations with the guys with the lasers and their efforts to determine, once and for all, the rate of the universe's expansion.

Lauren sums up.

"Okay, that was different; but I've got to say, listening to this stuff gives me a huge headache. It's so bizarre. I can't believe there are people who spend their lives just thinking about this. And they tell us *our* disease is all about escaping reality."

What can anyone say to that?

"I do have one more question. With the universe getting bigger and bigger, how does your book end?"

She asks as if I'm writing a novel. My answer's brief.

"There are several theories. Regardless, keep in mind that it'll be billions of years before anything happens; so not to worry. Most scientists support the Big Freeze, when all the energy in the universe just runs out; but my personal favorite is the Big Rip, where everything down to the last atom tears apart."

"Oh my God, those poor people!"

At this, she queues up some Phil Collins and chows down the remaining cookies. In another fifteen minutes, we reach the small coastal city of Antofagasta, and pull up to a modern ten story box-type hotel situated on the Pacific shore. It's dark out, and I'm looking forward to bed. What a fucking long day.

CHAPTER 57

Opportunity

I'm alone in my hotel room, finally. I lean over the sink in my gray boxers and tee-shirt to brush my teeth. I glance up at the mirror to see an unappealing reflection of myself: bloodshot eyes, like those of a heavy drinker, a teenager's oily complexion, and a multitude of course black hairs, like poppyseeds on a bagel, overtaking my face. I look like crap. Too tired to floss.

Lauren's in the adjoining room, I assume. We parted ways in the hall, where she agreed that she'd be packed and ready by eight. Inside, we're separated by a thick wooden dead-bolted door. I don't hear a peep from her, and that's fine.

I'm so relieved the day is over. The race to the geezers seems like weeks ago; and with Isabel's surprise illness, a chase up a small mountain, and near death in the desert, I'm done with the babysitting gig, at least until tomorrow. Let's face it, I'm one person. Any surveillance on Lauren at this point would require a Secret Service detail.

Yet, I do have a heightened appreciation for Isabel's situation. Poor thing. I haven't heard from her since our brief talk earlier and dare not to wake her with another call. Wish she were here, for more reasons than one.

I spit, rinse, and walk over to the window where I brush aside the blackout curtains. My seventh floor view is over a brightly lit pool patio supported on one side by stacks of giant boulders that emerge from the ocean bottom. Pacific waves crash against the rocks, spraying white foam caught in the artificial light.

I find my baggie of mini-bottles in my backpack and pour out a vodka into a plastic cup, setting it by my bedside. I link my iPad to the hotel's Wi-Fi for a quick game of solitaire. I'm not worried about tomorrow's interview, for which I'm prepared. I just need the drink and a moment to chill before sleep, at least that's what I tell myself.

I hear a knock at the door.

"Uno minuto!" My reflexive response.

How do you say in Spanish, "Who the f is there?!"

Without thinking, I grab a white terry cloth towel from the bathroom and wrap it around my boxers, and open the door, but no one's in the hallway.

What the hell?!

I hear the knock again, louder this time. It's from within. Shit!

"Henry, are you up?"

Oh Lord! It's Lauren, calling in a muffled voice through our common portal. What now? Can I ignore her?

"Are you there?"

Pretend I'm asleep?

"Henry!"

Oh my God.

"Yeah, what's up?!" I yell.

"I need a favor," Lauren pleads as if her life depends on it.

"I'm in bed. Can't it wait until tomorrow?"

"No, it can't. I need it now. It's an emergency."

Really? Crap!

"Okay, one second."

I lay the towel aside and throw on my jeans. I stash the cup of vodka and bag of mini's in the bathroom. She's just starting to believe I *don't* have a problem.

I unlock the door between our two rooms. She barges in past me, wrapped in her own terry cloth towel. It covers only the bare minimum, and she's damp from a shower.

"Lauren, what the hell do you want?!"

"Don't get all riled up at me. You took me through the fucking desert today and now I've got lizard skin, it's so dry. I need you to put some lotion on my back."

"Really? That's your emergency?!"

"Yes."

"Really?!"

"Yes, really!"

"Oh, Lord."

"I haven't asked you for anything all day. You nearly got us killed. You weirded me out with your story about the accident back in Tucson, and you bored me to tears for two hours talking about your cosmic fixation. I can't sleep until I know my skin is soft."

"Okay, fine! Where's the lotion?!"

"I'm sure you have some in the bathroom."

Seriously? What is this about? She's half naked, and asking me to rub lotion on her? Why is she doing this?

I head into the bathroom and find a little bottle of Verbena and Lavender. I return to see Lauren sprawled face-down on the bed, her breasts pressed against the sheets, with the towel covering only her ass, nothing more.

"Lauren, what are you doing?!"

"What?! I thought it would be easier if I just lied down."

"Easier for what?!"

She giggles into a pillow.

"I don't know what the hell you're thinking, but you've got me all wrong," I insist.

I've never had such a perfect specimen of a young woman in my bed, ready and waiting. For a fleeting instant, and not for a millisecond longer, if I didn't have so much to lose, I think I might go for it.

Times up.

"You've got to leave, Lauren. This isn't right!"

"Henry, do you think I'm pretty?!"

Holy shit.

"Yes, of course, you're very pretty. But I'm in love with your mother! Not you! I thought that was obvious."

She giggles again.

"Don't worry, I'm just teasing. Put the lotion on me and I'll stop bothering you. Promise."

"No, I don't think the lotion's a good idea. Why don't you just go, and I'll see you tomorrow?"

"No, I'm not moving until you put the lotion on. Maybe you need the towel to come off?"

Oh my God!

"No, fine. I'll do it. Don't move!"

Hands shaking, I twist open the bottle, lean over her, and pour the fragrant lotion between her shoulder blades. From there, and with haste, I rub it all around with the palm of my hand, up to her neck and shoulders, down her contoured sides to the small of her back. The towel starts lower from there, but I venture no further. I try to not feel, but she's soft as velvet. Lizard skin, my ass.

"Ooh, that's nice," she exclaims.

"Ooh, you're done," I say, moving away from the bed.

"A little more, please?"

"No, that's it. Get out now! I mean it."

Again, she titters, innocently, like a young girl.

"Okay. Why don't you turn around while I get up?"

I happily obey and hear her rise from the bed to adjust the towel.

"You can look now."

Afraid what I'll see, I face her, and indeed we're back at square one, when she first came in.

"Thanks. Sleep well," she says.

Lauren leans over, lifting her right leg behind her like a ballerina, and kisses me on the cheek. She saunters toward the common doorway. I keep my eyes fixed upon her, as if to assist with her departure. As Lauren crosses the threshold, she pauses, then drops the towel to her feet. She stands there motionless, facing forward into her room.

My focus is instantly narrowed: not at her backside, per se, which is as supple and perfectly formed as anything in nature; but at something that doesn't belong, a conspicuous anomaly: thick, dark and slightly-raised horizontal scars; four, maybe five in number, defacing her bottom, like a vandal's angry slashes in the canvas of the *Mona Lisa*. Then, without looking back, Lauren pushes the towel forward with her foot, and vanishes into her room, shutting the door behind her.

I slide the deadbolt, walk into the bathroom and down the vodka in two gulps. I refill the cup with the last of the five shots, lay it on the nightstand, take off my jeans and slip into bed. I forego my iPad, and instead, prop pillows against the headboard, sit up, and while savoring the calming heat of the alcohol, contemplate what just happened.

CHAPTER 58

Revelation

It's eight a.m. I knock on Lauren's door from out in the hallway. It quickly opens, and she stands there, with a hint of mascara, glossy lips, and a bright smile. Her rolling duffle and purse sit in front of her on the floor. Her dark brown hair is in a single braid, and in her blue slacks, sandals, and a crisp white blouse, she might be heading to a job interview, or a photo shoot, and she seems ten years older.

"Morning, Henry! How did you sleep?"

At least *she's* in a cheery mood.

"Fine, I guess. Looks like you're ready to go."

"I told you, I've been getting up early for five months. It's not so hard." She's still beaming.

I'm dumbfounded. I figured on having a hard time getting her up and on the road. I feared the lunacy from last night carrying over to this morning. Still imprinted on my mind, is that last image of her: raw beauty coupled with the aberrant evidence of violence; a magnificent figure cut from marble, course and abrasive in spots, finely polished in others. She's Rodin's *La Danaïd*: fragile, vulnerable, desperate; her pain and sorrow concealed by a seductive veneer.

Now, it's almost as if last night never happened. How do I deal with this? Regardless, I won't be telling Isabel about it, at least not anytime soon.

"New outfit?" I ask Lauren, trying to keep up a conversation.

"Yeah, I made Mom take me shopping before we left."

"Very nice, but will you be comfortable looking so . . . ?"

"Looking so what, Henry?"

"Professional?"

"Yeah, I'm totally fine," she answers easily. "You're the one with the important meeting today. I didn't want to embarrass you looking like some messed up kid. But what about you? Are you really doing your interview in that?" She titters, pointing at me.

I'm purposely wearing my *I Need My Space* tee-shirt. I thought if anyone would get a chuckle out of it, it would be a research astrophysicist stuck for weeks at a time in the desert.

"No, I'm cool with it. It's my good-luck tee-shirt. I met your mom in it."

"And it worked?"

"Yeah, I guess it did, but it's a long story. How about breakfast before we leave?"

"Good idea. I'm starving."

We make our way down the hall and onto an elevator. I smell a hint of lilac on her. She presses "1" and starts to hum a song.

"Gosh, you're in a good mood." Wish I slept more.

"Yes, I am. Enjoy it while you can." She grins.

The hotel restaurant is filled with local business types sitting at small white linen tables for a typical Chilean breakfast of toast and sweetened tea. As we make our entrance, heads turn to stare at Lauren, who seems oblivious to her own allure. We eat eggs, sausages, and pancakes off the buffet. I drink plenty of coffee. Lauren recounts yesterday's most notable events, as if to assimilate them now after the easing of tensions.

She reviews the race to the geysers, the strange warnings spoken by the old Atacameña at the llama stand, her own escape from the hotel on the bicycle and, with good-natured giggles, my frantic pursuit up the steep rocky hill. She tells me about looking out onto the great volcano, as if I weren't there to share the same view.

She's animated and laughs heartily through breakfast. She teases me and pokes fun at herself at every opportunity, but only mentions her mother's illness in passing. She also says little about our near-accident in the desert. As for her late-night stunt with the lotion, it may just as well have been my strange dream.

We're on the road to Paranal in less than an hour. I set the rent-a-car GPS while Lauren hooks up her iPhone. We stop for gas. While I fill the tank, my phone rings. It's Isabel.

"Iz, I'm so glad you called. How are you?"

Thankfully, she continues to improve, but will give it one more day in bed, reading and watching Chilean TV. I'm so relieved. Of course, she asks about Lauren.

"Lauren? Sure, everything's fine. Things became easier once we got on the road. She's actually in a really good mood today."

Now, it's Isabel who's grateful. Then she apologizes for getting sick and thrusting her daughter upon me.

"Don't be silly, love. Things couldn't be better."

I'm surprised how easily these lies roll off my tongue. I need to square this all up with Lauren. It's two hours to Paranal, enough time together to coax a serious discussion about last night, if only to get it behind us.

I open the door on Lauren's side, and hand her the phone to say hello to her mom, while I replace the gas cap and wait for my automated receipt. She hands me the phone back as soon as I get behind the wheel. I hear Isabel promise to ping me later in the day, and we say our goodbyes.

As we pull away from the petrol station and onto the desert highway, Lauren's loquacious and carefree mood continues.

"Can you tell me why it's so fucking dry here?" she asks as if only first noticing our barren surroundings.

I explain the topographical reasons for the Atacama, as we continue our drive through the desert.

"Is Mars really like this?" she wonders.

She then goes on to question me about the other planets, generally continuing where we left off from yesterday's ride. We discuss astrology and the constellations. She asks about Earth's position in the galaxy, and she wants to hear again about dark energy and the ever-expanding universe. I can't figure her out. Has she really gotten into this stuff, or is she just humoring me? It doesn't matter. After a while, she's reached her limit.

"Okay, enough of this science stuff!" Lauren exclaims. "How does Mom listen to this twenty-four-seven?" goading me.

"I swear, we don't talk about this more than six hours a day." I can't help but grin. "Seriously? There's a beauty to it, like that mountain you stared at so long up on Pukará. Your mom's into it also because it's new to her, and she's smart and inquisitive. She asks a lot of questions."

"Way too many," I hear Lauren mutter.

I talk over her. "You have to dig down deep into something to really understand it, appreciate it." I pause. "Same goes for people, sometimes." As I say this, I turn my head for a moment to look at her with a knowing glance. She purses her lips, and I focus back on the road.

"You know, I'm sort of proud of myself for getting your mom to open her eyes to the cosmos, but that's all I did. She was the one to open her mind to it."

We're silent for a minute. Did any of this register with her? I have no clue. We switch our focus back to her music playing through the car's speakers. I'm impressed. Her collection goes as far back as the fifties. She starts with Johnny Cash's "Folsom Prison Blues" and plays a little of the Isley Brothers and Chuck Berry. Then she nails it for me by selecting the best of classic soft rock: *Crosby, Stills & Nash Greatest Hits.*

First up is, "Suite: Judy Blue Eyes", and we hear ourselves quietly singing along with the band. Any reticence soon falls by the way-side, and we take turns belting out a nasal rendition of "Southern Cross", starting from the chorus. After a few stanzas, she hits the pause button.

"What's so special about the Southern Cross?" she asks me.

"We saw it that night at the hotel, remember?" I reply.

"I guess."

"It's the smallest of all constellations, but the most important down here in the southern hemisphere. It was a key to naviga-tion, and the ancients believed it to be their portal to reincarna-tion. Without knowing their fate, the souls of the dead would walk through the center of the Southern Cross hoping for another life."

Lauren hits play as she lets this sink in. We listen quietly.

Then I glance over at her, and see tears sliding down her cheeks. Oh, no.

I reach over to turn off the sound, keeping one eye on the road.

"Hey, what's up? You okay? You were so happy a minute ago."

"No, I'm *not* okay. I'm a real idiot. I can't get anything right," she replies, between sobs.

I look up at the rearview mirror. There's not a soul in sight. I pull over into the sand, as if we're in a Mars rover, and stop. I undo my seatbelt and turn to her.

"Are you talking generally, or are you thinking about something specific?"

"I guess, generally. I make such awful decisions. All the time. I can't seem to stop. I'm so ashamed."

"Listen. You've been through a lot for such a young person, but hey, there's no shame in it."

The tears flow faster, and mascara runs.

"Did Mom tell you?"

"Sure, about some of it. Maybe not everything."

"Did she tell you about that night at the bar?"

"Yes," I reply, recalling Isabel's tormented account of her daughter's rape.

"Did she believe me, then?!" She says, still crying.

"Yes. Why wouldn't she?"

"I don't know. I wasn't sure. Jack didn't."

"Your dad. Why didn't he believe you?"

"'Cause he's an asshole."

I sense an opening, aware of the risk.

"Lauren, I can't imagine what you endured. Tell me, but only if you want, did the guys at the bar give you, you know, those scars too? Not that I want to pry, if you don't want to talk about it."

"No! Anyway, that's not your business! You do want to pry!"

I refrain from pointing out that it was she who laid bare her violent history for me last night. Instead, I take the high road, with the first thing that pops into my mind.

"Okay, sure, I'm concerned! You're the daughter of the woman I want to marry!"

Lauren stops crying.

"Does she know that?!"

"No, not exactly."

"Have you talked about it with her?"

"No."

"So, she doesn't even know what you're thinking, does she?"

"Maybe not. You're the second person to know."

What I don't say is that I didn't exactly know it myself before I just said it.

"Wow, Henry. That's a big fucking deal. Do you think you can handle it?!"

"Meaning you?! Do I think I can handle you?! Is that what you mean?"

"Yeah. That's exactly what I mean."

"Yes. I got this, Lauren. You're not as badass as you think."

Tension falls away, and her lips turn upward.

"So, do you think she'll say yes?"

"I'm not sure, really."

"Well, maybe you should wait, then."

"Maybe you're right. Anyway, this was supposed to be about you. What were we talking about?"

"Something private." Lauren lowers her visor to look at her face in the mirror. She opens her purse for a tissue to wipe the mascara from beneath her eyes.

"Not that private," I respond.

"Shut up!"

"Yes, no doubt I will. So, it wasn't those assholes from the bar?"

"No, not them."

"Was there something else like that, that your mom may not have told me?"

"No. That was the worst she knew."

"Ah, so she doesn't know about this." I'm not surprised.

"No. I couldn't tell her."

I sit there and ponder. She waits, refusing to come out with it, but unwilling to shut the conversation down. Then it dawns on me. It's awful, but it fits: her rage and her inability to confide in Isabel.

"It was Jack."

Nothing.

"It was Jack, wasn't it?"

Her silence speaks a thousand words.

"Oh my God. It *was* Jack. Your own father. Damn!"

She trembles and starts to cry again.

"I was high as a kite, out of my mind. I stole from him."

"I don't give a shit what you did!!"

My own anger doesn't help, and I rein it in.

"Sorry. What I'm trying to say is that no matter what, you didn't deserve this. It's just wrong."

"He was drunk. He drinks, Henry. He found me. I was at the beach. He was insane! He lost it on me!"

She sobs quietly now. I put my arm around her. She buries her head into my lucky tee-shirt. For an instant, I'm back at Three Points. Then I sense relief in her, and within me. I release her, and we face each other.

"You can't say anything to Mom about this. I can't believe I told you," Lauren says, softly.

"My lips are sealed. I swear."

She pauses.

"Thank you," she says in a hushed tone. "I'm sorry."

"For what? Last night?" I ask.

Lauren nods.

"It's okay," I reply. "I guess you needed to tell someone. Thank you for trusting me."

There's nothing more to say, and I drive the car back onto the highway, toward Paranal.

CHAPTER 59

On the Precipice

Henry takes a right turn off Highway 710 South onto a perfectly paved two-lane driveway and starts the gradual westward climb to Paranal's main gate. The asphalt roadway winds its way up through the smooth, undulating foothills of the Chilean Coastal Range. But for the highway sign to the *Observatorio*, Henry might have missed the turnoff altogether, as the driveway's tan color blends with the surrounding pebbles and sand.

It's two miles to Paranal's entrance. Halfway there and over the rise, the mountaintop comes into view. Cerro Paranal stands at 9,000 feet, typical for this cordillera by the Pacific, but dwarfed by the Andean giants on the opposite edge of the Atacama.

Four shiny structures, the telescopes' housings, jut out from the summit. From this distance, they look like aluminum trash cans, but are in fact closer to the size of grain silos. Henry and Lauren can see the entire mountain as they approach the blue steel security gate. Beyond, the driveway snakes its way up to the flattened peak.

Each of the four great instruments alone make the list of the world's ten largest optical telescopes. Four smaller auxiliary telescopes, each with their own protective domes, are mounted on tracks, along which they're maneuvered to an optimal location each evening. All eight telescopes are linked below ground, and in combination, comprise Earth's most productive land-based research telescope, second only to the space-telescope, Hubble.

Paranal is the flagship of the European Southern Observatory. Next on ESO's list is ALMA. With a bit of whimsy, ESO named the Paranal installation the *Very Large Telescope*; or simply, VLT.

Henry presents his credentials. The lone security guard has been expecting them, and the gate opens. Henry is instructed in broken English to pull in front of the small white concrete visitor center, immediately to the left, and to go inside. Here, arrangements are quickly finalized. They're told to proceed back on the driveway to the Residencia, a mere five hundred feet on the left, and park in any of the visitors' spots.

They make their short drive to the hotel. They immediately come upon a compound of twenty or so white rectangular buildings off to the right. Henry studied online photos of Paranal for months, and he recognizes the compound at once.

"What do you think those are?" Lauren asks, pointing to the white buildings.

"Mainly maintenance and power supply for the whole facility, but there's a warehouse, a gym, even a gas station over there."

He pulls into the lot on their left. Lauren's puzzled.

"Where's the hotel? I don't get it."

"You'll see," Henry reassures.

As they leave the car, Lauren flicks the last of a smoldering cigarette onto the ground. They grab their bags from the trunk and head toward an area, an acre in size, of small rocks and sand. It appears like the natural desert, except completely flattened. A white glass dome, a hundred feet in diameter, protrudes a few feet from the surface. Looking toward it, they see into a concrete adobe-colored open-air corridor, that slants down into the earth.

"The hotel's built into the desert. See that rounded white glass bubble? It's the top of a skylight. The residence starts there, underneath. This ramp will bring us down to the entrance."

Lauren's still confused.

"You'll understand in a minute," Henry says. They proceed down the ten foot wide corridor. Its walls increase in height as they slowly descend. In a hundred feet, they're confronted by black double doors.

"Cool!" Lauren exclaims, as they push through the portal and into the hotel. They find themselves on a mezzanine walkway that leads to the reception area. The walkway circles around a tropical garden that emerges one level down and beneath the skylight they first saw from the outside.

"Yep, very cool. They put it underground to minimize light pollution. They used this hotel in a Bond movie, you know."

"Really? Which one?"

"*Quantum of Solace*. It was where the bad guys met in the Bolivian desert. The hotel got blown up, and Daniel Craig left the villain in the middle of nowhere with just a can of motor oil to drink, if he got that thirsty."

"Gross! I think I've seen it," she replies.

"It could easily happen here; I mean about leaving him in the desert to die."

The Observatory is surrounded by the Atacama, fifty times drier than Death Valley. Nothing more than a microbe can survive. It's desert sand, rocks, and mountains from Paranal to the Pacific, nine miles west. Even the coastline there, a narrow strip between the craggy foothills and the ocean's blue waters, is desolate, where the only sign of development is an empty dirt road identified as Route One. From Paranal, there is only barren, dry wasteland in every direction for hundreds of square miles.

As they make their way further into the Residencia, Henry notes the low roof lines, squared-off features, and the use of light wood, metal, and stone, all suggestive of a one-time modern design with a Scandinavian influence. They reach the front desk, and Henry confers with the clerk. Lauren turns to take another look at the garden, where tall green jungle plants reach almost as high as the skylight.

The clerk's been notified that Henry's interview has been put off until three, but that he's scheduled for a tour of the summit at 1:45. She offers to show them to their rooms, after which they will have time for lunch.

Henry's thoughts are now of Steinmetz, who not only introduced him to ALMA's Ralston, but who hooked him up with a room here at Paranal. The Residencia was built for scientists and staff, who otherwise must endure other-worldly conditions. Journalists are infrequently allowed. It's just dumb luck that a room was made available last minute to Lauren.

Henry also anticipates this evening. *This may be the best place on Earth to see the night sky. Conditions should be perfect. If only Isabel were here.*

The restaurant is more an upscale self-serve cafeteria. The food looks good, and there's plenty of it. A dozen men and women in animated discussions dine at long butcher-block tables. Some turn their heads to stare.

Henry and Lauren help themselves and sit across from one another at an empty table. Two young men carrying lunch trays soon approach to ask if they might join them. Lauren consents before Henry can get a word out. Introductions are made.

"Nice to meet you. My name is Thomas, and this is my colleague, Anders."

"Hello. I'm Henry, and this is Lauren."

"She is your daughter, maybe?" Thomas asks without hesitation.

"Yes," Lauren responds.

"No," Henry answers simultaneously.

After a slight pause, Henry splits the difference.

"I'm her stepfather," he says.

Lauren nods her head, smiling.

Both young men are first-year ESO Research Fellows who recently earned their doctorates. Thomas, who's Swiss, got his PhD in Astrophysics at the University of Texas, Austin. He spent four years in the USA, speaks fluent English, and is the more outgoing of the two. He's tall and athletic, and with his blond hair combed to the side, and deep blue eyes, he could just as easily be a footballer on the Zurich Grasshoppers as an astrophysicist.

Anders, on the other hand, although blond as well, is thin with rounded shoulders and a sallow complexion. He's beyond shy, but this doesn't stop Henry from engaging him.

"So, where are *you* from?" Henry asks.

"I am Danish," Anders responds, looking down at the table.

Lauren giggles like a teenager.

"So, do they have Danish where you come from?" she teases with an impish grin.

"Sure, I have heard dis before." Anders replies drolly, in a heavy accent. "I always say 'we have best Danish in de world'."

Thomas grins, but Anders seems bothered by the silliness. Nevertheless, Henry presses him further. Anders got his PhD at Lund University in Sweden, and is researching exoplanets, trying to find them in habitable zones within distant solar systems.

"I belief dare is life out dare," Anders confesses.

Henry nods in agreement. Lauren turns her attention to Thomas. She asks how long he'll be at Paranal, and if he's at all homesick. Thomas briefly describes his family back in Switzerland, but he confides that it's his Texas pals he misses most: their jocular attitudes, poker nights, and football. He never understood the fascination with guns, but he loved all that barbeque and beer.

"They really had me going my first year. They'd tell me, 'You eatin' roadkill, don't you know'," he says, faking a Texas drawl in his German-Swiss accent. "Up there, that means armadillo. I didn't care what it was, it was so good."

"I've never seen an armadillo," Lauren admits.

Henry describes it to her as a big rat wearing medieval armor.

"Seems that their instinct is to jump straight up when they sense danger," Henry adds. "So instead of running across the road, they get creamed by a pickup truck."

There's a brief gap in the conversation, then the young Swiss PhD turns toward Henry.

"I like your tee-shirt. So, are you a scientist?" Thomas asks. It's at this point that Anders excuses himself. He busses his tray and leaves.

"No. A science writer. I'm writing a book. I have an interview with Dr. Hernandez-Navarro at three."

"DHN. I know him well. He works closely with my mentor."

Before Thomas picks up his tray, he asks Lauren if he can show her around later. He'd meet her in the lobby at five. She's seems surprised but looks over to Henry for approval.

"Okay with me," Henry says, shrugging. "What will you do until then, Lauren? You can come on the tour with me if you want."

"No thanks, *Dad*," she says with a twinkle in her eyes. "I thought I would go outside for a smoke and maybe relax; catch some rays. I was promised a vacation, you know."

"Hope you have a good sunscreen with you? The UV here is very high," Thomas warns.

"I'll be careful."

"We have an indoor pool if you want to swim," he suggests.

"Good idea. Glad I brought my suit." Turning back to Henry. "I'll figure it out; don't worry. We'll meet back here for dinner; 'round seven?"

Henry nods, happy for a respite from fatherhood.

Henry and his guide, Sophia, stand together on the one-acre concrete platform atop Cerro Paranal. It's kidney-bean-shaped, with the inner, concave side comprising the summit's western edge. Three of the four Unit Telescopes sit evenly-spaced along this rim. The fourth is located on the platform's northeast corner. The control center is situated at the southwest corner, just outside of the platform and below grade.

Henry and Sophia stand on the concrete near to Unit Telescope 1, along the mountain's western rim. In their white ESO hard hats, they look like mismatched construction workers.

Sophia is a twenty-four year-old short, dark, and buxom woman from southern Chile. Serious and smart, she's part of a two-year ESO scholarship program, working on her PhD in Astronomy at the Universidad de Chile, in Santiago. Sophia's doing a three-month stint at Paranal under DHN's guidance. It's a long time for a student to be on site, but her advisor doesn't have the time to train someone else mid-project. He asked Sophia to show Henry around before the interview. She describes their west-facing vista.

"Those tall grasses and the security fence behind are at the rim of the mountain. Beyond that, what you see down there are the foot-hills of the Chilean Coastal Range, and there," she says, pointing to a gray-blue shimmering plane in the distance, "is the Pacific Ocean."

"Wow! How far is that?"

"The ocean? Fifteen kilometers from here."

"It's amazingly clear. Beautiful," Henry declares.

"Yes, the view from here is often changing, but it is always beautiful."

"And we're about 9,000 feet up?"

"Yes. 2,750 metros."

They admire the scene silently for a minute before moving toward Unit 1. Sophia describes the technical details of the telescope to Henry, who laps it in like a thirsty dog. Sophia then goes on to explain that each of the four unit telescopes is known by the Mapuche word for a certain planet or star in the southern sky.

"It is good to call these instruments by Mapuche names," she says. "Like most indígena, the Mapuche believe that men and woman are of the Earth, but also tied to the universe."

Henry and Sophia pass through the telescope's housing and go inside. The size and complexity of the main instrument astound him. It's shaped like an upside-down cone that supports a main mirror of eight meters. It's the mirror that captures and concentrates the light from the night sky.

Henry now scans the full interior of the silo-like enclosure to see the intertwining of giant motors, gear boxes, electrical panels and conduit, air ducts, and hydraulic lines, on or near the instrument or along the housing's perimeter.

"Amazing," he exclaims.

After exploring the interior of Unit 1 for a few minutes, Henry and Sophia find the exit. They come upon an outside staircase that leads down to the control center. It's filled with scientists and other staff working at Formica desks with laptops and open black loose-leaf manuals. LED monitors are mounted on the walls. There are fiber-glass drop ceilings, tiled floors, and acoustic partitions.

Henry muses. *Not very impressive for the brilliant work that gets done here.*

The tour is over, and they head back to the Residencia for Henry's interview with DHN. As they climb into her old Jeep Cherokee and start the drive down the mountain, Sophia asks Henry if he'll be heading back to Antofagasta afterward.

"No, actually, I managed to get a room in the Residencia."

"Oh. You are lucky. Look for Saturn this evening. She is in opposition and very near to Earth. She will be the earliest to rise," Sophia says, smiling for the first time.

"I will. Thank you."

"Also, the rooms are small, but the food is very good here."

"Yes, we had lunch with two of your research fellows. They seemed very nice."

"Oh, are you here with your wife?"

"No, her daughter," Henry responds, perpetuating the deception.

"Do you remember which fellows you met?"

"Yes, for sure. Anders and Thomas."

"Ah," she says, and her smile disappears.

It's 5:15. Thomas leans over the railing in the lobby to find Lauren doing a breaststroke underwater in the pool, adjacent to the tropical garden. She's in a black bikini, and when she surfaces, he shakes his head, whistles out a breath and calls to her.

"Lauren! Hello, down there! Sorry, I'm late. Do you still want to look around with me?"

She hears her name, glances up, and waves.

"Hi! Give me a minute. I'll throw on some clothes and meet you upstairs!"

"Great!" he shouts down to her. "Put on jeans and sneakers and bring a sweatshirt!"

Lauren climbs the pool's ladder, dons a coverup and flip-flops and hurries to her room. She arrives in the lobby twenty-five minutes later, showered, made up, with the arms of a brown hoody looped around her neck. Thomas, in khakis and a thin leather jacket, kisses her three times on her cheeks. She blushes, but smiles.

I love that; it's so French, she thinks.

"Are you up for an adventure?" Thomas asks.

"Sure!" she replies.

"C'mon, then, we don't have much time," he says.

"For what?"

"A little trip," he replies with mischief in his eyes.

They exit the Residencia, and he leads her to the parking lot.

They pass Henry's rented Altima and stop at a metallic blue BMW R1200RT, a powerful sport-touring motorcycle, that rests on its kickstand. The bike evinces sleek speed from its adjustable windshield to its passenger back rest.

Lauren's excited, yet hesitant.

"Is this yours?!"

"Yes. Why don't you come with me for a ride?"

"A Magic Carpet Ride?" she asks, playfully.

"Huh?"

"It's Steppenwolf. Never mind," she responds, discouraged. "I don't know, Thomas, I'm not so good with speed."

"It doesn't have to be fast."

"Honest, I'm a little nervous. I've never been on one before."

"As they say in America," he retorts in his bogus Texas accent, "thar's a first time for everythin'."

And here comes another bad decision, she thinks.

"Okay, fine. But I don't want to ride in the desert, I mean, like, *on* the desert, and you have to promise to slow down if I panic."

"No problem. This bike doesn't do dirt. I've got another one for that."

She nods. *A real superhero, huh?*

"And I never go *that* fast." Thomas unlocks each of the side cases.

"Now I know you're shitting me."

"Well then, you're smart *and* pretty. Don't worry, I'll explain what you have to do."

He pulls out a white helmet from each of the hard-sided saddlebags and gives her a quick lesson on being the passenger. After she pulls on her sweatshirt, they buckle up their head gear, he straddles the bike, and starts the engine. As instructed, she holds onto his shoulder, locates her left foot peg, and stands up on it, and, as if mounting a horse, swings her right leg back and over until she's seated behind him.

"Good job!" Thomas says.

She grabs him around his waist. He puts the bike into gear and they slowly make their way to the main entrance.

"This is great!" She exclaims.

"You ain't seen nothing yet!"

Thomas waves to the guard on duty, who opens the security gate just wide enough for the motorcycle to pass. Then the Swiss biker revs the engine, and in an instant, they're doing forty-five in second gear. Even at this speed, Lauren feels the radial forces against her body, as the bike serpentines its way down through the foothills. The engine growls through its aftermarket titanium exhaust, while Lauren's long dark hair, hanging below her helmet, over her sweatshirt's hood, flaps wildly in the rushing wind.

"Holy shit! This is so fun!" she yells, in between rapid and shallow breaths.

They reach Highway 710 in under three minutes. Without stopping, Thomas looks both ways, and makes a quick left. In a half mile, he pulls right onto a newly paved, two lane, black asphalt road. They pass through an s-curve, and he guns it. In an instant they're doing seventy in fourth-gear on a straightaway.

"Are you okay back there?"

"Okay," she mutters, holding on tight, looking ahead over his right shoulder, gently leaning as he does.

"You're doing great!"

Lauren's heart pounds.

"Are we almost there?!"

"Not too far!"

When the road opens into three-miles of straight asphalt, Thomas again pulls back on the throttle, and they're suddenly at eighty, then ninety. Lauren's whole body tightens like a fist, and she screams through his helmet.

"Fuck! Slow down! You're going to kill us!"

He squeezes on the brakes, and the bike comes to a swift stop. He turns around to speak.

"Wow, you weren't kidding, were you?!"

"I told you not to go too fast!" she shrieks.

"Relax. I hear you."

"I told you!" she says, trying to maintain her composure.

"It's okay. I'll keep it under sixty. You were doing good."

She takes a long deep breath.

"I panic. I told you. I have a problem with speed."

"I can see that."

She pauses.

"How much further?"

"Not much."

"Fine. Let's go."

Thomas puts the bike into gear and takes it to a steady sixty-five mph. It's another four miles before Cerro Armazones stands before them, 10,000 feet high.

"Are we going up there?!" Lauren asks.

"Yes, if you can handle it!"

"Okay."

Thomas starts the winding ascent up the mountain. A campus of rectangular buildings, akin to Paranal's service installation, appears at the mountain's base. It's fronted by a giant sign with the phrase "E-ELT Project". Below that, the sign depicts a telescope's housing, appearing like the top-half of a giant globe, mounted on a circular table. In the picture, there are huge, rectangular concave doors, like those of a Lamborghini, shown in an open position ready to retract laterally into the housing's façade.

"What is this?!" Lauren shouts.

"It's the ELT!"

"What?!"

"Hold that thought!"

The road first heads north from there, then circles the mountain twice in a wide clockwise arc that becomes tighter and tighter, until the pavement ends at the summit. They park the bike, and he leads her on foot toward the center of the flat mountaintop. It's a vast construction site, but late enough in the day that all activity has ceased. They're alone.

"So, what are we doing here? Are we even allowed?"

"Don't worry. I've ridden up here a dozen times after hours. This is ESO's grandest project ever: the ELT; one freaking Extremely Large Telescope. It will be the most powerful in the world and will capture images sixteen times sharper than even Hubble."

"I thought the one we just came from was supposed to be so big."

"This one will dwarf Paranal, and all the others. Just look right here at the telescope's foundation."

He gestures to a giant ring in front of them, some eighty yards in diameter, centered upon the mountaintop. It's comprised of contiguous, concrete, rounded rectangles, emerging from a basement ten feet below the surface. The area's roped off as a warning to unauthorized visitors. This casual attempt at security serves no purpose now, as Lauren has no interest in exploring further.

"The ELT will be a monster of a telescope: twenty-four stories tall with a diameter that's nearly the length of a Texas football field."

She says nothing.

"Look. We can see Paranal from here," Thomas says, pointing westward to a nearby mountain, atop of which Lauren can just make out the telescopes' aluminum housings glistening in the sun. Then she shifts her gaze beyond Cerro Paranal, slightly to the right, to the ball of fire that sits low in the cloudless blue sky. The sun illuminates the foreground, a rough, mountainous tan and brown terrain: a Martian desert here on Earth.

"So beautiful," she remarks softly.

They stand in silence for a minute.

"How far did we come?" she asks, looking again at Paranal.

"It's twelve miles in a straight line. Shall we head back? I want to show you the best sunset in the world."

"Sure. I guess."

They're back at Paranal in just under half an hour. Thomas passes the Residencia and heads up the mountain road. Near to the top, he makes a sharp left up to the control center, one level below the main platform. The two-story building bends around to the right along the contour of the mountaintop. Just before they reach the windowless side wall of the control center, Thomas stops, and turns off the bike's engine. They dismount here, and he pushes the bike against the building, where he hoists it up onto its kickstand.

Lauren's happy to be done with the noise and vibration of the fearsome motorcycle, at least for the moment. Thomas stows the helmets back in the side cases and grabs Lauren's hand. He leads her away from the control center, across the driveway, and toward Paranal's rim.

"You're not scared of heights too, are you?"

"No," she responds with a bit of a scowl.

They step over a metal guardrail onto bare earth and rocks, and he releases her hand. Here, the peak slopes gently to the bottom. They turn right to follow an uphill footpath along the rim toward the telescopes' platform. They are invisible to anyone who happens to look through a window from the control center.

When they reach the higher level, the mountain's downward angle steepens, and Lauren's body tenses. She sees the start of a cyclone fence along this hazardous section of the rim and realizes they're on the wrong side. *This better be good,* she thinks.

They continue along the narrow sandy path that hugs the fence line. In a minute, Thomas stops at a rocky ledge that protrudes over the steep slope. He sits on the shelf and dangles his feet over the cliff.

"Here. Best seat in the house," he says smugly.

Lauren walks past and carefully sits down beside him.

"Sunset in about ten minutes," he announces.

She looks toward the orange radiance.

"What's the flat area beneath the sun?" she asks.

"That's the Pacific."

"The ocean? I had no idea."

"We couldn't see the water from the ELT, but it's only nine miles from here. Part of it's hiding beneath that thin layer of low clouds."

The sun's rays reflect against the sea and cast broad shadows on the hilly terrain between the Pacific and Paranal. *He may be full of himself, but he was right about the sunset,* she thinks. *It's stunning.*

"I wish I brought my iPhone," Lauren says.

"Don't worry, I can share a dozen shots of this."

"Oh, I guess I'm not the first girl you brought up here, am I?" she says lightheartedly.

Thomas looks serious before he replies.

"I could lie, but I don't think you'd fall for it."

Why are all the hot men so dense?

"It's true," he continues. "I've met my share of women, even in the desert. I must say, Lauren, I've never come across one that's quite as pretty as you."

And he's as subtle as a fucking train wreck.

"And here I thought you just wanted to educate me about telescopes, Thomas."

"I do want to educate you, Lauren."

Ugh. He's worse than I thought. Whatever.

"How sweet," she answers. "Can we just watch the sunset?"

"Certainly. That's why we're here."

The two are silent as the sun descends near to the horizon. Lauren brushes aside her mild annoyance with the young, eager scientist and contemplates the real beauty before her.

Clouds hover over the ocean. They brush up against the higher of the inland foothills, the peaks of which protrude through the wispy layer and so, appear as small islands unto themselves.

The sun sets, and the blue sky above darkens. An intense narrow gradient of colors appears close to the horizon: a line of bright yellow atop a band of gleaming red-orange, as if from a fiery magma. The last beams from this day's dying ember radiate up and outward in perfect symmetry. The arid and desolate Atacama, devoid of light and life, filled with perils and unfathomable secrets, appears as a silhouette in front of it all.

She snuffs out a cigarette as her mind wanders. Thoughts go to the celestial view from on top of the rocky mount where Henry caught up with her, and to the volcano, Licancabur, a monument in the desert. She envisions the tragedy at Three Points, and reflects upon Brittany's all-too-short life, and the irony of her own violent yet ongoing existence.

She thinks about her father and of the insanity that they perpetuated together. She also feels, for the first time, a sense of empathy for his suffering, for his pain from failure, and for the disease that consumes him; and with all of this comes the beginnings of absolution.

She smiles inwardly at the notion of her mother with Henry, then she thinks just of Henry. He poses an enigma and, at the same time, presents an answer.

She's never known a person like Henry. He's smart and even funny sometimes. But he's nothing to look at, he's no millionaire, and he's infatuated with space. He's a total geek. *Yet, he and Mom are in love!* It's so strange, but it works.

And there's something else about him that goes deeper, Lauren thinks. Even in such a short time, she can talk to him, tell him things that she can't tell her own mother. He's like Sandy, in a way, except he's a man. It's nice to be able to talk to a man. And there's this weird connection around the music. *We've got something in common. Something important to me.* What a surprise!

It's this that she considers, when the sun dips below the horizon, the radiance fades, and desert, ocean, and sky become indistinguishable. It then enters her consciousness that everything before her has become one.

Lauren grasps at this realization like a struggling bather grabs for a life preserver in a fast-moving current. She's in awe of the infinite expanse. It's all around her: the earth, the sea, the eternal sky, all one and the same. It's Henry's cosmos, and she's a part of it.

Lauren seizes the moment with passion, for she's not diminished by the vastness of what lies before her. It's like some sort of galactic rock concert where, instead of cell phone flashlights, first planets, then stars will shine in acknowledgment of the wondrous miracle. Her own imperfect voice amplifies the stellar song in brilliant harmony, and she's empowered by her small role in this cosmic performance.

It is only her suffering that is diminished by this new frame of mind. The beating, the rape, her overdoses, even the awful accident, all of the horrible incidents that have been part of her own life - all are overshadowed by the truth that she recognizes for the first time: how small these events are in relation to the universe.

Lauren again recalls the words of the old indigenous woman. *Alone in the desert is dangerous.* Yes! She *has* been alone in a dry and lifeless desert, she thinks. Distant from the world in her self-doubt, anger, and despair. Untrusting of, and untruthful with others, and herself. And yes, it's been dangerous, so much so, that she's all too familiar with the hollow eyes and cold hands of death.

Climb the mountain. See things from there. She's traveled for years on a long desert road, to finally reach this pinnacle of understanding, of belief. She's made the ascent to behold the magnificence of the natural world that lies before her, and she's in awe of its unified splendor.

Lauren breathes deeply, contented in this enlightenment. Eventually, she turns to her Swiss companion.

"Thomas, you were right. That was the most beautiful sunset I've ever experienced. Thank you so much."

Thomas is surprised by her tribute.

"That was only the first act, Lauren. The second is even better. It starts in twenty minutes."

Despite mixed feelings about the young scientist and his capacity to kill the mood, Lauren stays put. *If it's as good as the sunset, the stars will be awesome. Maybe I can find the Southern Cross. That might shut him up.*

Lauren only half listens while Thomas makes small talk. He describes day trips on his dirt bike. He compares the contrast between American and European women with the differences between American and European football. He reveals secrets behind the best Texas pulled pork. He shows interest in Lauren but one time, when he asks her about her love life.

But Lauren is happy, and just smiles, and nods, and keeps him talking with a few well-placed questions. Part of her is back in rehab, at Dusty Palms, with Sandy.

Lauren would tell Sandy about her trip to Chile: the native woman she met at a llama stand, the magnificent view of the volcano, her mother's sickness, and her trip with Henry. She'd have a lot to say about Henry. She even might discuss her crazy antics over the lotion, and what was said in the car this morning. Most of all, she would describe her view of this special sunset.

Lauren's high spirits and reverie are suddenly interrupted when Thomas does the unexpected. He reaches inside his jacket and pulls out a flask-size bottle. She sees a reflection of Saturn as a spec of light on its glassy surface. He unscrews its cap and takes a big swallow.

"Here," he offers. "Have some."

Lauren hasn't been so directly confronted with the possible taste of alcohol since the night of the accident. She says nothing.

"Come on. Don't be shy. If you're afraid of germs, this stuff is a great antiseptic, too." He laughs.

"No, I better not," she answers.

"What's wrong? Try it. It feels good going down."

Lauren says nothing, pauses, then reaches for the bottle.

CHAPTER 60

End of a Search

Holy crap! What's wrong with this girl? How many times can she do this to me? She said around seven. It's closer to eight! The sun set twenty minutes ago, and it'll be dark by nine. I'm not going to miss this.

Where are they? I've looked everywhere. Well, not in *his* room; fucking awkward to start asking about him now.

I'm outside the restaurant on a lounge chair, waiting, worrying, pissed off. Is this another one of her insane tests? Or is she just being obnoxious and irresponsible. How does Izzy put up with it? Is this my future? And we had such a good morning together, an important discussion, I thought. She's so goddammed erratic!

My phone rings, and as I fumble to get it out of my pants pocket, I think, maybe it's Lauren lost in the desert, calling for a rescue. Then I realize she's got no cell service. I look down at the screen. Oh shit, it's Isabel. Great timing! Do I just let it ring?

"Hi, honey. How do you feel?"

"Much better. In fact, I feel fine. The hotel's been great. The doctor, too. I'm so glad you kept your appointment. How was your interview?"

"Good."

"Did I catch you at a bad time, Henry?"

"No, of course not."

"Well, tell me about it, then."

My two-hour meeting with Hernandez-Navarro flashes through my mind in an instant. We discussed Paranal's collaboration with the Nobel laureates on gravitational waves, the implications on dark energy of the dual method of detecting the merger of neutron stars, and its possible use as a substitute standard candle in gauging distance. DHN was relaxed, affable, and quite willing to hook me up with his colleagues at other observatories.

"Yeah, Iz, it was good. I'll fill you in tomorrow, okay?"

"Sure, Henry. I just thought you might want to talk to me, being that we haven't really spoken in two days."

"I do, Iz. I do. So, what's been happening there?"

A stupid question, yes, but it's all I got.

"Let's see," she responds. "I slept. I ate soup. I watched TV, and I slept some more. That's it, Henry. Anything else you want to know?" The answer I deserved.

She changes the subject. "How's Lauren?"

"Fine. We're supposed to have dinner. I'm at the restaurant waiting for her."

"So late? What's she been doing while you were at your good interview?"

By this point, further lies are off the table. Anyway, what could be wrong with a young astrophysicist showing her around an observatory in the middle of nowhere?

"We met a nice post-doc at lunch who offered her a tour of the place after work."

"When was that?"

"Lunch?"

"No! When was he supposed to take her around?"

"Oh, about five."

"Five! That's three hours ago. What time was dinner?" she asks.

"About seven thirty." I suppose small lies are back on.

"Let me guess. Was the post-doc young and good looking?"

"Yeah, he's in his twenties."

"Maybe you should check her room."

"She wasn't there."

"What about his?!"

"I didn't check. I don't even know where it is. Anyway, she's not that late, and I don't want to make a fuss about it."

"Henry, I would give her another ten, fifteen minutes max, then make all the fuss you have to; just track her down, please. That's not a problem, is it? I'm sorry she's such a handful, but I'm concerned."

"No problem here, Iz; and don't worry. She can't go anywhere. We're in the middle of the desert with a bunch of scientists. What could go wrong?"

"Are you freaking kidding me?! She's a drug addict; an alcoholic; and you know what trouble she's gotten into with guys."

I do indeed, but I push back anyway.

"There's good in her, Iz. Maybe you should cut her some slack?"

She goes silent; then responds.

"Maybe you're right, but what if you're wrong? Listen. You signed up for this. You can bail anytime you want, dear, but first you have to find her, and call me back when you do."

"Fine. I will. Talk to you later."

"Wait, Henry. You do know that I love you, yes?"

"Yes; yes. Love you, too," as I touch the red telephone icon.

Crap! Time to get moving.

I make for the lobby and explain the basic situation to a nice middle-aged Latina at the reception desk. She tries and fails to reach Thomas on his cell and explains how service can be iffy in the desert.

She has a maintenance engineer check Thomas's room. No luck. She suggests that I look outside, around the hotel.

"Is it possible that they went up to the mountain?"

"Yes," she replies, "this is possible. Thomas has a motorcycle, but he should not be up there unless he is on the schedule."

Wouldn't you know it. A fucking motorcycle, and who's to say the young buck doesn't fancy himself another Evil Knievel.

"Can I go up to look?"

"No, you are not authorized on the mountain. I will call the control center to ask if they have seen them."

In a few minutes, the clerk confirms that Thomas has no business on the mountain this evening; nor has anyone spotted him.

"I am sorry," she says.

I express my thanks and return to my room to retrieve my binoculars and pull on my hiking boots. Then I exit the hotel the way we first came in. I look overhead and see a bright planet through the twilight. It's Saturn. Damn! I should be searching the heavens and not looking for some crazy-ass girl.

I hike around the Residencia through sand and rocks. I reach the back of the hotel, where its long and narrow rectangular wing is wedged between two hills. It's here, where the desert floor is at its low point, that all four stories of the structure are visible from the outside.

I walk northwest along this section of the Residencia. The mountain, standing directly ahead, but a mile away, stops me dead in my tracks. This is stupid! They're not at the hotel. They're up on that freakin' mountain! Sure, you can see the starry night from down here, but that's not for another half hour. Before the stars, comes sunset, and what could be more romantic? You can't see the sunset from here, the mountain's in the way; but I bet it's beautiful on top of Paranal. So, if it's desire that drives Thomas, he took her to the mountain.

Shit! Screw the rules. I've got to get up there.

I look through my binoculars. At this angle, I can't see anything on the telescopes' platform except for the housings' silhouettes. I lower the lenses and make out a dirt path that winds its way down from the mountaintop to the corner of the hotel; a path that I noticed earlier driving down in Sophia's Jeep.

I walk with purpose and find the trailhead. Its verified by an arrow-sign with the words "Al Observatorio." I check my phone's battery: ninety-two percent of its life remains. I strap my binoculars over one shoulder and start out at a fast pace. I can see the path well enough for the first half of the climb, but the sky darkens, and the trail becomes steeper, so I tap on my phone's flashlight for the rest of the way up.

As I climb, I deliberate over the risk in my violation of Paranal's rule, expressed to me by the front desk clerk not more than ten minutes ago. I wonder if DHN will be so generous with his professional contacts once he learns of my felonious hike up the side of his mountain. I pray that my actions, once discovered, won't result in a black eye for Steinmetz, the one who vouched for me. I push on.

In fifteen minutes, my shirt is damp from sweat despite the dry air. I reach the control center driveway. The half-moon has just started its rise, but the sky is still dark. I shut off my phone's lamp to avoid detection. I stay put for a few minutes until my eyes adjust. Then, without a plan, I start to prowl on this lower level. In no time flat, I find a motorcycle inconspicuously parked on the side of the building. The speed at which I have been vindicated in my missing-persons theory surprises even me.

I climb the stairs to the telescopes' platform. I see the outline of a man in a hardhat. He carries a flashlight and walks across the concrete slab toward Unit 2. I duck behind one of the auxiliary telescopes until he shuts the housing's door behind him.

So far, I've not been seen, and as far as I can tell, there's no security staff up here. Perhaps an element of trust exists within the science community, a bond that is surely to be weakened once I'm found out. I worry that they've installed infrared cameras that are trained upon me at this very moment.

I tip-toe past Unit 1, toward the mountain's westward rim. I reach the exact point where Sophia and I started our tour this afternoon, and I pause. While I'm buoyed from my discovery of the motorcycle, I'm no Sherlock Holmes. With all this sneaking around, a tension has risen within me. I feel a tightness in my throat, and I take note of my rapid and shallow breaths. I'm concerned about the young lass and, should my mission fail, my relationship with her mother.

I try to refocus. The moon has inched up in the sky. Continuing toward the mountain's edge, I reach a narrow bed of tall and thick desert grasses and make out the wire-mesh security fence through it all. Regardless of the protective wire, I shudder at the thought of standing so near to what I know is a perilous cliff.

I turn right along the patch of grass. Within seconds, I hear young voices. I stop to listen. It's them! I'm sure of it. Thank goodness! I start to relax.

What's next? It's a bit of a ticklish situation. I can't see them, but if I barge into their little tête-à-tête, I embarrass all of us, lose Lauren's trust, and may even cause a row between mother and daughter. No, I'll go high on this one, and just eavesdrop for a while.

I inch closer to the sound of their conversation. It's quite strange; their voices seem to emanate from beyond the mountain. In any case, I stay still, and listen.

"What's wrong? Try it. It feels good going down," I hear Thomas say.

Going down? Did I just hear that? They just met! Who the fuck is this guy?!

I creep toward his voice, imagining the worst. I'm well-hidden in the darkness. I make out their shapes through the vegetation and chain link, and it dawns on me. They're on the other side. They're on the precipice! They're not more than twenty feet away, on the edge of the mountain, on the wrong side of the fence! I can't do a damn thing about it. I can't get to them, and I dare not whisper a word lest I startle somebody over the cliff. I'm scared to death just thinking about the possibilities.

"What is this, anyway?" I hear Lauren ask.

Now I'm confused. I may have jumped the gun.

"That's good ole Kentucky bourbon, don't you know?" Thomas says, in an overdone Southern accent.

"Yeah, I'll never forget that smell. My father's a bourbon drinker." She pauses. "Why'd you bring me here, Thomas? Because I'm pretty?"

"Yes, I told you, you're very pretty. I'm attracted to you, and I think you're attracted to me."

In the faint moonlight, I see his larger silhouette slide closer to her own, until the two shapes merge into one.

"Well, I'm not. You know nothing about me," Lauren asserts.

I hear the alcohol gurgling out, into the void, I assume.

"What are you doing? Stop! That's top shelf. 20,000 pesos. Give it here," Thomas demands.

"No! I won't be beaten by a bottle of bourbon again!" she exclaims.

Way to go, Lauren! You tell that son-of-a-bitch; but be careful on that ledge.

"Who said you had to drink it?" Thomas asks.

"You did!" she replies. "Guys like you think you're so special, like we should fall all over you. Do you think you're smart, Thomas?"

I see him edge back to his prior position, and there's moonlight again between their two shapes.

"I know I'm smart," Thomas says, sounding indignant. "Smarter than you'll ever be."

"That's where you're wrong! I hear you're faking it. You think you know everything. Turns out it's only four percent of everything.

You have no fucking clue about the rest, yet you pretend you do. Isn't that so, Thomas?"

Damn right, Lauren; more or less. You *were* listening!

"Actually, dark energy's not my field. I'm researching quasars," Thomas admits, sheepishly.

She talks right over him.

"You guys never considered the alternatives. Maybe we're not supposed to know about dark energy, like some never-ending mystery. You ever think about that?!"

Thomas fails to respond. God knows what's in *her* head. She pauses. I imagine her struggling with the same endless mystery she just now proposed. I hear her take a deep breath, then launch back into her cosmic homily.

"Maybe it's not dark at all. Maybe it's invisible to us because it's so bright. Maybe it doesn't want us to see it." She pauses again, lowering her voice. "Maybe, we're just not ready."

All is quiet. I look up. The sky is perfectly clear. The half-moon, a brilliant white beacon, continues its rise. Stars become radiant, and Saturn glows, like an extraordinary jewel in the heavens, her life preserver at the ready. As I strive to put Lauren's bemusing words into context, I hear her voice once more: insistent, confident, full of conviction.

"Take me back to the hotel, please. I want to see the stars with Henry."

I'm so proud, I could cry.

EPILOGUE

I t was an exquisite night sky, and we saw it all with utter clarity: the moon, Saturn and other planets, meteors, nebulae, galaxies, and thousands upon thousands of individual stars. Lauren pointed out the Southern Cross, but it was the Milky Way's galactic plane that was the most breathtaking and unforgettable feature that dominated our vista that night.

While Lauren and I lay back on a big blanket in the sand, eyes on the spectacle, we played songs on our iPhones. In a game of "name that artist," each of us tried to outdo the other with our mastery over the music. She claimed victory. I would've called it a draw.

It was weeks after Chile before I came clean with Isabel about my harrowing trip across the desert with Lauren. Iz took it in stride, but she shamed me some for not telling her earlier. But I'll never say anything to Isabel about Lauren's scars, or how I came to learn of them.

I often recall the short time Lauren and I spent together in the desert, and what she said to the Swiss astronomer that night on the mountaintop. Was Lauren speaking of God: the never-ending mystery, a force not ready to be seen? Could it be that simple - the hand of God that brings about the expansion of the universe? A theory, maybe; but not necessarily at odds with the vague and unproven proposition of dark energy. After all, Einstein believed in God, and it was Einstein, over a hundred years ago, who first predicted the expansion of the fabric of space.

But I don't know what Lauren intended to express on top of Paranal. We never discussed it. She's still unaware of my chasing her up there. What *is* certain is that she found *something* on top of that mountain. If it wasn't God, it was at least a broad perspective—to me, a vital element of good character. Without it, Lauren won't know up from down, nor how to forge straight ahead. Without perspective, she won't recognize the truth: the truth about the world, the people around her, or even about herself.

As for me, things are grand. I have a good woman in my life, and with her, the possibility of a small family. Perhaps that's purpose enough. Nevertheless, I'm forever reminded of the risks, and the inexorable fact that, one day, for all of us, the tide shall recede.

ACKNOWLEDGMENTS

T hanks go first to my wife, Jeanette, the love of my life. I've been thinking about this novel for some five years and writing it for three. She and I started off raw in this business; but it's Jeanette that gets the most-improved-player award, over time becoming an increasingly insightful critic of my writing. In the end, as I read a passage aloud to her, and she made yet another intelligent suggestion, I heard myself say, lovingly, "Why don't *you* just write the damn thing?!" She and I know that I wouldn't have been able to do this without her. Now you all know.

Then there's my editor, Jessi Rita Hoffman. She taught me so much. Jessi encouraged me about my talent as a writer, but never failed to remind me that if I didn't make the corrections called for in her side notes, my book would be doomed. You know that you've got a good editor on your side when you realize that, after giving it some thought, you agree with nearly all her suggestions. Jessi nailed it.

I'd like to thank the rest of my family next. My wonderful children have been supportive throughout, and I am proud of them all. My loving sisters and their families have also been encouraging along the way, and their constant help in other areas allowed me to focus.

My ninety-seven year-old mother deserves honorable mention. She always told me, in jest, that one day she would be an actress; and so, Mom, when a movie is made from this novel, I'll make sure you have a significant part. It could not be a greater role, however, than the one you played in all our lives.

I only wish that my father had lived to see this day. He died last year at ninety-nine. I believe he would have been proud.

Finally, there are a host of family members and friends who, at various stages of this process, acted as my beta readers, also known as guinea pigs. I cannot thank them enough: for their unbiased criticism, their honesty, their time and energy, and their encouragement. A few said that they felt privileged to act as a beta reader. Quite the contrary, my friends, the honor was all mine. Here they are:

Kelly Bolus, Tommy Bolus, Karen Fichter-Venners, Lawrence Fleder, Elizabeth Froemke, Joyce Gianatasio, Alyson Hadley, Michelle Higgins, Jim Higgins, Anne Kleinert, Debbi Klopman, Monica Kolzet, Cathy Lehman, Philip Mintz, Kelly Nash, Shane Nash, Gabrielle C. Prosnitz, Erez Rotem, Gonza Salamanca, Lauren Williams.

Many thanks to all.